GREENCLOAK

GREENCLOAK

LYNDSEY LUTHER

All rights reserved.

Audiobook read by Mario Bueno.

Cover art and title page by J. Caleb of JCalebDesign.com.

Suken Anisaria concept art by Ben McSweeney.

"Lady Chance's Prayers" section divider symbols and artwork by Salvatore Virgilio.

All other interior artwork by Trenton Rose. (IG: @forloveofnerd)

Adunare map by Felix Avenier of www.avenier.org.

Set in Libre Baskerville

Designed by Lyndsey Luther

Dedicated to Salvatore Virgilio and Kylah Coffey,
without whom this book would not exist.

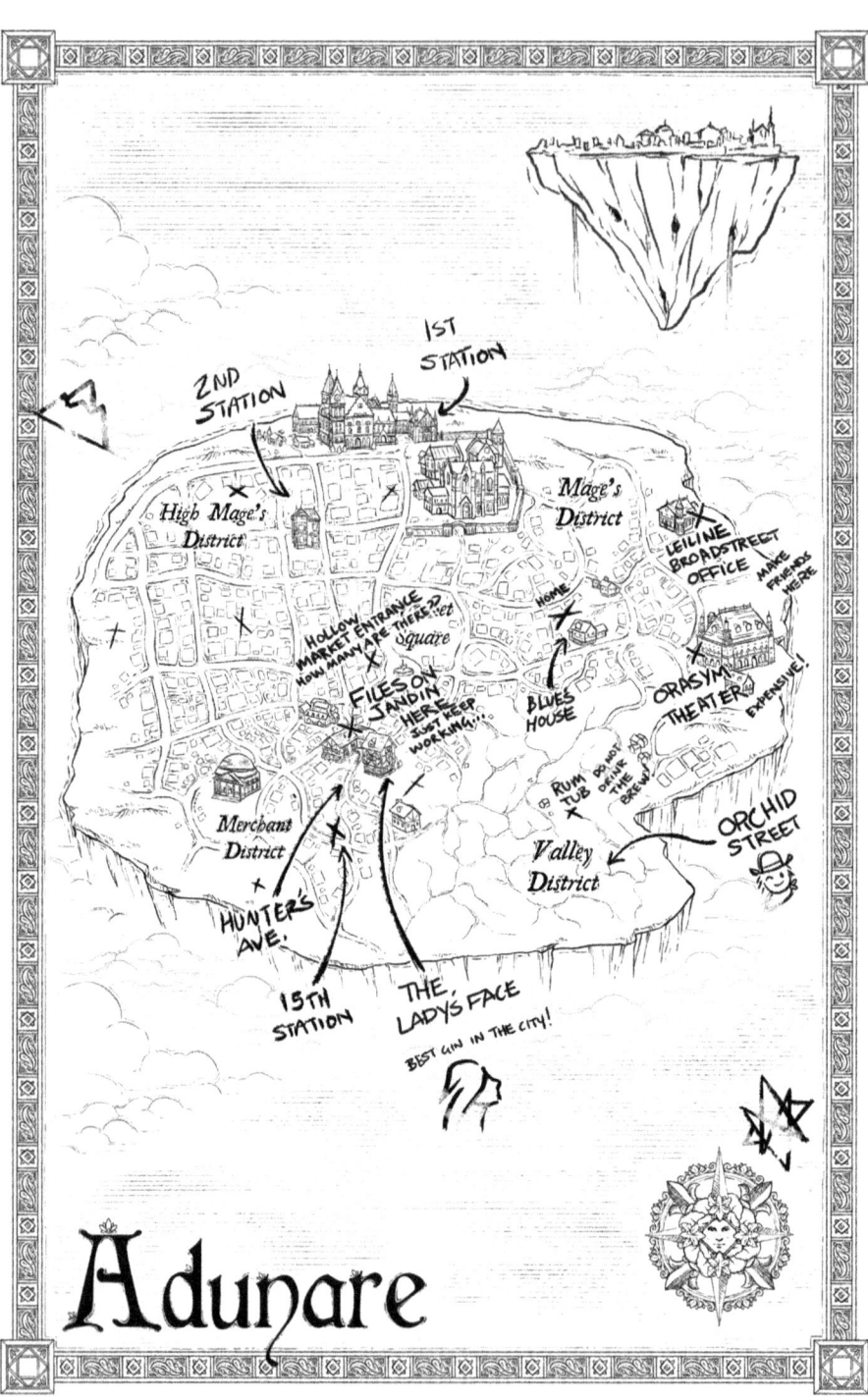

1ST STATION

2ND STATION

High Mage's District

Mage's District

LEILINE BROADSTREET OFFICE

MAKE FRIENDS HERE

HOLLOW MARKET ENTRANCE
HOW MANY ARE THERE?
HOW MANY ARE THERE?

Street Square

HOME

FILES ON SANDIN HERE
JUST KEEP WORKING...

BLUES HOUSE

ORASYM THEATER

EXPENSIVE!

Rum Tub
DO NOT DRINK THE BREW!

Merchant District

ORCHID STREET

Valley District

HUNTER'S AVE.

15TH STATION

THE LADY'S FACE

BEST GIN IN THE CITY!

Adunare

Chapter One

It's dangerous, knowing something, Suken thought as he looked down from the rafters at the crying girl and her kidnappers. These idiots *know* their plan is foolproof. *Know* that the girl's parents will pay any ransom to get her back. *Know* that the abandoned dye factory they've chosen as a hideout is safe and secure.

They were so secure in their *knowing* that the thought of anything going awry was unthinkable. Unplanned for.

And something was about to go very awry. The best up-and-coming bounty hunter in Adunare was about to spectacularly ruin their plans, and all the *knowing* in the world wouldn't help them.

There are only two of them. I've faced worse odds, Suken thought, flipping a thin golden prayer-coin across the backs of his knuckles. The edges were smooth from the fingers of all the bounty hunters who had used it to ask for the Lady's favor, the symbols on front and back nearly worn away.

This job was supposed to have been a simple missing persons case, but in Suken's admittedly limited experience, nothing was ever as simple as you expected it to be. A runaway child, the warrant had said. When he'd discovered that she'd been kidnapped, he should have brought that information to the Bounty Hunter's Guild. But if he did, he'd have to share the reward, fame, and prestige a successful rescue would bring. He needed to pay off his uncle's debts to the cartels, but more importantly, he needed his reputation to spread.

It's not like the girl's in any real danger. Criminals they may be, but even criminals aren't going to kill a ten-year-old girl. Especially not when keeping her alive will get them more ransom money.

Suken looked at the girl again. She huddled against an empty vat fifty feet away from the box of crystallin where the two men were sitting, playing cards. She watched them and sniffled quietly, a purple bruise blooming on her left cheek. He couldn't remember her name, so he named her Flower.

"What we waitin' for?" One of the men asked, tapping a deck of cards on the box of crystallin. Suken wouldn't sit with a box of that flammable shit between his legs for all the aerans or prayers in the city.

Add another point to the stupidity tally, he thought, rolling his eyes. And, to make matters worse—or better—they'd left a metal-bound dagger lying on the table. Silver inlaid into the steel of the blade and wrapping the hilt indicated that the weapon was imbued with stored power by some mage or another.

The man began shuffling, thick fingers deftly maneuvering the battered cards. His arms were muscle-bound and covered with remembrance blooms. *Looks like he could squeeze the piss right out of you if he managed to get those arms around you,* Suken thought, pulling a heavy cloth from his belt and pulling it tight around his mouth and nose, tying it behind his head. *Python, then.*

"We got the girl, don't we?" Python continued, dealing out a hand to his partner. "What else we need? I could go now, deliver the bloody ransom note, and we could be hittin' the Rum Tub by midnight."

Suken unslung his crossbow from his leg and pulled a bolt with a silver tip from the case at his belt, placing it into the channel, careful not to touch the silver.

I'll only get one shot at this. But then, when have I ever needed more than one shot? He couldn't toss a prayer to Lady Chance; not now. But he mentally promised the goddess her rightful tithe, knowing that she'd hear him. That done, he crouched down and waited for Descent, his heart thundering in his chest.

"I'll deliver the note," the second man said, and as the words left his lips, his face ran like melted wax, shifting and changing into that of a nondescript man in his early twenties.

Suken grinned, clenching his fist around the prayer in his left hand. Bringing in a pair of kidnappers and saving a little girl was great and all, but a *shifter?* That would put him up to rank three at least.

"You're being paid well for your time," Shifter continued.

"Not well enough," Python said, examining his cards. "'specially when I ain't heard what we're ransomin' for. How much we gettin'?"

Shifter threw him a dark look over his hand of cards. "You'll get what you were promised, and not an aeran more."

Right on time, the beam below Suken's boots began to vibrate. Below, the kidnappers braced themselves, placing their hands on their possessions so they wouldn't rattle off of the box.

Suken reached down and tapped on the little nub of silver protruding from the back of the bolt with one finger.

Five.

Tiny white and purple sparks began to spit from the silver as the convergence activated, bouncing off the crossbow's wooden handle.

Outside the windows, Suken saw the familiar mist beginning to roll through the streets as the city descended deeper into the perpetual cloudbanks shrouding the rainforest below.

Four. Three. Two. . . .

The shuddering stopped, and the lights in the dye factory

flickered and went out as the city drew upon all remaining magical energy to stabilize.

One.

In the moment of darkness, Suken released his pent-up breath and squeezed the trigger. The string released with a *twang* and the bolt whistled towards the box below as Suken's hands, quick as caal-fire, yanked back the lever to reset the string and drop a new bolt from the magazine into the channel. This new bolt wasn't metal-bound; it was too dangerous to keep those in a magazine.

Suken heard a thud as the metal-bound bolt implanted into the box. Then the lights came back on.

For half a heartbeat, Shifter and Python stared at the new decoration gracing their table. They scrambled away as blue-white energy crackled from the bolt to arc over the scarred wood and across the metal of the dagger, activating whatever convergences had been stored in the blade in a dull *whump*. The box went up in a great gout of fire which smelled of bad fish. The explosion rattled the rafter Suken crouched on.

Bad luck for you, boys, Suken thought with a grin hidden by the cloth. *Excellent luck for me. As usual.*

Dust poured from the ceiling following the concussive blast and smoke rose from below. They met in the middle like two stormclouds crashing into one another, shrouding the factory in an acrid, swirling fog mirroring the mist outside. Between the smoke and the afterimages dancing in his eyes, Suken didn't see if either of the men had been knocked unconscious by the blast. Oh well. He'd find out soon enough.

He kicked the coil of rope lying beside his foot. It unraveled down towards the floor as shouts of alarm and pain began below.

Suken hung his crossbow from the hook on his belt and grabbed the rope in both hands, lowering himself hand over hand into the roiling smoke. One of the two of them was roaring at the other, and Flower's panicked cries joined the cacophony.

Hold on, Suken thought. *I'm gonna get you out of here, kid. As soon as I knock your new buddies around a little.*

He dropped to the floor, the cloth blocking the worst of the smoke. His eyes stung and watered, making it difficult to make out which blurred shape in the billowing clouds was which. Flower let out a loud cry, followed by a bout of coughing.

Suken knelt and waited, listening. Nothing. Apparently the kidnappers were waiting, too.

Well, he couldn't sit here all night. The smoke was going to clear out eventually. *Time to throw a prayer and hope the Lady likes me today.*

"What kind of idiots," he called, "would choose a *dye factory* for their base of operations?"

A grunt, and footsteps to his right.

Suken raised his crossbow, tracking the footsteps with it. "All the good locations already taken by the *real* criminals?" he continued. "You know . . . the ones not resorting to kidnapping ten-year-old girls?"

Python burst from the smoke and skidded to a halt, his eyes widening, staring at the loaded crossbow pointed right at him.

"Hey," Suken said. He loosed the bolt towards the man's leg. A shattered kneecap was a damned good way to keep a mark from making a run for it. But Python took a hurried step backwards, tripping over a broken chair. Suken's bolt, intended for the man's knee, buried itself in his abdomen instead.

"Damn it," Suken said through gritted teeth. Such a wound was often fatal, and Suken wasn't the type of hunter who brought his warrants in dead. Criminals were assholes, yes, but it wasn't Suken's place to pronounce guilt or sentence them. That was for the law to decide, no matter what the warrants said.

He hurried forward and knelt beside Python. The older man groaned, both hands pressed over the wound. His shirt was already soaked through with blood.

"Stop pressing on it," Suken snapped, reaching into a case at his belt and pulling out a little vial of bloodweir. The stuff was worth a mage's ransom, but Suken could save up for another couple months and get more. This man would die without it. He pulled the stopper free with his teeth, yanked the bolt from the wound, and poured the bloodweir over it to mix with Python's blood.

It wouldn't stop the bleeding completely, but it would slow it enough for Python to get medical care in time to save his life.

He heard the footstep behind him a half a second too late.

Something slammed down onto Suken's shoulder with a blinding burst of pain. Suken swayed for a moment, the already hazy smoke-filled world growing dim and unfocused. He gritted his teeth against the pain and lurched his way into turning to face his attacker, then dodged back to avoid a broken piece of wood lashing at his face. The jagged end of the broken chair leg Shifter was wielding knocked Suken's wide-brimmed hat off backwards, but it blessedly missed damaging anything important. Suken dropped to his hands and knees, then darted to his right into a thick bank of smoke.

Shifter tried to follow him, but he wasn't quick enough. Suken dodged back and forth through the smoke, blinking and trying to ignore the pain in his left shoulder. He took a moment to try to lift his arm, and managed to get it to shoulder height before a wave of blinding pain shot from his shoulder up his neck. He gasped and let his arm drop back to his side. Not good. He pressed his back to a stack of boxes and peered around the corner. No sign of Shifter. Suken rested his crossbow against the ground, bracing it with one foot so he could pull the lever back with his good hand to reload it. He'd nearly finished when a dark shape loomed out of the smoke to his left.

Suken ducked under Shifter's first clumsy swing, spinning and bringing his crossbow around to crack against the side of the man's head. Shifter took the hit, reeling back into the smoke bank. He didn't reappear. Suken glanced at his crossbow, but in the smoke he couldn't tell if it was damaged.

No time to worry about that now.

Shifter probably wasn't feeling too great after that blow to the head, and Flower wasn't screaming anymore, which could be either very good, or very, very bad. Suken had thought that Shifter wouldn't risk killing a ransom. Could he have been wrong?

He shoved those doubts aside and concentrated on the present.

The smoke was beginning to clear, blown to wispy shreds by a warm, wet wind smelling of ash and rot from the nearby incinerators. Suken saw the curved wall of one of the vats looming out of the smoke, and darted over to press his back to it, his shoulder alternating between throbbing and jagged bolts of pain. He winced and braced his crossbow against the ground again. The lever pulled back harder than usual, and the weapon made a strange clunking noise as the bolt fell into the chamber.

Suken winced. *That didn't sound good.*

"You're not bad," a gruff voice called, and coughed. "Whoever you are. But you're not good enough."

Shifter. The smoke had dispersed enough for Suken to see that his hiding spot was little more than a narrow alleyway between two huge vats, closed off on the far side by the outer wall of the factory. The voice had come from the other side of the vat he had his back pressed against, the same area where he remembered seeing Flower.

Chances were good that Shifter had no idea where he was. He could use that. He reached down into the prayer-pouch hanging from his belt as the man continued, "This ends here, hunter. Come on out, nice n' slow. Lay down your weapons, and no one needs to die." The girl cried out, then the factory went silent save for her muffled sniffles.

Suken hesitated, the thin beaten gold of the prayer warm against his fingertips. He wanted to take these men, but even he wasn't willing to put anyone's life at risk to further his career, especially that of a little girl.

He won't kill her, Suken reminded himself. *If he does he'll get no ransom, and he'll be bumped up from a fourth rank warrant to third. Maybe even second. No one's stupid enough to risk the scaffolds for a kidnapping.*

If I let Shifter walk away now, he'll go to ground with her. He'll give her father his ransom demand, and the old man'll pay it. But Shifter won't hand her over. Why should he, when he can continue to bleed a desperate father dry?

Suken read stories like this in the broadsheets twice a month. Honesty wasn't a trait that the criminals of Adunare held in high regard, not when there was a rain-barrel full of aerans to be made.

Suken didn't care about how much money the kid's father stood to lose. But he did care about Flower. An experience like that would scar a kid for years, if not a lifetime. He'd already irreparably scarred one child in his life. He wouldn't see it happen again, not if he could stop it.

He balanced the coin on the back of his thumb and his bent index finger, whispered a prayer to the Lady for luck, and flicked it.

The coin flipped end over end towards the far side of the factory before hitting the ground with a dull clink and bouncing across the wooden floor. Suken stood and stepped around the curve of the vat, his crossbow already raised. He adjusted his aim as Shifter came into view, kneeling with the girl in front of him, a knife to her throat and his head turned towards the place where Suken had thrown the coin.

Suken took a half-second longer to aim than he usually did since he didn't have his other arm to support the bow, and squeezed the trigger.

As the string released, the bolt jammed in the channel, wood splintering and flying in all directions. The string snapped with a dull twang, one end whipping back to slice across the back of his hand, lashing through his thick leather glove and the skin beneath it. Suken dropped the weapon on reflex, and it *thunked* to the floor.

Shit, he thought with a wince. *Of all the bloody—*

Shifter whirled towards him, hurling the knife he'd been holding to the girl's neck. Suken ducked back behind the vat, panting. That had been a near miss. He'd felt the wind of the knife's passing. *Auriss's kiss,* his uncle had always called it.

He edged close to the side of the vat again and peered around the rounded corner. The smoke had dissipated enough to give him a clear view of Shifter and Flower. The kidnapper faced him, his eyes narrowed, one hand clutching the girl's shoulder. He must have drawn another knife from the bandolier slung over his shoulder, for he had it pressed against the girl's throat again.

Suken took a deep breath and stepped out into the open. He raised his right hand, palm out. Blood soaked his sleeve from the gash in the back of his hand, staining the cloth the crimson of a sicario's tattoo.

"Don't hurt her," he said, spotting his crossbow lying on the ground a few feet away. It was too far for him to reach without giving the man ample time to part the girl's skin and let her life drain out all over the floor. Oh well. Not like the weapon would have done Suken much good with a snapped string and a jammed bolt anyway. He'd have to rely on brains instead of brawn. Thankfully he was almost as quick with his wits as with his hands.

"Get out," Shifter snarled, his eyes fixed on Suken. The hand holding the knife was rock-steady. "You have no idea what you're doing."

"I'm stopping you from making the biggest mistake of your life," Suken replied.

Shifter tightened his grip on the girl. "I'm leaving," he said, "and she's coming with me."

He had the look of an animal backed into a corner. His eyes were too wide, his posture too still. Suken had seen that look before, and knew better than to make any moves that the man might construe as threatening. He bit back the gibe that rose to his lips, instead taking the time to consider his words and the effect they would have on the man standing in front of him.

Shifter had reasons for what he was doing. Money, probably. It was almost always about money down here in the Valley. He probably needed it to pay off the cartels, and unlike Suken, he didn't give a monkey's diseased shit who he hurt in the process so long as it saved his own skin.

The girl shuddered, her red-rimmed eyes fixed on Suken's face. Tears had tracked clean lines through the dust caked on her cheeks. She knew that Suken would help her. That he'd save her. He saw it in her eyes.

Suken wasn't about to let her down.

"You're not getting out of here," Suken said. "Not with her, or without her. But if you let her go and come quietly, you won't be charged with the murder of a child. The child of a rich lord, I might add. Old Garron'll be able to buy any judge in the damned city. Kill her and you won't live to see daybreak."

"Lord Garron," Shifter snarled, "isn't who he pretends to be."

"I don't give a damn who he is," Suken said. "The way I see it, you've got two choices." He lifted one blood-stained finger, ignoring how his hand throbbed. "One, you drop that knife and get charged with kidnapping and aggravated assault. Two," he lifted a second finger and pitched his voice down, "You kill the girl, and I make sure that you regret that decision before I turn you over to the guards. You'll keep regretting it until they march you to the Arrival Circle and fit the noose around your neck." He took another step forward, lowering his voice still further. "It's not too late. No one has to die here today."

Shifter's eyes darted to the closest door and back to Suken.

Suken saw what he intended in one moment of horrified re-alization.

He'd *known* that Shifter wouldn't kill Flower.

But knowing things was dangerous.

Shifter grabbed the girl's wrist and whirled her around, pulling her arm up. Suken started towards them, but he was too far away. He'd only made it two steps before Shifter sliced the girl's arm from wrist to elbow, digging the knife into the flesh and along the vein. She screamed, blood beginning to spurt from the open wound.

Shifter dropped the girl and ran for the door. Suken let him go, dropping to his knees beside Flower and pulling his cloth from his face.

"Hey," he said, giving her a smile as he grabbed her wrist and pressed the fabric of the cloth against it. "Look at me, kid. Everything's going to be all right. You hear me?" Warm blood suffused the cloth alarmingly fast. Flower didn't reply. She cried in huge gasping sobs, tears streaming from her face.

He reached for his case, but cursed when he realized that he'd already used his only vial of bloodweir on Python.

Suken glanced towards the door. There would be people out there by now, drawn by the smoke and the shouting. Probably standing around chatting with one another about what was going on inside.

"I need help in here!" he shouted. "Someone, please!"

The girl kept crying, and Suken kept pressure on the wound, but no one entered the door.

Bloody Valley district, Suken thought, gritting his teeth. *Someone ready and willing to fuck you over on every street corner, but Chance forbid you ever find yourself in need of some help.*

He heard a groan to his right, and turned to see Python roll to his hands and knees, crawling towards the door.

He was going to lose them. Lose them both.

But that didn't matter. Not anymore. There was only one person in this warehouse Suken was concerned with losing now.

"We're going to go and get you help," he told Flower, giving her his most reassuring smile. "But I'm going to need to pick you up, and while I do that I need you to press down hard, right here where my hands are. Can you do that for me?"

She met his eyes, her crying fading into hiccupping sobs. She was growing pale, little red splotches standing out on her pale cheeks. "I want my d-daddy," she whispered, her lip trembling.

"I know," Suken said, his heart constricting in his chest. Somehow he managed to keep that reassuring smile on his face. "I know. We're going to go and find him. But to get to him, we have to play a game. To win, you have put your hand here, and press down real hard. As hard as you can."

She looked down. At the sight of the blood coating his hands and soaking her dress, her eyes rolled back in her head and she went limp.

Suken swore under his breath and looked at the door again. Still no one. Lady's breath, he'd seen at least fifteen people out there from the roof before he'd come in. Someone *had* to be within hearing distance.

"Help!" he tried again. "For fuck's sake, there's a little girl *dying* in here!"

Nothing.

He shook his head and turned his attention back to Flower. Putting pressure on the wound was helping, but not enough. She was still losing blood. He had to get her to an ardein. The closest Temple was a half hour pathway ride away, but as long as she held out until they got there, the ardein could save her. The guild could pay the damn fee out of his wages. He didn't care . . . as long as she lived. He hesitated another moment, took a deep breath and pulled his hand away, tying the cloth as tightly around the girl's arm as he dared. "I'll make you a deal," he said to her unconscious form as he pulled the knot tight. "You hold on until I get to an ardein, and I'll make sure the bastard who did this to you gets a pounding he won't forget. All right?"

Her eyelids fluttered, but didn't open. He lifted her, ignoring the pain in his left shoulder, and starting loping towards the door. He exited into the warm wet air of the Valley District and the reek of trash, urine and soot. The buildings lining the street through the mist were mostly abandoned factories or warehouses with their windows boarded up. One leaned forward over the street like a drunkard, half of its second floor collapsed inward. People in soot-stained uniforms or beggars' rags wandered by, giving the dye factory a wide berth. They ignored Suken and the blood-soaked girl in his arms, and he wished them all the Rotting Death.

He began to run through the Valley District. Buildings and beggars, slaves and pickpockets lurking in dark alleyways all blended together as he ran. He ignored his pain, ignored the wary looks the poor gave him, ignored the piles of trash he leapt over and the calls of whores and the taunts of men lounging outside of bars.

He ran as fast as he ever had chasing a mark, but it wasn't enough. Halfway to the pathway station, he felt Flower give one little shuddering breath and cease breathing.

He stopped in the middle of the street, panting, staring at her. People walking by gave him furtive looks as they passed. Suken set Flower down on the soot-stained cobblestones, uncertain of what he should do. He tried untying the cloth, planning to put pressure on the wound again, but as he did, he saw that the bleeding had stopped.

There was no longer a heart beating to drive it.

He looked up at the people walking by him. Some threw him disdainful looks, but no one stopped. Another dead kid in the Valley. . . . nothing to write a broadsheet story about. Not one of them cared.

I care, Suken thought, reaching up to press a finger against Flower's chin to close the girl's mouth. He brushed her hair back from her still face and reached into the pouch at his belt to pull free a prayer, unable to wrench his gaze from the girl's face. With trembling fingers he took her hand and placed the prayer on her palm, closing her fingers over the blood-smeared gold.

Her hand was so small. Like his brother's had been, the last time Suken had seen him.

"I'm sorry," he whispered, bowing his head and closing his eyes. "I'm so sorry."

He sat there holding her hand in the middle of the street until the guards finally showed up an hour later.

Chapter Two

Suken made his way down a narrow street towards the edge of the merchant's district in the bright light of early morning, houses and stores looming over him on either side. Suken barely noticed the crowds of people as he walked, head down, wide-brimmed leather hat pulled low to hide his eyes and the bruise blooming high on his right cheek. People glanced at him as they passed, but they didn't stop to question him or ask if he were all right, despite the blood spattered on his tan pants and soaking the sleeves of his off-white shirt.

The crossbow probably had something to do with that. Citizens recognized a bounty hunter when they saw one, and knew that it was a good idea to keep their distance. Even from one as young as Suken.

A lot of good the bloody crossbow did me last night, he thought, kicking at a loose stone as he walked. Chance, the girl's mother . . . her eyes, when the guards had told her. . . .

Suken tried to shove the memory away, but it lingered like a bad hangover. He hadn't been permitted to go with the guards to deliver Flower's body, so he'd followed them and waited across the street, concealed in the shadows of a vine-covered glass awning. He'd watched as a servant opened the door, then ran to fetch

Flower's mother and father. Suken had a horrible suspicion that that mother's eyes filling with horrified disbelief and tears would haunt him for the rest of his life.

Flower's father had stared in disbelief. He'd reached out once, his fingertips brushing against his dead daughter's cheek, then turned and walked away, leaving his wife to collapse to the floor, screaming in anguish.

Lord Garron's not what he seems, Suken had remembered Shifter saying.

From where he'd stood, Lord Garron had looked like any parent would after hearing that they'd lost a child.

After he'd left, Suken had stopped at one of the many remembrance artist's parlors dotting the merchant's district. The woman had asked no questions, going about her business in quiet efficiency, the lei-powered machine buzzing as she added another remembrance bloom to the ever-growing garden climbing up Suken's left forearm. This was the fifth bloom he'd gotten, the inked lines tracing memories and regrets across his flesh.

He stopped at a pathway crossing as a rail-car swept along the silver tracks set into the street, bluish white streaks of magical energy trailing in its wake. The pathways crisscrossed the floating city like a spider web, looping over and under the streets to convey their passengers from place to place. Like most things in Adunare, they were powered by the energy mages bound into metal. The wind from the rail-car's passing pulled at his serape, and he raised his uninjured hand to hold the brim of his hat. Suken glimpsed faces staring out of the well-lit windows; barely blurs, suggestions of eyes and hair and hats. The last car swept past with a rattling shriek and one last rush of warm, humid wind, revealing the fifteenth precinct of the City Guard.

The precinct was a riot of activity even this early in the morning. Suken opened the door, ignoring the twinge of pain in his shoulder, and held it for a guard in iridescent armor dragging a criminal through the doors. The guard nodded to him, and Suken lifted his bloody fingers to the brim of his hat in response. The criminal, a brawny man wearing a scarred leather vest and a ragged shirt and pants, growled curses under his breath as he struggled against the chains binding his wrists behind his back. Suken followed the two into the lobby of the station, glancing around. Hunters and civilians filled the benches lining the walls, waiting to sign up for warrants or fill out paperwork. There weren't enough seats, so the rest stood in a loose crowd near the front desk, where a harried-looking young woman sat, surrounded by stacks of paper. A few guards filtered through the crowd with papers clipped to wooden boards, calling out names. The only guard wearing his armor was the one with the brawny criminal who had now made it to the front desk. The others wore well-pressed grey uniforms under their iridescent cloaks.

Some of the hunters wore small crossbows like Suken's, but just as many favored metal-bound knives, clubs, or swords. One man in the corner had a spear. *Idiot*, Suken thought as he followed in the wake of the guard and his catch. Hunting was difficult enough without a weapon like *that* sticking up over the heads of the crowd, giving away your position to every potential mark in a ten yard radius.

He took a deep breath of the warm air and let it out slowly. He wasn't looking forward to this report, but it had to be done.

Suken waited as the young woman behind the desk, Kora, directed the guard to an open cell. Suken stepped forward. She looked up at him, the necklace of glass beads around her neck catching the light of the luminaries in flashes of various colors. Those beads must have cost her a pretty prayer—mage-glass, unless Suken was mistaken. Kora was pretty, with a heart-shaped face and full lips and thick dark hair pulled back into a braid. Unfortunately, a scowl soured that prettiness.

"Anisaria," she said flatly.

"You remember me," Suken said with a forced smile, resting

his elbow on the counter and lifting the brim of his hat. "I'm flattered, Kora. You know—"

"State your business."

Suken allowed his face to fall. "Can I at least ask you how your vacation was?"

"Do I *look* like I have time for chit-chat?" She gestured to the crowd of people in the lobby. "State your business." She picked up a stamp and slammed it down onto a piece of paper so hard that it made Suken flinch and handed it to a guard who approached her from the side.

"Here to make my report on last night's job."

Kora gave another piece of paper a mild concussion with her stamp. She set it down and pulled an unbludgeoned piece of paper from one of the stacks, handing it over the counter to him. "Take this and have a seat. They'll see you when they can." Suken turned, scanning the crowd. All the spots on the benches were occupied. He took his form and walked over to an empty stretch of wall between two benches.

Filling in the form and returning it to Kora took ten minutes. Suken spent the next hour leaning against the wall with his sketchbook open in one hand and his pen in the other. Sketching usually helped to clear his head. He started with Kora, removing that scowl (it added about ten years to her looks. She looked much better with a smile) and moving on to a quick sketch of Flower, smiling as she played with a puppet. Maybe he'd deliver it to Flower's mother, anonymously, of course.

"Suken Anisaria?"

Suken sighed and snapped his book closed, wondering how much of a chewing-out he was about to get.

A guard in a pristine grey uniform gave him a disinterested look over the top of his clipboard. "This way." He turned, and Suken pushed himself away from the wall to follow him, muttering apologies to the people he pushed past in the crowd as he went. The guard led him through a thick wooden door and down a narrow hallway lined with open and closed doors. The open ones displayed rooms small and large, most holding only a single desk and two chairs. In one, a guard leaned forward over a table, his face red and cords standing out in his neck. The criminal he was staring down looked back at him across the table with a smarmy smile and a relaxed posture. The next room boasted a gigantic map of the city, taking up the whole wall and criss-crossed with colored strings, the wall beside it haphazardly covered with notes and warrants. The guard paused outside of a closed door and rapped on it once.

"Come," a muffled voice from within said. The guard opened the door and stood aside so Suken could step in. As he did, the floor began to vibrate in Ascent. The empty ceramic mugs on the man's desk rattled and several pieces of paper fell from the corner of the desk. The man sitting behind the desk muttered a curse under his breath, reaching out to steady a framed picture. It was clearly a family portrait; similar to the one Suken had hanging in his own study. A much younger version of the man behind the desk stood in the center of the drawing, with his arms around the shoulders of a pair of little girls, their hair bound in twin braids and their faces lit by huge smiles. A woman stood behind him, her dark hair hanging loose to below her shoulders.

It was a decent drawing. Suken could have done better. Outside, the mist faded into sunlight and the vibration of Ascent ceased.

The man himself was a stark contrast to the disorder of the room. His grey uniform was neatly pressed and he wore three knots of rank on the shoulders. *Three knots,* Suken thought with a sinking feeling. *That'd make you Corporal Niden.* The highest-ranked officer at the precinct.

That didn't bode well.

Niden's ash-blond hair was held back in a tail at the nape of his neck, and his short beard was meticulously trimmed. He was paler than most people Suken knew, his skin nearly as light as cream. Niden glanced up at Suken, his eyes hard and cold as brushed steel.

"Anisaria," he said. "Sit."

The guard who had led Suken here closed the door, trapping him in the room. As Suken sat down in a hard-backed wooden chair, Niden turned his gaze back to a piece of parchment in front of him, picking up a simple pen. "You're making a bit of a name for yourself," he said.

"Just a bit?" Suken said, though his nerves felt like exposed metal-bound silver. "Pretty sure I'm the youngest hunter ever to receive his license, and I brought in more warrants in my first year than—"

"Four low level cases," Niden said, flipping one of the papers in front of him over and looking at the back. A remembrance bloom of his own peeked out from the hem of the sleeve of his uniform, mirrored by another on the other wrist. "Two mid-level, not counting the ten or so rank fives you brought in before you got your license." He looked up. "Clearly, you have talent. So perhaps you can enlighten me as to why such a promising young hunter with a sterling record wouldn't come to us for backup as soon as he knew that he was outnumbered?"

Suken winced. "I thought I had a better chance of taking them out on my own, sir."

"Not a mistake you'll be making again, is it."

No, Suken thought, looking down at his blood-stained hands. *No, I won't be making that particular mistake again.*

"I see from your report that you tracked the girl to the factory, where you managed to take down one of the two men," Niden said, still not looking at Suken.

"Yes."

"Your report claims that the one who escaped was mage-born. A shifter. Are you certain?"

"Yes, sir. Positive."

Niden's expression soured at that, but he only nodded. He

picked up a pen and began scribbling something on the paper in front of him. "Anything else you can tell us about him? Physical identifiers, other than his face?"

Suken gave him as good of a description as he could, and Niden jotted it all down, though Suken had included a sketch with his report. He waited a moment as the corporal finished writing and took a deep breath. "Sir," he said. "The man I shot . . . is he all right?"

"Yes, though it wouldn't have been a great loss had he died." The corporal sifted some sand over whatever he'd been writing to blot it. "He's worked as a sicario for the cartels in the past."

Suken let out a breath in relief, feeling as if a weight had lifted from his shoulders. "I was hoping," he said carefully, "that I might be able to continue on this case. I know that it's probably a rank two now, but seeing as how I was the only one who actually saw him . . ."

"You're being pulled to work on a different case."

Suken blinked. "But, sir—"

Niden speared him with a hard look.

Suken swallowed and closed his mouth.

"All hunters not currently on assignment are being assigned to the Greencloak case," Niden continued.

Suken looked up. "*All* the hunters?"

"That's what I said."

"I . . . thought Greencloak was a rank one, sir."

"He's been given priority," Niden said, sliding a copy of the Greencloak warrant across the table along with a signed permit. "Word came down from the High Mages last night."

Suken had seen the Greencloak warrant a hundred times, tacked up on walls everywhere hunters were likely to show up. The sketch was vague and shadowy, depicting a man in a cloak with his face half-hidden in the depths of the hood. Below the picture, a block of cramped text listed the man's crimes.

Larceny. Grand larceny. Forgery. Several counts of each. In the case of grand larceny, the number was in the double digits, almost a hundred.

And three counts of murder.

That's new, Suken thought. The thief had been getting a reputation in the past couple of years as being uncatchable. Rumors about him flew more thickly than flies around a rotting fruit. But Suken had never heard anything about the thief killing anyone.

He looked up. "Sir, about the shifter—"

"Forget it," Niden interrupted. "If I see you walk in the door with that shifter before the Greencloak case is closed, you can kiss your license goodbye, Anisaria. This is your highest priority. Any information you find about Greencloak, you bring directly to me. Understood?"

Guy's wound tighter than a cocked crossbow, Suken thought. *Well, at least I'm not being demoted a rank, or having my license taken away.* His relief was tempered by a touch of anger that the shifter was going to be free to run around until Greencloak was eventually caught.

"Understood, sir," he said.

"Dismissed," Niden said, turning his attention back down to the clutter on his desk.

As he walked out of the precinct, Suken paused to pull a prayer from the pouch at his belt, thinking.

Word among the other hunters was that Greencloak was well-nigh uncatchable. Dozens of first rank hunters had tried to find him, and had as much luck at it as trying to catch a cloud in their bare hands. Suken had never tried, being fifth rank. But now that he had a shot . . .

Could he find Greencloak? He had a lot of contacts in the Valley, where Greencloak was rumored to operate. And he was good, better than most of the first rank hunters who had tried, despite what the guild believed. Suken started idly flipping the prayer along as his knuckles.

If I catch him, *he thought slowly,* the reward will be . . . well, more than I've earned on any of my other jobs combined. Not to mention the marks towards my rank. It'd definitely put me up a rank, maybe two.

But what about Shifter? Suken flipped the coin up and caught it, looking at the symbol carved into the gold. Seven lines, forming a crude crown shape. Suken closed his hand around the coin. *Something heroic, eh?* He thought. *What could be more heroic than bringing in the killer of a ten-year-old girl?*

But he couldn't show up here with the shifter before Greencloak was caught.

So I'll find Greencloak first. While I'm chasing him, I'll ask around after Shifter. I'll get a few solid leads on the shifter, bring in Greencloak, then get the jump on any other hunters on Shifter's trail. He'd be able to kill two birds with one bolt: secure his career and reputation as the best hunter in the city, and bring Shifter to justice.

He'd just have to make sure that he found Greencloak quickly. The sooner he brought the thief in, the sooner he could begin chasing Shifter in earnest.

No one stays uncaught forever, he thought, starting down the steps and tossing the prayer back over his shoulder. *Not even Greencloak.*

Chapter Three

Fletch Greencloak glared at the iron chain leading from the manacles around his wrists to the ceiling. He sat on a cold stone floor, wearing only a pair of thin cotton breeches and shirt. The chains gave him enough leeway to lie down on the unforgiving rock floor, but he couldn't move farther than a foot from the wall. He'd long since lost feeling in his hands from the manacles locked tightly around his wrists, and dried blood from the gash in his head had stiffened the back of the thin cotton shirt his captors had given him.

"You know," Fletch called to the locked door across the room, "You could at least have the common decency to *pay* me if you're going to tie me up like a fetishist's plaything!"

No response. Either his guards weren't out there, or they were ignoring him. As usual.

Footsteps coming down the hall pulled him from thoughts of his discomfort. Fletch turned his head slightly towards the wooden door, the muscles in his neck and shoulders protesting even that small movement. The footsteps grew closer, then stopped, only to be replaced with the metallic jangling of a ring of keys. The door swung open inwards to reveal two stocky men wearing black cloth masks over their faces flanking a young boy carrying a platter. The boy's skin was grey with shifting patterns of black, like smoke. Vethin, the boy, wore a similar outfit to Fletch, with the addition of a steel collar around his neck. Behind them strode a man wearing Fletch's own damn cloak, the hood drawn up to cover his face. The cloak faded from dark green at the hood to leaf green at the bottom hem, the inner lining a deep midnight blue so dark it was nearly black. As usual, the man wearing it leaned back against the wall, arms folded, silent. All three of them wore dark brown clothes, unremarkable in every respect. In short, nothing that would give Fletch any sort of indication as to their identities.

"If it isn't the asshole squad and their silent fucking guardian," Fletch said, leaning back against the wall. "So what's it going to be today? Questions about my career? My history? My bloody love life?"

One of the two guards flicked the chain leading from his hand to the boy's collar, and Vethin flinched.

Don't give them the satisfaction, Fletch thought savagely. When he'd first been brought here a week ago, he'd refused to eat or drink, or to answer their stupid questions. A day later, they'd brought Vethin in. They hadn't said anything, just nudged him forward with the food and water and met his eyes. Fletch had understood the threat. Cooperate, or the boy would suffer. Fletch had no idea how they'd known about the boy's connection to him—but then, Fletch had no idea how they'd captured him, either. All he remembered was kneeling at the door of a mage's house, pulling out his lock picks . . . then the world blacking out around him. No sound, no pain, nothing out of the ordinary. And then he'd woken up *here,* chained to a wall, his head aching and all of his clothes and personal belongings stripped from him.

After they'd brought in Vethin, Fletch had begun eating and drinking, and feeding them lies in answer to their myriad questions, each more outrageous than the last. He knew that it wouldn't be long before they grew tired of him jerking them around, and then the serious threats against Vethin's well-being would begin. But in the meantime, he took savage pleasure in keeping them guessing as to which of his answers were real, and which were fake.

Hopefully by the time you get tired of my attitude, I'll have figured out a way to get out of this shithole, Fletch thought, his eyes fixed on the guards. *And I'll be sure to leave you bastards with a few parting gifts on my way out.*

Vethin straightened his back and glared at the guard, who rolled his eyes and gestured towards Fletch. "Go on," the guard said, his voice muffled. "Feed the bastard." His eyes shifted to Fletch and crinkled at the corners in what was probably an unpleasant smile behind that mask. "Maybe this time you'll give us some straight answers, thief."

"I'd say it's about as likely as you turning around and ramming your partner's sword up his own ass," Fletch replied.

The guard's eyes narrowed. Fletch didn't know exactly what the men wanted of him. He'd been approached by an operative of one of Adunare's many criminal organizations—he wasn't sure which one, not that it had mattered to him at the time—the night before his abduction. The hooded man had asked him to take part in some sort of plan, something that would supposedly pay well and required his particular talents. Fletch had promptly told him to go piss off the side of the city. He worked alone, always had, always would, and there was no way he was letting the bloody cartels get a chain on him.

But they'd managed to get a chain on him anyway. A real one. Fletch shifted position slightly, his numb hands resting in his lap.

"Where were you born?" the second guard asked.

"The moon."

"Who were your parents?"

"The fire god and his favorite pet bitch."

The guards shared a look. "Where do you keep your stolen goods?" the second guard tried.

"In a warehouse on Farris Street," Fletch said.

Both of the guards blinked at that. "Really?" one asked.

"No," Fletch said. "Also, fuck you."

"If you don't give us serious answers," the guard said, "we're going to have to do things we'd rather not." This one was softer-spoken than the first. The old good guard, bad guard routine. It was as old as a mummer's play and just as likely to fool Fletch into thinking it was real, but at least they were finally getting around to the legitimate threats.

"It's about time," Fletch said. "I was getting tired of the fore-play." He grinned viciously at them and lounged against the wall, crossing one ankle over the other. "So where are we starting, boys? I prefer whips to branding, but I'm willing to make concessions."

"Bloody thief," the bad-guard muttered. "Don't know why we bother. I think we should kill the both of them and be done with 'em."

"What fun would that be?" Fletch asked. "Any cartel henchman worth a shit knows that you can't pull answers from a corpse's lips. C'mon . . . torture's clearly the way to go. Your boss'll approve, I'm sure." *Come on,* Fletch thought savagely. *Come within grabbing distance. I dare you, you bloody bastard.*

The guards ignored him, as usual. So did their silent hooded partner.

Fletch narrowed his eyes, trying to peer into the shadows of the hood. It was made specifically to keep anyone from seeing the wearer's face, and unfortunately it worked as well for the strange man as it did for Fletch. *Does he have any idea how expensive that bloody thing is? If he puts so much as a mark on it, I'll have him gelded.*

Vethin shuffled forward and set the platter down on the stone floor beside Fletch. A simple clay cup of water. A wooden plate with a wrap filled with rice, beans and pork. The same thing he'd eaten every day for the last three days. Enough to keep him alive, but not enough to restore any modicum of strength to his limbs. Fletch met Vethin's eyes, asking silently if the boy were all right.

A small stubborn smile was his reply. Fletch took the water, grasping it awkwardly with his bound and numb hands, and downed it in one long gulp. He ate the wrap next, careful not to waste a bite. He'd need every bit of strength he could muster for when the opportunity to escape presented itself. And it would. If there was one thing Fletch had learned, it was that new opportunities *always* presented themselves. Eventually.

Vethin gathered up the empty tray and started to stand. But he lost his balance briefly and fell forward, jamming his shoulder roughly into Fletch's chest, the tray clattering to the floor and the plate rolling across the stone towards the wall. Fletch let out a pained cry, but the pain wasn't jarring enough to keep him from noticing Vethin dropping something on the floor. Fletch shifted slightly to sit on whatever it was, hiding it from the guards' view.

"Git off him," the guard growled, yanking on the chain. Vethin fell on his side, barely avoiding the kick the guard aimed at his ribs. He rolled to his feet and edged away from the guard, who snorted and tugged on the chain.

"C'mon," he said. "We ain't got all day."

Vethin bent and picked up the dropped tray and plate, meeting Fletch's eyes long enough to drop him a wink. The guard shoved Vethin out into the hallway, followed by the good-guard and the man wearing Fletch's cloak. Fletch stared at the wood of the closed door for a long moment, listening as the footsteps receded. Once he was certain that they were gone, he shifted his weight and looked down at the object Vethin had brought him.

A lockpick. Gods bless the bloody kid, he'd managed to palm a lockpick. And not just any lockpick, either. It was one of Fletch's own.

Ten minutes later, Fletch massaged his wrists, the blood returning to his hands with dull tingles and frequent sharp jabs of pain. *If these bastards damaged my hands,* he thought, *I'll not only kill them, I'll kill everyone they ever loved. Gods below, I'll kill everyone they ever* met.

As the hours went by, he forced himself to stand and begin pacing the room, continuing to rub the life back into his fingers. He didn't know why these people had taken him, but it obviously wasn't for the damned bounty on his head. If it had been that, they'd have turned him in to the cats or the pearls by now. The questions he'd been asked hadn't given him any clues either. They'd asked everything from his opinion on politics to his favorite foods.

He couldn't figure out why they would want to know things like that. It was a mystery, but not one Fletch wanted to know the answer to badly enough to stick around and find out.

By the time he heard keys jangling down the hall, he almost felt back to his old self again. Fletch stood with his back to the cold stone, his heart beating a staccato rhythm in his chest. His hands were still numb, but he could move them easily. It would be enough. It would have to be.

"Bloody stupid, if you ask me," one of the guards said, his voice muffled through the locked door. "Ain't he got enough by now?"

"Don't know. Maybe it's harder than he thought," the other guard replied. "Thief *is* a bloody sharp-tongued bastard."

"So? Ain't like anyone knows him."

"Someone must." The footsteps stopped right outside the door. The keys jangled again. "Ain't nobody got *no* friends or family."

"Other than the kids?" A snort. "Why'd we have to take one of the mongrel ones, anyway? I heard they got diseases. You know if they got diseases?"

Fletch bent his knees a little, the metal of the lockpick cold in his hand. He ran the ball of his thumb along the edge of the metal. It was thin, but the edge was sharpened to a razor edge. He heard the key slide into the lock and the familiar *thunk* as the tumblers fell into place.

"Dunno," the second guard said as the door began to open. "Never heard one way or—"

Fletch spun towards the door as it opened to slam the lockpick into the guard's eye. It sank in as easily as a knife into hot butter, the eyeball beginning to ooze a white mucus. The man's other eye widened. Before he could let out a cry that would alert any other guards to what was going on, Fletch yanked a knife from the guard's own belt and used it to slash the man's throat from ear to ear, spilling a flood of warm blood over his hand. The man began to stagger, gurgling as his lifeblood spurted from his neck. Fletch stepped back, lifting one foot to kick the dying man in the gut. He fell back into the second guard, who was cursing and struggling to pull his sword from his scabbard. Fletch glanced at the knife in his hand, noting the thin traceries of silver that marked it as a metal-bound blade. The uninjured guard opened his mouth to shout a warning, but Fletch leapt forward, slamming him against the doorjamb and pressing cold metal-bound silver and steel to his throat.

"Now," he said, his voice low and dangerous, "normally in this sort of situation you and I would have a long discussion about who hired you, how you found me, and how you caught me. But I don't know how many of you there are, and even if you told me you two came alone today, I wouldn't trust you. Don't take it personally." Beside them, the first guard collapsed to his knees, his hands scrabbling at his throat in a vain attempt to staunch the bloodflow. The eye Fletch had punctured was slowly deflating, clearish mucus oozing from it. The other was wide, terrified. The guard with Fletch's knife to his throat watched as his friend fell to his side on the stones, the spurts of blood from the jagged wound in his neck coming slower, more sporadically.

"So this is how this is going to work," Fletch said. "You're going to tell me where the boy is, and where my personal effects are. If you do, I'll kill you quick instead of leaving you to bleed out in agony for the next three hours."

The man's dark eyes darted back to Fletch's face. "Please," he whispered. "I've got a son, he's only—"

"Should have thought of that before you took this job," Fletch said, a hard note creeping into his voice. "The boy, and my things. *Where?*" He pressed the knife hard enough to draw a bead of blood.

The guard let out a strangled sound, his adam's apple bobbing above the blade. "S-second door on the left," he whispered, his upper face pale. The lower half was still shrouded by his dark cloth mask. "The boy's there. Your things are in the next room down. But please . . . please, my son . . . he'll be alone, I—"

Fletch reached up to grab the man's hair. He pulled the guard's head towards him and slammed it back against the stone wall with a dull *thwack*. The guard's eyes rolled back in his head, and he slid to the ground bonelessly. Fletch stared down at him for a long moment, then he knelt and began methodically stripping the guard of his clothes.

"Don't think I spared you for your own sake," he muttered to the unconscious man as he pulled his boots free. "Just don't want another bloody orphan to take care of. I've got more than I can handle already."

Each step was agony. The adrenaline from the attack had worn off before Fletch was even done pulling the guard's outfit on, leaving Fletch exhausted, his limbs trembling. He hadn't realized he was as weak as he was. He forced himself onwards, though. He was used to being weak. He'd experienced enough of it in his youth.

Dim light from luminaries set in the walls illuminated the tunnel he found himself in when he exited his cell. He was obviously in the undercity, the twisting warren of tunnels which bored beneath the city of Adunare like an anthill. Fletch knew a good portion of the tunnels under the city, but this part was foreign to him. They were probably under the Mage's District somewhere, given the fact that the stone had been covered over with dark wood paneling both on the walls and the floor. The ceiling had been left uncovered, exposing lichen-encrusted damp rock.

As Fletch reached the second door, he paused. When men feared for their lives, they were considerably more honest. But there was always the possibility that this guard had lied. There could be fifteen armed men behind this door.

He knelt and knocked lightly on the door in a predetermined pattern. He heard the gentle pad of a thief's footsteps from the other side of the door, then a series of knocks came back to him. He nodded. Vethin was in here, and alone. Good. He picked the lock deftly. He could have taken the guard's keys, he supposed, but that would have seemed like a slight against his professionalism. Two heartbeats after he'd begun (one longer than it would have taken him if his hands hadn't still been shaking), the door swung open to reveal a room containing a small bed with a threadbare blanket. Vethin stood in the middle of the room, grinning, his teeth startlingly white against his mottled soot-grey skin.

Fletch glanced around the room. "Terrible accommodations," he said. "I think we can do better. Don't you?"

"Lady's breath, yes," Vethin said, the grin widening. "I got the right lockpick, then?"

"Guess you were paying attention in Rossin's lessons after all," Fletch replied, twirling the little tool around one finger. "Where'd you get it?"

Vethin gestured to the wall to his right. "The room next door," he said. "It's the same one as where they keep the food n' water. Saw your things in there while I was waitin' for 'em to hand over the tray, so I spent the first two nights pullin' that paneling out." Fletch glanced at the indicated board, his mood darkening as he saw the dark blood staining the edges of the wood panel. The kid had worked at it until his hands were torn and bloodied. No wonder he was hiding them behind his back like that.

"Took hours," Vethin said, the pride apparent in his voice.

"You're lucky there wasn't a stone wall between the rooms," Fletch said.

"Nah. Rooms're too close." He looked up at Fletch, all big dark eyes and aching need for approval. Fletch nodded to him.

"Good job."

The smile that spread over his face could have lit the room with light to spare. Fletch turned and stepped back out into the hallway, glancing to his left and right. Empty. Good.

"So now what?" Vethin asked, bobbing up beside him.

"Now," Fletch said, "we collect my things and get you home."

The boy beamed and hurried ahead of Fletch to the closed door of the store-room, which wasn't locked. Fletch opened it to find a small room well stocked with stacks of dried meat, flatbread, a wooden barrel half full of water, and a disorderly pile of pouches, leather scabbards, and cases. Fletch heaved a sigh of relief and picked up the pile. He'd spent the last five years commissioning these tools and knives from various merchants around the city, never using the same merchant twice. He'd have hated to have to do all that work again.

He pulled the belt around his waist and cinched it tight, then searched the rest of the wooden shelves, though he didn't have much hope of seeing his last missing item.

"Cloak?" he asked.

"Don't know," Vethin replied from the hallway. "The quiet one was always wearing it when I saw him. I didn't like him. He felt ... wrong." Fletch glanced back over his shoulder at the boy. Vethin had remained out there, staring down the hall with an intent expression.

Keeping a lookout. Good. According to Rossin's reports, this one had been a particularly quick learner.

Fletch turned back to the shelves, looking a little more carefully, just in case. This search was as futile as the last. Damn. He turned back to Vethin. "Were there more than two guards and the bastard wearing my clothes?"

"Yes," Vethin replied, turning his completely black eyes to Fletch. "I saw at least four others, and another one who wore a hooded cloak sort of like yours all the time. Never saw any of their faces. Dunno if they all stay here, or sleep somewhere else."

Fletch stepped out into the hall. "We'll—"

The twang of a crossbow interrupted him mid-thought. Without thinking, he leapt forward, shoving Vethin against the wall. Hot pain seared into his calf. He didn't have time to stop and inspect the damage. He whirled, keeping his weight off of his injured leg, hands darting to the hilts of the short throwing knives in his belt. A man stood in the hallway ten paces away. He was pulling back the lever on the crossbow in his hands, his brow furrowed, his eyes darting back and forth from the weapon to Fletch.

Crossbows. Stupid weapons. Took too long to reload to be much good for most people. Well, this idiot's penchant for the newest moronic weaponry would be his undoing.

Fletch pulled the knife he'd taken from the guard from his belt and twisted his body, throwing it with all his meager strength. It whistled through the air, but Fletch's aim—not very good at the best of times—was off, and he barely nicked the man's shoulder. He cursed, reached for his other knife . . . and found the scabbard empty.

Vethin ducked around Fletch, his hand darting out, Fletch's knife leaving it in a bright flash. This knife caught the attacker dead in the chest. He cried out and dropped the crossbow, staggering back a step. Fletch lurched forward as quickly as he could, crashing into the attacker in a chaos of flailing limbs and grasping hands.

He didn't bother punching, not at this close of a range. Fletch wasn't much good at it anyway, and he knew it. Instead, he raked his fingers across the man's face, aiming for his eyes. When that failed, he rammed the knee of his uninjured leg up into the man's groin and was rewarded with a moan of pain. He managed to work his hands past the attacker's flailing fists, gaining a couple short rabbit-punches to the ribs and an elbow to the eye for his trouble, but it was worth it as his hands closed around the other man's windpipe.

The stranger's struggles grew more feeble as his air supply dwindled, then ceased entirely. His arms fell limp to his sides, his fingers twitching once or twice as his eyelids fluttered closed. Life bled from him like aerans slipping from a cut purse. Fletch held on long enough to be sure that the man was dead, then stood shakily, his sides burning and his eye slowly swelling shut, and turned.

Vethin stood near the door, staring at Fletch's leg, his eyes wide.

"Get those knives," Fletch said. "And search him, see if you can find anything else, like a letter or some sort of identification." Vethin rushed to obey. He fished through the man's pockets and looked up, shaking his head.

"All right," Fletch said. "You go on ahead of me." He took the knives from Vethin, tucking them into his belt, and pressed one hand against the wall. The luminaries in the walls around them wouldn't continue past this section of tunnel, so he pulled one of his own from one of his cases and tapped the silver nub on it. The little glass sphere burst into light as the metal-bound energy reacted with the chemicals contained inside it. He tossed it to Vethin, who caught it nimbly, and Fletch pulled another out and hung it from a thin silver chain around his neck, activating it and pointedly not looking at his injury. As long as he left the bolt in, the blood loss probably wouldn't be bad enough to kill him. Probably. He felt warm blood running down his leg, filling the boot he'd stolen from the guard. It squelched as he stepped forward, using the wall to help keep his balance. A flare of bright, stabbing pain shot up his leg, and he winced.

The boy stood there, staring at him, the luminary held in one dark hand.

"I said go," Fletch said between gritted teeth. "I'll meet you at the den."

Vethin didn't answer. Instead, he made his way to Fletch's side and ducked so Fletch's arm was over his shoulders.

"I *said* to go," Fletch said as the kid grabbed his wrist.

"Ain't leavin' you," Vethin said.

Bloody stubborn kids.

"This is how you're going to die, you know," Fletch muttered as he reluctantly put some of his weight on the kid. The phrase was part of a ritual all the kids knew—Fletch had taught it to them himself. It was the only thing he had taught them personally. *Determine your weak point, don't deny it,* he'd told them. Denying your weaknesses got you killed. Facing them made you stronger. "You die from not bloody doing what you're told."

"Nah," Vethin said, holding Fletch's wrist and throwing a grin at him. "I'm gonna die jumping from one rooftop to another. Gonna miss and wind up with a broken back or neck in some alley. Besides, ain't you always told us not to listen to anyone 'cept ourselves?"

Fletch rolled his eyes. Leave it to Vethin to turn Fletch's own words against him. Well, no use arguing, not when they might have more guards arriving at any moment.

They made their way deeper into the twisting tunnels. The wood paneling stopped after about a hundred feet, transitioning into the more familiar stone walls, moss, and dripping water. Fletch tried to keep an eye out for familiarities, but as time wore on he had to focus more and more of his concentration on putting one foot after another. Once or twice he thought he heard voices and running footsteps echoing in the tunnels, but Vethin guided Fletch into darker, less upkept tunnels until the voices passed, hiding the luminaries in a closed hand. The voices could have been people Fletch knew, but they were far more likely to be thieves who wouldn't hesitate to slit Fletch and Vethin's throats and rob their corpses of every last item they owned.

The pain grew with each passing minute, and after what felt like a mile of lurching, limping steps Fletch noticed the world beginning to fuzz at the edges, like a slow mist creeping in through the alleyways of the Valley. Whenever the mist began to encroach on him, Fletch brought his full weight down on his injured leg. The resulting surge of pain cleared away some of the haze, but each time it retreated less. It wouldn't be long now before the darkness claimed him, and if he fainted down here, he'd certainly die.

"Fletch," Vethin said. Fletch looked up blearily. How long had it been since the last time he'd looked up? He wasn't sure. He'd been concentrating too hard on holding the unconsciousness at bay. Vethin pointed.

The dim light of their luminaries illuminated a stone carved into the form of a willowy woman set into an alcove in the tunnel wall ahead of them. The denizens of the undercity had painted her in several garish shades of red in mocking imitation of the Empress of Tyrodames, the desert land to the east. The Red Lady pointed the way towards the surface, her slim hand extended to point eastward.

"We're almost home," Vethin said, worry hovering at the edge of his voice. "Can you make it?"

"Yes," Fletch said. It felt as if he were hearing his own voice from somewhere far, far away. "I'll . . ." He swayed, the world spinning around him. "I'll . . ."

The pain faded. The mist encroached, and Fletch smiled in relief as darkness claimed him.

Chapter Four

One of the three men sitting behind the desk of the Hunter's Guild looked up from Suken's permit, one eyebrow raised. His hands were stained with green ink and he'd shoved a pen behind one ear so that it stuck out of his hair like a displaced feather. The other two clerks were busy filling out paperwork for the hunters at the counter beside Suken. A pair of hunters stood to Suken's left, their backs to a wall covered with hundreds of overlapping warrants. Their voices added to the gentle hum of conversation and the distant calls of clerks deeper in the building.

"Taking another job already?" the clerk asked. "Didn't you turn one in last night?" Another clerk pushed open the pair of thick oak doors behind the desk, revealing an aisle running between towering shelves stacked with wooden boxes, dimly lit by a few scattered luminaries. Suken's gaze was drawn irresistibly to the dark shadows of the records room. As always, he found himself wondering which one of those thousands of boxes held the classified case-file he really wanted.

The clerk cleared his throat. Suken gave him a forced smile, pulling his attention from the records. "They pulled me to work on Greencloak's."

The clerk looked at the line of fifteen hunters behind Suken, all holding permits and shifting their weight impatiently. He sighed and shook his head, slamming a heavy stamp down onto the permit to mark it with a ji'Ahiran symbol in green ink. Each symbol stood for a word, or in the case of the more complicated symbols, entire phrases. The mages used them in their casting somehow, but Suken had only ever seen the stupid things used as signatures since he'd left school when he was fourteen.

"Here," the clerk said, sliding a folder across the counter. "Remember, return it before you leave the guild or—"

"Yeah, yeah." Suken bit back his frustration at being treated like a kitten, as usual. "Thanks."

He touched the brim of his hat in farewell, ignoring the other hunters as he turned and made his way past them towards the door which connected the Guild to the bar next door. He folded the permit and tucked it into his bolt-case as he walked. He was about to reach for the handle of one of the glass doors adjoining the Lady's Face to the Guild when a hunter stepped out of line and began walking towards Suken.

Suken pretended he hadn't seen and pulled the door open, hoping that the older man would take the hint.

"Anisaria! Hold on."

Today was apparently not his day. He stopped and turned, plastering a smile on his face.

"Ezin," he said. "What can I do for you?"

Ezin o'Fairis was of a similar height with Suken, but he had lines etched into the corners of his dark eyes and wings of grey hair at his temples. Suken couldn't walk down the street without a broadsheet carrying stories about Ezin blowing past him in the wind.

The old hunter wore a crossbow strapped to one leg and a thin-bladed short sword in a leather scabbard at his other hip. His clothes were typical of a hunter, almost identical to Suken's save for an unbuttoned maroon vest worn over his off-white shirt. The red was so dark it was nearly black, but it was still technically against the law for him to be wearing it. Any non-mage who dared to wear a color usually got slapped with a stiff fine, but Suken supposed Ezin's reputation and popularity protected him from such trivial annoyances as adhering to the law.

And worst of all, the old busybody had taken it upon himself to keep an eye on Suken. *I've got enough people claiming I've gotten where I am on someone else's merits without the most famous hunter in the damn city trying to play mentor,* Suken thought.

"I heard about what happened last night," Ezin said quietly, stepping closer. "Lady Chance can't be watchin' all of us at once, but even so, that's rough luck, son. You doin' all right?"

"Yeah," Suken said. "Lady'll make it up to me eventually." Out of the corner of his eye, he noticed every hunter in line watching them. *Great. Just great.*

Ezin nodded. "Good to see you've got the right outlook. Got a decent warrant this time out?"

"Greencloak," Suken said. "Along with everyone else, apparently."

"I'd wish you luck, boy," Ezin said with a grin, "but if anyone's going to take in Greenie, it's going to be me."

Not bloody likely, Suken thought. "We'll see," he said out loud.

"Myself and a few other hunters are working together to bring 'im in. And about time too, if you ask me. The boy's damn talented, but this business in the Valley . . ." he shook his graying head, his expression reserved. "He's gone rabid, I suspect." He paused, and leaned in closer. "You want in on it?"

For half a heartbeat, Suken considered it. But he discounted the thought as quickly as he'd had it. Joining Ezin would reinforce the view the rest of the hunters had of him, and worse, he'd get less money and marks if he joined with a team than if he brought Greencloak in alone.

"Thanks," Suken said. "But I work better alone."

"Optimistic! I always liked that about you. Well, keep up the good work." He clapped his hand to Suken's shoulder with a good-natured smile.

"Well," Suken said, tipping his hat and hoping that Ezin took the hint. "See you. Try not to get yourself killed out there."

"I always do," Ezin said with a smile. "Been pretty successful so far." He raised his hand to rub at the stubble on his jaw. "You know . . . if you wait around for a few minutes, I could join you in the bar. Give you a few pointers."

No offense, old man, but I'd rather eat my own hat.

"Appreciate the offer," Suken said, somehow managing to sound grateful. "But I've got some people to talk to after this."

Ezin nodded and leaned closer. "Keep it up," he said under his breath. "They're starting to warm up to you." He clapped Suken on the shoulder again, turned, and rejoined the line. Suken stared after him, raising one eyebrow despite himself. *Did he just make a scene in order for me to turn him down in front of everyone? If so, I'll need to remember to buy him a drink when I make it to fourth rank.*

Suken turned, pushing open the door and entering the Lady's Face.

Hunters weren't allowed to leave the guild's premises with case-files. Before the Face's opening, the rooms on the second floor had been filled with sweaty, dirty hunters hunched over dusty case-files for hours on end. Suken had a few vague memories of this, from being dragged along with his uncle when his uncle was supposed to be watching him and his brother. But five years ago, an ex-hunter named Marxen had worked out a mutually beneficial deal with the Guild. He'd cut a hole through the wall adjoining the two buildings and made an agreement to collect the confidential case-files at the end of every shift, returning them to the guild's clerks. In return, he got all the business he could ask for in the form of bleary-eyed hunters who were all too happy to pay for the convenience of some coffee, hot food, or booze while they studied their case-files. The guild came up jewels on the deal too, as they now had the free space to refurbish most of the rooms upstairs into administrative offices.

A wave of raucous laughter rose to greet him from the group

of men and women seated around one of the ten round tables in the room. Only two other tables were occupied, one by a pair of men playing cards, the other by a young woman poring over a thick stack of case-files. Spherical luminaries hung in simple glass tear-drop holders from the exposed rafters, casting their warm light over the tables. Weapons and warrants hung on the walls in lieu of the sculpted glass greenery that most other taverns boasted, and the entire back wall was taken up by a well-worn bar with fifteen simple wooden stools lined up in front of it. The mirrored shelves behind the bar held bottles of various shapes, sizes, and colors.

Beside the door leading to the guild, a huge stuffed jungle-cat snarled in frozen fury, its ivory fangs a stark contrast to its black glossy fur. Several hats were balanced on its head and back. Suken paused a moment, searching for an empty spot, but apparently Lillon was full of hats for the day. He carefully inserted a single prayer in between those sharp teeth to slide down her gullet and into the hollow where her stomach used to be and turned his attention back to the room.

Some of the hunters had turned to glance at Suken when he walked in, but after a single disinterested once-over, all save one turned back to their conversations. Tuorin, one of the two men playing cards, met Suken's eyes briefly and nodded with a hint of a smile playing across his lips. Suken was about to return it and join him at his table when he heard his uncle's name mentioned by someone at the bigger table, followed by a round of derisive laughter. The smile died before it could be fully born, his desire for companionship dying right along with it. He made his way to the back instead, collapsing onto a stool at the bar and resting his elbows on the dark wood.

The bartender, Marxen, glanced up as Suken sat down. He set aside the rag he'd been using to clean glasses and made his way over to face Suken, pulling his long dark hair back into a tail at the base of his neck and binding it with a tie before resting his hands on the bar with a lop-sided smile. A pair of thin white scars ran from his jaw down his neck to vanish under the collar of his spotless white shirt, souvenirs of the injury that had knocked him out of the hunting business and spurred him on to buy this bar. He looked at Suken's head pointedly.

Suken sighed and pulled his hat off, setting it on the empty stool next to him. He ran his uninjured hand back through his hair and rested the other on the bar, wincing. "Sorry. Lillon was full."

"Busy day," Marxen acknowledged. He looked at the blood-stained bandage wrapped around Suken's right hand, his gaze drifting up to the blood-soaked sleeve. "Looks bad."

"Eh. Most of it's not mine." Suken reached down and flipped open the straps holding his crossbow to his leg. He hefted it and placed it gently on the bar. The weapon was longer than his forearm, the cartridge holding spare bolts jutting out at an angle from the haft. A bolt was still jammed at an odd angle into the channel, the wood around the steel tip splintered. He'd tried to pry it free with a knife on the rail-car ride to the dead girl's house, but after a few tries he'd given up, fearing that he'd do more harm than good. One of the bows was broken, too, and the string hung from the weapon to drape on the bar like a dead snake, still stained with Suken's blood. "*This,*" he said, nodding to the bow, "is bad." He ran a hand along the weapon, his fingers intimately familiar with every curve of the wood. "Avara's gonna kill me."

Marxen eyed the weapon. "That bolt metal-bound?"

"I wouldn't be putting it on the bar if it was," Suken replied, a note of annoyance creeping into his voice. Even Marxen treated him like a kitten sometimes.

"Well, Lady Chance knows you won't be the first to get a tongue-lashing from Avara. Coffee?"

Suken shifted on the stool, moving his arm to display his new remembrance bloom, the skin around it still inflamed and puffy.

It was a simple plumeria blossom, half the size of the other flowers spreading their petals across his skin. "Lost someone last night. I'd prefer something harder than coffee."

Fifth-rank hunters like Suken were allowed into The Lady's Face, but Marxen refused to give them hard liquor until they reached fourth. Any fifth-rank hunter who sauntered in and asked for rum, aguardente, or other hard drinks found himself with a tall, cool glass of milk and a round of jeering comments about kittens knowing their place. But Marxen did make an exception for those in mourning.

Marxen's mouth drew down. "Who?" he asked.

"A mark," Suken replied, staring at the plumeria and seeing Flower's blue eyes. "Little girl. Barely ten."

"You get a remembrance bloom for every mark you lose, you're gonna run out of space before you hit thirty," Marxen said dryly.

"You're suffering under the delusion that I'm like the rest of these talentless hacks," Suken said, jerking his thumb back over his shoulder. He winced as the movement pulled on the raw edges of the cut on his hand.

Marxen snorted, but he bent to pull a small empty glass from under the bar. He set it down in front of Suken. "Suppose you'll be wantin' gin, like yer uncle did?"

Suken nodded, flexing his fingers again.

"Got the aerans for gin, boy?"

"Yes," Suken replied. *Barely.* Uncle Lorrin had once told Suken in a confidential whisper that he liked gin so much because it came from Darashan, far across the northern ocean. Supposedly the liquor was distilled from some sort of tree that didn't exist in the jungles below Adunare, and import fees from Darashan were steep.

Suken certainly harbored no desire to be like his uncle. But the first time he'd come here, gin was what Marxen had given him and his brother. He'd tried other liquors, but none of them held quite the same sweet and sour pang of memory.

Marxen set the bottle down on the bar in front of Suken with a dull clunk. "What went wrong?" he said as he pulled the stopper free. The pungent scent was as familiar to Suken as the ever-present sound of the rain against the windows.

Suken picked up the glass, staring into the gin. Flower's pale face floated before his eyes, as clear as if she were lying in front of him now, and not swathed in linen in some dark room waiting to be burned. "I did," he said softly. "I expected a criminal to make the right choice—to be noble. That'll never happen again." He brought the glass to his lips and threw his head back. The liquor went down like caal-fire, burning his throat. He shuddered and set the glass down, tapping the bar beside it with his index finger, just as Lorrin had used to do.

Marxen stared at him, his expression solemn. "Can I give you some advice, kitten?"

"Something gives me the feeling I'm going to get it even if the answer is no."

"Criminals are people too," Marxen said, leaning forward to rest one elbow on the bar. "Most of 'em just run into hard times, is all. Treat 'em as such and you'll get a lot farther, a lot faster, in this business."

"I've run into hard times," Suken said, a brittle edge creeping into his voice. "I never went out and kidnapped ten year old girls for ransom."

"Maybe you haven't been pushed far enough," Marxen said with a shrug. "You push a man to the edge of the city, you'd be surprised at what he'd be willing to do to keep from falling. Remember that, all right?"

Suken tapped his finger beside the glass again, more insistently this time.

Marxen picked up the bottle, refilling Suken's glass. "Risarin was in here earlier asking after you," he said, a little too innocently. "Told me he was headed to the precinct. Bet you could catch up with him, if you hurry."

Suken gave a non-committal grunt and picked up his glass. Marxen had a habit of trying to play match-maker among the hunters, but Suken was in no mood for that today. Marxen hesitated for a moment, but when Suken didn't reply, he shrugged, put the glass stopper back on the bottle of gin, and turned to slide it onto the shelf. He moved on down the bar to begin chatting with another hunter as Suken pulled out the Greencloak case-file and set it on the bar, flipping it open. A serving girl sidled up to him.

"Breakfast?" she asked.

"Coffee," Suken replied, his eyes already skimming the file. "And a plate of rice with pork."

"For *breakfast?*"

He smiled up at her. "Not breakfast for me, little lady. I've been up since before daybreak."

The girl flushed before curtsying and taking her leave, and Suken turned his full attention to the file. The first thirty pages were reports on Greencloak's early counts of petty theft. Suken skimmed those, picking up bits of information here and there as he went. At some point the girl returned with his coffee and a plate of brown rice, slathered with a generous helping of sauce laden with chunks of slow-roasted pork and peppers. Suken scooped a heaping portion onto a piece of flatbread and ate an occasional bite as he flipped the pages, chasing the food down with sips of coffee.

Eyewitness accounts of Greencloak were scarce. Each time he'd been spotted he'd been wearing the long, hooded green cloak which had led the broadsheets to give him his nickname, and each time he'd vanished into the shadows before the witness in question could get more than a glimpse of him. In the early days this had led many to think that there *was* no "Greencloak." Some had claimed that he was a spirit, others that he was some sort of new mage-born, created without the Council's approval.

The cloak was the only thing that every story agreed on.

Ground-length, leaf-green at the hem and fading up into a dark forest-green at the shoulders. A hood that completely shrouded his face. A dark lining. He probably flipped the cloak around and wore it inside out when he needed to be more discrete, but discrete didn't seem to be his style. The very fact that the cloak was green was a slap in the face of the status quo.

He obviously had a flair for the dramatic. Some people claimed that he *allowed* himself to be seen at his heists, wanting the attention and the renown. One popular story ran that he'd broken into a mage's manor late one night, dressed the mage and his wife in the soot-stained uniforms of incinerator workers without waking them, and proceeded to rob them blind. Suken had heard at least ten different variations on that one. Other stories were less dramatic but no less popular, told in taverns and rum-houses over glasses, the audiences bursting into laughter at all the right places.

Public hearsay was often more useful than the information the guards provided for a case-file, but in this case Suken had no way of knowing which of the stories were true and which were false. There were too many, and the man himself too damn mysterious. He turned his attention back to the case-file, turning a page. His eyes widened as he scanned over the first few lines, and he went back over them, reading more carefully.

Lightsday 29, Terras, approximately half past midnight. Report collected from Orwyn Sirkor, Mazarine Guard, regiment twenty-three. Captain Sirkor reports that he was on guard detail at the Council's Library on First Street, and upon hearing an unusual noise entered the third Great Hall. As he entered, he saw a man of average height wearing a green cloak kneeling in front of the door to the Second Repository. When confronted, the suspect turned. Captain Sirkor reports that the suspect's hood was down. He described the suspect as young, perhaps in his late teens to early twenties, with long dark hair pulled back from his face, a Majitanian complexion, and a dark well-trimmed

*mustache and beard. His features were described as sharp, his
build slim. The suspect fled. Case still open to investigation.*

Suken read over the Captain's report a second time, but other
than the physical description he didn't find anything he could
use.

After that came the list of grand larceny charges. Greencloak was indiscriminate in his thieving when it came to
difficulty, breaking mundane and metal-bound locks with
apparent ease, but he was certainly picky when it came to his
targets. Mages, usually, and only those who were particularly
wealthy. The last ten pages of the larceny report were thefts
in which his guilt hadn't been proven due to a lack of evidence or a witness to the crime, but they fit with his profile. A
priceless manuscript on convergence theory reported stolen
from Lord Pertwith. Three hundred thousand aerans stolen from a thrice-locked metal-bound chest in Mage Tork-
id's private study. A statue practically dripping with silver and
emeralds taken from the Academe's bustling front entryway,
apparently during class hours. Interesting, but there was little to nothing he could use here, either. He turned the page,
and stiffened.

This was clearly the first of the murder reports. It began with
an artist's sketch of the scene. Suken knew that it was common
practice to call in sketch artists in order to properly document
the scene before the bodies were removed, but this was the first
time he'd seen such a sketch in person. He pushed his half-
eaten meal away with two fingers, his appetite lost. The drawing depicted a room in one of the tenement housing sections
of the Valley District. The adobe walls were patched and moss
and mold spread outwards from the corners. The simple bed
shoved into one corner was little more than a misshapen lump
covered with tattered blankets. All of that was fairly normal
for a Valley dwelling. The corpse sprawled in the center of the
room was not.

One of the man's arms jutted out at an unnatural angle, his eyes staring up at the ceiling. His face was strangely blank, as if the skin had been pulled taut over the bones of his face, erasing any wrinkles or expression. *A shifter,* Suken thought. *Like the one who killed Flower.*

When they died, their skin relaxed and took on a blank, expressionless quality that made it near impossible to guess their age or properly identify them. The victim's throat had been slit, and his stomach opened to spill his bowels around him in a half-circle of gore. It looked as if the man had tried to gather his own innards back up, judging by the way he was clutching them to his stomach. Blood had drenched the front of the simple shift he wore and lay pooled around him for a foot in every direction. And on the wall, scrawled in what was apparently the man's own blood, was a single word.

Enough.

Suken shuddered and looked away from the drawing. He didn't usually have trouble with blood. Lady Chance knew he'd seen his own often enough, and spilled plenty more in the last couple years. But this scene . . . Chance. Something about the way the man held his spilled organs raised the hair on the back of Suken's neck. This wasn't a killing in self-defense, as many in the Valley were. It wasn't even a cartel hit, which were business-like and professional. The shifter had been disemboweled and left to die in agony.

Suken took a moment to let his mind settle and turned back to the papers, scanning over the written description of the crime scene.

The victim had been in his mid-to-late thirties, but it was difficult to tell for sure with shifters. He had no family that the guards could find, and had apparently gone by a different name to everyone who had ever spoken to him. He paid the tenement-lord on time and his neighbors described him as quiet and polite.

As a shifter, his occupation was probably illegal. Most people only undertook the dangerous procedures to transform into mage-born as a last resort, in order to pay off debts to the cartels or keep themselves from the slavers or the scaffolds. There were always Hollow Market mages looking to experiment on living humans, and willing to pay outrageous sums for the privilege. If the hapless individual survived the process (the chances of that were apparently little better than half), they were 'reborn' with abilities which lent themselves well to illegal activities like thievery, spying or assassination. Each mage-born was subtly different, as the convergences linked to their internal leis rarely worked the same way twice. Some results were slightly more predictable than others, creating people with abilities similar enough to classify. Shifters, who could change their faces and the color of their hair with a thought. Haunts, their skin as black as night but marked with grey patches which shifted like clouds across the sky, able to render themselves nearly invisible at night or in the shadows. Sylics, hauntingly beautiful and said to exude some sort of scent which made them irresistible. And, so rare that most people considered them mere myth, readers. Men and women able to see your innermost thoughts with a touch. The only reader Suken had ever heard about personally was the TruthSeer, a mage-born the High Mages kept around to determine guilt in high-profile cases.

Most of them looked perfectly normal, which gave some people the creeps.

Suken flipped to the next page. This victim had been a shadow-sprite. Suken looked down at the drawing of its deflated body, like a shed snake-skin, with a touch of pity. Shadow-sprites looked something like children in build and height, with pitch-black skin and huge eyes through which you could see the glowing stores of energy which powered them. They were slightly more intelligent than dogs or cats, but less likely to defend themselves if attacked. Suken wasn't sure if they felt pain, but he was certain they were capable of fear. Since shadow-sprites lacked blood, the word at this crime scene had been written in ink. In order to have killed a sprite without an explosive backlash when the creature's stored energy was released, Suken realized that Greencloak must either be a mage, or have had access to a metal-bound item to draw the energy out safely. He filed that little bit of information away.

The third victim was mage-born, too—a sylic. The victim had been found in one of the brothels on Orchid Street, and had managed to let out a cry of warning. One of the bouncers had kicked down the door in time to see a man in a dual-toned green cloak leaping out the window. The word written on the wall in blood was rushed, the blood trailing off from the "h" in a jagged smear like a bolt of lightning.

Suken ran his hand back through his hair, leaning back to look up at the ceiling. Why the sudden change from thievery to murder? Greencloak clearly had some sort of vendetta against the mages, based on his thieving preferences. Maybe that vendetta had shifted to the mage-born.

Suken wondered uneasily if Greencloak had fallen in with the Coalition. The movement believed that mage-born were diseased, or something. Suken had never paid much attention to them, other than to avoid the people begging for money for their cause in the markets. They'd slowly been gaining support for the last two years in the Valley, but they'd yet to take any actions more drastic than speeches at the Arrival Circle, marches, or letters written to the High Mages' Council.

Well, motives were unimportant. Suken's job was *finding* the thief, not learning why he did it. That was a job for the judges.

Suken sighed and internally listed off the things he knew. He knew vaguely what the man looked like without his hood up. But other than that? Majitanian, presumably, so Suken wasn't looking for a Tyrodamian, Darashanian, or Eldressi. *Good*, he thought with a wry twist of a smile. *That'll cut my potential targets down to . . . oh. About a million or so.*

Greencloak's targets for thievery were rich mages, which meant the High Mage's District. But his murder victims were mage-born, which meant the Valley. *So, the whole city, then.*

The best way to find a mark, generally, was to find the people they were close to. Someone was always willing to sell out a criminal, for the right price. In most case-files, the Guild included a list of known contacts and places the mark was known to frequent. In Greencloak's case, this page was surprisingly sparse. There were a few names there, people who had come to the guild for a small reward, claiming that Greencloak had bought their wares or sold them fenced goods. But each of their descriptions varied from one another, and none matched the guard's report.

He realized that someone was standing beside him. Suken looked up to see his serving girl staring down at one of the crime scene drawings he'd shoved aside, her eyes wide and her face pale beneath her dusky skintone. Suken immediately flipped the case-file closed. The serving girls knew they weren't supposed to look at the case-files, but he supposed he couldn't blame this one for catching a glimpse. "Did you need something?" he asked.

She jumped, her eyes darting from the case-file guiltily. "I didn't mean to look, it was just—"

"Totally my fault," Suken interrupted her, waving one hand. "Don't worry . . . um . . ." He'd met her before, though it took him a few heartbeats to place her name. *Chiana.* Her long dark hair was tied back, but several strands had escaped to frame her face. "Chi, right?"

She nodded, pushing an errant clump of hair back behind her ear.

"No harm done," he said. He eyed her as she reached over to take his empty cup of coffee. Chiana had made a few shy advances towards him in the past, but he'd never reciprocated. Not because she wasn't pretty—she was, very—but because he didn't have time for anything serious.

Chi glanced around. "Is that Greencloak's file?" she asked in a whisper.

"Yeah," Suken said. "Seen a lot of copies today?"

"Almost every hunter who's come in has had a copy of it."

Suken sighed and gathered up the papers, tapping them once on the table to straighten them. "Don't suppose you know anything about Greenie, do you, Chi?"

She shrugged. "What everyone knows." She reached across him to take his plate. Her shoulder brushed against his, and she gave him a shy glance before drawing back. She was wearing a tight-fitting bodice under a buttoned vest which displayed her bosom not quite to its fullest, but nearly so. Suken's heartbeat picked up, but he reminded it (and other interested parties) firmly that he was on a job.

"If you should happen to hear anything," he said with his most charming smile as he pulled his hat on, "I'd be interested to hear. Maybe you and I could sit down and chat about it over a drink." He glanced around. "Somewhere else. You probably see enough of this place during the day."

She raised her hand to brush her hair back behind one ear. "That would be nice," she said. "A drink, I mean. With you." She looked away, biting her lip. Then she glanced around, leaning closer and dropping her voice into a whisper. "They all say he's guilty. Do you think it's true?"

He raised an eyebrow, trying to ignore how good a view that position of hers was giving him. On purpose, he was sure. Sometimes he wondered if the young men and women of the city had all attended classes on this sort of thing, and how he'd missed out on them. *I was probably out hauling around supplies for Avara or Ni'darrisana,* he thought, and pulled his thoughts away from well-shaped bosoms and back to the conversation at hand. "Why wouldn't Greencloak be guilty?"

"I don't know. It's just . . . I've heard things." She lowered her voice still further. "Nice things, you know?"

"About *Greencloak?*"

Chiana flushed and stepped away from him. "It's stupid. Never mind."

"Wait," Suken said, reaching out to catch her wrist. *Any information can potentially be the information that leads you to a mark,* he remembered his uncle saying once. *No matter how small it might seem.* She hesitated, glancing at his hand around her wrist. He didn't release her, instead giving her another smile. "Whatever it is, you can tell me."

"Well," she said, the flush creeping higher, "some people say he helps the people in the Valley, sometimes. Gives them money. Medicine. Things like that."

"Some people? Like who?"

She shrugged. "Lots of people."

Interesting. That wasn't a rumor he'd heard before. Greencloak might even be spreading this one himself. Trying to get on the peoples' good side, so they'd refuse to turn him over to the guards.

Or . . . if it's true, Suken thought, *then it shouldn't be too hard to find out who he's been helping, and keep an eye on one or two. If he's helped them before, he might again.*

"Oooh, the kitten's on the Greencloak case. How *cute.* You think you can run with the big cats, kitten?"

Suken closed his eyes for a heartbeat. *Of all people to run into today. . . .* He turned on his stool to give Rilana a broad smile. The lean huntress stood with her arms crossed over her serape, rain dripping from her long dark braid, obviously having just come in. Her face was pinched and gaunt with high cheekbones, and she had a habit of puckering her lips in a way which always made Suken wonder if she'd eaten half a lemon. Beneath the serape, she wore a dark tunic belted tight to her waist and a black shirt with tight sleeves. A pair of wickedly curved knives hung from the belts crisscrossed over her serape.

Chi vanished in a swirl of skirts behind the bar and through the door leading to the kitchen.

"Rilana," Suken said. "Charming as always, I see."

She swung herself onto a stool three seats down and nodded to Marxen, but her words were directed at Suken. "Don't bother trying for Greencloak. Other, *better* hunters are already on it. Hunters who worked their way up from the bottom on their own merits instead of riding their uncles' serapes." She eyed him with a mildly disgusted twist of her features.

"Right," Suken said. "Hunters like you?"

She snorted and turned to watch as Marxen poured her a small glass of rum. Suken narrowed his eyes at her, feeling the familiar anger churning inside him. He'd worked hard to get where he was, harder than most. But everyone always assumed he'd pulled in favors in the guild to get his hunting license. Instead of ignoring the anger—and Rilana—like he knew he should, Suken threw her a wicked smile and put on his most innocent, "I'm-just-curious" tone of voice.

"How long's it been since you brought in a mark alive, Ria?" he asked, reaching over to pick his broken crossbow up from the bar. He strapped it to his leg as he continued, "Has the guild knocked you down to rank four yet, or do you have another three or four murders—I mean, botched jobs, sorry—to go before they do?"

"You're one to talk about botched jobs," she said with a sidelong look at him, a sly smile playing across her lips. "Least on my jobs only criminals wind up dead."

"Watch it," he said with a dark look.

"Or what? You'll kill me?" She snorted and picked up her glass. "Last I checked, I was over the age of ten."

Suken's stool tipped backwards and fell to the ground as he leapt to his feet with a growl, his hand darting to the hilt of the knife at his belt. Ria reacted almost as quickly, dropping her glass and grabbing her own knives as she whirled towards him smoothly. Before he could make a move towards her, the resounding bang of a bottle slamming down on the bar brought them both up short. The conversation of the six hunters sitting around the table behind them quieted. The pair of men playing cards stared at Suken and Ria with considering expressions, and the woman with the case-files had half-stood, a knife in one hand. For a moment, watchful silence cloaked the tavern. Suken slowly and deliberately lifted his hand from the knife at his belt. Ria dropped her hands from her weapons as well, and the other hunters turned back to their conversations, cards, or contracts.

"You," Marxen said, pointing at Ria with the empty bottle. "Far end of the bar. Now." Ria paused long enough to right her fallen stool, throwing a single venomous look back over her shoulder at Suken. "And you," Marxen said, turning to Suken, "are going to get yourself killed one day, whether by that bloody smartass mouth o' yours or your high n' mighty morals, or a combination of the two."

Suken opened his mouth to reply, but Marxen lifted a hand, forestalling him. "I don't wanna hear it. Go chase Greencloak like the rest of em. Or, even better, take a day off. Relax and get your head back on straight."

"Right," Suken said, rolling his eyes. "like Terri'll let me take a day off."

"She will," Marxen interrupted, jabbing him in the chest with the bottle, "or I'll pay a visit and have a talk with her myself."

Now there was something Suken would have paid good aerans to see. Marxen facing down Suken's lithe little housekeeper and account manager would be a battle for the history books. Better than the Amaranthine War. More entertaining, at the least.

Suken drew out a half-aeran and laid it on the bar. "Thanks."

Marxen picked up the coin and Greencloak's case-file and nodded to him, his expression solemn. "Take care of yourself."

Suken stood and glanced at Ria as he walked by her. She pointedly ignored him, staring into her rum.

Time to call in a few favors in the Valley, Suken thought as he exited the front door into a warm drizzle of rain. *With all the people I've helped down there over the last four years, at least one or two is bound to talk.*

Chapter Five

Fletch awoke in a haze of pain and nausea. He rolled to one side, eyes already sweeping over his surroundings, but the tension in his body eased as he recognized one of the small back caves attached to the den. Vethin was fast asleep near him, sitting up with a ratty blanket draped over his shoulders.

He got me here safely, Fletch thought, but forced down the wave of gratitude and pride. If he showed any hint of it on his face, the kid would latch onto it and the hero-worship would get even worse. He stood, having to brace himself against the stone wall as pain shot up from his injured leg. Someone had bound it, but they'd done a good job. Fletch limped out of the little cave and into the main cavern of the den.

The kids emerged, yawning, from behind draped sheets and blankets. They poked their heads out of side-tunnels leading out towards the city. One or two dropped down from a series of wooden platforms against the wall which they called The Bruiser, built to help teach them to climb and keep their balance.

They filled the open space behind Fletch with wary eyes and nervous mutterings, a small rippling sea of snarled hair, dirty faces, tattered rags and rusty and discarded weapons shoved into worn leather belts.

Fletch carefully climbed his way up onto a flat section of The Bruiser and settled down on a pile of tattered blankets, stretching his injured leg out in front of him with a wince.

He looked down on a sea of expectant, frightened eyes in gaunt, dirty faces. The den, usually a din of laughter and yelling, was silent as a tomb.

"Someone's after me," Fletch said. His voice carried well in the cluttered cavern. "They might know about the den, so Two by Hand from now on."

Solemn nods from the older kids in the back. Two by Hand was a phrase from an old children's poem, supposedly written when the mages had been exiled from Darashan. It meant that one of the older kids was to partner with a younger, and no one was to leave the den alone. This happened from time to time, when one of the younger kids wasn't careful and unknowingly let someone follow them back to the den. Eventually the older kids would hunt down the trespasser and convince them to 'forget' the location by bribes or threats of violence, but until then, Two by Hand was the rule. This was the first time Fletch had brought danger to the den himself, albeit unwittingly. For five years he'd worked to keep this place safe, and his involvement in the children's dealings secret. He'd brought the children he found starving on the streets here and turned them over to the older ones to teach and take care of, and he'd personally hunted down more than a few people who'd thought to raid the den in search of children to sell to the slave markets or the whorehouses. But otherwise, he operated under a strict hands-off policy in regards to the kids here.

And yet, they still regarded him as some sort of father figure, crowding around him whenever he showed his face and clamoring for his approval. He put up with that as best he could. It was a fair exchange, he thought, for the knowledge that he was keeping them safe from the bastards who would buy and sell them on the streets above. If he had to put up with a little hero-worship, well . . . it was a sacrifice he was willing to make.

But now it looked as if this time in his life was coming to an end.

I knew this was coming, he thought, looking out over that sea of expectant faces. *The more infamous I got, the more chance someone could find out about this, and use the kids against me. I always knew that eventually I'd have to step back and allow the community to thrive on its own. . . . I just didn't expect for it to happen so soon.*

One of the younger ones, a little girl who had joined them a year ago, stepped forward. She wore a simple pair of trousers five sizes too big for her tied at the waist with a piece of twine, and a brown vest worn over a shirt that might have been white several hundred washes ago. "What happened?" she asked. "How'd they find you?"

A chorus of curious murmurs followed this.

Wouldn't I like to know. "I wasn't careful," Fletch replied. Turning this experience into a lesson might keep some of them from making a costly mistake. He saw Vethin emerge from the little cave, rubbing his eyes. He wouldn't say anything to refute Fletch's story. Kid was too smart for that. "Didn't check my corners. Turns out that's how I die."

The girl stood for a moment in grim silence, clearly digesting this, and nodded. "Did you kill 'em?" she asked. "The people who caught you? Is that why all the cats and the pearls are callin' you a murderer?" Another low murmur of curiosity at this.

Fletch blinked. The bounty hunters and the guards were *always* after him, but they couldn't possibly have heard about the man he'd killed down there, and no one knew about the handful of other people Fletch had killed in self-defense before donning his Greencloak persona. "Yes," he said. He'd ask some of the older kids what was going on later, when he didn't have three dozen pairs of eyes fixed on him. "I'll be leaving for awhile. If anyone comes looking for me, you tell them you don't know me.

You don't know who I am, or what I look like, or what my real name is. You've heard of me, of course, but that's it. Got it?"

Some of the smaller ones looked as if they were on the verge of tears, but they nodded.

"Good." He stood, keeping as much weight off of his leg as he could, and eased himself down from the scaffold.

Rossin stepped forward, pushing the younger kids out of his way until he reached Fletch's side. He was nearly twenty-six now, the oldest in the den and the only one other than Fletch remaining from the original group. His hair was dark as the soot from the incinerators and unkempt stubble shadowed his jaw. The other children broke into smaller groups, the noise level in the cavern rising as they began talking in hushed tones, deciding who would be paired with who for Two by Hand.

"What's going on?" Rossin asked, his dark eyes as solemn as those of the younger kids.

"I'm not sure yet," Fletch replied, keeping his voice down. "What was she talking about, with the cats and the pearls calling me a murderer?"

"You mean the warrants?"

Fletch stared at him. "*Murder* warrants?"

"They're everywhere," Rossin said, dropping his voice to barely a whisper. "Every pearl in the damn city is looking for you, and most of the cats. They say that the guild removed the rank-restriction from your warrant, and the price on your head is four hundred thousand aerans."

"Four hundred thousand? Good fucking gods, that's enough to buy half the bloody Academe! Who am I supposed to have killed?"

"They say you're butchering mage-born. A serial killer. Deranged."

"Murdering mage-born," Fletch said flatly. "*Me?*"

"That's what the warrants say. None of us believed them, of

course. But . . . maybe the warrants have something to do with the people who caught you?"

"Maybe," Fletch replied, thinking of the silent man wearing his cloak. "Wouldn't be the first time someone tried to frame me for something. If you so much as suspect that someone from the underside is shadowing the den, you bloody well get them all out. You understand?"

"Yes, boss."

"How many times have I told you, don't call me that." Fletch reached down to gently probe at his knee with a fingertip, and was rewarded with a fresh stab of pain. "You get 'em out, and you keep 'em safe 'til this is over."

"Where are you going?"

Fletch pulled the dagger he'd taken from the guard from his belt and ran a finger over the complicated nest of criss-crossed lines etched into the metal at the base. It looked like every other maker's mark to Fletch. . . . As if someone had dropped a skein of yarn and their cat had gotten ahold of it. He spun the knife around his index finger once and tucked it back into the belt. "To see a weapon-smith," he said.

Chapter Six

Night had fallen by the time Fletch scaled the metal gate blocking one of the narrow alleys in the mage's district, his lower leg still hurting like the gods' own aching balls. This place was practically a bloody mansion compared to the tenement homes in the Valley, though it wasn't quite as nice as the other three homes on the block. Thick curtains shrouded the windows, and the adobe walls were cracking and peeling in more than a few places. Mildew spread upwards along the wall, and a wind-chime hung at a skewed angle from one of the eaves, the glass bird in its center dangling as if it had a broken wing. Fletch had no doubt that on other nights the little quad between the houses hosted block parties during which puppeteers or student mages were hired to entertain the children while the adults sat around and sipped chilled aguardente in the gathering dark, but tonight it was empty.

He wore a midnight blue cloak with the hood up to hide his face, the fabric thick but not as comfortable as his own cloak. *When I find the bastard who's framing me,* Fletch thought, kneeling with a wince and inserting his pick into the lock, adjusting it slightly until he heard the familiar snicks of the pins lifting, *I'm going to strangle him with his own fucking intestines.* He inserted the torsion wrench, twisted it with a deft flick of his wrist, and stood as the door swung open on squeaky hinges. The mage's servants were gone for the night—Fletch had seen them leave a half an hour ago from his vantage point across the street. He made his way through a small sitting room with a stack of jumbled pairs of shoes in a corner, then through a hallway lined with framed drawings and paintings. Weapons on wooden racks stood in several corners, some half-covered by thin fabric shrouds. The place smelled of roasted pork and garlic, undoubtedly what the mage in question had had for dinner tonight.

The steps up to the second floor were a tricky matter, as the boards were loose and prone to creaks. Fletch stepped as carefully as he could, setting his weight with more care than a pawn shop owner weighing a handful of stolen gold, and managed to make it to the top with no telltale sounds. He avoided stepping on any of the scattered books or sheaves of paper scattered about the floor in the musty library at the top of the stairs. Light shone beneath a door between two large bookshelves, and Fletch heard muffled off-kilter humming from inside.

He walked to the door more silently than his own shadow and edged it open, not needing to apply any drops of the oil he kept on his belt to keep the hinges from squeaking. Inside, a young man sat on a wooden stool with his back to the door, his head bent over a battered wooden desk. The sleeves of his gold tunic were rolled up to the elbows and some sort of thin metal tool was balanced behind one ear. A leather strap running around the back of his head pushed his short brown hair into disarray, as if he'd often adjusted it. Rolls of wire and various tools that looked a great deal like Fletch's lockpicks lay scattered about the desk, and the scents of steel-oil and teak filled the air, along with an uncomfortable static sensation causing the hair on Fletch's neck to stand on end. The walls were as disorderly as everything else in the house, covered with a seemingly random collection of daggers, crossbow bolts, arrows, tools, wires hanging in loose strands or in rolls, and even one huge sword which looked as if it were taller than Fletch. Its hilt was a mess of silver wires poking out in every direction.

He made his way across the small room, picking his way carefully through the scattered piles of wood shavings, metal shards, and wires, until he stood directly behind the mage. Fletch touched the tip of his knife to the small of the man's back, just enough for the mage to feel it.

The mage stiffened, lifting his hands slowly from the complicated mess of wires on his desk. "Fletch?" he said. "Is that you?"

"Yes," Fletch said. "And you're damn lucky it is, Blue. You're *still* not watching your back." He poked the tip of the blade into the mage's back hard enough to give him a little discomfort. "Gonna get you killed one of these days."

"Well, so far you're the only one who's ever bothered to break in here," Blue said, not turning. "So I guess I feel pretty safe about taking my chances. Though if you'd pricked me with that thing ten minutes earlier, you might have interrupted a very delicate procedure."

"Gods forbid," Fletch muttered, drawing back.

Blue turned to look at him, the thick lenses of the goggles making his blue eyes look enlarged, like a bug's. That did nothing to detract from the mage's good looks. One corner of his mouth lifted upward in a smile. "Been awhile since you visited. How are you?"

"Shitty. You better be in the mood to answer some questions."

"These questions are important enough to warrant poking holes in my best tunics?"

Fletch drew back. "Don't mention that word," he said sourly.

"What word? Poking?" Blue asked with a smirk. "Hole?"

"Warrant," Fletch snapped.

Blue snorted. "I thought you *liked* attention."

"For things I actually did, yes," Fletch replied. "The warrants out for me now are for murder, if you hadn't heard."

Blue pushed the goggles up to the top of his head, mussing his hair even more. Dark smudges of oil stood out against the pale skin on his nose and his left cheek. Even half covered in grime and with his short hair mussed, he looked nothing short of a sculptor's masterpiece with those high cheekbones and that straight nose. His blue eyes, however, were wide and horrified. "Murder? What did you *do?*"

Blue must have been so immersed in his work for the last few weeks that he hadn't stepped outside of his house. On his way here, Fletch had seen badly-drawn depictions of his own hooded form staring at him from every lamp-post and plastered along every wall.

"I didn't do anything," Fletch replied, grabbing a chair and flipping it around to sit on it backwards and rest his arms on the back. He sighed in relief as some of the pain faded from his leg, now that he wasn't putting any weight on it. "Nothing more than I usually do, anyway. Someone's framing me, and doing so with considerably more success than the last three assholes who tried."

Blue let out a low whistle. He was in his late twenties, barely out of the Academe, but despite the fact that the mage was older, Fletch was more mature in many ways than Blue ever would be. Blue liked to think that he was living on the edge, selling metal-bound weapons in the Hollow Market once a month, but the truth of the matter was that he was something of a joke to the Valley dwellers that dealt with him. They didn't disabuse him of his little delusions of being a hardened criminal because he sold them quality products, and Fletch didn't enlighten him because Blue was surprisingly good in bed, for a mage. It helped that he was also devastatingly handsome. It was a bloody wonder that no eligible young men had snapped him up in the year that Fletch had known him.

"So that happens often?" Blue asked, pulling the goggles off and tousling his hair. "Getting framed for things, I mean. It's just . . . you don't seem too worried."

"I've got other things on my mind," Fletch said.

"Do you?" Blue gave Fletch a crooked grin. "The sorts of things I might be able to help you with, maybe?"

The rakish grin, that smudge of oil on his cheek, and the promise laughing in his eyes chased all of Fletch's worries and pain away and drowned them in a lake of arousal.

This hadn't been what he'd intended, but . . .

Aw, caal-fire. Why not. He could use the distraction.

An hour later, Fletch lay on his back in Blue's bed, naked. He stared at the ceiling in the darkness, thinking of the bastard who had been wearing his cloak, the one who had never talked. Clearly, he was the brains behind this operation, and the one Fletch needed to take out. He leaned over the edge of the bed to hook his belt with two fingers and drag it closer.

"Leaving already?" Blue said, his voice thick with sleep.

"No," Fletch replied. He pulled the knife from the scabbard and lay back down, holding the weapon above his face and twirling it idly, the tip of the blade jabbing into his index finger. Blue rolled onto his side and laid his head against Fletch's shoulder, joining him in looking at the knife. He smelled of sweat and steel.

"That's a handsome blade," he murmured. "Well made. But not as well made as . . ."

He voice trailed off as his hand traced a line down Fletch's stomach. Fletch grabbed his hand before it could reach its final destination and gave Blue a hard look.

"One of the people framing me was carrying this," he said. "I need to find out who made it."

"Oh," Blue said, drawing away. "So . . . this visit was business after all." The mage sat up, his back a pale curve in the darkness.

Fletch wasn't stupid. He knew what Blue wanted from him. But he couldn't offer what the other man wanted or needed to take. He'd been very up-front about that, as he was with all his partners. Some accepted it more readily than others.

Sooner or later, Fletch would stop coming, and the mage would move on and find someone who could give him more than just a night between the sheets now and then. But now wasn't the time to bring that up, not when he needed Blue's expertise.

"You're the only one I can trust with this," he said.

"I know." Blue reached over to the table beside the bed. He pulled out a small box, then sat back, looking at it. "I made you something," he said, and held the box out to Fletch.

Fletch sighed. "Blue. . . ."

"Take it," Blue said.

Fletch opened the box to reveal a silver ring, inlaid with thin golden traceries. He tightened his lips into a thin line. "I can't accept this," he said.

"Why not?"

Because it's symbolic of everything you want that I can't give you. He closed the box, holding it out to Blue.

The other man didn't take it. "I made it for you," he said. "With no expectations. It's metal-bound, with a high charge of tidi-lei. I . . . thought it might come in handy, someday. Keep you safe, you know? Just . . . take it."

Fletch sighed again and opened the box, removing the ring. He pulled it onto his middle finger. "Happy?" he said.

Blue let out a breath and shook his head, turning back towards Fletch and holding out his hand. "Give me the knife." Fletch handed it to him, glad to drop the awkward line of conversation. Blue reached over to the little table beside the bed and tapped a luminary to activate it. He began to examine the knife, running his fingers along the edge, then up the silver traceries wrapped around the hilt.

"Do you know who made it?" Fletch asked.

Blue laid the knife on his sheet-enshrouded lap. "Not yet," he said, looking up to meet Fletch's eyes. "It's not a maker's mark I recognize. But I can find out for you. Tomorrow night I can take it to the Hollow Market and ask around, I've got some—"

"No." Fletch reached over to make a grab for the knife, but Blue snatched it up.

"Why not? You helped me to make connections, got me supplies when I couldn't get them through the regular channels. . . . I'm actually making a living at this, a much better one than the damned Academe-sanctioned metal-binders." He leaned forward, his eyes hungry. "Let me help *you* for once."

"It's too dangerous," Fletch said, making another try for the knife. Blue held it out of arm's reach. Fletch glared at him. "Don't make me steal that," he said.

"I can do this."

"No," Fletch said again, his annoyance rising. "Tell me who to talk to in the Hollow. I'll go."

"They won't talk to you," Blue insisted. "These are trade secrets. We don't talk about maker's marks to anyone who's not a smith. It *has* to be me." He leaned closer. "Come on, Fletch. I can do this."

Fletch stood (carefully, keeping his weight off his bad leg) and ran both of his hands back through his hair. Blue was right, damn it. The smiths *wouldn't* talk to him, not about a Maker's Mark. But he couldn't pull Blue into this, not with murderers and pearls and cats on his tail. "You can't even watch your back in your own bloody house," he said, turning. "Gods below, Blue, the only reason they haven't killed you is because you sell your shit to them so cheap. These people who are framing me are dangerous, and don't think for a moment that they'd hesitate to torture you to find out where I am. If you go in there asking questions, alerting the wrong people to—"

"You think I don't know what they think of me?" Blue interrupted, his eyes hardening. "What *you* think of me?" He squared his shoulders. "You think I'm some kid, wet from playing out in the rain and dripping all over his mother's carpet, but I understand more than you think." He stood, wrapping the sheets around his waist. "I know so much more than you think, Fletch. I know there's nothing between us, and I know why you do what you do."

"Do what? Sleep around? I told you when we started this that it wouldn't be exclusive, that—"

"You want everyone to *think* that you steal from mages because you hate us," Blue said, his voice flat. As he continued, he rounded the bed until he was standing toe-to-toe with Fletch. "But that's a lie. You do it because you fucking enjoy it. You're a selfish bastard, *Greencloak,* and you always have been." A slow smile crept across his face. "But even selfish bastards need help sometimes. *You* need *me* for once," he said, punctuating the 'you' and 'me' with light taps of the knife's blade to Fletch's chest. "Admit it."

Fletch reached down and touched his fingers to the bead of blood those light touches had brought. *I'm not his fucking father, he thought. I'm not even his husband. I'm just someone who shows up from time to time for a roll in the sheets, and I have no right to tell him what to do with his own damn life.*

He sighed. "Fine," he said. "If you want to put your life in danger to prove a fucking point, I'm not going to stand in your way." He bent to grab his clothes. "But I'm going with you."

"They won't talk to me if—"

"Who do you think you're talking to?" Fletch said, rolling his eyes. "Some two-aeran pick-pocket? They won't see me. No one does, unless I want them to. I'll be outside, waiting, in case anything goes wrong. Watching your back, since you're incapable of doing it yourself. If something goes wrong, call out and I'll haul your handsome ass out of there."

"Fine," Blue said, sliding the dagger into its scabbard. He started pacing, avoiding the piles of mess around his room. "I should probably go to Tysm first. She's got the best—"

"Whatever," Fletch interrupted, sitting on the edge of the bed to pull his pants on. He winced as the fabric tugged against the blood-stained bandage wrapped tightly around his lower leg. "I'll meet you at the entrance to the Hollow three hours past night-fall, I have a couple things I need to check on in the meantime. If anything goes wrong, we meet back here." He stood, tying the lacing on the waistband of his pants, and turned to level a finger at the mage. "And as soon as you find a name, you're *out*."

"And you'll owe me," Blue said, that grin still plastered on his handsome face. "Don't think I'll forget that."

"Lovely," Fletch muttered, pulling his shirt over his head. "Just what I need, to be in debt to a *mage*."

"Don't act like you won't enjoy what I have in mind," Blue said.

Fletch glanced at him out of the corner of his eye. Blue sat on the edge of the bed, the sheets puddled around his waist, a crooked grin on his face. *He's a kid, really, despite his age,* Fletch thought. *Excited to be a part of something he sees as . . . as some sort of adventure.* Fletch had no intention of enlightening Blue to the realities of the world. *Let him keep his delusions, so long as he doesn't get hurt in the process.*

He pulled his cloak back on and left the room, his thoughts already turning to which of his storerooms he should check first.

Chapter Seven

Twelve hours after he'd left the Lady's Face, Suken walked along a street on the edge of the Valley District, his mood as black as the night sky above. Somewhere to the south the incinerators were running, their caal-fire fed vats turning the trash of the city into clouds of black, noxious smoke drifting down the alleys to mix with the cloud-mist.

None of his sources were talking about Greencloak. *None* of them. Street performers, orphans, courtesans, shop-owners, guards . . . some didn't know anything about Greencloak, but others clearly did and refused to tell him. A woman whose daughter Suken had saved from slavers had closed the door in his face. A tailor Suken had gotten dozens of good tips from had threatened to throw him out of his shop. A traveling singer had turned and walked away from him the moment Greencloak's name had left his lips. He'd begged, and bribed, and made promises he probably couldn't have kept, and even seriously considered getting down on his hands and knees once or twice.

And still, nothing. He wasn't certain why no one was talking, unless maybe Chi had been right and Greencloak was bribing the Valley dwellers with charitable acts. He hadn't had any luck asking after Shifter, either, but Suken got the impression that

that was just bad luck. He wasn't asking the right people the right questions. He had confidence that eventually, he'd find a lead on that front.

But Greencloak . . .

Suken sighed and pulled a prayer from a pouch at his belt to begin flipping it along the backs of his fingers as he walked down the nearly deserted street. This particular thin golden coin was inscribed on one side with the symbol for the Lady's Face and on the other with the symbol for the Jewel. Suken had already tried asking Lady Chance for her guidance by flipping a prayer, but he hadn't been able to decipher the answer. The coin had depicted the symbol for the Tree. That aspect had two meanings . . . *remain open to new ideas,* or *a child.* Suken didn't know many kids, and he was as open to new ideas as he could get short of cracking his skull open like an over-ripe melon and picking through the brain matter. He stopped and looked up at the stars glimmering in the smoke-enshrouded night sky, the few people on the street giving the broken crossbow strapped to his leg wary glances as they passed.

"Look, Lady," he said. "I'm coming up stars, here. I'm gonna need a little more than the Tree if I'm gonna catch this one. I've always been a good customer, haven't I?"

A warm wind tugged at his serape mockingly. He sighed and continued walking. Either the goddess was angry with him, or she was like everyone else and wasn't willing to talk about Greencloak.

Wonder if he pays her, too, he thought morosely, hand drifting idly to brush against the crossbow at his waist. Avara would probably have told him he was a bloody, rain-soaked fool. As a matter of fact, he could practically hear her saying it now. He was willing to bet that . . .

Suken paused, his forward momentum faltering. *Avara,* he thought, hope kindling in his heart. *She's always looked out for me. And she's got the best information in the Valley. But . . . Chance, no matter* how *much she likes me, it's gonna cost me.*

The rain falling to the street around him was light, barely a drizzle. Luminaries encased in blackened steel cages to prevent theft lit the streets well enough for him to see that he was only a few streets away from Avara's shop. Maybe that's why he had begun thinking about her. Or maybe Lady Chance had guided him after all. He took a deep breath, flipped the coin back over his shoulder to bounce across the broken cobblestones, and turned down a side-street narrower than the main one, the shops leaning inwards over it to nearly block out the night sky. A thin strip of cloud-obscured blackness between the eaves was all Suken saw when he looked up. Soot from the incinerators blackened the adobe walls, giving them a dull grey look. Lichen and moss grew halfway up most of the walls, coating the adobe with blankets of green, yellow and grey. The people here didn't bother trimming back the hanging vines which crept along the rooftops, either. Several thick vines brushed against Suken's hat and shoulders as he made his way deeper into the Valley.

The few people still out and about after nightfall hurried on their way, giving him a wide berth. Patches and tattered hems were prevalent, as were worn boots and expressions. Suken made his way past a restaurant serving meat pies with questionable filling, a small tavern, and a store with second-hand clothing displayed in the grimy front window before reaching a trim little building with a sword hanging over the door.

Not a sign painted to *look* like a sword, either. An actual steel one. Suken had often wondered how Avara managed to leave it out there without some enterprising thief taking off with it.

The shop was markedly cleaner than those around it, and the wooden sign beside the door with "Paress" burned into it wasn't weather-stained and cracked, the soot meticulously washed away each morning by orphans Avara hired for the job. Suken had asked once, when he'd been younger, why Avara hadn't moved the shop to a more wealthy district. She'd continued polishing the wickedly curved knife in her hands as she'd told him that her clientele came from either side of the Valley, and that the poor had as much a right to defend themselves as the mages did. Probably more so, since they were liable to get attacked more often and for less reason.

His uncle had often sent him to her store when he was younger to run errands, and she'd taken pity on him for his circumstances, allowing him to try out various weapons that she'd never let other children his age look at, let alone touch. It was she who had discovered his talent for the crossbow, and her work that was strapped to his leg right now. He'd paid for it with over two years' hard work, running various errands for her before he'd gotten his hunting license.

Avara had never been one to hold anyone's hand. She hadn't exactly *taught* him how to use the crossbow, she'd simply handed it to him and let him figure it out on his own. He'd managed to get his fingers caught in the triggering mechanism once and come to her with his hands covered in blood, crying. She'd taken him aside, bandaged his hand without a word, and asked quietly if he'd learned not to do that again. He'd nodded, and she'd clapped him on the shoulder before sending him off home. It was just how Avara was. She gave you the tools she thought you needed, and if you figured it out, all well and good. If you didn't, they obviously weren't meant for you to begin with.

She wasn't going to be in a good mood once she saw the damage he'd inflicted on her handiwork, but he might still be able to get something out of her if he could convince her of how much depended on it.

Right, he thought as he pushed the door open, the familiar silver and glass wind chime over the door tinkling over his head. *And maybe all those lizards scampering in the streets will sprout wings and take flight, like dragons in the old legends.*

He shook his head. *Stay positive, Suken. It can't hurt to try.*

The show-room smelled of leather, steel and wood-polish. Each wall save the back one was lined with racks of swords, longbows, spears, and other large weapons. The smaller weapons like knives and crossbows were displayed in a waist-high glass case taking up the entire back wall. Avara sat on a high stool behind the case, bent over a ledger-book. A pair of luminaries molded to look like glass birds perched on carved wooden stands on either side of her, shedding their light over the pages.

"We're closed," she called without looking up.

"Maybe you should lock your door, then."

She glanced up over the tops of her thin glasses. Light brown hair streaked through with grey was pulled up on top of her head in a pile as artful as it was disorderly. She wore a shirt with flowing white sleeves rolled up to her elbows covered by a leather vest open at the front and a full, dark brown skirt. A thin silver chain with a glass bead dangling from it hung around her neck, its delicate beauty a stark contrast to the utilitarian knife at her belt. After regarding him with a considering expression, she turned her eyes back down to the book.

"Where's Terri?" she asked.

Suken raised one eyebrow. "At this time of night? Home, I'd assume."

Avara looked up again, slowly. "You didn't come with her?"

A tiny thread of dread wormed its way into his mind. How long had it been since he'd been home?

Oh, Chance. Had he dropped off his latest payment in time for the tax collection? He couldn't remember. That was a bad sign.

"Um," he said, hoping his expression didn't betray his rising guilt. "No. Is she, um. Coming? Here, I mean?" Suken resisted the urge to look over his shoulder again. It definitely wasn't that he was afraid of his housekeeper. He just didn't want to deal with the speech he was certain to get when she saw him next.

Yeah. That was it.

"We're heading to our reading group as soon as she gets here," Avara said, flipping a page in her ledger book.

"Ah. I'll come back," he said, plastering on a fake smile.

"Wouldn't want to keep you from—" He started turning towards the door and nearly choked on his next words. A young, pretty woman a head shorter than him with full dark hair curling out around her face like the petals of a flower stood in the open doorway, her arms folded. Suken had never quite dared to ask Terriala how old she was, but he guessed that she was five years older than him. Her deceptively innocent face had led more than one man to underestimate her, assuming her to be a quiet, prim little merchant's daughter. It usually only took a few seconds for that particular illusion to shatter. Suken always enjoyed watching them scurry away after receiving one of Terri's scathing tirades, throwing bemused looks back over their shoulders as they went.

It wasn't nearly as much fun when he was on the receiving end of them, however.

Her eyes narrowed. "Suken," she said. "Fancy meeting you here."

"I was just leaving," he said, but she grabbed his arm as he tried to step around her.

"You haven't been home for ten days," she said, her voice brittle. "There are these little things called *bills*. Maybe you've heard of them?"

"Right," Suken said, giving her his most innocent smile. "The programs they give you when you go to plays, right?"

Her eyebrows rose a fraction of an inch. Suken knew he was wading into dangerous waters, but he couldn't help himself.

"No, wait. I know this. A written statement presented to a judge?"

"Suken," Terri said, a dangerous edge to her voice. Her fingers tightened on his arm.

"A type of halberd," Suken said, pointing to one hanging on the wall. "Am I getting close?"

"How about the things where, if you don't pay them, the government repossesses your property? Or the things where the cartel comes and breaks your knees before leaving you to die in a ditch? Sound familiar?"

"Right," Suken said, drawing out the word. "I knew that."

"How about my *salary*?"

He gave her an artfully curious look. "How much is that again?"

Terri let go of his arm and held out her hand palm-up. "Chance, it's like wringing water out a bloody stone with you, I swear."

Suken glanced back over his shoulder. Avara watched them with her chin propped in one hand.

"Don't look at me," she said with a grin. "It's better than a puppet show, watching her string you up to dry."

No help there. Not that he'd really expected it.

"Sorry," Suken said to Terri, taking a step back to prevent any potential blows to his manhood. "I don't have much. Been a bad week."

Terri heaved a sigh. "How bad?"

"The usual," he replied with a shrug. "Shot at some people. Got hit in the head a few times. Don't remember much else."

She stared at him. Suken relented and sobered.

"I'm on a big job now," he said. "I'll have it for you by the end of the week. Provided," he looked at Avara again, "I get some information."

"Don't give me those eyes," Avara snapped, sitting up. "They might work on half the eligible young men and women in the city, but not on me."

Suken stepped closer to Terri and lowered his voice. "I really am on a big job," he said, quietly enough that Avara couldn't hear. "But I need a few minutes with Avara alone. Can you wait outside?"

"How big?" she asked, and that disinterested expression she always wore slipped to reveal curiosity and more than a little worry. "Suken, the cartel's been sending men over. If you don't have a sizable sum to give them . . ." she glanced from side to side and leaned closer, lowering her voice even more. "They've started making threats," she whispered. "Said that if you don't have the money soon, they're going to force you to work for them to pay it off. I . . . Suken, I . . ." She trailed off, biting her lip.

Suken felt a stab of guilt. He had no family, and few friends. If the cartel was looking to find a leverage point to make Suken play nice, well . . . Terri would be the only card they could play. That meant kidnap. Torture.

As much as Suken teased her, he didn't want to see that fate befall Terri. *Couldn't* see it. Yet another reason why he had to find Greencloak, and fast.

"I know," he told her. "This is a big job, trust me. More than enough to keep them off my back for a few months, maybe a whole year." When his uncle had died, he'd left Suken with more than a house and a hat. He'd also left him with more debt to the cartels than Suken could hope to pay off doing anything legal, other than bounty hunting.

"Is it dangerous?" Terri asked. Suken knew that she cared about him in much the same way that she cared for her little brothers. She worried about him when he went out on his jobs, but she was usually good about hiding that care behind a mask of nagging and disapproving looks. It was the primary reason he kept her on, though he could barely afford her.

"It's not going to be a walk in the park," Suken replied with a smile. "But I'll be careful."

Terri sighed, and the mask slipped back on. She raised her voice. "Fine," she said. "But hurry up or we'll be late."

"Be out soon," Avara called. Terri paused long enough to give Suken a quick hug and turned and left, the little bell over the door jingling cheerfully as she exited.

"So," Suken said, coming up to the counter and unstrapping the crossbow from the holster at his leg. "For starters, I need a repair."

Avara's eyes narrowed when they alighted on the crossbow. "Give her here," she said, holding out her hand. Suken handed the crossbow over. Avara took it and turned it over in her hands with a sound like a mother cooing over an injured child, then looked up at him, her eyes hard. "I told you to take *care* of her, not smash her around like a gods-cursed club." She plucked something from the splintered wood and held it up, her expression darkening. "Is this *hair?*"

"Sorry," Suken replied, his look of chagrin unfeigned. "Didn't have much choice."

"You lot never do," she muttered, tossing the hair aside and wiping her fingers on her skirt before returning her gaze to the weapon. She ran her fingers over the wood lovingly, lingering for a moment over the bolt jammed into the channel. Suken waited, knowing better than to rush her. Weapon-smithing was as much an art as Suken's drawings, and he respected Avara deeply for the amount of time and love she put into each of her creations. Finally, she grunted and lay the weapon aside.

"Two days," she said.

He winced. "That bad?"

She leveled a hard look at him over her glasses. "Yes. In the meantime . . ." she reached under the counter and rummaged for a moment before emerging with another crossbow. The leather on the grip was nearly worn through in several sections, one of the bows was visibly splintering, and it wasn't a repeating model. "In the meantime, you can use this," she said, but pulled it back before he could take it. "Providing you bloody well take care of the old girl."

"I'll do my best," he assured her.

She speared him with a dark look, but shook her head and handed the weapon to him regardless. "I'll add it to your tab," she said as he tested the lever and sighted down the weapon. "So this information you need?" Her gaze flicked up to him. "This warrant won't require delicate instruments being used as clubs, I hope."

He ignored that and considered what he was going to say next. Coming right out and asking about Greencloak would probably be a mistake. If she were like all the others, she'd close up quicker than a night-flower at dawn. He'd start with Shifter, then. "Technically it's second rank, so it should net me a fair reward. Ever heard of a shifter who uses throwing knives?"

"Maybe," Avara said. "But you know my information doesn't come cheap, Suken, and you're already in the red."

"He was responsible for the death of a ten year old girl," Suken said, his own voice hardening. "She died in my arms."

She stared at him for a moment and shook her head. "You know exactly which cards to play against me, don't you, boy?"

"Known you a long time," Suken replied with a hint of a smile. "But it's the truth, Avara. I want this shifter. He needs to face justice."

"Justice," Avara muttered, sliding down from her stool and picking up her ledger book. She closed it with a dull thump and picked it up to slide it under the counter. "Justice isn't going to make that girl any less dead."

"It'll stop any more from winding up like her."

Avara sighed. "I know of three shifters who favor throwing knives," she said, and lifted one finger. "One you can find in the Rum Tub most nights of the week, third table. Likes his gambling, though he ain't much good at it." She lifted a second. "Second is a bit trickier to find. He keeps to himself most times, but word is that if you want to hire him, you can ask around the Pelting Rain in the Hollow Market. The third," she raised a third finger, "spends a good deal of time on Orchid Street. Ask the courtesans at the Ruddy Amapola, I'm sure you know it well enough."

"I do," he said. "Just three?"

"All I know of."

"Thanks, Avara." The relief he felt at finding leads for Shifter was tinged by uneasiness about what he intended to do next. "It's nice not to have to worry about competition for once," he said, reaching down under the pretense of adjusting the straps for the crossbow. "Everyone else's on the Greencloak warrant." He lifted his gaze surreptitiously to watch her reaction.

"All the first rank hunters, you mean?" She picked up his poor broken crossbow again, sighting down it.

"No," Suken said casually. "*Everyone.* They opened his warrant up to all ranks."

Her eyes narrowed ever so slightly. If it were anyone else, Suken might have dismissed it. But he'd known Avara for almost eight years now, and he knew her worried expression when he saw it.

She knows him, Suken thought, somehow unsurprised. *Or at least, she knows about his supposed charitable works and doesn't want to see him caught.* Suken suspected that Avara donated anonymously to a number of Valley charities. He also suspected that she illegally sold weapons to Valley residents for self-defense, but he didn't know any details about those deals. Nor did he want to. What he didn't know for certain, he wouldn't feel obligated to tell the guards.

Regardless, he might be able to use this. If she did know Greencloak . . . or knew how to get word to him . . .

"Word at the Face is that the guild's telling the hunters to ignore the live-bounty," Suken lied, looking down at some of the knives in the case he was leaning on. He kept watching Avara's expression out of the corner of his eye. "Are these new metal-bound models?"

"What?" she said, sounding distracted.

"These knives," Suken said, tapping the counter. "Metal-bound?"

"Oh. Yes." She pulled a tool from her belt and jammed it into Suken's crossbow, prying the jammed bolt loose. "Never heard of the guild pressuring anyone to bring in a warrant dead," she said.

"They're saying he's too dangerous to risk taking alive," Suken continued, carefully keeping his gaze fixed on the knives. "Personally, I think it's ridiculous. He's a thief who's dabbling in murder, not a sicario." He pointed. "Is that one caal-lei?"

"New model," Avara said. "Caal and flauri."

"Oh, nice. What does it do? Explode?"

"Yes," Avara replied distantly.

"Rechargeable?"

"Of course. And well out of your price-range."

"Figured. I was just curious." He sighed and stretched. "I better get back to work. Warrant's not going to bring himself in."

"Mmm." She seemed to snap out of her thoughts, looking up at him. "Be careful out there. Don't want to see your name on page eight of any of the broadsheets." Page eight was where they printed the death-notices.

Suken smiled. "Come on, now. I only get hurt on three out of four of my cases."

She snorted and picked up the crossbow again, cradling it under her arm.

Sorry, Avara, Suken thought as he turned and left the store, the chime tinkling over his head. *Hate to lie to you like this, but . . . I need this warrant more than you know. I'll make it up to you someday. I promise.* He waved goodbye to Terri and, when he got far enough from the shop to be out of sight, ducked into an alleyway.

Suken crouched on the roof of a building across the street from a little cafe three hours later, his arm resting on his knee. He stared down into the street below as the little weapon-smith exited the cafe, laughing about something and waving goodbye to the people still inside.

As the door closed, the smile fell from her face and she turned left, heading towards the Valley District.

I knew it, Suken thought with a grin, standing and brushing clinging bits of vine from his pants. He walked along the roof-top in a low crouch, watching Avara as intently as if she were a criminal and not a trusted friend with somewhat questionable connections. Rain pattered against his hat and washed the ever-present soot from the off-white tiles and matted vines of the roofs. The gaps between the buildings here in the Valley were small, usually only a foot or two, and easily crossed with careful jumps, though it was rare to find adjacent buildings in the Valley of the same height. Some tilted slightly to the sides due to shoddy construction, others were angled steeply, some were as flat as the streets below. Some of the more creative thieves had built make-shift railings, ladders and narrow bridges across the wider gaps between the roofs, making them a viable means of transporta-tion after night fell, provided you were reasonably careful and watched your step.

As Avara traveled deeper into the Valley, the streets grew nar-rower and more populated by the ragged homeless, the drunk, or the clearly up-to-no-good. Suken saw one or two thieves scurry out of sight into rooftop gardens as they spotted him, but he ignored them, focusing on Avara. She moved through the crowded streets outside of taverns or brothels with fluid grace, throwing harsh looks at anyone who tried to stop her.

Once, she stopped and turned, scanning the rooftops. Suken froze, half-concealed behind a wooden rain-barrel. Avara stood there for another moment, sweeping her gaze back and forth, then shook her head and started walking again. Suken let out a sigh of relief and thanked the Lady's grace for his instinct to stay behind cover, even when he was relatively certain no one was watching him.

Avara turned one final corner and walked into an alley near Orchid Street, the walls barely wide enough for her shoulders. Suken hopped from one roof to another and padded along the roof above her, leaning slightly to one side to keep her in sight. After about fifteen feet, she stopped. Suken dropped into a crouch and watched, rain dripping from the brim of his hat in a steady stream right in front of his face. A small red and yellow snake poked its head out from beneath a loose tile to stare at him. Suken shooed it away.

"I know you're there," Avara called. Suken froze, but she continued, apparently talking to a pile of trash, "Got a message for him. It's important."

Suken let out a slow breath and leaned forward in order to hear her better over the rain, taking care to keep from putting his weight on any loose tiles.

A boy melted out of the shadows of the alley, his skin-tone shifting from black to light grey. His clothes were a flat black. He didn't answer, just stared at Avara, clearly poised and ready to run.

"Here," Avara said, tossing a leather tube at the haunt. The kid caught it deftly, never taking his eyes from Avara. "Make sure he gets it as soon as possible. The hunters are out for his head."

The boy snorted. "He knows that."

"Not the full extent of it, he doesn't," Avara said darkly. "Not unless he's got friends in the hunter's guild, and I sincerely doubt that he does. Go on."

The haunt spat to one side, tucking the tube into a pocket. "C'mon," he said. Another child stood up from the pile of trash, shaking loose melon rinds and tattered pieces of broadsheet from their clothes.

Avara turned as the two orphans scurried deeper into the alley, but Suken didn't follow her. He followed the orphans, and Avara's message to Greencloak.

Chapter Eight

The warehouse reeked of wet ash and wood long gone to rot. Moonlight beamed in through cracks between boards nailed up over the windows, illuminating broken boxes and half-burned bags spilling over with grain and squirming maggots. Most of the ash had long since been ground into the floor or blown away by the wind, but enough remained to coat everything with a layer of grayish black dust and reveal two sets of small footprints.

Suken followed those footprints around a corner of a stack of boxes and found himself looking down at a small wooden trap-door set into the stone floor. The wood was blackened from the fire which had gutted this warehouse Lady Chance only knew how long ago, but the door was still sound. He knelt and pressed his ear to the wood, listening.

The voices of the kids were muffled by the wood, and growing more distant. Suken reached down, grabbed the metal ring which served as a handle, and lifted the trapdoor open an inch, peering down into the darkness beneath the warehouse. A wooden ladder stretched down, barely illuminated by the fading glow of what was probably a luminary carried by the kids, given the steadiness of the light and the fact that it was growing dimmer by the second.

The undercity. It had *to be the undercity.* Suken grimaced but pulled the trapdoor the rest of the way open. He wouldn't be able to use his own luminary. . . . The kids would be able to see it. He'd have to follow them closely enough to see by their light, but without letting them see him.

It'd be tricky, but he'd done worse.

Suken swung himself down onto the ladder and took a deep breath, trying to ignore the fear that always clawed at him when he had to go down into the undercity. The series of tunnels and caves which twisted and turned beneath Adunare were dangerous, but Suken knew how to avoid or deal with the various gangs, creatures and other hazards associated with them. It was the tunnels themselves that caused his heart to beat faster and his throat to close up as he got deeper and deeper. He couldn't help imagining the tons of stone above his head, and how it would feel for that stone to come crumbling down, crushing him. He often awoke from nightmares in which he was trapped in a cave-in in the undercity, starving to death in the darkness, screaming for help . . . just as his parents had.

Suken shuddered, but he started lowering himself into the hole nonetheless. *Don't think about it,* he thought as the moonlight above faded into darkness. *Think about how it will feel to walk into the Lady's Face and have everyone know your name, and not because they knew your uncle.* He could barely see the rungs of the ladder now. The kids must be walking fast. *Think about the stories they'll publish in the broadsheets.* The grain of the ladder was rough against his hands, and as he descended further and further, his breath began to come shorter and quicker, almost panting. *Think about bringing Shifter in to face justice for poor little Flower.*

One of his feet slipped, and Suken's hands clenched into white-knuckled fists around the rung in front of his face. He could feel his heart thundering in his chest, and squeezed his eyes shut, trying not to think about the stones in the walls slowly sliding in closer, trapping him, crushing his breath from his body and—

Stop it, he told himself harshly. *It's never happened to you before, and it's bloody well not going to happen now.* He forced himself to take a slow, deep breath and open his eyes, and unclenched one of his fists from around the rung and moved it carefully down to the next. But the fear remained, not dissipating even when his feet found the wet rock of the floor of the tunnel. The air was muggy and thick, the silence broken only by the steady drip of water from the ceiling and the distant chatter of the two orphans. He reached down without realizing he was doing it, his trembling fingers brushing against the pouch hanging from his belt. The feel of the prayers inside did more to calm his nerves than anything else could have—except maybe a glass of gin.

Or a whole bottle, he thought wryly.

He let his breath out slowly. The sooner he got this over with, the sooner he could return to the roofs, where the sane criminals and hunters spent most of their time.

Suken looked to his sides. The tunnel stretched in a gentle curve away from him on either side, dimly lit by the receding light of the luminary far ahead. Moss and lichen grew half-way up the walls in striations of dark green and sickly yellow. Near the floor, a reddish type of moss grew in sporadic patches amongst the green and yellow. Suken drew back.

Bloodmoss. Great. Just what I need.

He rubbed his hands on his pants reflexively and turned to start off down the tunnel after the kids, careful not to brush against the walls. Suken never heard any people other than the kids, thank the Lady, but occasionally he heard a deep rumbling and felt a thrum in the floor through the soles of his boots. Whenever he did, he hurried his steps. The tunnels nearest the great metal-bound engines which held Adunare City aloft over the jungle of Majitan were the most likely to suffer cave-ins due to the vibrations.

After what seemed like an eternity but probably wasn't any longer than fifteen minutes, he reached a stone bridge over a rushing torrent of dark water. The aqueducts began beneath the High Council chambers, where a single magical Gateway opened onto the base of a river somewhere in the jungles below. The water rushed beneath the streets of the city, guided along stone tunnels to fill the public bath houses and supply the entire city with drinking water, but getting more fouled with refuse and waste the farther south it went. By the time it reached the Valley it was little better than a sewage system, which was why every tenement housing building had large barrels suspended from the corners of their roofs to catch rainwater for drinking or bathing.

He had to wait until they crossed the bridge completely before crossing himself. Once their luminary vanished into the tunnel on the other side, he stepped onto the thin arc of stone, barely wider than his shoulders and with no hand-guards or railings. He stepped carefully, not looking down at the unseen water below him. As he reached the middle, the light ahead abruptly blinked out.

Suken stopped. The rush of water drowned out most other sounds, but he thought he heard a few whispers ahead.

Then, silence.

Damn it. He glanced back over his shoulder, panic rising to claw at his chest. Blackness before him, and blackness behind. Churning water below, and Chance alone knew how much stone above. And below it all, the deep thrumming of those bloody engines, buried somewhere in the rock.

They spotted me, Suken thought, resisting the urge to run forward towards the last place he'd seen the light. Running across this bridge in pitch-darkness would be a spectacularly bad idea, and if he activated his own luminary, the kids would know for certain that he was back here.

So it's a game of Exile's Purge, then, Suken thought. *They're waiting for me to light my own luminary, to give myself away. Either that or they're creeping back towards me in the dark, and intend to unshield the light in time to push me off. . . .*

He knelt on the stone and ran his hands along it until he felt the edge. He took a deep breath, more to steady himself than anything else, and gently lowered himself over the edge, letting himself hang by his fingers over the rushing water far below.

He felt sweat beading on his forehead and trickling down his back as the darkness continued.

If he'd been wrong and the kids had simply continued on ahead, he might be lost down here now, and—

The light flared back into life on the far side of the bridge.

"See?" One voice said. "Nothing."

Another voice replied, too quietly for Suken to make out the words, and the light began bobbing away again. Suken hauled himself back up onto the bridge and lay there on his stomach, gulping the stagnant, moisture-laden air and thanking the Lady that he'd been right.

After a moment in which the light grew dimmer and dimmer, Suken heaved himself to his feet, quickening his steps to finish crossing the bridge but taking care to step lightly. He couldn't afford to spook them again. The light bobbed and flickered as the kids went around bends in the tunnels, and he heard voices ahead. He crept forward until he could hear them clearly.

"—fourteen rolls, one book and a used-up luminary."

"Why'dya keep that? Shoulda thrown it away." Suken recognized the voice as the haunt boy, the one who had spoken to Avara.

"Thought we could sell it," the other child said. "Might be worth something, yeah?"

The voices lowered to whispers, and the light dimmed abruptly. Suken pushed himself away from the wall and continued, stepping softly. He rounded one final corner to find himself facing a barricade of broken boards and half-filled sacks of sand in the tunnel ahead. One of the sacks of sand had burst, spilling its contents across the stone floor. He stopped, eyeing the construction warily.

This was probably the entrance to the orphans' lair, or whatever they called it. He had the feeling that eyes were watching him from the shadows between the boards. Orphans were more common in the Valley than rats, stray dogs or rabid monkeys, though not quite so common as the little lizards that seemed to take up residence in every corner.

Well, it had been too much to hope that he'd manage to follow them all the way into their lair without having to confront them. Best to play this out as well as he could. He reached down and tapped his own luminary, hanging by a piece of twine around his neck. It burst into bright white light.

"Hey there," he said, taking care to keep his voice friendly. "Anybody home?"

Silence.

"I'm a bounty hunter," Suken said, and continued, using a term they'd be more likely to respond to. "A cat. Looking for some information, and I'm willing to pay."

No answer, but that wasn't unusual. The street-kids were tight-lipped if they didn't see incentive with their own eyes. He reached into one of the cases at his belt and pulled out a pair of aerans. The silver caught the glow from his luminary and made the coins seem to shine with an inner light. He danced one across the backs of his fingers a few times.

"Piss off, cat." The voice from within the barricade was young, all right. Sounded like a boy, but sometimes it was hard to tell the difference even when you saw their faces up close.

Suken couldn't see this one yet. But then, he didn't need to. He knew how to deal with him, or her. "Come on now," he said, flipping the coin back down into his hand. "No need to be that way. I'm looking for information on a warrant, a big one. There's good—"

A wild cry from behind the barricade startled him into silence.

He drew back a step in surprise. Sand shifted beneath his boot, and he felt something draw tight around his ankle a half a second before it yanked his foot out from under him. As he fell, he slammed the side of his head against the ground, and the world faded into black as it turned upside down.

"Think he's here about Him?"

The voice swam up out of the darkness, tugging at Suken's attention. His head pounded, feeling like it had the morning after he'd drunk his uncle's entire flask of gin when he was fifteen. He was upside-down, hanging by a rope encircling his ankle. His arms hung on either side of his head, his fingertips brushing the floor.

The sand, he realized, feeling like the city's biggest idiot. *Talking about their haul was a front. They knew I was following them, so they concealed the trap under the sand, and waited for me to step right into it. Which I did, because I'm a fucking moron.*

Suken inwardly sighed and resolved to make the best of this situation. He didn't feel the familiar weight of his crossbow against his thigh, but they'd thankfully missed the thin knife tied to his lower arm beneath his sleeve. When the kids started talking again, he didn't open his eyes, choosing instead to feign unconsciousness.

"'Course he's here 'bout Him," the first voice snapped. It was the same one that had told Suken to piss off. "You heard what 'e said. Big warrant."

Greencloak, Suken thought. His spirits picked up at that, despite his situation.

"We oughtta kill him." This one was quieter, and sounded younger. A gentle murmur of other voices responded to this.

"Maybe we should find out how 'e found us first," a voice rose above the murmur. "No one else's come here, askin' 'bout Him. If someone's ratted on us, we should know who."

Murmurs of assent.

"Musta been Avara," the haunt boy said. "She gave us a message for Him, and that's when the cat started tailin' us."

What the . . . how in blazing caal-fire did he see me?

"Ain't Avara," the first voice said firmly. "She'd never rat us out to the cats. Maybe he was playin' her, too."

A new voice piped up from somewhere behind Suken. "Maybe this one can help. Y'know He'd never ask, but He needs help. Most of the hunters after Him, all the pearls, and half the thieves, too. . . ."

"Maybe he can—"

"He's a bloody *cat,* and you know what—"

"—never know, He—"

"SHUT IT," the first voice shouted. The others quieted. "Can't trust a cat," he continued after the voices had stilled to silence. "Y'know that's what He'd say. Best kill 'im now, afore he gets a chance to sell us. Or use us to find Him."

Suken didn't like the way this conversation was going. Just because they were kids didn't mean they wouldn't slit his throat. Valley orphans made harder choices every day than most people had to in their entire lives . . . including killing in self-defense. He let out a groan and opened his eyes, looking around himself. He hung upside down in the middle of the tunnel, half-surrounded by a semicircle of bedraggled children. The Valley orphans shared a uniform composed of the tattered and stained cast-offs of those better off than themselves—which was pretty much everybody. Their hair was almost always long, hanging around their faces in dirt-caked clumps. And their faces . . . well. Emaciated was probably the best word for those. Their eyes were the worst, though. Either they stared up at you with a kind of dull desperation, or with the wary wildness of a cornered animal. This bunch looked like most of the orphans he'd worked with in the past, save that they seemed to be better fed and slightly better clothed. An older boy with short-cropped black hair stood within the ring of children facing Suken, his dirty arms folded and his expression grim. Suken's luminary hung around the boy's neck, and his pouch of prayers from the boy's stained and tattered leather belt. A younger child with long dark hair circled around from behind Suken to stand next to the older boy. He or she tilted their head to one side, looking at him.

"He's awake," the soft-spoken one said. Judging by the kid's voice, it was the same one that had suggested asking him for help instead of killing him.

The other children stiffened, their eyes darting to Suken's face, and several hands holding shards of sharpened wood came up into defensive postures.

Suken couldn't tell if the kid who had suggesting asking him to help was a boy or a girl. The baggy, nondescript tunic and the dirt darkening their skin made it impossible to tell the difference. Another child held Suken's loaned crossbow in both hands, loaded and pointed in Suken's direction. Suken felt shivers creep up (or was it down?) his back at the thought of the kid's finger on that trigger. Towards the back of the group, a child who looked barely old enough to walk wore Suken's hat. It hid the kid's face entirely, the brim nearly resting on his shoulders. He looked something like a turtle hiding in its shell.

Suken reached up (*down? Blast this bloody trap,*) and gently touched the side of his head. He felt a sizable lump, and his fingertips came away smeared with blood. The kids watched him warily, obviously poised to flee or attack.

He had to give them incentive to free him, and quickly. They'd obviously already taken his money and anything else they'd have deemed valuable, but he hadn't been carrying much. A group this size needed a lot to live. He took a deep breath to calm his nerves and smiled at the older one.

"Been a long time since I've been caught in a trap," he said, letting his hand drop back to hang at his side. "Well done. Hidden under that patch of sand, eh?"

The older boy's eyes narrowed.

Not in the mood for flattery, Suken thought with a wince. *Right to business, then.*

"Look. You've got me in a rough spot, but I'm willing to pay you to get out of it." The rope he was dangling from creaked, and he began rotating slowly to face away from them. He reached down and walked his hand along the ground, pulling himself back to face the kid directly again. He smiled.

Would a smile look like a grimace if he was upside down? Chance, he hoped not.

"Pay us with what?" the older boy said. He had a pinched face with a long, thin nose and stringy hair hanging into his eyes. Those eyes had the same wary, street-wise quality Suken associated with city-rats. The soft-spoken one beside him looked more like a mouse. Slightly rounder face, big ears poking out of the snarled mess of long hair, little snub nose.

"I'm not rich," Suken admitted. "Not by a long shot. But I've got a little stashed away for emergencies. When I get home, I'll send it to you."

Rat snorted. "We let you go, you run back to the Hunter's Guild or the slavers and send 'em after us. We ain't stupid, hunter."

"My name's Suken Anisaria," Suken said, hoping that some of these kids had heard of him, or worked with him before. He'd always been fair and honest with the Valley residents—the ones that were abiding by the law, anyway—but no recognition flitted across any of the kids' faces at his name. *Damn it.*

He realized that he was starting to feel dizzy. *If I don't get out of this soon,* he thought, *they won't need to stab me. I'll die from all the blood rushing to my head.* He could feel his heart thudding deep in his ears, and his face and hands felt heavy.

"How much would ya give us?" Turtle asked, lifting up the brim of Suken's hat enough to give him a curious look.

Rat gave him a withering look. "Dun you be listenin'? He ain't gonna give us nothin'." He faced Suken. "We got yer aerans, yer light, yer crossbow, and this." He reached down to touch the pouch of prayers hanging at his side. "Feed us all for near a week, I figure."

Chance, the little bastard was smug.

"I've got three times that at home," Suken said, a note of desperation creeping into his voice. All those criminals he'd hunted, and to be taken down by a bunch of orphans not even half his age? "You could send one or two of your own with me," he continued. Rat's expression soured even more.

Stupid, Suken berated himself. *The minute I got out onto the street, I could call to the guards, get them all arrested.* "All right," he said, "keep me here as ransom, but let me send a message to my housekeeper. You could look it over after I've written it, to make sure that I didn't put in anything about where I am. She'd send the money back with your messenger, then you could let me go."

"Do we look like we can fuckin' read?" Rat said. Suken raised his eyebrows at the language, but none of the other children so much as batted an eye.

The haunt boy Suken had originally followed down here stepped out of the shadows, grey shifting across his skin like drifting smoke. "And who's to say you won't turn around once you get out an' lead a band o' bloody-handed slavers down on us?"

"Who's to say you wouldn't kill me after I wrote the message?" Suken threw back at him. "Way I see it, we'd both be taking a risk. I'll trust you not to kill me, you trust me to leave you alone once our business's done. You walk away with full bellies for a month, I walk away with my life." He continued carefully, "And, if I know that you're trustworthy, I might come back to you in the future for information. Any you'd be willing to sell, that is. You know we're always looking for good sources. This might turn out to be a good deal for both of us in the long run. You get steady payment, I get information." He paused. "Providing all our interviews don't wind up like this, that is. Generally speaking, I work better when I'm right-side up."

Mouse cracked a smile at that, but Rat and Haunt didn't. Suken held Rat's gaze, keeping his face impassive. The orphans in the Valley adhered to an honor system. If they gave their word about something to another Valley dweller, they held to it. Hunters operated on the boundaries of that system. If Rat and his crew gave Suken their word, Suken trusted them to keep it.

They'd get their money and he'd keep his life . . . until he got home and had to face Terri, that was.

Rat, Haunt and Mouse turned their backs to Suken, the other children gathering in a loose knot around them. After a few minutes of quiet deliberation, they broke apart and turned back towards him.

"How many aerans?" Haunt asked.

"Four hundred," Suken replied, trying not to picture Terri's face when she got the note.

"Seven," Rat said.

Pushy bastard, aren't you? "Five."

"Six hundred an' fifty."

Suken shook his head. "Six. Any more than that and the cartel will have my skin hanging from their wall, and you can't get any further payments from me if I'm dead."

Rat's mouth twisted in a dissatisfied grimace, but he nodded once. "Fine. Six. And *we* set the price for any information we give ya."

"A tenth-aeran is the going rate for low-profile intel, one half-aeran for high-profile. I'll give you that, and half again as much if the information you provide leads to a capture. That's better than you'll get from any of the others." He glanced at Turtle. "And I get my things back, minus the aerans."

Rat looked down at the glowing luminary strung around his neck and back up, arching one eyebrow. "Lumins're expensive."

Lady's breath, Suken thought. *Someone taught this kid how to drive a hard bargain.*

"Fine," he said, rolling his eyes. "You keep the aerans and my luminary. I get everything else back, in addition to a lantern or a torch or something so I can find my way out of here."

"And you never come here again. You need us for intel, you leave us a token in the big-house, and a time 'n place to meet."

"Big-house?"

"The warehouse we entered the undercity through," Haunt supplied.

Rat nodded sagely.

Suken had hoped that he might be able to watch this place, in case Greencloak had a habit of stopping by. But if he gave his word now, he couldn't break it. A hunter's reputation was like a glass awning. Once broken, impossible to mend. He looked at the half-circle of grimy faces half-illuminated by his luminary. *Your life or this warrant, Suken? Which is more important to you?*

"And I never come here again," he finally repeated, his voice low. "Without an invitation, anyway."

"Swear it."

Suken met Rat's eyes. "On the Lady's name. I won't come back here without an invitation."

Rat looked down on him and nodded once, decisively. "Done."

Two children stepped forward and unwrapped the end of the rope from a metal stake in the wall, slowly lowering Suken to the stone floor. He groaned as the blood began rushing back into his legs, reaching down to pull the rope from his ankle and massage some life back into his tingling calf. The children watched him, tenser than before. He saw the glint of light reflecting from knives in a few hands. Mouse nudged Turtle, and the boy walked up slowly, pulling off the hat. He paused for a moment, then held it out at arm's length. Suken took it, and the kid scurried over to hide behind Mouse as soon as the hat left his fingers.

"There should have been a leather case with my things," Suken said to Mouse, pulling his hat on. Now that he was right-side up, he noticed the distinctly feminine set of her eyes and mouth. "With a bunch of papers in it, and a pen." Mouse looked up at Rat, who nodded. The girl reached behind herself and picked up Suken's bolt-case, fishing his pen, a handful of warrants, his hunting permit, and his sketchbook from a compartment behind the bolts.

"Just the book and the pen," Suken said. The girl handed them over, snatching her hand back as soon as she could, as if she were afraid that Suken had the Rotting Plague. "I don't bite," he said. "Promise."

She eyed him, stepping back.

Terri, Suken wrote, turning his attention down to the paper. *Send six hundred aerans back with messenger. Do not follow, or contact Guards or Guild. Sorry. Will explain when I get home.* He signed it with his unique ji'Ahiran gylph, ripped it from the book, and held it out towards Mouse.

The girl took it and scanned over the words. She looked back up at Rat and nodded. *Clever,* Suken thought with a small smile. *Telling me none of them could read, so they could check it over and see if I were honest. I wonder if they considered the possibility that I might have used some sort of coded phrase.*

Not that he had, of course. But suspicion and a healthy dose of paranoia kept these kids alive.

Rat instructed Suken to give two young boys directions to his house, which Suken did, hoping that Terri was actually there and not out on an errand. They took his letter and scampered off, leaving him with Mouse, Rat, and four other children, including Turtle and Haunt. They seemed to be more at ease with him now, though they hadn't put away their knives or sharpened sticks. Suken looked around.

"We'll be waiting awhile," he said to Mouse. "It'll take them at least an hour to make it there and another to get back, providing my housekeeper's not out running errands. Don't suppose there's anywhere more comfortable we could wait?"

Rat scowled, but the other children gave him plaintive looks. It was cold here, and damp. They probably wanted to sit on the moss-encrusted floor as much as Suken did—which was not at all.

"He's already this far," Haunt said.

"Fine," Rat snapped, more to the other children than to Suken. One of the orphans shoved a part of the barricade to one side, revealing a narrow passageway through the broken bits of carriages and crates. Suken stood slowly, his legs and feet still tingling. He had to admit that he was a bit curious about the den. He'd heard of them, but never actually seen one. Half of the children ducked into the passage, the other half—including Rat—waiting to follow Suken. He had to bend nearly double to walk through, and followed the children ahead of him as they wound their way through another hundred feet of tunnel and two more barricades.

The last barricade was far better built than the others. Suken had to drop to his hands and knees and crawl through the passageway, cursing under his breath as his sleeve momentarily got caught on a rusty nail sticking from a broken board. He exited into a cavern lit by a few torches and stood, pushing the brim of his hat back. Children were everywhere, some sitting on piles of rags while others stood in a loose clump near the back of the cavern. One group sitting in a circle near the entrance turned from the bedraggled green and red parrot they were feeding, their faces full of mingled curiosity and wariness. Tattered tapestries with holes worn through them had been hung on the stone walls and draped over ropes crisscrossing the cavern to form a set of temporary dividers. For privacy, Suken assumed. Someone prodded him in the back.

"Get movin'," Rat said. Suken obliged, taking a few steps forward into the cavern. All of the children, some fifty or sixty all told, stared at him as he entered. They ranged from barely of an age to begin walking to their late teens, though those last were rare. The cavern was warm, and smoke from the torches on the walls drifted near the high ceiling in a haze. The smell of baking flatbread wafted up from a small caal-fire oven in a corner, presided over by a young man wearing a tattered brown cloak.

Judging by the man's height, he was the oldest one here, maybe even older than Suken. His dark hair was cropped so closely to his skull that it was barely a fuzz. He turned, raising one eyebrow at Rat, Mouse, and the rest of Suken's ragged entourage.

Probably not Greencloak, Suken thought as they got closer. *He looks nothing like the description in the case-file. But I can't discount the possibility. Keep your mouth shut for once, Suken, and listen. Maybe they'll let something slip.*

"Who's this?" the cook asked, raising a thin wooden flatbread paddle to rest against his shoulder. Under his cloak, he wore an off-white, patched shirt with the sleeves rolled up to his elbows and dark tightly-fitted pants. Very tightly fitted pants, Suken noticed, raising an eyebrow. He cleared his throat and forced his gaze back up to the man's face, placing his age at about four years older than himself. He was handsome under the layer of dirt coating his face, with brown eyes sparkling with good humor. That humor was tainted at the moment by the usual wariness all of the kids were displaying, regardless of age.

Rat took a step forward and gave Suken a distrustful look from the corner of his eye before replying. "He's a cat. We think he followed Vethin and Tam. And there's this." He handed Avara's note to Cook, who unrolled it and scanned over the words.

That's the second one who can read, Suken thought, glancing at Mouse only to catch her staring at him. She looked away immediately, flushing. *Wonder if Cook taught the others . . . or if someone else did.*

"Well," Cook said, rolling the note up. It vanished into his belt with a quick flick of his fingers. Suken immediately felt a twinge of distaste. Whatever else this young man was, he was most certainly a thief. Suken could forgive the smaller children for some thievery, but once you reached adulthood, there were jobs aplenty provided you actually *looked* for them instead of taking the easy way out and stealing from those who *worked* for their aerans. "We'll make sure this gets where it needs to go. As for you . . ." He cocked his head to one side, considering Suken. "What warrant you on, cat?"

"Looking for a shifter," Suken said. Best not to mention Greencloak, not given the kids' reactions in the tunnel. "Killed a merchant's little girl in the Valley last night."

"Fair number of shifters in the Valley," Cook said, sounding amused. "That all you know?"

"Liked to use knives."

"Oh, really?" Rat smirked at the others. "Well, that narrows it down."

A round of laughter from the other children. Suken ran his tongue along the inside of his teeth and considered his next words carefully. "Like I told them," he said, nodding to Mouse, "I'm willing to pay well for information on him."

Cook raised an eyebrow. "What made you think we'd know anything?"

"Well," Suken said slowly, "one of my leads was for a tavern in the Hollow Market."

Rat laughed. "Cat wants to visit the *Hollow*," he said to the others, a mean glint in his eyes. Chuckles from the other children.

Suken had two options. Either he could continue to play on the defensive, placing each hand with care . . . or he could take this bluff to the next level.

Why not. The Lady owes me one for that damned trap earlier.

He ignored Rat, meeting Cook's eyes. "Look," he said. "I'll be straight with you. I'm new at this. Still a kitten, so far as the bloody guild and everyone else's concerned. My name's not well known enough to hire a guide into the Hollow. But everyone knows that orphans can get in and out as easily as rain-water. When I saw these two," he nodded to Haunt and Mouse, "I thought maybe that's where they were headed, and that I could follow them back there."

Silence. Cook and the other kids stared at him, their gazes piercing. Suken felt as if he were being flayed by tiny knives determined to ferret out his secrets and lay them bare.

"Tam?" Cook asked without breaking Suken's gaze.

"Could be tellin' the truth," Mouse (whose real name was Tam, apparently) said. She looked up at Cook with obvious affection. "We noticed him followin' us before the big-house. Led 'im to the trap at the third barricade, and he made us a deal. Givin' us six hundred aerans, Rossin."

"Why did you bring him back *here?*" Cook's eyes hardened, never leaving Suken's face. "Why not keep him at the barricade?"

"We needed someplace to wait 'til his payment gets here," Rat said, stepping in front of Tam. "'Sides," he threw a sidelong look at Suken, "what's he gonna do? Mew at us?"

More laughter.

Get your laughs in now, Suken thought, clenching one fist. *When you're older and still out there thieving, and I catch you and haul you in, you won't be laughing.*

"Well, someone take him to the back corner and stay with him, make sure he doesn't wander," Rossin said. He leveled the spatula at Rat and Haunt like a sword. "Not you, though. I need to talk to you about . . ." He trailed off, his eyes darting up to Suken. Suken tried to look innocent. "Things," Rossin finished, and turned to the oven and the three small children standing beside it. All of them stared at Suken with wide eyes.

"I'll take 'im," Tam piped up.

Rossin waved a hand in clear dismissal, Rat and Haunt approaching him. The mousy little girl stepped up to Suken, looking him up and down with fists planted on her hips like a miniature tyrant.

"You're tall," she said.

"You're not," he replied.

"How old're you?"

"How old are *you?*"

"I asked first."

Fair enough, Suken thought. "I'm twenty-two."

"Don't look it."

"That's what they say."

"Who's they?"

"Everyone." Suken couldn't help a small smile crossing his lips. "I told you my age. Turn and turn about, little lady. How old are *you*?"

"Don't know. This way," she said, turning and walking past several of the hanging dividers.

Suken followed. He hadn't learned anything yet. . . . But he still had at least two hours before the other kids got back with his ransom.

He'd make the best of that time.

Tam led him to a corner of the cavern, the floor covered with several layers of quilts and blankets. Suken dutifully sat down and gave Tam his most charming smile as he pulled his hat off and set it down beside him on the patched quilt, ignoring the lizard that skittered out from under the edge to scurry deeper into the cavern.

These kids looked up to Greencloak, and Tam had mentioned that he needed help. Well, with all these hunters after him, maybe Greencloak was looking for a way to escape the city for awhile. Suken might be able to use that, if he could get the kid talking. He'd always been pretty good with kids.

And, truth be told, he sort of liked this one. Maybe he could talk some sense into her before she completely ruined her own life.

Tam plunked herself down on a rug barely out of Suken's reach, folding her arms. The heads of other children poked through the various tapestries and pieces of cloth hung over the ropes nearby, ducking back into cover as soon as Suken turned his gaze towards them.

"Shy, aren't they?" he asked.

She glanced at the other kids, then obviously dismissed the question as unimportant. "How long you been a cat?"

"I've had my license for a little over a year now, but I used to take small jobs before then."

"Why are you cats always throwin' money away?" Tam asked.

"Money?" Suken blinked, then realized what she meant. "Oh. These?" He reached into the pouch at his belt, noticing as he did so that it was considerably lighter than it had been before he'd found himself hanging from the kids' trap, and pulled out one of his prayers. He let it dance across the backs of his fingers once or twice, watching as the expression on Tam's face shifted from wary curiosity to awe. "These aren't money," he said, flipping the prayer down into his palm and holding it out towards her. "Want one?"

She looked up, eyes wide. "Really? I can have it?"

"Sure."

She reached out with grubby fingers and deftly plucked the prayer from his hand, turning it over to inspect both sides. "If it ain't money, why does it look so much like it?" she asked, pressing a thumbnail into the soft gold gilding.

Suken leaned back on his elbows. "Lady Chance likes to be paid for her help," he said. "So we make her prayers look like money, to honor her. But they're not worth much. Gold's cheap, and they're only gilded with it. The inside's iron. I can buy a whole bag's worth of prayers," he patted the pouch, "for one aeran."

"Who's Lady Chance?" the girl asked. The prayer vanished into her clothes somewhere, quicker than a blink. "She like . . . a weaponsmith, or somethin'?"

"She's a goddess," Suken said. "Like the god of Light's Harmony that the ardein worship. Only not as stuffy."

Come on, kid. Ask something that'll let me steer this conversation back onto the pathway I need.

"Where'd she come from?"

Suken shrugged. The Lady wasn't nearly as forthcoming with her past as the Light's Harmony. From what Suken knew, He had ardein to spread His word, and to use His power to heal people for extravagant fees. He had Rules and Laws and Temples. The Lady had the hunters, and they didn't much care about her past.

All they cared about was that she was there when they needed her, and she seemed to like it that way.

"An' she helps you?" Tam asked, leaning forward. "Like the ardein help the high-an-mighties?"

"Nah," Suken replied. "When we're not sure where to go or what to do, we ask her a question and flip one of her prayers. The symbol on it is her way of telling us what to do." He grinned at her. "Want to see?"

Her eyes lit up with curiosity and she shuffled a smidge closer to him, then seemed to realize that she was being as transparent as a sheet of glass. She shrugged and looked away. "I guess."

"All right. Ask a question."

"A question?" she looked puzzled. "Like . . . any question?"

"Questions about where things are usually work the best."

The girl chewed on her lower lip for a moment, and nodded once. "A'ight." She looked up at the roof of the cavern over their heads. "Where's the best place to go pickin' pockets tomorrow?"

Suken bit back a grimace of distaste and dug into the pouch, letting his fingers sift through the coins. He pulled a random one free, flipped it, and caught it, looking down at the symbol scratched into the gold. "The Jewel," he said reluctantly. Now that the question had been asked, he couldn't very well lie about it. Lady Chance wouldn't like him putting words in her mouth. "Lady's telling you to go somewhere rich." He flipped the prayer to her. "Now you have to pay her, like any source. When you get up to the streets, toss it over your shoulder."

Tam looked down at the prayer skeptically and back up at Suken. "What if another kid picks it up?"

"Then obviously the Lady wanted him or her to have it," Suken said, leaning back against the wall and folding his arms behind his head. "Once you give it to Her, it's Hers to do with as She wishes."

"Fletch says it's stupid," Tam said, examining the other side of the prayer. "He says you throw your money away."

Suken resisted the urge to lean forward and made his voice as nonchalant as he could as he asked, "Who's Fletch?"

Tam started, then flushed and looked away, towards the other kids. "One of us," she said stiffly.

An orphan? Or . . . maybe someone she respects more than just another orphan. He didn't reply, hoping that she might say something else, but she only shifted and looked back at him. "The other cats ain't like you," she said.

Suken wanted to ask more questions about this Fletch character, but if his suspicions were right, doing so would probably make her close up as quick as a bar's doors at last call. Instead, he shrugged. "Most of them are all hiss and no claws."

"Ain't what I meant." She tilted her head, regarding him. "You ain't treatin' me like somethin' you stepped in."

"That's how other hunters treat you?"

"Mostly."

"Hmm." Suken looked up at the smoke-shrouded ceiling high above. "When I was fourteen," he said, "my parents died. Both of them, in an accident. I know what it's like to be an orphan."

Tam stared at him with rapt attention, as if he were telling her a story. *Might as well keep going,* he thought. But the next words came hard to his lips.

"After they died, my little brother ran away," he said, picking at a stain on the blanket. "He was only six." His heart constricted at the sudden flash of memory that phrase called up, but he continued. "From what I managed to learn, he wound up in a place like this for awhile. This is the first time I've actually seen one, though. Are all of the street gangs this big?"

"We *ain't* a gang," she said vehemently. "We're a *family.*" She pointed at a group of young children sitting in a corner. They were looking at a girl barely into her teens who sat in front of them, a tattered book open in her lap. She appeared to be reading to them. Every so often one turned to give Suken and Tam a furtive look. "We find the little ones," Tam said, the pride in her voice evident, "and watch out for 'em. Feed 'em 'til they can feed themselves, teach 'em what they need to know to get by. We all share everything here. The other gangs work together 'cause it's easier and safer, but the bigger kids still get more of the bloody take. We're the opposite. The littlest ones get the most, and the oldest get the least, since they can get most of what they need by themselves." She looked fondly at the young man in the cloak. "Rossin's like . . . our uncle. He's the oldest. He's the only one still here from before."

Suken raised an eyebrow. "Before what?"

She looked away, a slight flush creeping onto her cheeks again. *Interesting,* Suken thought. He turned the conversation back to territory she was obviously comfortable with. "How long have you all been down here?"

She seemed relieved that he hadn't questioned her about her sudden silence. "Two years. Rossin says that the boy who started the family, he got sold to the bloody rot-infested slave markets eight years ago."

Suken grimaced. Poor kid. That sort of thing unfortunately happened about once a day in the Valley, if not more.

"But the ones he taught," Tam continued, "like Rossin, they kept it going. The family changes as we git older and leave, but most of 'em come back to visit, sometimes." She scooted closer to him and lowered her voice. "You find people for money. Right?"

And we're back to the inquisition about my job. Suken had hoped to glean more information about this "first," or the Fletch character she'd mentioned, but it wouldn't do to press her.

"That's the job description, yes," he said.

"All kinds of people? Even murderers?"

"Sometimes," he said slowly. Technically he'd only taken one of those, and it had been in partnership with his uncle, not alone. But this kid didn't need to know that. "Usually it's thieves, runaways, or malcontents, though."

"Mal . . . contents?"

"People who start fights," Suken explained.

She shifted her weight. "So how many murderers have you caught?"

She's awfully hung up on murderers. Because that's what Greencloak's doing, maybe?

"People who kill other people are nasty sorts," he told Tam, hoping for a reaction. What reaction, he wasn't sure. He'd know it if he saw it. "Hard to catch. They don't care about other people. They can turn on friends or family like *that.*" He snapped his fingers. "Something's broken in their heads. They can't tell what's right or wrong anymore, like a normal person can."

Tam screwed up her face in thought. "Rossin killed someone once," she said slowly. "A gang surrounded him, and he had to stab one to get away. Right here." She gestured to her throat, and her voice turned surly. "*He's* not broken."

Suken reached up and rubbed the back of his neck. *I can't believe I'm debating ethics with an eight-year old.* "That's self-defense, not murder. According to the law, that's the only time that it's all right to kill someone else . . . if they're about to kill you, and you don't have a choice. A murderer, though, is someone who *likes* to kill. Someone who does it over and over again. And someone like that . . . they're dangerous, Tam. Even to people they might have cared about once, before they broke."

She shifted on her rug. "So if someone who wasn't a pearl paid you to catch a murderer—a *real* murderer, not like Rossin —would you do it?"

"I guess that depends," Suken said.

"On what?"

"On who the murderer is."

She fidgeted, rolling a piece of twine between her fingers. She looked up and met his eyes. "Can I tell you a secret?" she asked softly.

He leaned forward, resting his elbows on his knees. "Of course."

"Promise you won't tell anyone I told ya?"

Suken smiled. "Swear on the Lady's name, little lady."

Tam took a deep breath and let it out slowly. "A'ight. So . . . I have a friend."

Here it comes. Suken refrained from leaning forward more, anticipation waxing.

"He's in trouble," Tam continued, "because everyone thinks he killed some people." She leaned forward, her eyes wide, insistent. "But he didn't. I *know* he didn't!"

She still trusted Greencloak. Why? What could he have done for these kids to get them to trust him so completely?

Suken looked around the den, and a possible reason slowly dawned on him like rainwater seeping through the cracks in a leaking windowpane. These kids were well fed. Organized. They had protection and stability. All things that could be bought with a steady flow of aerans.

Like, say, the amount of aerans one could make by stealing from seventy-something rich mages.

Suken grimaced. *Regardless of where he's spending it, he didn't come by those aerans honestly.* That was beside the point, though. Tam trusted Greencloak because Greencloak provided for her and the other kids, like a father figure. But he'd moved on from thieving to outright killing people. Suken knew how hard it was to accept that someone you loved had changed, but Tam had to understand that her life could be in danger, as well as the lives of all the kids in this room.

"Why do you think he's innocent?" Suken asked.

"I don't *think* he's innocent," Tam snapped, bristling like a house-cat facing a bath. "I *know* he is! He and Vethin vanished days ago. Then the murders started, and everyone was sayin' he did them. But then he came back, an' he was hurt. Bad. Vethin told us they had 'im chained up, and were askin' him all sorts of questions." She met Suken's eyes fiercely. "If he were chained up, ain't no way he was killin' people. So I figure there's somebody else out there pretendin' to be him. If you caught the *real* murderer, then the pearls'd know that Fletch didn't do it. Right?"

Chance. She had to give him *that* look. It was the same look his brother had used to give him when he was pleading for something, complete with quivering lower lip.

He sighed and ran a hand back through his hair, wording his next question carefully. "Did Greencloak say where he was being held?"

Her eyes narrowed. "Didn't say nothin' 'bout Greencloak," she said, her voice growing wary again. "Said it was my friend. *Fletch.*"

"Fletch," Suken corrected himself quickly. "Right. Sorry. You're talking about a different set of murders than the ones Greencloak's supposed to be doing?"

"Yeah," she said. "These ones're poor people. Just normal people. Not mage-born."

She was a poor liar.

"So this Fletch . . . he's one of you?" He gestured, encompassing the den with a wave of his hand. "Like your haunt friend, or Rat-face over there?"

"Rat-face?"

Suken nodded towards him. Tam looked and snorted a little laugh, turning back to him. "Yeah. One of us." When Suken didn't reply, she relaxed and started giving him that damned pleading look again. "So . . ." she said, "if we paid you, you'd help?"

Suken leaned back, chewing the inside of his cheek as he thought. If, Chance forbid, she was right and Greencloak was being framed, this job had gotten about ten times as complicated. Not only would Suken have to track down the real killer with no leads and bring him to justice, he'd have to provide some sort of evidence that he was guilty. Evidence the guards would believe. Like a witness, or a murder weapon, or the killer's clothes soaked in blood, or something.

Or, Suken thought, s*he's wrong. This is just the sort of trick someone like Greencloak would use to deflect suspicion. Hire someone to beat you up and limp back home, convince everyone that you* *couldn't possibly have done it. A smokescreen so you can continue killing at will.*

Of the two possibilities, Suken was far more inclined to believe the latter.

Tam stared at him, chin hidden behind her knees, eyes wide and pleading.

How did he always seem to get himself into these things? "I'll ask around," he told Tam. "See if I can find any leads."

She brightened, straightening and grinning. "Really?"

"Yeah. But in return you've got to do something for me."

Her expression darkened, and she drew away from him.

"Not that," Suken said, briefly imagining what he'd like to do to the sorts of people who would ask for sexual favors from the orphans on the streets.

Tam didn't relax. "You want us to pay you?"

"Well, that would be nice. But I meant something else. Can you get me into the Hollow Market? There's someone I'm looking for there, and maybe we can dig up some information on your murderer as well."

"Oh." She finally relaxed, the tension between her little shoulders easing. "Sure. You really think you might be able to find the murderer?"

"I can try," he said.

She beamed at him.

He spent the next hour and a half teaching her how to play Exile's Purge with a tattered set of cards one of the kids had stolen, though it was hard when half the cards were missing. Once she got the hang of the rules, she proved to be an apt player, though she had to work on not grinning whenever she found herself with a good hand. Suken was about to let her win her fifth game in a row when he glanced to his left to see the two kids they'd sent to Suken's house entering the den, a thick leather case clutched in one's hands. *Terri really is going to kill me for that.*

"Journey's End," he said, indicating the end of the round, and laid his hand down, face-up.

"Low War Council?" Tam asked, looking up at him.

He nodded.

She lay her own cards down. "Safe Quarter," she said smugly.

"Remind me never to play you when we're betting," Suken said, watching out of the corner of his eye as the two boys handed Suken's money over to Rossin. The young man opened the case, whistled, and nodded. The boys vanished behind one of the hangings, and Rossin walked over towards Suken and Tam. Tam leapt to her feet when he arrived.

"I'm bringin' him to the Hollow," she said before Rossin could say anything.

He blinked. "Why?"

"Cuz he's payin' me." She crossed her arms.

"I need a guide," Suken put in with a shrug. "Willing to pay for it."

"Fine," Rossin said evenly. "But you're not going alone. Two by Hand, Tam. You know the rules."

She pointed one grimy finger at Suken. "*He's* my Two."

Rossin raised an eyebrow, glancing at Suken and back at Tam. "He's a *cat*."

"He's an orphan," Tam said stubbornly. "Like us. And he's big. And he's got that." She pointed at the crossbow strapped to Suken's leg.

Rossin stepped closer to Suken and lowered his voice. "You fuckin' with her, mate?"

"No," Suken said, holding the young man's gaze. "I really do need a guide to the Hollow, and I'll keep her safe."

"Why?" Rossin said. "What does she matter to you?"

"Every cat knows that orphans are some of the best sources on the street. No one sees you, but you see everything," Suken said. "Ruining my reputation with you lot would be as good as shooting myself in the foot. I'll make sure she gets back here safely. You have my word." He held out his hand, reflecting sourly that he'd made an awful lot of promises to thieves in the last two hours.

Rossin hesitated a moment, then took Suken's hand and shook it once. Before Suken could pull away, Rossin tightened his grip and pulled Suken forward to hiss in his ear, "You get her killed, cat, I'll find you and make you eat that bag of fucking coins you wear."

He let go of Suken's hand, pulling back, his expression amiable. "Be back by Ascent, Tam," he said, and turned and walked away.

Tam gazed after the young man, a grin on her face. "Rossin's great," she said. "Ain't he?"

"Sure, kid," Suken said, shaking out his hand before bending to pick up his hat and pull it on his head. "Great."

He felt his gaze drawn down to the little girl at his side, and felt a moment of doubt that this was actually a good idea. The last time he'd put a little girl in danger to further his own career, it had ended in blood.

This time'll be different, he told himself firmly. *I'll make sure of that.*

Chapter Nine

Hundreds of tunnels led down to the Hollow Market, but only one was open per week. All the others remained closed off by magical or mundane means, and the knowledge of which entrance was open was a closely guarded secret by the denizens of the underworld. This week's entrance was through the back corridor of an old abandoned restaurant owned by one of the cartels, the glass-tiled hallway opening onto a set of steps leading down into a cavern several hundred times larger than the one Fletch had appropriated for the den. The roof curved three stories over the floor, completely coated with the sprayed-on liquid metal used in the pits to help reinforce the bottom of the city and keep the stone from gradually eroding away. Rain trickled along the steel in rivulets and gathered in pools which stank of piss and rotting trash. The light of luminaries reflected eerily off the glimmering, wave-like metal and gave the entire place the feel of being underwater.

Several rows of markets and shops lined the three long streets stretching from one end of the oval cavern to the other. They'd been built one upon another until some simply caved in, creating piles of wreckage, wares, and bodies that had to be hauled away before the next stack of buildings could take its place. The streets teemed with people, most wearing dark colors or clothes so stained with soot and ash that they might as well be black. The richer ones spat tobacco juices into the trash lining the street or onto the orphans half buried in it, and all of them, young or old, rich or poor, laughed and fucked and bought and traded with a reckless abandon that Fletch had always found quite endearing.

And the wares. . . ah gods, the wares. You could buy anything in the Hollow. Slaves, liquors, weapons, foods, drugs to enchant or to heal or to poison, stolen goods, pleasures of the flesh too risqué for Orchid Street, alchemical potions, or the services of a sicario. You could buy everything and anything in the Hollow, provided you could pay the price.

Fletch wasn't here to find a fence, as he usually was. He was here for information, which, as luck would have it, was the second most common commodity bartered for within these walls.

He'd spent the day checking on some of his various bolt-holes and stashes of loot, and had found all of them being watched by nondescript beggars. *All* of them. His mouth twisted down into a grimace as he considered how much it would have cost to hire that many eyes, and at how thoroughly the people framing him were fucking him over. They must have been following him for *months* to find all those locations.

And I didn't even notice. Some master thief I am. He kicked at a half-rotten melon rind as he walked along Third Street (so clever with the names, the founders of this place were), and pulled the hood of his nondescript cloak up to better conceal his face. *How could I not have noticed? I've* always *tagged my tails before, and lost them. Gods below, who* are *these people?*

He shook his head and forced his mind to the present. Whoever they were, they didn't know where he was now, or they would have moved on him already. *Focus on what you're doing, Fletch. You can question the bastards framing you* after *you've caught them.*

Ahead of him, Blue sauntered into the midst of poverty and

crime like a pudgy puppy bounding into a nest teeming with red ants. *It's a wonder he's survived as long as he has,* Fletch thought, watching as the mage walked along in his work-stained gold tunic, completely ignorant of the considering looks following him. Fletch knew what thoughts hid behind those veiled eyes. Theft was undoubtedly the most pleasant of them.

But Blue seemed to have something watching over him—other than Fletch, that was—for he made it to the end of the street without incident and stopped in front of a ramshackle two-story building with peeling, moss-encrusted walls sagging outward like the bulge of a fat mage's stomach against the fabric of his tunic.

Don't you dare turn and look for me, Fletch thought.

Blue turned, obviously searching the crowd behind him. Fletch's hand itched to strike his own face, but he managed to fight down the urge and side-stepped into an alley instead, just far enough that he could still see Blue but wouldn't be clearly visible from the street. *Go on, you bloody, handsome, stupid bastard. Into the shop.*

Fletch leaned back against the wall of the alley, crossing his arms. A bedraggled rat scampered over the toes of one of his boots, but he ignored it as Blue gave up his search, took a deep breath, and ducked into the shop.

About fucking time. Fletch waited for a count of ten and pushed off from the wall, slinking out into the street. Anywhere else in the city, furtive movements would be as obvious as an orphan in a jeweler's shop. Here, no one looked at him twice as he made his way past the shop and turned into the narrow alley beyond it. Like most alleys here in the market, the thing was barely wide enough for Fletch to walk through without his shoulders brushing both walls. He stepped over a sleeping or dead drunkard, hopped up onto a broken box full of reeking meat, and crouched there motionless as a statue, cloaked in the stinking shadows. He glanced back at the drunkard once. The man let out a rasping, gurgling snore.

From the window a few feet above, he heard voices.

"—to know who made this dagger." Blue's voice.

"Aye, do ye, laddie?" The woman's voice that answered him was high-pitched but with the quiver and rasp of old age. Her accent marked her as coming from the western end of the Valley district. "And what're ye willing to trade, eh? A night with you wouldn't be so bad, nay, not at all!"

Fletch counted at least three distinct low, rumbling chuckles in the room with Blue and the old smith-bitch. There could have been more in the room that hadn't laughed, but Fletch didn't think so. It couldn't possibly be big enough.

The creak of a chair was followed by shuffling footsteps. "Aye, aye, bet you'd do right well. Hard as a rock, and lastin' well through the night, eh? Ye'd give me a poundin' like I'd never forget, maybe make me old heart burst like a ripe star-fruit!"

"Ma'am," Blue said, his voice grave, "with all due respect, I'd rather fuck a piece of pork."

Silence.

Fletch had to give it to him. Blue might be naïve, but the man had balls of metal-bound steel.

The silence continued to stretch, and Fletch's hands crept for the hilts of his knives. Then uproarious laughter burst from the room above. First the old woman's, followed by the rumbling baritone of her bodyguards, like boulders rolling downhill.

"You," the old woman said between chuckles, "are tough as a year-old strip of jerky, m'boy. I like that." The creak of her chair again. "Pass me the pig-sticker, then."

Fletch adjusted his posture ever so slightly to relieve some of the tension in his injured leg and heard a rustle behind him. He glanced over his shoulder, but it was only the drunkard rolling over. The man stumbled to his feet, groaned, and leaned against one of the walls, fumbling with the lacing on his pants. He finally got it undone and proceeded to piss into the trash. Fletch rolled his eyes and turned his attention back to the discussion going on above.

"—get this?" the old woman was saying.

"A client," Blue replied.

"Oh, aye," the old woman said, her voice taking on a keening tone Fletch didn't like one bit. "A client, 'e says. Ain't they all, aye, ain't they all?" Unpleasant laughter from the men.

Blue was silent.

"Word been goin' round," the old smith crooned. "Word 'bout a certain thief who might've stolen a certain knife, and what should be done if it were to show up, aye."

Shit, Fletch thought. It was time for them to leave, but Blue wasn't getting out of there without help. Even if Fletch hadn't been injured, there was no way he would have been able to get in and fight off three bodyguards. The best he could hope for was to give Blue a diversion, then meet the mage back at his house.

"You ain't Greencloak," the old smith continued. "Ain't sly enough, not by half. But ye know where he is, don't ye?"

Fletch reached into one of the pouches at his belt, pulling out a glass sphere. It was about the size of his palm, and cool to the touch. Inside it, two liquids were separated by a thin barrier of glass, one a murky grey, the other blue. Fletch looked up at the oil-paper window above his head.

The sphere would punch through it easily enough. He drew his arm back to throw—

And a hand closed around his wrist.

"Now den." The drunkard gripped Fletch's wrist more tightly, raising a thin blade between them as Fletch turned to look at him. He stank of rum and piss, but his gaze was steady. His dark hair was pulled back into a clumsy tail and one side of his face was pocked with old scars, his skin the color of roasted coffee beans.

A flash of bitter anger swept over Fletch's mind, mostly at himself.

He was here, waiting for me. That means that someone sold me out, and the only person who could have done that. . .

Was Blue.

Betrayed again. Fletch's jaw clenched, his teeth grating together painfully. He should have known. Should have *known* that he was getting too close.

No one was too good not to be bought out sooner or later, if the price was high enough. If Fletch had learned one thing in his life, it was that.

"Notch my usual job, catching men indead of killing dem," the man continued, his voice low and gravelly. "Might make a mistakie," he raised the blade higher, his eyes glinting dangerously, "and dat'd cost me a boondle of aerans and *you* your life. So just come alung—"

Fletch twisted and dropped his center of gravity before the man could finish his sentence. He wrenched his wrist from the man's grasp, dropping the sphere as he did so. It hit the stone and the glass shattered, the two liquids inside meeting and igniting with a low *whoomph*. Fletch threw himself back in time to avoid the resulting cloud of smoke, but his bad leg gave out on him and he tripped, falling onto the box he'd been standing on. The wood broke under his weight and the rancid reek of rotting meat assaulted his senses. Smoke washed over him, blotting out the world in a haze of swirling grey. He heard his attacker coughing and cursing behind him and cries of alarm from above. Maggots squirmed between his fingers as he pushed himself up, holding his breath to avoid inhaling any of the smoke. It wouldn't hurt him, not like some the alchemists sold, but it certainly wouldn't be good for him, either.

Every instinct screamed at him to run. He gained his feet and lurched down the alley towards what he hoped was the entrance. He'd lost his bearings when he fell, and the smoke completely blinded him.

Judging by the people's voices rising in alarm around him,

Fletch had chosen the right direction. Fire was the only unforgivable offense down here in the Hollow Market, as the smoke easily became trapped in the cavern and half the dilapidated structures would go up in flames at the touch of a mere spark. The people nearby couldn't know that Fletch's weapon had released smoke alone, so criminals of all types raced towards the smith's shop, shouting and calling for buckets. Fletch limped out among them, their forms fading in and out of the smoke like phantoms.

He spared a single venomous thought for Blue, still up in the smith's shop. *You're a dead man,* he thought as he began limping down the street, weaving his way through the crowd. *No one betrays me and lives, Blue. No one.*

Suken walked out of the Pelting Rain Tavern into the wavering light of the Hollow Market, his mood grim. He and Tam had visited both of the places Avara had told him about, but neither of them had yielded results. Flower's murderer had vanished into thin air the night Suken had foiled his ransom, or so it appeared. No amount of aerans, promises or threats had gained him so much as a single lead.

This is not my week, he thought, hooking one thumb into his belt as he stopped on the narrow street to wait for Tam. The Hollow was pretty much what he'd expected, he reflected as he looked around. It was a smaller, more condensed version of the Valley. . . full of crime, grime and illicit goods.

Tam bounced out from beneath a nearby cart and joined him in the dank, stinking air outside the tavern. He hadn't let her follow him in, though she'd insisted that she'd have been fine. Suken already had one little girl's blood on his hands this week—literally—and he hadn't been willing to risk it happening again.

"Fiiiiiind anything?" she asked, hands clasped behind her back, rocking from heel to toe.

"No," Suken replied. "Nothing." He threw her a small smile. "Did manage to win a few aerans, though."

A man bumped into him, his head down, mumbling incoherently to himself. Suken dropped his hand to check his purse, but it was still there. The man looked up at him, his wiry hair hanging in his eyes.

"Anisaria?" he whispered. He grabbed at Suken's arm, his fingers coated in soot and grime. He growled and glanced back over his shoulder. "Didn't ask you, did I?" he snarled. No one was standing near enough to him to have said anything.

Suken's lips tightened into a thin line. He pushed the man aside and reached down to grab Tam's arm, pulling her away. The man started laughing and gibbering to himself, all the other people on the street giving him a wide berth.

"Who's that?" Tam asked, straining to look behind her.

"No one," Suken replied. "Not anymore, anyway."

"Why's he talkin' to himself?" She kept pace with Suken easily. "Is he broken? Like a murderer?"

"Yes," Suken replied, troubled. He hadn't seen Janin in nearly a year. The man had been a liar and a mean drunk, but no one deserved what had happened to him.

"Think he might be the murderer?" Tam asked.

"No," Suken replied. "He's just a man who's gone mad."

"How?"

Obviously she wasn't going to let this go. Suken led her back towards the entrance. The street was lined with small portable stands, their owners hawking stolen goods. They had to raise their voices to near shouts to be heard over some of the vendors. "A hunter I knew made a mistake," Suken said. "Thought Janin there murdered someone, and brought him in. But Janin insisted that he was innocent, so the High Mages brought him in to be Truthread."

"Truthread?"

"You've heard of the TruthSeer, right?" Suken said.

"Them's just stories," Tam said dismissively. "Everyone over the age o' five knows they ain't real."

"That man," Suken said, nodding his head back in Janin's direction, "would disagree with you."

Tam screwed up her face in thought. "So the TruthSeer read his mind, like in the stories. And he went mad?"

"Yes. And the hunter who wrongfully accused him was executed."

"Oh." Tam trotted along beside Suken, completely nonplussed by this.

"Liquors here," a dirty man shouted as Suken and Tam passed him. He brandished a dark bottle that could have held anything from mud to the finest gin. "Straight from Kerisan Port, cheaper an' stronger than ye'll find elsewhere!"

A short man tugged on Suken's sleeve, looking around furtively. "Metal-bound bolts," he whispered, pulling his serape aside slightly to display crossed bandoliers packed tight with bolts. "Best in de city, cat."

Suken pulled his sleeve free of the man's grubby hand and pushed him aside, ignoring his squawk of indignation.

Tam peered up at him as they walked. "So. . . now what?"

Suken rubbed his thumb along the edge of the prayer in his hand. "Usually, I'd wait outside one of the locations for the mark to make an appearance."

"Sounds boring."

He let his gaze sweep over the people clogging the street around them. Ragged, dirty, dangerous. Any one of them would likely be willing to stick a knife in his guts for the right price.

And any one of them could be his mark.

Uncle Lorrin did always say that shifter warrants were difficult.

"It *is* boring," he said to Tam. "Very boring. The boring-est job ever. That's why I'm taking you back to the den. Wouldn't want you getting bored too."

"You *could* start looking for. . ." Tam trailed off, glancing from side to side before continuing in a hushed voice, "*him*. The serial killer. That ain't boring!"

She was right about that, whether the serial killer turned out to be Greencloak or not. But Suken had even less of an idea of where to start on that than he did on the shifter, now that Avara's leads had turned up stars.

"Do you have any idea where your friend Fletch might be?" he asked carefully. "If I can talk to him, I might—"

Suken broke off mid-sentence, realizing that the atmosphere around them had shifted, like the change in the air before a storm. Voices were taut, some raised in outright alarm, and heads began to turn to the south, behind Suken. A beggar-woman in torn and dirty clothes raised one hand, pointing with a bared finger, her glove fingerless and tattered. Suken turned, his hand dropping to his crossbow.

Smoke billowed in a cloud somewhere deeper in the Hollow, rising towards the polished steel cavern walls. Screams rose in that direction.

A small hand grabbed his.

"Come on," Tam said, her voice tense. She pulled him after her, darting and weaving through the crowd like a swallow flying through the narrow, winding streets of the Valley. Suken tried to mimic her, but he knocked into more people than he avoided, dropping apologies like prayers in his wake.

As the girl led him deeper into the warren of backstreets close to the wall of the Hollow, Suken realized why she'd been so adamant that they get out of the crowd. Behind them, he heard cries and the clash of metal on metal, and the unmistakable sounds of brawls starting.

Apparently the denizens of the Hollow were quick to latch onto any opportunity for a riot. Tam rounded a corner and ducked into an alleyway so narrow that Suken had to turn sideways to enter, the brim of his hat touching both walls. He was forced to side-step, slowing his speed by half.

Tam's hand pulled against his, and she turned to look over her shoulder at him. Kid was so tiny that her shoulders didn't even touch the walls. He ducked his head to avoid hitting it on a rusted pipe going from one building to the other.

"Hurry *up,*" Tam said, tugging his hand more insistently. Suken heard the sounds of shouts getting louder behind him.

"Going as fast as I can, kid," Suken said. "In case you hadn't noticed, I'm not quite as small as you."

Tam let out a frustrated noise and let go of his hand. She darted forward twenty feet, stopped, placed her palms flat against the lichen-encrusted wall of one of the buildings and pushed.

A section of the wall swung inward. She turned and gave Suken a gap-toothed, dirty grin. "Here," she said, pointing into the darkness. "This is—"

A hand shot out of the opening and grabbed her wrist.

Tam let out a panicked cry as the hand jerked her forward into the darkness.

Chapter Ten

Suken fumbled in his pocket for the cheap luminary he'd traded two of his metal-bound bolts for, finding it just as he stepped into the opening in the wall. He tapped the silver at the base of the sphere, hazy white light flooding the opening and revealing a ragged beggar with one dirty hand clapped over Tam's mouth. He held the girl from behind, a hood covering his face. As Suken's light washed over him, he flinched back a step, dragging Tam back with him.

For one fleeting moment, Suken saw not Tam, but the bright blond curls of Lord Garron's daughter, held in Shifter's grip. Then the illusion shattered, leaving only dread and paralyzing fear.

"Don't hurt her," he said, raising both hands and remaining as still as he could.

"Who are you?" the man growled. Tam struggled feebly against him, but the man retained his grip. "What're you doin' with her?"

"I'm a bounty hunter," Suken said, not moving. "She was helping me chase down a lead. Please, don't hurt her. I'll give you anything you want. . . . Everything I have."

The man didn't respond. Tam stared at Suken over the man's hand. Suken was surprised to notice that she didn't look frightened. If anything, she looked annoyed.

She's not afraid that he'll hurt her, he thought, furrowing his brow. *Which means. . . she probably knows him.*

A suspicion loomed in his thoughts. He took one step forward, bringing the luminary down far enough to cast its light under the man's hood.

He was young, Suken's age maybe, but his well-trimmed beard made him look years older. Dark bags of bruised flesh hung under piercing eyes, the rest of his skin ashen. Shoulder-length dark hair poked out from under the hood around his neck. It looked as if he hadn't had a decent wash in weeks.

"Not a step closer," the man rasped. "Got a knife to her back, I do. Ain't afraid to use it."

Suken felt a chill run down his spine at how similar this situation was to the one he'd faced last night, but Tam's fearless gaze steadied him.

"That's a lie," he said, but didn't move forward. "You're not going to hurt her. Are you," he paused, putting emphasis on the next word, "*Greencloak?*"

The flash of surprise which flitted over the man's face was all the confirmation Suken needed. It was gone as swift as a blink.

"Drop all yer aerans," Greencloak said, "and get the fuck out of here." Tam struggled briefly, trying to say something, but it only came out a muffled "mmph." She rolled her eyes and heaved a dramatic sigh.

"Tam's told me everything," Suken said, keeping his voice calm and even. "So you might as well drop the act."

"Everything?" The Valley accent Greencloak had been using dropped from his voice, and he let out a single snort of laughter. "Bloody kid knows more than I do these days, then."

Suken watched the other man's face carefully. What he saw wasn't a cold-blooded killer who used his victims' blood to write on the walls. This was a man teetering on the edge of desperation.

Suken's certainty of Greencloak's guilt wavered.

"Is she right?" Suken asked. "Are you being framed?"

"What do you care?"

"If you're being framed, then the pearls are all chasing the wrong man, leaving the real murderer free to slaughter at will."

Greencloak barked a short laugh. "And you're going to stop him all by yourself, are you?"

"Yes," Suken snapped. "If I know where to start. If you're really innocent, tell me where—"

"If you think I'm trusting a bloody cat," Greencloak interrupted, "you're out of your fucking mind." He leaned in close to Tam and whispered something in her ear.

Suken had trained for months in reading lips. It came in damn handy in taverns and dance-halls where the roars of laughter and music drowned out words, and he'd used the talent often to glean information he otherwise wouldn't have been able to get. This time, he read the words "Tell the others not to trust Blue," before Greencloak shoved Tam at Suken. The girl crashed into him, and Suken dropped the luminary as he reflexively reached out to catch her. The luminary shattered on the stone underfoot, releasing a small puff of glowing vapor before extinguishing and casting the alley back into darkness.

Suken swore under his breath and pushed the girl gently aside, darting into the inky blackness of the opening in the wall. It took a moment for his eyes to adjust. When they did, he found himself looking down a tunnel leading beneath the building. The darkness only ten feet into the tunnel was absolute. Without a luminary, Suken had a better chance of finding a dropped prayer in the middle of the Valley than he had of chasing down Greencloak. He turned to Tam.

"Where would he go?" he asked.

The girl looked into the tunnel, her brow drawn down into a frown. "I don't know. He's got places like this all over the city. He showed us most of 'em, in case we ever needed a place to hide. This is the only one in the Hollow, but the tunnel leads to more.

Lots more." She lifted her left hand, looking at it. Blood stained her fingers.

"Are you hurt?" Suken asked, all thoughts of Greencloak briefly fleeing his mind. He knelt beside her, taking her hand and inspecting it. She didn't seem to be cut.

"It's his," she whispered, meeting Suken's eyes.

Suken stood, looking at the tunnel. By the time he got back with another luminary, Greencloak would be long gone. He slammed his fist against the wall, standing there for a moment with his eyes closed as he fought his anger. *I had him. For a moment, I had him.*

And what was I planning on doing with him? If he's innocent, I can't very well turn him over to the pearls.

But on the off chance he's not, I just let a psychotic killer slip through my fingers.

Suken let out his breath in a slow, trembling sigh. He opened his eyes and turned to Tam. "Let's get you home," he said, fighting to keep the edge from his voice. "Must be almost time for Ascent by now, and I promised I'd get you back safe."

"We can follow him," Tam said, peering into the tunnel. "We—"

"No," Suken snapped.

The girl flinched away from him, her eyes widening at his tone.

"No," he repeated, more softly. "I'm not putting you at risk. Come on." He reached down and took her hand, the one not covered in Greencloak's blood.

The walk back to the den was silent and uneventful, Tam leading him through the darkness. Suken distracted himself by going over Greencloak's features in his head so he could draw a sketch later. If nothing else, he'd have that. He could bring the sketch around to a few of the sources he hadn't talked to yet, ask if they'd seen anyone who looked like him. Maybe if he didn't mention the name Greencloak, people would be more willing to help. And there was that phrase Greencloak had whispered in the girl's ear. . . "Tell the others not to trust Blue."

Who—or what—was Blue?

After they crossed the bridge over the underground river, Suken stopped. If he was going to ask, he'd better do it now, before they reached the den. "Who's Blue?" he said.

The girl stopped, her back to Suken.

"Fletch told you not to trust him, or her. Maybe this Blue knows something about whoever's framing him."

"He's a mage," she said softly, not turning. "They're friends, I think. Fletch brought him here once, months ago. He was. . . nice. Showed us magic, and gave some of us li'l metal-bound knives."

"Do you know where he lives?" Suken asked.

She shook her head.

Suken sighed. It wasn't much. But it was more than he'd had before.

"Thank you," the girl said, finally turning. Her eyes shone with unshed tears which he could barely see in the dim light of the tunnel. "For helping."

Suken looked away, feeling guilty. If Greencloak was lying about his innocence, Suken would turn him over to the pearls, and Tam would probably never look at him again.

Wouldn't be the first time he'd betrayed a child. That thought stung, adding a bright flare of anguish to the guilt. *I hope you're right, kid,* he thought. *I really do, if only so I never have to see the look in another kid's eyes when they find out I've let them down.*

He stepped forward, taking her hand and letting her lead him back to the barricade he remembered from earlier tonight. He shoved the wood aside and followed Tam in, meaning to ensure that she made it all the way home safely before leaving her.

As soon as they entered the den, Suken knew that something was wrong. The kids stood clustered at the rear of the cavern, silent. Two near the door stiffened when Tam and Suken walked in, but Tam waved a hand at them and they relaxed.

"What's goin' on?" Tam asked one of them.

The boy's expression, already drawn, darkened. "It's Vethin," he said. "He's dead."

The haunt boy? Suken turned to look towards the back of the cavern, where the children had gathered in a loose circle. A still body lay on the floor in their midst, visible in the gaps between the kids.

The grey patches on the boy's skin had ceased moving, like clouds in a still sky, and his eyes gazed at the ceiling, wide and staring. Suken turned back in time to see Tam shake her head, taking a step back as if she could distance herself from the body. The color bled from her face, leaving her starkly pale beneath the layer of grime.

"But. . . he was. . ."

The boy opened his mouth as if to reply, but the approach of Rossin silenced him. The young man reached Tam and Suken, looking them both over. "I'm sorry, Tam," he said softly.

She stood for a moment, swaying slightly as if she were being pushed by a strong wind. Then the tears broke free. Rossin knelt and opened his arms. Tam rushed into them, burying her head against his shoulder. He looked up at Suken as the girl began sobbing. "This ain't your business, cat," he said. "You got what you came for."

"What happened?" Suken asked. It had probably been an accident, or an attack by one of the street gangs. But Suken couldn't walk away without finding out for sure.

Rossin scowled. "Just said it ain't your business."

Suken didn't move. Rossin stood, picking up Tam as if she were no bigger than a kitten and resting her against his hip, holding her as she cried. "The man calling himself Greencloak killed him earlier tonight, in the Mage's District. 'Bout an hour ago."

Right about the time Tam and I were talking to him, Suken thought, a shiver running down his spine. *There's no way he could have gotten all the way to the Mage's District in time to kill the kid before or after*

I saw him. Lady's breath. . . he really is *innocent.* One part of him was relieved. The other part shrank away from the knowledge that his job had just become five times harder.

"Witnesses?" Suken asked.

"Vethin's Two-by-Hand," Rossin said, looking to his right. Suken followed his glance to see Rat sitting against a wall, his knees drawn up to his chest, staring towards the group of children at the back of the room with eyes a little too wide.

"Can I talk to him?" Suken asked, keeping his voice down.

"Why?"

Suken looked at the ring of children again, his heart going out to them. He knew how hard it was to lose a member of your family. Chance, but he wished he didn't. "Tam's hired me to find whoever's framing Greencloak," he said simply.

Rossin blinked at him. Tam's hand clutched his shirt collar, Greencloak's blood dried on her fingers. Her shoulders shook in silent sobs.

"I'll be quick," Suken said. "I know he's hurting."

Rossin glanced at Rat, sighed and nodded.

Suken walked over to crouch down next to Rat. "Hey," he said softly. Rat looked up at him, his gaze distant. "I know about Fletch," Suken said. "I know that he's being framed, and that that bastard who killed Vethin is part of it. I want to find the killer, make him pay for what he did and clear Greencloak's name. But in order to do that, I need you to tell me everything you remember."

Rat reached up and wiped his nose with one dirty shirtsleeve. "He was wearing Fletch's cloak," he said softly, all trace of the harsh tone he'd used before missing. "Came. . . came outta nowhere. Pushed me. I tried to stop him, but. . . but he grabbed me, hurt me." He shuddered and hunched his shoulders, wrapping his arms around his legs. "I tried," he said, voice trembling.

"Did you see his face?"

Rat shook his head.

"Did he say anything?"

Another shake of the head. Suken reached out and laid his hand on the boy's shoulder for a moment, a simple gesture of comfort and solidarity. He'd only known these kids for a few hours, but somehow he felt connected to them. As if he were a part of their family, somehow. Because he was an orphan, too?

Maybe. Maybe they were just connected through the universality of grief.

He withdrew his hand and stood.

"He was tall," Rat said suddenly.

Suken looked down at him. "How tall?"

"Not as tall as you," the boy said, looking up at him. Tears had marked clean paths through the grime on his pinched face. "But almost. And strong. And he had remembrance blooms on both his wrists."

"Thank you," Suken said, the gratitude in his voice unfeigned. "That'll help." The boy buried his head in his arms, and Suken turned back to look at the group of kids standing with their backs to him near the back of the den.

The majority of the people in the city had remembrance blooms, so that wasn't much of a help. Neither was the fact that he was tall. But he'd had to tell the kid something.

Suken had to find Fletch. The thief must know more about who was trying to frame him, and talking to him was the only way Suken was going to get that information. But first Suken had to go back to the station. The guards and the guild had to be told that they were chasing the wrong man.

Both of those things were important. But that ring of silent children pulled at his heart and refused to let go. He joined them, standing beside Rossin, who held a still-sobbing Tam. In the middle of the group, the cloth-wrapped bundle lay still and motionless, Vethin's sightless eyes gazing up at the ceiling.

"What are you going to do with him?" Suken asked in a hushed tone.

"The same as we do with all our dead," Rossin replied. Burning the dead in a Temple to the Light was a privilege that only the rich could afford. Most of the Valley residents bid farewell to their dead the same way they disposed of their trash. . . over the edge of the city. Tam looked up from Rossin's shoulder, face streaked with tears. She reached out one hand, and Suken took it.

"Can he come?" she whispered to Rossin.

The young thief sighed, but nodded.

A half an hour past Ascent, Suken stood beside Rossin on the edge of the Southern Ridge, his serape snapping behind him and his hat tucked under one arm. The other children stood in a long line along the edge to either side, the wind tossing their hair and the rags they wore. The edge of the city fell in a sheer cliff from their feet, curving down and inwards towards the center of the city like an upside-down mountain. Clouds stained orange and pink from the light of the rising sun drifted across the sky between the floating city and the verdant jungles of Majitan far below. Fifty feet behind Suken, a line of refineries and incinerators belched dark smoke into the air. The ground between the buildings and the edge of the city was broken and uneven, littered with broken bricks, adobe chips and shards of metal and glass. A single squat palm tree sprouted from the wasteland, its sooty fronds clattering in the gusts of wind. Rossin held Vethin's body in his arms, wrapped in a long swath of dirty cloth. One of the boy's arms protruded, his dark-skinned fingers limp.

Rossin glanced at Suken. "You follow the Lady," he said in a quiet voice. "Right?"

"Yes."

"Never much held with the Light," Rossin said, looking out over the expanse below them. "Ain't never done nothing for us. But your Lady. . . she feeds us, sometimes. The prayers you cats throw away, they've been enough to keep us alive, when times are hard." Tam stood beside Suken, still clutching his hand. She sniffed and nodded, pulling the prayer he'd given her earlier from her clothes.

"Figure if we're gonna ask anyone to watch out for him," Rossin continued, "It'd be her. So are we. . . supposed to say anything?"

"Lady doesn't stand on ceremony," Suken said gently. "Say whatever you feel is right. She'll hear you. And. . ." he held out his hand to Tam. "We need to give Vethin something to give her. A payment, to thank her for guiding him wherever he wants to go."

Tam placed the prayer in Suken's palm. He freed his other hand from hers and took Vethin's cold hand, closing the stiffening fingers over the prayer with some difficulty. He repressed a shudder at that.

Rossin waited for Suken to move back again, and stepped up to the edge of the city. "This is Vethin," he announced to no one in particular. "He died because he wasn't quick enough. But he was a good thief, and family. So you'd better make damn sure he lands somewhere nice."

A murmur of assent ran down the line of children. Rossin hesitated for another moment, the warm wind tossing his hair. He opened his arms. The corpse tumbled in the wind as it fell into the clouds and disappeared from sight.

Suken watched it fall, and for a brief moment envied it. Vethin's life would be simple, now. Drifting on the Lady's blessing, doing whatever he wanted.

Suken, on the other hand, had to convince the entire governing council of Adunare that the most notorious thief in the city was innocent of murder. With no evidence, witnesses, or money.

He turned and trudged back towards the city with a heart which felt as if it were made of lead.

Chapter Eleven

Anisaria?"

Suken started, his hat falling off of his face. He looked blearily to his right at the guard standing beside him, the man giving him a disgusted look.

He didn't remember falling asleep. He didn't even remember walking into the fifteenth precinct's lobby, which for once was relatively empty. When was the last time he'd slept?

He couldn't remember that, either. Never a good sign.

Suken reached down and picked up his hat, putting it on gingerly. He still had a sizable lump on his temple from where he'd hit his head in the tunnels. It seemed to have gone down, but Suken suspected that he needed to get some sleep on a real damn bed before he could start feeling better.

"How long was I asleep?" he asked the guard standing next to him, and ran his tongue along his teeth with a grimace. It felt as if he'd been chewing on cotton in his sleep.

"About an hour," the man said. "Corporal Niden will see you now." He gestured back over his shoulder, where Niden stood with a group of guards. The man's uniform was rumpled and his short grey hair was sticking up. It looked as if he'd hurriedly tried to comb it down, but hadn't been successful and decided to let it be. Another man stood beside him, older, with a weathered face that looked as hospitable as a bar after closing time. He wore a simple shirt, vest and trousers and a short-sword strapped to his back, a crossbow at his hip.

Oh, Chance. Suken stood slowly, feeling as if he'd swallowed a glass full of oil. *What in caal-fire is* Ulric *doing here?*

Uncle Lorrin had always spoken of the guildmaster with awed fear, and told Suken to mind his manners if he ever had to face him. Suken had met the man personally twice after that. The first time, the meeting hadn't gone well. Not at all. The second hadn't been much better.

"Corporal," Suken said. Then, with an unintentional chill creeping into the title, "Guildmaster."

"You wanted to speak with me?" Corporal Niden said. The man's face couldn't have been colder if it had been carved out of ice.

I must have asked to see him before I passed out on the bench. Suken swallowed hard and nodded.

"I hope you won't object to your guildmaster joining us," Niden said, turning and starting towards the administration door. Suken followed, resisting the urge to turn and look at his guildmaster. He was certain the man was prowling behind him like some sort of giant, wizened bird of prey, ready to pick Suken's bones clean.

When they reached the door to Niden's office, he opened the door and gestured for Suken to go in ahead of him. Suken obediently stepped inside, taking one of the two seats. The guildmaster took the other, sitting back and staring at Suken with heavy-lidded eyes beneath a wide-brimmed hat that could have been twin to Suken's.

"Got to admit, it's taken you longer than I expected to land yourself in a vat of molasses, boy," he said in a slow drawl dripping with smug self-assurance. Ulric bared his teeth in a predatory smile. "Taking your license is going to be a bloody pleasure."

He can't take my license without due cause, Suken thought. *That means I can poke the ugly old bear a little with no repercussions.* He sat back and regarded the man with a cool expression. "Not as much of a pleasure as taking your daughter's maidenhead was."

Ulric let out a low growl, one hand clenching into a fist.

Niden sat and folded his hands. "I see you two have something of a history," he said dryly.

"Little bastard came into the guild ranting and raving about a rank one warrant some four years past," Ulric said, his eyes never leaving Suken's face. "Threw a tantrum like a ten-year-old girl when we wouldn't let him see it."

"That warrant has information about my gods-damned *brother,*" Suken snapped. "As a family member, I should have the right to—"

"*Shoulds* don't pay the taxes," Ulric interrupted him, his voice rising. "The law's the law, boy, as well you know. If you hadn't scored higher than any other hunter in the damned history of the guild I'd have rejected your license based on your attitude alone."

"You wouldn't have da—"

"*Enough!*" Niden roared, standing and slamming both hands down on his desk.

Suken swallowed the rest of his sentence, turning his attention from the heavy gaze of the guildmaster.

The corporal stood for a moment in silence before sitting slowly and folding his hands on the desk. "I was told that you have information about the Greencloak case," he said.

"Yes, sir," Suken said.

Corporal Niden leaned back in his chair, his expression unreadable.

"I have a trustworthy source who claims that the thief's being framed," Suken said. "And I . . . well, I saw him, sir. At the same time that a witness claimed to have seen Greencloak killing a haunt down in the Valley last night."

"You're sure it was Greencloak you saw?" Niden said.

"I am."

"Did you see his face?" Niden's voice sharpened at this.

Suken raised an eyebrow. "Yes. But—"

"You've done warrant-sketches for the guild in the past," Ulric said. He leaned forward, staring at Suken almost hungrily. "Could you draw him?"

Ulric probably only wanted a drawing so he could hunt down Greencloak himself for the bounty. Even without the murder charges, the thief had a sizable reward on his head, and the guildmaster wasn't above taking in a warrant or two when he needed a few extra aerans.

"I'll draw him," Suken said, "as long as you revoke the death reward on the warrant so he has a chance at a fair trial. I—"

"This isn't a negotiation, boy," Ulric cut him off. "You'll draw him or you'll regret it."

Before Suken could reply, Corporal Niden said, "Where and when did you see the thief?"

"Last night in the Hollow Market," Suken said, watching the guildmaster out of the corner of his eye. "Maybe three hours before dawn."

"Did he say anything?"

Suken shifted uncomfortably in his seat. He'd been on the giving end of too many interrogations to not recognize when the same tactics were being used against him. "He said something about not trusting someone named Blue."

"That's all?"

Suken nodded. Niden leaned back in his chair again, tapping his fingers on the dusty desktop. "One of our guards did find another message a few hours ago," he said to Ulric. "Written on the wall in blood, like the others. But no body."

Vethin, Suken thought.

Ulric folded his arms, keeping that hard glare fixed on Suken.

"When you saw Greencloak," Niden said to Suken, "was he wearing his cloak?"

"Well. . . no," Suken said.

"Then how do you know it was him?" Ulric asked.

"My source insisted that it was," Suken said. "And he matched the description in the case-file."

Niden eyed him. "Very well. Draw a sketch for your guild-master and tell us who this source is, and the witness who saw the crime take place. I'll send some men to question them. If you're right, and their testimony casts substantial doubt on the case, I'll pull the death-warrant."

Suken stared across the desk at Corporal Niden, his heart sinking. He couldn't tell the guards about the den. If he did, they'd come down on those kids harder than a storm in rain season. All of them were thieves, and Suken was willing to bet that most if not all of them had warrants. They were only stealing to survive, but the guards couldn't draw the line between hard criminals and orphaned kids struggling to find a scrap of bread to eat. It wasn't their job to judge, just find the criminals and bring them in, exactly like the hunters. Suken couldn't take the chance that even one of those kids might end up at the end of a length of rope or sold to the slave-markets because of him.

Not again.

"I'm sorry, sir," he said, knowing even as the words left his lips exactly how deep of a pile of shit he was wading into. "I can't do that."

Ulric rolled his eyes. "What did I tell you?" he said. "Blatant disregard for authority."

Niden didn't respond to that, keeping his eyes fixed on Suken instead. "We don't deal in confidential sources here, Anisaria. If this source of yours knows Greencloak personally, we might be able to use him or her to catch the thief. Even if he's not guilty of murder, he's still got almost a hundred other warrants on his head."

"How do we know Greencloak's not paying you to spread

rumors of his innocence?" Ulric said, stabbing one thick, calloused finger into Suken's chest.

Suken shoved the man's hand away. "He's not."

"The cartels have their hands around his neck," Ulric said to Niden, jerking a thumb towards Suken. "Kid's so balls-deep in debt it's a wonder he ain't suckin' cocks for Jesro o'Carfin down in the Hollow. Ain't hard to believe that Greencloak'd use some of those aerans he's got to—"

"I *said* he's not paying me," Suken snapped.

"S'posed to take your word for that, are we?" The older man stood, glaring down at Suken. "Easy way to convince me, boy—Tell us who your sources are."

"Withholding information from the guards is a punishable offense," Niden said coolly. "You know that."

Suken did. He'd been trying not to think about what that punishment might entail. But it looked as if he were about to find out, whether he wanted to or not.

"The last time I turned over a source to you," he said to Niden, unable to keep the anger from his voice, "my little brother got sold to the fucking slave markets right under your noses. So you can see why I'd be hesitant to do the same thing now."

Niden and Ulric both stared at him, their expressions hard. Suken let his breath out slowly, getting a handle on his temper. "Look," he said, "I'm more than willing to help with this investigation. I'll—"

"Name," the guildmaster growled, looming over Suken. "Now."

Suken stood. He was taller than the guildmaster now, but not by much. "No," he said. The word fell from his lips with the finality of a stone dropping from the edge of the city.

The guildmaster's face creased into a hard smile. "I was hoping you'd say that." He turned to Niden. "Take his license and his weapon. If he won't cooperate, he's of no use to us." He turned and pulled open the door, stalking out into the hallway.

Suken stood in Corporal Niden's office, staring blankly at the open door and the hallway behind as Ulric's footsteps faded. Niden stood. "Stay here," he ordered, and hurried after the guildmaster, leaving Suken alone in the room.

Suken felt dazed, as if he'd been hit in the head. He collapsed back into the chair, the strength temporarily fading from his legs. *He . . . he didn't mean that. He couldn't. He can't revoke my license for protecting the confidentiality of my sources. Can he?*

Suken mentally ran through the laws he'd memorized and felt his mouth go dry again.

Hunter's Charter, Subsection A, article 27. In cases in which the lives or wellbeing of civilians are threatened, no source is to be considered confidential. All information gathered in the course of a hunt must be turned over upon request by guild or city officials.

Suken closed his eyes and leaned forward to put his face in his hands.

I just lost everything, he thought, feeling as if the bottom had dropped out of his stomach. *Everything. I can try appealing for my license to be returned in a year, but there's no guarantee that my appeal will be heard. Even if it is . . . my reputation will be shot full of more holes than a crossbow training dummy.*

His training. His career. All of his hard work, and his chance to get his hands on his brother's case file . . . gone. All to protect a bunch of orphaned kids in a cave, and because he couldn't keep from mouthing off to Ulric. Suken ran both hands back through his hair slowly. *Maybe . . . maybe I can still salvage this. Go after him, beg for another chance, tell him . . . tell him . . .*

Tell him what? He was willing to do a lot to further his career, but putting children's lives in danger was where he drew the line. *Not again,* he thought, thinking of the little girl he'd doomed with his own arrogance. Thinking of the betrayal on his brother's face as he'd turned him and his friend over to the guild. *Never again.* If he wanted to protect those kids, he'd have to pay the price.

But Lady's breath. . . what a price.

Footsteps approached. Someone entered the room and rounded the desk. Suken didn't look up. He heard a squeak as someone eased into a chair. "I talked him down," Corporal Niden said.

Suken looked up, hope flaring in his chest like the energy from a released caal-lei convergence. "Really? My license isn't revoked?"

"Oh, it's still revoked," Niden said, leaning back and lacing his fingers on his stomach. "But the revocation is off the record, and if you stay out of trouble for the next month, I'll see to it that you get it back."

Suken managed to refrain from groaning out loud. This was the best he was likely to get. It would ruin his chances at finding Shifter and the murderer, but. . .

But it would save his career without putting the kids in danger. *And what about Greencloak?*

Suken shoved the thought, and the memory of those panicked, hunted eyes from his mind. *Your career is more important than a thief's life, Suken.*

The words rang hollow.

"What about Greencloak?" He found himself saying anyway. "If he really is being framed. . ."

Niden regarded him placidly. "I'll do what I can to pass along the information you've given me, but without evidence I can't revoke a death-warrant. And you are *not* to get involved. If you do. . ." he shrugged. The implication was as clear as glass.

Get involved, and you might as well kiss your license goodbye. Permanently.

"Thank you," Suken said, standing. Despite the good news about his license, he felt as if he had lead weights attached to all his limbs.

"Oh, and Anisaria. . ."

Suken turned back towards him.

"Leave your weapon and your license with the clerk at the front desk, along with that sketch."

Avara was *not* going to like that. "Yes, sir."

"*Six hundred aerans,* Suken?! What were you thinking? For the Light's sake, next time you get held for ransom just write them a deed for the bloody house."

Suken sat at the table in his kitchen, a bag of cool water pressed against his head. Terri's voice wasn't doing anything for the headache that had begun throbbing behind his eyes, and it sounded as if she was just getting started. She stood next to the sink, her fists planted on her hips. The morning sky through the window behind her the color of a bruise, rain pattering against the glass. Suken's fat black and white cat, Chance, was rubbing against his leg, but Suken wasn't in the mood to pet him.

"I know that you don't give a damn about your finances, but—"

He closed his eyes, her voice becoming little more than an annoying buzz in the back of his mind.

A month, he thought. *A whole month. What am I supposed to do for a living?* All he'd ever practiced and prepared to be was a bounty hunter. He had no other marketable skills, no trades, no crafts.

Well, except his drawings. He supposed he could do what his mother had done and draw sketches for people on the street, but he doubted he would be able to make enough at it to keep the cartels from clawing their way into his life. Not to mention the fact that it felt. . . wrong. If he wasn't a bounty hunter, what—who—was he?

A sap, he thought sourly. *A sap who's going to stand aside and let an innocent man hang for murder.*

"—food? Do you think it appears out of *nowhere?* I have to—"

"Terri," he interrupted her, not opening his eyes. "I'm afraid I'm going to have to let you go."

Silence, broken only by the patter of rain against the window.

"That's not funny, Suken."

"I'm not joking. I'm on probation." He opened his eyes and looked up in time to see her expression shift from exasperation to worry. All he wanted to do was go upstairs, collapse on his bed, and sleep. But he owed it to her to tell her what had happened. "It's only for a month, but . . . any money I make's going to have to go towards my debts."

Terri blinked at him, looking as lost as he felt. After a moment she visibly collected herself, shaking her head so that her hair swayed around her face. She pulled a chair out, sitting and resting her elbows on the table. "What happened?" she asked quietly.

"I went after Greencloak. And I found him. But . . . he's being framed, Terri."

Terri didn't say anything. She stared at him over her folded hands.

"I went to the station. Told the corporal, and the guildmaster. They ordered me to give up my source." He pulled the pack of cool water from his head and set it down. "They were orphans," he said, knowing that she'd understand. He'd told her about what had happened with his brother once, when he'd come home drunk. "I couldn't turn them over to the pearls."

"Of course you couldn't," she said, as if it were the most obvious thing in the world. If she hadn't been . . . well, *Terri*, he could have kissed her for that.

"I'm sorry," he said, looking away. "You can stay here if you want, until you find a new job, or until the tax collectors or the cartels come to claim the place. I doubt I'll be able to make enough to keep them away." He looked up at her. "How much would I need to make a month?"

"What are you planning to do?" she asked. "Sell your smiles?"

"Drawings, actually," Suken said. "Unless you think people would pay more for smiles?"

She snorted and sat back, folding her arms. "And Greencloak?"

Ah, chance. She had to ask that question. He felt the headache return with a vengeance. He raised two fingers to massage his temple. "What about him?"

"Did those idiots at the station at least believe you about his innocence?"

"Maybe," Suken said. "I don't know. It doesn't matter. I can't get involved."

Silence. Suken looked up to see her staring at him, her expression as blank as a sheet of new paper.

"What?" he asked.

"Do you know why I work for you, Suken?"

He shrugged. "I'd assume it has something to do with the two hundred aerans a month I pay you." He sighed. "*Paid* you."

She raised one eyebrow. "Now you remember how much my salary is? Maybe you should get hit in the head more often."

He couldn't force himself to laugh. He could barely keep a shadow of a fake smile up for her benefit.

"Suken," she said with a sigh, reaching across the table to take one of his hands in hers. "I could do this job for a rich, fat merchant or a mage and get paid twice as much. I chose to work for *you* because you've got a good heart, try as you might to hide it."

"I suppose the fact that I'm charming and talented and handsome had nothing to do with it?"

She ignored that. "You didn't tell the guild and the guards about those kids because you knew what would happen to them if you did. You didn't do anything wrong. In fact, I would have thought less of you if you'd done any differently."

"Is there a point behind this flattery?" Suken said, shifting his weight. "Coming from anyone else I'd be grateful, but from you . . . honestly, it's starting to make me feel uncomfortable."

"The *point* is, I know you, Suken Anisaria, and I know that you're not the kind of man who would let an innocent man hang. Not if you could stop it."

Suken sighed. She was right. Why was she *always* right?

His eyes fell on a broadsheet sitting on the table between them.

He'd thrown it to the table after walking in ten minutes ago, and Terri had set down the glass of water she'd been drinking on top of it. Beneath the glass peeked three letters—BLU.

He reached over and moved the glass aside, picking up the broadsheet.

MAGE RALOR BLUVAEL FOUND DEAD IN HOME AT DAWN, the headline read. Beneath that, in smaller letters:

In a shocking development, respected mage discovered to have been selling illegal metal-bound weaponry under the pseudonym "Blue." Neighbors aghast, claim that he was . . .

Suken looked up slowly. "Tell them not to trust Blue," he whispered. Tam had said that the person Greencloak had referenced was a mage, and had given them metal-bound weapons. Could this be the same man?

It wasn't much of a lead, especially since the man was dead. But if he was right . . . maybe he could find something in the mage's house that would help him to figure out who was framing Greencloak. Or find Greencloak himself again.

He skimmed over the rest of the article. Mage Bluvael's home was only seven blocks away. He could make it there in about fifteen minutes if he walked fast, and . . .

Suken hesitated. *What are you thinking? Hasn't this case gotten you in enough trouble as it is?*

But Terri had been right. He *couldn't* walk away and let an innocent man die. The thought made him feel ill. Someone had to do something. And other than the orphans, no one was likely to.

Either Suken saved Greencloak's life, or no one would.

He sighed and stood, picking up his hat. "You probably shouldn't stay here," he told Terri. "If something goes wrong and word gets around that I'm helping Greencloak," *oh Chance, had those words actually left his lips?* "the other hunters might come looking for you. Or the cartel might send some men by, since it looks like I won't be making this month's payment."

She rolled her eyes. "The day I can't handle a few—"

"Terri," he interrupted her. "Please."

She eyed him and sighed. "Where should I go?"

"Avara's," Suken said immediately. He could think of nowhere safer than with the aging weaponsmith and her husband, except maybe the Lady's Face. And as much as he trusted Marxen, he certainly *didn't* trust all of Marxen's clientele.

"Fine. But when this is all over, you owe me." She bent and lifted Chance. The cat hung from her arms like a piece of wet laundry. "We'll leave as soon as I get some things together."

Suken nodded and pulled his hat on. "Wish me luck?" he asked her with a crooked grin.

"I would, if I thought you needed it," she said. "And Suken . . . try not to get yourself killed." She shouldered the door open as Chance gave Suken a tortured look from her arms.

Chapter Twelve

Mage Bluvael's home reminded Suken of a hornet's nest. Guards swarmed all over it, entering and exiting, carrying arm-loads of metal-bound weapons and blood-stained items to a cart standing on the corner. Two large shadow-sprites stood in the cart's yoke, looking about with eyes which glowed like embers. Other guards stood in the midst of the crowd across the street, speaking to neighbors or shouting for passers-by to continue on with their business.

Suken stood in the crowd, trying to look inconspicuous. He needed to get into that house, and soon. If Bluvael had anything about the people framing Greencloak, it was possible the guards might collect it up as evidence, not knowing what they had. So far as they knew, this wasn't connected to the Greencloak case. And if they removed a piece of evidence, Suken wouldn't be able to get his hands on it until they released the man's belongings to his family in a month or two. That would be too late for Greencloak.

But *how* to get in? He flipped a prayer over and over between his index and middle fingers as he considered his options.

There weren't many. If he told them that he was on a warrant and needed access to the crime scene, he was certain they'd ask to see his license. He supposed the one guard he recognized in the crowd might not ask for his license, but Weyav was from Niden's precinct. Suken couldn't risk Niden hearing that he was still poking around where he shouldn't be.

Well . . . he couldn't ask Weyav for access to the scene. But that didn't mean he couldn't try to get a little information. Suken broke from the crowd and headed towards the man, raising his hand in a wave.

Officer Weyav's light brown hair stuck out from the edges of a tight-fitting grey cap that wasn't strictly uniform-issue. He was in his mid-thirties and had a nose so thin Suken wouldn't have been surprised if he could cut paper with it, along with a pair of high cheekbones and arching eyebrows that gave him a somewhat condescending appearance. As Suken approached, Weyav looked up, his tired expression fading into a warm smile.

"Anisaria," he said, holding out his hand. "Here on a warrant?" Suken took his hand and shook it once, firmly.

"Taking a few days off," Suken said, looking at the house. "I was on my way home when I saw all the commotion. What's going on?"

"Murder," Weyav said, putting one hand on his hip and looking back over his shoulder towards the house. "It's not pretty, and we can't start cleaning it up until the gods-be-damned sketch artist gets here. Bastard's taking his bloody time, and I promised Syrenna I'd be home to take the kids to play practice."

"Really," Suken said slowly. He reached down to run his fingers along the edge of the case at his belt. They'd taken his weapons, they'd taken his license . . . but they hadn't taken his sketchbook.

"You know," he said, "if you need a sketch artist that badly, I could do it for you. I'd hate to see you late to pick up Perra and Torlin. And I wouldn't mind a few extra aerans. Warrants have been scarce lately."

"I don't know," Weyav said, looking at the house and fingering the hem of one of his sleeves. "You know that our sketch artists all work under contract."

"I've already got confidentiality access. How different is seeing the scene in person from seeing it in a case-file?"

Weyav bit his lip, looking back and forth from Suken to the house. Then he nodded once, sharply. "All right. Can't hurt to ask, right?"

Suken smiled. "Right."

"This way." Weyav led him up to a thick-looking man with captain's knots on his shoulders who filled out his uniform like half-solidified butter poured into a mold. Weyav saluted crisply, and the man turned towards them, handing a sheaf of papers over to one of the other officers.

"Weyav," he said, his voice raspy. "Who's this?"

"Hunter who dabbles in sketching," Weyav said. "Not by the book, I know, but by the time that bloody sketch artist gets here that body'll be half rotted in the heat and we'll be able to smell the stench from here."

"I was on my way home when I saw all of this and thought you fellows could use a hand," Suken put in. "As you can see," he pulled his sketchbook from his case and flipped it open to a random page, showing it to the captain. "I'm more than capable."

The man grunted, not even sparing the book a glance. "Well, this is your unlucky day. Get yer ass up into that house and start drawin' so we can wrap this shit up."

"*Un*lucky?" Suken asked.

The captain didn't answer, turning instead to another guard who approached him with a bag of what looked like coils of metal wire.

Weyav took Suken's arm and pulled him away towards the front door of the house. "Best get to work quick," he said under his breath. "Captain's in a ripe mood. If you don't have these done soon, he's liable to order us to remove the body without the sketches, and to hell with protocol."

Suken followed him towards the front door of the house, dodging other guards as the men and women walked or ran around, conveying messages or carrying objects draped in sheets to a nearby covered cart. Suken saw blood smeared on one of the sheets.

Weyav hesitated, one hand on the door handle. "Have you eaten recently?"

"No," Suken replied, resisting the urge to roll his eyes. "I've seen bodies before, you know."

"Not like this," Weyav said in a dark tone, opening the door.

Suken stepped into the house and stopped, the hand holding his sketchbook going numb. The victim had definitely been a mage, judging by the gold tunic he wore. It was smeared with ash and soot, as were his tan pants. He lay half on the stone floor with his legs stretched up the steps, one arm bent in an unnatural angle behind his back, the other above his ruin of a face.

Eight thick parallel channels had been gouged into the man's face, almost like claw marks. Each one wept crimson blood in dried sheets and ran all the way from his forehead down his neck. Suken glimpsed the dull white of bone peeking through the strips of flesh remaining on the man's face, and one blue eye gazing up sightlessly from a mass of pulpy muscle and pooled, congealed blood. His hair was dark and mostly matted to his skull with blood which spread around him in a puddle two feet wide. A trail of dried blood ran down the steps and patches of the walls were spattered with it.

The room smelled of the coppery tinge of blood, urine, and the dull, wet reek Suken could only attribute to fear. He felt the bile rise in this throat and raised one hand to his mouth, looking away.

"Told you," Weyav said, a hint of sadness tingeing his voice. "Bastard was selling metal-bound weapons illegally, but even the worst of criminals don't deserve this."

Suken nodded, not trusting that he'd be able to keep from vomiting if he opened his mouth.

Weyav sighed and gestured to the bloody mess. "Sooner you get started, sooner you finish. I'll buy you a drink tonight at the

Lady's Face, we can chat about anything that's *not* a damned murder case."

"Sounds good," Suken said, though his voice was choked. Weyav clapped him on the shoulder and turned to kneel down beside an overturned vase splattered with blood near the doorway.

Suken lifted his book, took a deep breath, and began to sketch.

It was different from every other sketch he'd done, but also the same. Start with soft lines to delineate the boundaries of the room. Next, simple shapes. A series of ovals instead of a corpse, a circle for the arch of the stairwell. The stick of lead flew across the paper for this part, but slowed as he reached the details.

The bent angles of the arms were unnatural, and felt strange to draw. The spatters of blood on the walls became blotches of lead on paper. And the face . . .

Suken realized he'd have to do a close-up sketch of that. He shuddered as he filled in the last few bits of shading on the overall room sketch, and flipped to a new page. He walked over to the corpse, carefully avoiding stepping in the blood. He squatted down beside the body and rested his pad on his knee.

He let his gaze drift over the man's body, from feet to bloodied face. He wasn't quite certain what he was looking for. A note or letter, maybe, or some sort of indication as to where this man had been recently? Suken glanced back over his shoulder. Weyav was chatting with one of the other guards, and the one at the top of the stairs seemed to have moved on to somewhere else in the house. He turned back to the body and lifted one corner of the man's tunic, trying to avoid touching any blood.

Nothing in the man's trouser pocket. Nothing visible, anyway, and Suken wasn't about to go sticking his hand into a dead man's pocket. He shuddered at the thought and let the corner of the tunic drop, looking at the soot smudging his fingers.

He brought his fingers to his nose and sniffed. It smelled and looked like soot from the incinerators. So before getting killed, Mage Bluvael had been in the Valley.

That made sense, if the man had been selling illegal metal-bound weapons like the broadsheets claimed. Weapons . . . like the one at the mage's belt. Suken cocked his head to the side, looking at the knife more closely. He began to sketch it without thinking about it, his hand moving over the paper as his eyes traveled across the knife.

It was ornate, with delicate silver traceries woven into the hilt and the cross-guard. The blade had been pulled free of the scabbard a bare inch. . . . Maybe Bluvael had tried to draw it to defend himself. Suken could make out the maker's mark etched into the blade, several ji'Ahiran symbols all stacked one upon the other resulting in a tangled mess like a clump of string. It looked familiar somehow, but he couldn't quite place why—the things were too chaotic and confusing. He drew that, too. This blade was probably one of Bluvael's own making, but it couldn't hurt to check.

He heard footsteps approaching, and flipped the page to a clean sheet before Weyav crouched beside him. "How's it going?" the guard asked. "Almost done?"

"Almost," Suken said, beginning to draw in the base lines of what was left of the man's face. "So who was this fellow, anyway?"

"Mage," Weyav said, looking at the corpse. "Not a terribly successful one, but apparently his failures in academia were more than made up for by his extracurricular activities. You wouldn't believe how many metal-bound weapons we've found in this house. Captain's never going to hear the end of it. Illegal weapon-manufacturer in his own district, and he had no idea."

Suken nodded, beginning to sketch in the gouges in the man's face. It was far, far harder than he'd anticipated. A face had certain proportions, rules that you adhered to while sketching. But it was as if all those lines had been erased here, and replaced with a nonsensical mess of blood and flesh and pulpy mess.

Suken wasn't even sure where to start. He sent a brief, fervent prayer of thanks to Lady Chance that he hadn't found himself in this line of work.

"He's a mess," Suken said, gesturing to the soot stains on the mage's tunic. "Any idea where he was before he got himself killed?"

Weyav didn't reply. Suken glanced over at him and found the man giving him a considering look.

"What?" Suken asked. *Was I being too obvious?*

"You lied to me outside," Weyav said. "You *are* on a warrant, aren't you? For someone who kills like this?"

Damn. Weyav was on the wrong pathway, but Suken didn't want him on a pathway at all.

"No," he said, drawing in a jumble of shaded mess that he hoped looked enough like the remnants of the corpse's ear to be passable. "I'm hurt that you think I'd lie to you, Weyav."

The door to the street opened, saving Suken from coming up with anything else. He looked up to see who had entered, and felt his mouth go dry.

Fletch stood in the crowd in front of Blue's house, watching as the guard and the bounty hunter entered the front door. It was the same cat that had been with Tam last night in the Hollow Market, the one who claimed to believe that Fletch was being framed.

That was a load of shit, of course. He'd only been trying to get close enough to grab Fletch for the bounty, and Tam had swallowed the story like a piece of sugared fruit. The kid was an excellent pick-pocket, but by the *gods*, he'd have to have a talk with her about how easily she let herself get conned by a pretty face.

Not that he should talk, apparently, given how thoroughly Blue had done the same to him.

Fletch set his jaw and turned his attention back to the hunter. He'd nearly abandoned his plan and melted back into the streets when he'd seen the tall man, but the hunter hadn't seemed to notice him in the crowd. How had he known to come here? He couldn't have followed Fletch, that was a certainty. So how?

Doesn't matter, Fletch thought. The hunter was a danger—he'd seen Fletch's real face, for starters—but he was a danger Fletch was willing to face in order to find out what was happening in that house.

Looked as if someone had ratted on Blue. Fletch was annoyed by that, if only because it meant that the pearls might find him before Fletch had time to hunt the bastard down himself.

He sidled closer to the crowd, eavesdropping.

"Can't believe it," one woman said, shaking her head. "Illegal metal-bound weapons, in our neighborhood! It was supposed to be so *safe* here!"

"Well, at least he won't be making any more," an old woman beside her said acidly. "Good riddance, you ask me."

Fletch furrowed his brow.

"Have they brought out the body yet?" a little boy asked, trying in vain to peer around his mother's skirts. Every time he moved, his mother stepped with him, deftly blocking his line of sight.

What if he'd been wrong? What if Blue *hadn't* betrayed him, and had instead come back here, as they'd planned?

But Fletch hadn't been here. He'd taken his time, making his way through the undercity slowly and thinking about all the ways he'd like to kill the man who'd betrayed him.

Dread rose in him, cold and numbing, but Fletch forced it down. It was possible that that weapon-bitch from the Hollow had sent someone here to ransack the place and found one of Blue's servants. Fletch took a deep breath, anger, doubt and fear waging a battle for control of his mind.

He had to find out what was going on in there. He tilted his head side to side, working out some of the kinks in his neck, and slumped his shoulders. He limped over to the nearest guard.

"S'cuse me," he rasped, taking care to keep his head down so his hood obscured his face in shadow.

The pearl turned towards him, his expression shifting from bored to wary. Fletch knew that he looked out of place here in the Mages' District in these beggars' clothes, but he hadn't had time to find or steal anything else.

"Saw somethin' suspicious in that alley," Fletch said, nodding towards it. "A man, skulkin' about in the shadows, there." He hesitated, putting on an embarrassed smile and hoping the man would hear it in his voice. "Could be nothin. Bet it is. Jumping at shadows, with all the commotion, you know? But maybe, if it *is* somethin' . . . a reward, you know . . . ?" He wrung his hands.

The pearl sniffed, his nose wrinkling. He was apparently too well-bred to make mention of the fact that Fletch still reeked of rotting meat. "You sure it wasn't just another beg—one of you?"

"Could be," Fletch said, looking in that direction and wiping his nose with the back of his hand. "But I didn't recognize him."

The guard sighed and adjusted the hilt of the short-sword he wore at his belt. "Wait here," he said, and turned to stride into the alley.

Fletch waited. The guard crossed the street and entered the alley, picking his way around flowering plants and wrought-iron fences enclosing little balconies. Once Fletch figured he was far enough in, he followed, moving through the crowd like an otter through a river, hindered by his limp. He slid into the alley and slunk from shadow to shadow, far slower than he was used to, but quick enough to make it to the guard's side as the man bent to examine the bundle of trash and blankets Fletch had carefully arranged there.

Fletch's hand flashed out, a thin steel needle held carefully between his thumb and forefinger. The steel jabbed into the back of the guard's uniform below his left shoulder-blade.

The man stiffened for a heartbeat, hand moving to the hilt of his sword. He collapsed forward with a low moan, falling on the pile of trash. Fletch glanced back over his shoulder. No one had seen. They were all paying too much attention to the guards entering and leaving Blue's house, and this section of the alley was nicely shadowed. He bent and began stripping the guard of his uniform, pulling each piece on as he discarded the disguise he'd been wearing.

The poison on the tip of the needle would keep this guard asleep for an hour, maybe more. Plenty of time for Fletch to get into the house, find out what was going on in there, and get out. He straightened and pulled the guard's opalescent cloak around his shoulders. It wasn't *his* cloak, but he supposed it would do, for now. He ran his hands back through his dark hair. The incessant rain had wetted it, and Fletch used the moisture to push it back into a more respectable-looking style than usual. He turned and walked slowly out of the alley, adjusting the collar of the jacket.

The crowd parted for him without a word. Fletch walked slowly to try to mask his limp as much as possible and headed straight for Blue's front door.

No one stopped him. The authority of an Adunare guard was a far more effective cloak to wear than the physical one around his shoulders, and he used it effortlessly, striding up to the front door and opening it.

And there he stopped, the blood draining from his face.

Blue lay dead in the entryway, his blood pooled around him, his dark curly hair matted with it and his face gouged and practically unrecognizable. But Fletch knew it was him.

Oh, gods, he thought, staggering a step to the side to lean his shoulder against the doorjamb for support, his eyes fixed to the corpse. He raised one shaking hand to cover his mouth.

I thought that he'd betrayed me, so I didn't get here as quickly as I could have. If I'd trusted him . . . If I'd refused to let him get involved in the first place. . . .

I got him killed.

"You all right?" someone asked, but Fletch didn't see them, didn't see anything except the body.

I came to him for help. If it weren't for me, he'd still be alive.

Emotions clouded his mind in a murky swirling mess, like rainwater in the gutters. Pain. Guilt. Sorrow. That last surprised him. He'd never thought that he felt anything for Blue, not really. A sort of . . . aesthetic admiration of his looks and his carnal talents, maybe, but nothing deeper. Nothing *real.*

Apparently he'd been wrong.

"—room before he vomits," someone was saying. Fletch forced himself to pull his attention back to his surroundings, away from the one blue eye he could see staring at the ceiling, away from the stark contrast between dark blood and polished wood.

A guard with a stupid-looking hat stood in front of him, the bounty hunter standing from where he'd been crouched beside Blue's body. The former was looking at Fletch with concern, the latter with wariness.

Fletch had assumed that the hunter would have moved on to the upper rooms by now, allowing Fletch to avoid him. But that apparently wasn't the case. He turned to bolt out the door, but the guard caught his arm.

Suken stared at the guard who walked in the door. Long dark hair, pushed back from a gaunt face. Green eyes, fixed on the corpse now, but Suken remembered a similar pair staring at him over Tam's shoulder, like those of a hunted animal. *No,* he thought, shocked speechless. *It couldn't be.* Greencloak wouldn't have been stupid enough to come here himself. . . . Would he?

"Must be his first murder scene," Weyav said to Suken. "We should get him out of the room before he vomits."

The man's eyes finally shifted from the corpse to Weyav and Suken, and Suken saw them narrow as they settled on him.

He recognizes me. It is *him.* Suken felt a surge of elation as he stood. He'd found Greencloak again. Well, more like he'd stumbled onto him for the second time in twenty-four hours, but that didn't matter. What mattered was that he had the man, and this time he wouldn't let him get away.

Greencloak turned towards the door, but Weyav grabbed his arm. "Hold on there," the guard said, his voice gentle. "If you're gonna be sick, best to do it away from where the civvies can see."

Suken approached them, noting how tense Greencloak was. He was like a coiled spring, ready to release in any direction. The man's eyes darted back to Suken, and Suken could guess what thoughts whirled behind them.

He doesn't believe that I want to help him. He thinks I'm going to turn him over to the guards.

He had to disabuse Greencloak of that notion, and quickly, before the thief broke Weyav's grasp and vanished into the street.

Suken looked out the door, cocking his head slightly to the side. "Did you hear that?"

"Hear what?" Weyav said, following Suken's glance. Across the street, the captain had his head bent over something one of the other guards had brought him.

"I think the captain called your name," Suken said, putting his arm around Greencloak's shoulders. The thief shot him a sharp look. "Go on. I'll take him out back, and bring you the sketches when I'm done."

Weyav glanced between the captain, Suken, and Greencloak, and nodded curtly as he hurried down the steps to the street.

"If I'd wanted to turn you over for the bounty," Suken said in a quiet, friendly tone, "I would have just done it."

Greencloak pulled away from him, his eyes narrowed, his hand hovering over the hilt of the guard's sword at his belt. Suken glanced up at the top of the stairs, where one of the other guards had reappeared, carrying a stack of swords. "We need to talk," Suken said, keeping his voice low and returning his gaze to Greencloak.

The thief hesitated for another moment, his hand still on his sword-hilt. Then he straightened and nodded towards a doorway under the curve of the stairs. He headed off in that direction, Suken following closely behind him.

Greencloak led him down a hallway decorated with portraits, stepping over scraps of metal and books in haphazard piles on the floor before turning into a doorway. He palmed a silver panel on the wall with casual familiarity, and a luminary burst into light above them, illuminating a large kitchen. A wooden table took up most of the middle of the room. One wall was lined with shelves holding plates, glasses and silverware. Another was dominated by a table topped with a thick slab of steel heated by metal-bound convergences and used to cook food. Greencloak stopped beside a counter on which rested a half-eaten plate of pork and apples, the flatbread hanging half on and half off the plate.

"You've got two minutes," he said.

Suken closed the door and walked over to stand on the opposite side of the table from the thief. "You," Suken said, "are the infamous Greencloak."

"I hope you're not trying to play to my vanity. I'm not in the mood."

Right to the point, then.

"I know that you're innocent," Suken said.

"Of murder, you mean," Greencloak said, picking up a star-fruit from the counter and casually tucking it into a pocket of the guards' uniform he wore. "Congratulations. What do you want?"

Suken blinked. "Want?"

"You're a hunter," Greencloak said, examining the plate. "But as you pointed out in the lobby, you're not clapping me in cuffs and dragging me to the nearest precinct, so obviously you want something from me." He reached down and picked up a chunk of meat, tossing it in his mouth. "Better spill it quickly," he said around the food as he chewed. "They'll be coming back to check on us any time now."

"What could I possibly want from you?" Suken asked.

"Information. Sex. Money." Greencloak shrugged. "Blackmail's a popular option, one that better men than you have tried." He ate another piece of the pork.

"I'm not going to blackmail you," Suken said. He had to get control of this conversation, and quickly. "Someone's pretending to be you, using your reputation to kill mage-born, for some reason."

"No," Greencloak said, his eyes widening in faux surprise. "Really?"

Suken ignored that. "I tried to get the guards to retract the death-warrant so you could get a fair trial, but without evidence they won't listen to me."

"Shocking," Greencloak said.

"Most of the other hunters will be out for your blood. But if you come with me to the precinct, the guards can keep you in a cell for a few days. When the killer strikes again they'll know for sure that it isn't you. They'll have to retract the bounty on you and start looking for the *real* killer."

Greencloak barked a laugh. "Just go to the pearls and let them lock me up. Of course. Why didn't I think of that?" He shook his head. "If you seriously thought that was going to work, you're not going to make it far in this business." He turned, but Suken darted forward and grabbed his arm. Greencloak tried to pull away, but Suken tightened his grip.

"Let me help you find him," Suken said. "We can pool our resources, our knowledge. You must know things about all of this that I don't, and I have skills that you don't. We can work together, and when we find the real killer I can bring him in."

"Right," Greencloak said caustically. "And I'm sure that as soon as we find the real killer and turn him over, you'll let me walk free, despite all the *legitimate* bounties on my head."

The reminder that this man was a criminal irked him, but Suken bit back his dislike, reminding himself that Greencloak might be a thief, but thieves didn't deserve death. "Until this is taken care of, yes," he said. "We can form a . . . a kind of temporary alliance. A truce. You have my word."

Greencloak raised one eyebrow. "The word of a bounty hunter? I've had too many of your friends try to kill me for that to carry any weight." He yanked his arm free of Suken's grasp and turned towards the door.

He's from the Valley, Suken thought with an edge of desperation. *Self-preservation should be something he can relate to.*

"They took my license," he said, raising his voice. "Because I wouldn't turn over your kids to be questioned. If I don't find this killer and clear your name, my career is ruined." It was only *half* a lie, but a necessary one. "Please. This is the only way I'll get it back."

"Ah," Greencloak said, turning back towards him with a grin. "So you *do* want something."

"It's in both of our best interests to work together on this."

Greencloak snorted and started limping towards the back door of the kitchen. "I don't need your help, and I don't care about your bloody licen—"

"But you *do* care about those kids," Suken interrupted him, raising his voice. "The ones in the undercity."

Greencloak froze. "Was that a threat?" he asked, looking back over his shoulder. Suken didn't like the glint in the thief's eyes.

"No," Suken said quickly. "I just thought that, if the killer's gotten to one of them, chances are he might try to kill more, to draw you out. I can help you stop him before he gets the chance."

Greencloak turned to face him. For the first time, Suken saw genuine confusion on the man's face. And, deep in his eyes, fear. "What are you talking about?"

Suken felt his blood run cold. *Oh, Chance. He didn't know.*

For years the thief had been built up as a legend in Adunare, a man that knew a hidden way into every home, a man who could melt into shadows better than a haunt when he chose to, a legend among thieves.

But Greencloak wasn't a legend. He was just a man, a man who was injured, and on the run, and hadn't had time to stop and check in on those he cared about. Suken tried to make his voice as soft as he could. "After I lost you in the Hollow Market, I escorted Tam back to the den. One of the kids . . . I'm sorry, but . . . he'd been killed. By the person pretending to be you."

"Which one?" Greencloak's voice was stiff, emotionless.

"A boy named Vethin."

Greencloak stood for a moment in silence. Then he slammed his fist down on the counter, rattling the pans and metal spoons laid out on it. He stood there for a long moment, eyes closed, jaw clenched.

"I'm sorry," Suken said softly. "I thought you knew." He glanced back over his shoulder at the closed door of the kitchen. If anyone had heard that, they'd come to investigate. He needed to end this quickly. "You're injured, and you're tired. If you do manage to find the killer on your own, you won't be able to chase him if he runs, or fight him." Suken leaned forward. "But I can. I can bring him to the guards, and get your name cleared of murder."

"The last person who tried to help me is lying in that entryway in a pool of his own blood," Fletch said, his voice cold. "Whoever's framing me isn't working alone, kitten. You stick your nose in this, and it might get you killed."

Greencloak was wavering. He wanted to be convinced. . . . Suken only needed to push a little harder.

"I'm a bounty hunter," Suken said. "I've had years of training. I can protect myself. And you, if it comes down to it."

Greencloak raised one eyebrow. "And you'll do that—play bodyguard to a *thief*—for nothing more than a piece of paper?"

"For a *career*," Suken said. "A livelihood. One I've worked hard to get."

A knock came on the door to the hallway. Greencloak tensed, his eyes darting to the back door.

"Anisaria? Everything all right in there?"

"Fine," Suken called back over his shoulder without taking his eyes from Greencloak. "Knocked some things over getting him to the sink. Looks like he's about finished up now, we'll be out soon."

Once Weyav's footsteps had receded down the hallway, Suken turned his full attention back to Greencloak. "Well?"

The thief looked at the door, idly playing with a ring on his middle finger. "Blue had a dagger," he said. "He was trying to find out who made it. We need to get it back. It's the only clue I have as to who's doing this to me."

"We?" Suken couldn't help it. A grin spread across his face.

"Yes, we. Since you insist on tagging along, you might as well make yourself useful." He started towards the door, but Suken stepped in his way.

"If you're trying to find out who made it, you should just need the maker's mark, right?"

Greencloak's eyes narrowed again. He did that a lot. "Why?"

Suken pulled his sketchbook from his case and flipped it open to the page with the dagger, and turned it around to show it to Greencloak.

The thief took the sketch and examined it. "This is accurate?"

Suken bit back an irritated retort at that. "Yes."

"Well," Greencloak said, ripping the page free, folding it twice and stuffing it in the pocket of his uniform, "let's go find ourselves a weapon-smith." He tossed the book back. Suken caught it and glanced at the door. He'd promised these sketches to Weyav, but he couldn't very well go back out there now, nor could he let Greencloak out of his sight. He ripped the pages free and set them down on the table, turned, and followed Fletch Greencloak out the kitchen's door, hoping that he hadn't signed himself up for more than he'd bargained for.

Chapter Thirteen

Fletch sat on the pathway seat next to the bounty hunter, eyeing him. The cat had insisted that he had a weapon-smith he trusted who might give them a lead on the maker's mark, so Fletch had grudgingly agreed to try there first. The pathway was mostly empty at this time of day. The few people sharing the car with them were minding their own business, reading broadsheets or napping with their heads leaning back against the windows.

The bounty hunter looked at him out of the corner of his eye. "Isn't it illegal to wear a guard's uniform if you're . . . you know. Not a guard?" he asked. He wore a simple but comfortable-looking outfit, like most of the hunters did. Off-white shirt with long sleeves covered by a dark, thin leather serape. Dark brown pants, rugged boots that had obviously seen a lot of wear. A wide-brimmed leather hat covering short dirty-blond hair and throwing the man's eyes into shadow. The petals of a remembrance bloom peeked out from under the hem of his left sleeve, the colors of the flower faded from age. Overall, your average hunter . . . save for the empty straps at his leg where a weapon was supposed to be, and the fact that he looked barely as old as Fletch himself. He was probably in his early twenties if he was already a licensed bounty hunter, but he looked years younger. The criminals he tracked probably had a tendency to underestimate him based on that. Not a mistake Fletch would be making.

"You know who I am," Fletch said dryly. "Do you really think I care about legality?"

One corner of the hunter's mouth twitched down into a frown. "Guess not."

Fletch was certain that there was more to this man's motives than he was letting on, but he had to grudgingly admit (if only to himself) that having someone over the age of sixteen who believed in his innocence was a bit of a relief.

"If we're going to cooperate," the hunter said, "maybe it would help if we were, oh, I don't know. Cooperative?"

"Meaning?"

"We should know each others' names," he said. "I can't exactly go around calling you . . ." he glanced from side to side and lowered his voice. "You know."

"Caiman," Fletch said, giving one of his many aliases.

The hunter raised the brim of his hat with two fingers to give Fletch a measuring look.

"What?" Fletch snapped.

"That's not what the kids called you," the hunter said evenly.

"Well if you knew my bloody name, why'd you bloody ask me?"

"Because that's what polite people do when they meet one another for the first time," the hunter replied. "*Fletch.*"

Fletch flipped him a rude gesture, and the hunter sighed.

"I'm Suken. Suken Anisaria. I'd say it's a pleasure to meet you, but . . . well."

Fletch raised one eyebrow. He'd heard that name before, here and there in the undercity. That was a rarity for a kitten who didn't look old enough to be rank four yet. The rumor going around amongst some of the orphans and whores was that if you needed help but didn't have the aerans to pay the guards to put up a proper warrant, you could contact Anisaria and he might help you, if he had the time.

For free.

Fletch shook his head. Everyone had an angle, and nothing was free—especially with hunters and guards. Anisaria was probably trying to get in good with the Valley dwellers with this good-guy act of his, so he could call on them for information when he needed it. Fletch had seen other hunters trying that angle. They played nice with the poor when it suited them, but didn't think twice about turning on them once a warrant went up.

"So," Anisaria said. "Since we've decided that cooperation is in order . . . That dagger. Where did it come from?"

"Someone who asked too many questions," Fletch said. "Sound familiar?"

"You got it from the people who captured you, didn't you?"

How could he possibly . . . The thought trailed off as Fletch remembered who he had seen Anisaria with last night. *Gods below. I'm definitely going to have to have a talk with Tam about how much she talks, and with whom.* Well, if the hunter knew, he knew. No use trying to repair broken glass. "Yes," he said in a brittle tone.

"That's the only lead you have on them?"

"Yes."

"Are you capable of answering questions with something other than 'yes' or sarcasm?"

Fletch gave him a mocking smile. "Yes."

Anisaria rolled his eyes. "I can see why you work alone."

"This weapon-smith of yours," Fletch said. "Do you trust them?"

Anisaria threw Fletch's own mocking smile back at him. "Yes."

Cheeky bastard. Fletch bit back a retort. Throwing insults back and forth with the kitten wasn't going to get him any farther towards finding the assholes framing him. "You're sure they'll know the maker's marks for the Hollow Market smiths, too? I know how your type despises associating with we lowly criminals."

Anisaria pulled one of those stupid coins from a pouch and began letting it dance along the backs of his knuckles. Fletch didn't believe in that Wind-bitch nonsense, though he had a bit of grudging respect for whoever had come up with it. A religion that conned people into *literally* throwing their money away? Bloody brilliant. But no one would ever catch Fletch Greencloak throwing his hard-earned money at a woman, imaginary or otherwise.

The hunter flipped the golden coin up and caught it, then continued dancing it across the back of his fingers. "Definitely," he said. "Avara knows—"

"*Avara?*" Fletch interrupted him, his surprise overriding his common sense. A few people in the pathway car glanced at him over the tops of their broadsheets. He lowered his voice and leaned in closer to Anisaria to hiss, "Avara *Paress?*"

"I thought you might know her," Anisaria said, meeting Fletch's eyes. "After I told her about your warrant, she tried to get a message to you."

So that's how he found the kids. Either Avara was getting sloppy in her old age, or this kitten was better than Fletch had thought. *Something else to add to the list of things I need to look into once this business is over with.*

"We can't go to Avara Paress," Fletch said, leaning back and folding his arms. He glanced to his left, letting his vision sweep disinterestedly across the man sitting on the farthest seat from them, a hood up over his head, pretending to sleep. He'd been tailing them since they'd left Blue's. Fletch wasn't sure if Anisaria had noticed him yet—if the hunter had, he hadn't given any indication of it.

"Why not?"

"Because I said so," Fletch snapped.

"I'm not a child," Anisaria replied evenly. "If I'm going to work with you, you're going to have to explain things to me eventually."

Don't hold your breath, kitten. I'm not giving you a drop more information than you need.

Silence stretched between them, broken only by the quiet conversation of a couple sitting in the corner, the constant squeak-sway of the pathway car, and the wind rushing by outside the windows.

"I trust Avara," Anisaria finally said. "She tried to warn you, so she's probably not going to turn you in. But if you'd rather wait outside while I ask about the maker's mark . . ."

That could work. Fletch absently slipped a prayer-coin from the hunter's pouch, thinking. Avara *was* the next best choice other than Blue.

Blue.

The memory of the mage's corpse burst upon his mind like a metal-bound caal convergence being released. For one awful moment, he was back in that entryway, staring at a glimpse of bright blue peeking up at him out of the pulp of flesh that had once been a face. All he saw was death, all he smelled was blood, and all he felt was . . . was . . .

He looked away from the hunter. Not now. He'd grieve later, after the people responsible for Blue and Vethin's deaths were whimpering and pleading for their lives under Fletch's knife. And yet . . . he found himself touching the ring on his right hand, the one Blue had given him.

Now it was all he had to remind Fletch of him.

"Fine," he said, standing as the pathway car swayed to a stop. Anisaria stood as well, straightening his wide-brimmed hat. "You go in, I wait outside. And *don't* mention my name."

"Did you steal from her?" Anisaria asked as they pushed their way through the crowd of people outside the doors waiting to get in. The man following them stood as well, lurching as if he were tired or drunk. People moved aside for him with looks of mild disgust. "Did you break one of her weapons? She hates it when I do that."

Fletch rolled his eyes and headed north, towards Paress's shop. The tail followed, of course. *Can't be a hunter,* Fletch thought, climbing the steps up from the station to street level. *He's not carrying a weapon.* The man weaved expertly between people, leaving just the right amount of space to keep Anisaria and Fletch in eyeshot while at the same time remaining inconspicuous. *Too good to be a guard. One of the people framing me, then.* He must have been waiting outside of Blue's house, watching, hoping that Fletch would show up. Maybe while Anisaria was wheedling information out of Avara, Fletch could lose the tail and circle around, get him into a position where Fletch could use—

"Oh, I know. You insulted Jodrif. Am I right?" The hunter grinned at him under the brim of that stupid hat.

Gods below, Fletch thought, pushing past a gaggle of children watching a wandering puppet-show. *Does he ever shut up?*

"So you're not willing to talk about Avara," Anisaria continued after a moment of silence from Fletch. "All right. How about these people who are framing you? If I'm going to help I'm going to need to know everything you do."

"Thought Tam told you everything."

"Everything *she* knew," Anisaria countered, his eyes following a passing woman with an appraising expression before turning back to Fletch. "I'm willing to bet you know more."

Fletch shrugged. "Someone came to me with a job offer a couple of weeks ago. I turned them down."

"That happen often?"

"A few days after that," Fletch continued, ignoring the question, "someone caught me."

"How?"

Fletch gave him a flat look.

"Professional curiosity."

Even if I knew, I wouldn't tell you. "They kept me in a bloody cell for a week," Fletch said. "Chained up. Feeding me scraps. They came in and questioned me every day, and the bastard who stole my cloak was always there, listening. Never got a look at his face."

"What sorts of questions did they ask?"

"Stupid things," Fletch said, turning to side-step around a crowd of people watching a street performer as the man juggled metal-bound knives. "Nothing important." The calls of merchants from the stalls lining the street would probably mask their conversation from anyone nearby, but Fletch made certain to keep his voice down nonetheless.

"Like?" Anisaria pressed, drawing out the word.

"Are you always this annoying, or only when you're on a case?" Fletch snapped.

"Depends on who you ask. So they asked you a bunch of stupid unimportant questions and the killer was listening in on the answers. Were you as forthcoming with them as you're being with me, or were you truthful?"

"What do you think?"

"Sarcastic and mean-tempered. Right."

The bastard was smiling. Why in all the gods names was he *smiling?*

Anisaria hooked his thumbs in his belt and continued, "Did you ever stop to think that maybe they were trying to figure out your personality, so the killer could impersonate you believably?"

"Impersonate me to *who,* exactly?"

"I don't know," Anisaria replied. "Who do you know in a less-than-professional capacity that our cloaked friend might interact with?"

"A less-than-professional capacity?"

"Well, I assume you don't wear that cloak *all* the time," Anisaria said. "You-Know-Who is a professional persona. Do the people you interact with on a more . . . personal level know that you spend your nights thieving?"

Fletch considered this. The list of people who knew his real name *and* his thieving persona was very, very limited. He went back over his interactions with people over the last few years. So-Riya was dead; unfortunate complication with the cartels. Kenril hadn't been seen in months. Petha and Enratel were still peddling stolen goods in the Hollow, so that was a possibility.

"The only people who know me that well wouldn't be fooled by someone pretending to be me," he said.

"Your kidnappers didn't know that, then. Good."

"I fail to see how anything in this situation is *good*."

Anisaria gave him a considering look as he walked. "It's good because it means that none of the people who are close to you are working with them. If they were, they'd have passed that information along and the kidnappers wouldn't have bothered finding out about your personality. They'd have just killed you outright."

Fletch blinked. That was surprisingly paranoid thinking from a kitten. Immediately jumping to (and discounting) the possibility of a traitor was something that Fletch would have expected out of a thief, but certainly not a hunter. *Maybe he's not as naive as I thought.*

"So," Anisaria said. "We know that they're worried about the possibility of having to pass their impersonator off as you. What could they possibly be hoping to gain from all this? Finding out where you keep your money or stolen goods, maybe?"

"If that was all they wanted, they wouldn't have bothered framing me."

"Where *do* you keep it, anyway?"

Fletch rolled his eyes, deftly plucking a purse from a well-dressed merchant that passed too closely to him.

"Can't blame me for trying," Anisaria said, half to himself. He walked along beside Fletch, barely watching where he was going. "Maybe they're planning to ruin your reputation?"

"Well, they're certainly succeeding at that," Fletch muttered, glancing at a wall plastered with warrants and playbills as they passed it. He saw at least ten copies of his own warrant up there.

"Made anyone angry lately?"

"Other than the hundred-odd high-and-mighties I've stolen from, you mean?" Fletch shrugged. "Only about half of the Hollow Market and three of the cartels."

"Hmm. Let's go back to your captivity for a minute. How did you get out?"

"Vethin," Fletch said.

"He rescued you?"

"After a fashion."

"Where were you being held?"

"I don't know," Fletch replied, getting more and more fed up with the unending stream of questions. "I was a little busy keeping myself from passing out from the pain of getting shot in the leg."

"And after you escaped? What did you do next?"

"After that I had tea with the High Mages, went to my day job as a singer at the theater, and fucked Joswyn Orin on-stage in between the second and third acts," Fletch said. "We got a standing ovation. Happy?" He glanced back over his shoulder. Their tail was two blocks away, blending into the crowd and keeping a steady distance.

"Not quite," Anisaria replied. They rounded a corner and the familiar squat little weapon-shop came into sight. "One more question."

"Lovely."

"What are you planning on doing about our friend?"

Fletch looked at Anisaria, surprised. "You noticed him?"

"I'm a bounty hunter," Anisaria replied. "In case you missed that. Following people's my job. You think I wouldn't notice when someone was doing it to me?"

"Congratulations. I'll be sure to steal you a prize from the next shop we pass," Fletch said. "Get in there and find out who made that bloody dagger. I'll take care of the tail."

"How?"

"I thought you said you only had one more question."

Anisaria stopped, grabbing Fletch's upper arm to pull him to a stop, too. "You're wounded," he said, gesturing at Fletch's leg.

"What gave it away? The limp or the fact that—"

"Stop being snide for a minute and listen to me," Anisaria said. All the joviality vanished from his voice, replaced by severity. "These people who are after you caught you once. You don't think they could do it again?"

"I wasn't *expecting* it the first time," Fletch replied, heat rising to his face. "Now I'm—"

"*Injured,*" Anisaria over-rode him, putting emphasis on the word and stepping closer, lowering his voice. "I didn't put my career on the line so you could trip at an inopportune moment and get captured all over again. . . . Or worse, *killed.* Either we take care of him before I go in there, or you're coming in with me. Your choice."

Fletch stared at him, taken aback. People didn't give Fletch Greencloak ultimatums. It just . . . didn't happen. Not since he'd been young enough to need help walking, anyway. Yet strangely, he didn't find himself angry. Probably because deep down, he knew that Anisaria was right. Fletch *was* injured, and he had never been much good at combat even when he was healthy. He didn't like depending on other people, but this situation was so far out of the norm for him that he honestly wasn't certain how to handle it. Anisaria, on the other hand, was a bounty hunter. He did this sort of thing day in and day out, and Fletch knew a little about the tests the cats had to take in order to get their licenses.

Using Anisaria's skills was like choosing the right lock-pick for the job. This wasn't giving in to a demand. . . . It was realizing that the tool he'd needed was sitting right in front of him, asking to be used.

And the fact that it was a particularly good-looking tool didn't hurt either, he supposed. For some reason, he hadn't noticed that until this moment.

All right, kitten. Let's see how good you really are.

"How would you propose that we take him out?" Fletch said.

The smile crept back onto Anisaria's face. He looked up at the low roofs above them, then at the nearby alley. "Simple," he said, meeting Fletch's eyes. "We use you as bait."

Fletch raised an eyebrow.

"I go into Avara's, as we'd planned. You wait there," he gestured with his eyes towards the alley without moving his head, "as if you were waiting for me to come out. I'll go out Avara's back door and circle around up over the roofs. He'll take his time coming for you. . . . He'll want to be certain that I'm staying in there for a while. When he makes his move, I'll drop down on him from above and take him out." Anisaria nodded to himself as if this were the wisest plan ever conceived. "Then we can question him, find out who sent him. If the knife thing doesn't work out, maybe we can find a lead that way."

"Let me get this straight," Fletch said slowly. "You want to use *me . . .* as bait . . . in a *trap.*"

"Right."

Fletch stared at him for a moment and shook his head. "You're lucky you're pretty."

"Why complicate a tried-and-true method?" Anisaria said. "I've done this sort of thing before. Dozens of times."

Well, the kitten knew more about catching people than Fletch did. And if it didn't work, Fletch had his needles. No one ever seemed to expect those.

Unless these are the same people that kidnapped me. They had a good long time to go through my things while I was chained up, and I have so many of those damned needles that I'd never notice if one were missing.

Fletch glanced down at what he was wearing, and scanned the street. A pair of guards were sitting under the awning of a nearby meat-pie restaurant, chatting over their meals. *If neither Anisaria nor the needles work, I can always scream bloody murder. Guards won't sit by and watch while one of their own gets ambushed in an alleyway, that's for certain. Then I can duck into the undercity while they deal with him.*

It wasn't ideal, but Fletch felt considerably better about the situation now that he had a couple of backup plans.

"Fine," he said to Anisaria, waving one hand. "Get going."

"It'll work," Anisaria said with a grin. "You'll see." He turned, walking across the street and into Paress's shop. Fletch turned into the alleyway and leaned against the wall, ignoring the people giving his guard's uniform curious looks as they passed. He reached into his pocket, keeping his movements stealthy, and plucked a needle from the wooden box.

Their tail hesitated on a corner a block away, his cowled head turning from Fletch (who pointedly inspected his fingernails) and the shop.

He started walking. Fletch felt his muscles tense, and fought that old familiar instinct to flee.

But the tail didn't turn towards him. He followed Anisaria into the shop.

Chapter Fourteen

Suken entered Avara's shop, the little glass chimes jingling over his head. He couldn't seem to keep the smile from his face. Hundreds of other hunters and guards and thieves looking for Greencloak, and Suken Anisaria was the first to find him. Even the prospect of taking out whoever was following them didn't seem too daunting. How hard could it be, when Suken had already done the impossible?

And he was learning things. Not much, but a little here and there. Greencloak had avoided most of Suken's bigger questions, as he'd expected, but the little hints he was gleaning about the thief's life were invaluable. When this was all over, and the murder warrants taken down, Suken might actually stand a shot of catching the thief for his legitimate crimes.

After he'd found Shifter, that was.

Avara's husband Jodrif sat behind the glass case this time, hunched over a complicated mass of thin silver wires, steel, and wood. With his hulking shoulders, bushy beard and massive height, he looked something like a bear balancing itself on one of those tiny chairs they set up in the traveling performer tents in the marketplace. One gloved hand clutched a metal tool that looked something like a lock-pick, the sheer size of Jodrif's hand making the instrument seem as thin as the wires he was deftly manipulating. He held his other hand suspended in the air about five inches above whatever he was working on, his thumb and forefinger pinched together and his other three fingers splayed out. Whatever convergence he was holding, it must be a complicated one. His brown curls hung forward over a forehead creased in concentration, and the sleeves of his golden tunic were rolled up nearly to his shoulders to reveal thick arms. A tuft of dark hair poked up out between the lacings of the white shirt he wore under his tunic.

A spattering of blue sparks leapt from one of the silver wires to scatter across the glass. Jodrif muttered something under his breath and adjusted the position of his ungloved hand slightly, poking deeper into a coil of silver wire with his pick.

It wasn't wise to surprise a mage when he had a convergence already drawn, so Suken coughed into his hand politely. Jodrif didn't react. Suken rolled his eyes and reached out to rap gently on the edge of the glass with his knuckles. The burly man's head came up at that, revealing a set of brown eyes with laugh-lines at the corners and a puzzled expression that swiftly resolved into a smile.

"Suken!" He shook his hand free of whatever invisible lines he'd been holding and pulled his tool from the mass of wire, extending his ungloved hand over the case to clasp Suken's forearm in a friendly grip. The thing he'd been working on sent up a sputtering fountain of blue sparks before vanishing in a puff of acrid smoke. Jodrif glanced down at it, shrugged, and hauled Suken half across the counter to wrap one huge arm around his shoulders, clapping him once on the back. Suken winced as his injured shoulder cried out in protest at the rough treatment.

"Heard you're doing great!" the big man said as he pulled back. "Almost rank four now, eh?"

"Yeah," Suken said. "Look, Jodrif. I need to use your—"

"AVARA!" Jodrif bellowed. Suken flinched. The man's voice

rattled half the swords on the wall and made dust sift down from the rafters. "LORRIN'S KID IS HERE!"

Suken heard footsteps approaching from the back, and the door behind the counter opened to reveal Avara, her hair down and her glasses pushed up on top of her head. She held Suken's crossbow cradled in the crook of one arm, and glanced at the mess on the counter before shaking her head and gently placing the weapon down beside it.

"Shout a little louder next time, dear," Avara said. "There might have been a mage or two in the Council who didn't hear you."

"Last time I was quiet, you didn't hear me and yelled at me for not interrupting you," Jodrif replied with a smile.

"Perhaps you can work at finding a mid-point between whispering and bellowing so loud that half the swords shake free of their sheaths."

Suken shifted his weight impatiently. He didn't have much time before the person tailing Greencloak made his move. "Avara," he said.

She shot him an imperious look. "I'll get to you in good time."

The chime over the door behind Suken jingled, heralding the entrance of another customer. "Help you with somethin'?" Avara called.

"Just looking," a man's voice replied.

Avara nodded curtly and returned her gaze to Suken.

"I need to use your back door," Suken said.

"Why?"

"I don't have time to—"

Someone bumped into him from behind, knocking him off balance. A sudden small sharp stab of pain, like getting pricked with a needle, radiated up from the center of his back.

A normal patron looking at wares wouldn't come so close, Suken thought with a sinking feeling as he started to turn, *which means . . .*

The man who had been following them stood behind him, something metal vanishing up his sleeve, a slow smile spreading across his face and pulling a scar on his cheek into a half-moon shape. Before he could say anything, the door burst open with a wild jangle of chimes.

Greencloak stood in the doorway, a small thin throwing knife held between finger and thumb. "Down," he shouted, and Suken obligingly threw himself to the floor. He landed on his bad shoulder and cried out in pain, looking up in time to see Greencloak draw his hand back over his shoulder to let the little throwing knife fly, blue sparks trailing after it.

Their attacker dodged the weapon easily, ducking under it in a whirl of fabric. It thudded into the wooden cross-section of Avara's counter. She glanced down at it and the sparks leaping from the metal, swore, and grabbed Jodrif, pulling him down to the floor with her.

Suken threw his hands up in front of his face as the convergence released a concussion of sound and an array of blue-white arcs of energy which raced over the glass, shattering it. Two of the weapons in the case must have been metal-bound as well. As the energy arced over them, they exploded into balls of white-hot heat that sent shards of glass flying in all directions. Suken felt some embed themselves in his leg and arms, but forced himself to ignore the pain as he staggered to his feet.

Thin, acrid smoke drifted around the room, and the discharged energy made the hair on the back of Suken's neck stand up. Greencloak still stood in the doorway, tense, his eyes fixed on the man who had been following them. The attacker shrugged out of his cloak. He raised one hand, palm-out, towards Greencloak. The thief's face visibly paled.

Suken didn't wait to find out what had elicited that response. He launched himself at the scarred man, intending to tackle him to the floor. Out of the corner of his eye he saw Avara shoot up from behind the case, stabbing her hand into the broken glass to make a grab for something.

The man turned towards Suken at the last second, moving

fluidly to one side and out of Suken's path. Suken tried to make a grab for the man as he passed, but his grasping fingers found nothing. He stumbled to a halt and whirled to see Avara pulling a knife from the glass with bloody fingers, the scarred man stepping towards her, drawing his fist back. . . .

"Avara!" he shouted, but the man was too fast. His fist connected with her jaw with a sharp crack and she reeled backwards, her eyes flashing in anger and pain.

Bad idea, Suken thought as he took three big steps back. *But you'll find that out soon enough.* The wall behind him was lined with wooden racks of quarterstaffs and spears. Suken reached back and grabbed the closest one, a staff thinner than his wrist. He'd always been shit with short-range weapons, but it was better than nothing. The attacker turned towards him.

His clothes were simple, nondescript. They wouldn't have looked particularly out of place anywhere in the city, from the Valley to the Mage's District. His face was similarly plain save for the old scar marking the right side. Dark skin tone which could have been either Majitanian or Tyrodamian, dark hair, a face that was neither ugly nor handsome.

In short, all the characteristics of an assassin.

Suken held the staff out in front of him in both hands like a long club and took a step to his right, towards the broken case and Avara. And his crossbow, which now lay in the midst of a pile of shattered glass and scattered knives. He sent a silent prayer to the Lady that it was fixed.

Jodrif scrambled to his feet in the open doorway to the back room, his mouth hanging open.

"Jodrif!" Avara shouted. "Supply room! Now!"

His mouth snapped shut and he ducked back through the doorway.

Suken took a careful step to one side, towards the case and his crossbow. He eyed the assassin. Long nose, slightly hooked under, like a beak. Quick motions. *Like a hawk.* "You know," he said to Hawk, "sneaking up behind me and attacking without warning isn't very conducive to a good trade of amusing banter." He took another step to his right, keeping his eyes fixed on the assassin. "Honestly, it's almost as if you don't want to get famous."

Hawk reached up under the back of his jacket and unsheathed a short-sword.

"Anisaria," Greencloak said from the doorway. "This isn't—"

Hawk lunged at Suken. Suken used the staff to clumsily bat the sword to one side, but the man spun with the motion, whipping around to slice the blade horizontally through the air in a follow-up, aiming at Suken's neck. Suken barely managed to get the staff up in time to block it, the sword sinking deeply into the wood and sticking there. The assassin tried to yank the blade back, but it was stuck too deeply in the wood.

"It's all right," Suken said. "I'm willing to give you another chance." He pushed the staff towards Hawk, putting all his weight behind the shove. The man look two steps back towards the wall covered in swords, putting Suken only a few feet from his crossbow. "You start. Say something menacing."

The man snarled and yanked on his sword again. This time it pulled free, and Hawk staggered back a step.

"Good enough," Suken said. He raised the staff, preparing to strike out again.

"Suken," Avara snapped. Both Suken and the man reflexively turned to look at her. She stood behind the counter, blood coating the lower half of her face, a long-bladed knife in each hand. "Catch," she snapped, and flung one of the knives at Suken.

This was something of a game between the two of them. When he'd come to visit when he was younger, she'd pulled out small blunt knives and had him stand on the other side of the room. Then she'd throw the knives at him. The game was to see how many he could snatch out of the air before they hit him. If he could catch more than half, she'd let him practice with the crossbow for an hour. If not, he'd have to go home.

When they'd begun to play, he hadn't been able to catch any, and had gone home covered with bruises. But as he got older, his reflexes had gotten faster. They didn't play as often as they used to, but these days he could catch three or four out of five of the knives she threw at him.

Unfortunately, he hadn't been ready for this one. He let go of the staff and brought up his right hand a half a second too slow. The knife sank to the hilt into his left shoulder, and he let out a half-surprised, half-pained cry that sounded remarkably like "Ow!"

It didn't hurt, not really. Yet. But Suken knew from unfortunate experience that it was only a matter of time before his body realized that something was sticking out of him that shouldn't be.

Avara gave him a flat look. "Catch with your *hands,* Suken."

Suken looked at Hawk. "Now see," he said. "*She* gets it."

The attacker lifted one boot and planted it in Suken's abdomen, shoving him back three feet and knocking the breath out of him. He turned to stab his hand into the case, wrapping his fingers around the haft of Suken's crossbow.

Damn it! Suken fought to regain his breath, looking up in time to see Avara try to grab the attacker's wrist. The man twisted out of her reach with a savage snarl and spun to level the crossbow at Suken. Suken saw that it was loaded. He watched as Hawk's finger tightened around the trigger. Then something slammed into Suken from the side as the bolt released with a *twang.* He crashed to the floor half-buried under the weight of a guard.

Or someone wearing a guard's uniform, anyway.

"Get *off,*" Suken grunted, shoving Greencloak away and looking up to see Hawk dropping the crossbow with a dissatisfied expression. As the man brought his hand up to a guard position, Suken caught a glimpse of a red tattoo on his palm.

The man started to step forward, then let out a low grunt of pain and whirled, dropping his sword to clatter to the floor as his hand reached up towards his shoulder. A knife, twin to the one currently protruding from Suken's shoulder, was buried to the hilt in his back, to one side of the shoulder-blade. Avara placed one hand flat on one of the intact wooden section of the counter and vaulted over it, planting her feet squarely in the man's side in a swirl of brown skirts.

Hawk let out a pained exhalation and fell, cracking the side of his head on the floor. Avara ran to the wall and grabbed a short-sword in each hand, grinning. Suken hauled himself to his feet, doing his best to ignore the pain beginning to bloom in his shoulder. She'd *had* to hit him in the one that he'd hurt in his job the other night, hadn't she? He reached up and grabbed the hilt, pulling the blade free. Blood dripped from it to spatter the floor as Hawk rolled lithely to his feet, swaying before gaining his balance.

Oh, Suken thought as a wave of agony swept over him. *There's the pain.* He gritted his teeth and drew his right hand around his body, whipping it toward Hawk, the knife leaving his fingers and whistling through the air before burying itself with a distinctly satisfying *thunk* in the floor behind the man.

"Gods below, and they said you were *good?*" Greencloak said.

Hawk started forward, but before he took two steps the knife exploded. Suken threw his hand up in front of his face as a wave of heat washed over him, his ears ringing from the concussive sound. The force of the explosion threw Hawk forward into a stagger, and Suken dashed forward, balling his right hand into a fist and coming around in a wide cross.

The other man's hand shot up, blocking Suken's punch with a quickness that rivaled Suken's own. Suken ducked under Hawk's retaliatory blow to his ribs, trying to bring his leg around to sweep Hawk's legs out from under him. Hawk side-stepped neatly and somehow managed to get a fist through Suken's guard to slam him in the jaw. The world faded out of focus for a moment before snapping back into clarity, and Suken danced back a step. His ears were still ringing, but not quite as badly as before. He could make out shouts in the street outside. The place where the knife had been was little more than a smoldering, blackened crater in the wood floor.

"You're outnumbered," Suken said, wiping blood from his lip with the back of his hand.

Hawk looked from Avara, to Suken, to Greencloak, who had taken up a position near the door again. Greencloak held something small in his left hand that caught the light, but it didn't look like it would do much damage.

"Am I?" Hawk asked, dropping into a crouch.

Suken didn't like the man's tone. He was entirely too sure of himself. He must have something, like a metal-bound weapon, concealed on his person somewhere.

Enough banter. Time to end this before one of us gets really hurt. Or killed.

"Yes," a muffled voice said from the vicinity of the back door. "You are."

Suken glanced in that direction out of the corner of his eye. Jodrif stood in the open doorway, wearing a strange leather contraption over his lower face. In his hands he held a glass ball as big as a person's head. Some sort of blue gas roiled inside of it.

"If he has to use that," Avara said evenly from behind Hawk, "I'm taking its price out of your fucking hide."

Suken had no idea what the ball was, and apparently Hawk didn't, either. The assassin licked his lips once, nervously. Suken stayed where he was, poised and ready to move, watching Hawk. The man's eyes slid from Jodrif to Suken. He turned and stepped into Avara's guard as neatly and efficiently as a dancer, grabbing her wrist and swinging her around in a half-circle towards Suken. She stumbled, and Suken leapt forward to catch her before she fell as Hawk ran to the door. Greencloak stepped in his way, but the man lashed out with a savage punch that landed square in Greencloak's stomach, doubling him over.

He vanished out the door, the chimes jingling cheerily, as Suken helped Avara regain her balance.

"Fucking bastard," Avara spat, pushing herself away from Suken and starting towards the door. She stepped out into the street and yelled, "You'll pay for all these damages with aerans or with blood, you cowardly piece of shit!"

Suken spared a moment to be relieved that she was blaming Hawk and not him before kneeling beside Greencloak. The thief was on his hands and knees, alternately coughing and retching. "You all right?" Suken asked. Greencloak nodded and waved him away. Suken stood and started towards the door, but Avara caught his arm.

"Where do you think you're going?"

"I'm going to follow him," Suken said. "If he goes back to report to whoever hired him, then—"

"He's not," Greencloak wheezed, using the doorjamb to pull himself to his feet. "No self-respecting sicario is going to run back to his client like a dog with its tail between its legs after one failed attempt."

Suken's eyes widened. Sicario were assassins, highly skilled and very, very expensive to hire. He'd only ever heard of the cartels hiring them in the past. They operated under a strict set of codes and strange traditions which led many people to whisper that they secretly worshiped the God of Discordant Darkness. Suken knew that the bounty hunters' guild had some sort of an understanding with the sicario, though he wasn't privy to the details. All he knew was that warrants never went up for sicario, and sicario never killed hunters.

Either the loss of his license had negated whatever protection he'd had, or someone had paid that man a ludicrous sum of money to ignore the unwritten agreement. If the latter, he was working on his own, and without the approval of his guild. Suken suspected that an assassin working without the approval of his guild didn't have much of a life expectancy.

And a bloody good riddance to you if that's the case, Suken thought, reaching up to gently prod at his bruised jaw. "Well," he said with forced cheer, turning back to face Avara, Jodrif and Greencloak. "I'm still alive, so he must not be a very good assassin, right?"

Greencloak limped over to Suken and grabbed the back of his shirt, pulling it from where it was tucked into Suken's pants.

"Hey," Suken said, trying to turn, but Greencloak moved with him, peering at his back. He flinched as Greencloak reached out and pressed his fingers against his lower back for a moment.

The thief brought his fingers to his lips and sniffed, dabbed the tip of his tongue against them, and grimaced. Suken reached back to touch the same place. His questing fingers found nothing, but when he brought his hand back he saw that his fingertips were smeared with a few drops of blood.

"Avara," Greencloak said, turning towards her and wiping his fingers on his pants. "Got any pavendala root?"

Avara paled. "No," she said. "That bad?"

"Yes. I'd say he's got about two hours, give or take."

"Two hours until *what?*" Suken asked, paling.

"Jodrif, put that thing down and run to the Hollow Market," Avara said. "Now."

Jodrif gently placed the sphere on the counter and yanked the mask from his face, then lumbered out the door.

"What are you all talking about?" Suken asked. "Two hours until *what?* And what in bloody glass and caal-fire is pavendala root?"

"He poisoned you," Greencloak said, finally turning towards Suken. "Needle between his fingers when he first bumped into you. Like this." He pulled a thin needle out of seemingly nowhere and wrapped his hand around it so the tip poked out between his index and middle fingers, near the knuckles. "Nicely done, really."

"Nicely . . ." Suken trailed off, staring at him. "I'm *poisoned?*"

"Catches on quick, doesn't he?" Greencloak said to Avara.

"What . . . what do I do?" Suken asked, looking back and forth between the two of them. "Are we supposed to . . . to cut it, let the poison out? Or . . . should I lie down? Drink salt-water?"

"Sure," Greencloak said, shrugging. "If it'll make you feel better."

Avara smacked Greencloak on the back of the head on her way past him. "Suken," she said firmly, taking his arm, "You're going to be fine. Come in the back with me and have a seat while we wait for Jodrif. And you," she leveled a glare at Greencloak, "lock the door, then join us in the back before someone sees you. And get out of that damned guard's uniform."

"I'm flattered that you want to see me naked so badly, Avara, but you know you're not my type."

"I would have already thrown you out the gods-damned door if you hadn't saved his life twice," she snapped. "But comments like that are testing my resolve. Jodrif has some clothes in the spare bedroom in the back. Lock the door, get changed, then join us." Her expression darkened. "I think we should all have a little chat."

Chapter Fifteen

Suken sat on a long wooden bench in Jodrif's cluttered workshop, his shirt off and blood trickling down his chest. Avara sat on a stool in front of him, a bowl of water on her lap and a wooden case filled with rolls of bandages and salves laid open beside her. The skin around her eye was slowly blackening with a bruise, but she didn't seem to notice or care. She dipped a cloth into the water and paused. "Did he do this?" she asked under her breath, gesturing to the mass of bruises covering Suken's shoulder.

"Greencloak?" Suken said, glancing towards the door behind which the thief was changing his clothes. "No. This was from that other job I told you about."

"Sometimes I wonder if you bounty hunters get some sort of perverse pleasure out of getting injured," she said, shaking her head and grabbing another piece of glass with a pair of tweezers. She yanked it free from his shoulder, and Suken bit back a cry of pain.

"Well," Suken managed, "the scars are good conversation starters. The ladies love 'em. And the men."

She rolled her eyes, dropping the bloody shard of glass with a clink into a metal pan. He winced as she began cleaning the knife wound, his mind wandering back to the poison. How quickly would it kill him if Jodrif didn't make it back in time with . . . whatever it was he'd gone for? His heart was beating faster than usual. He tried to concentrate, to slow it. His heart beating faster would make the poison spread faster . . . right? But he couldn't seem to make his heart cooperate. He swallowed hard and tried to force himself to think about something else.

The sicario had attacked *Suken*, not Greencloak. Why? Who could possibly want him dead? And how long had the man been following him? The first time Suken had noticed him had been after leaving Mage Bluvael's home, on the pathway. It was possible that he'd been tailing Suken before then, but . . .

His blood ran cold.

"Did Terri make it to you safely?" he asked Avara, keeping his voice low. He wasn't certain if he wanted Greencloak knowing about Terri.

"She's at our house," Avara said, wringing out the bloody cloth. "Arrived here late this morning and explained everything. I sent her on over with a key. Gonna do some cleaning for me."

Suken let out a sigh of relief.

"She mentioned that you'd owe her extra for this month," Avara said, looking up from dabbing at his shoulder with the washcloth. The creases at the corners of her grey eyes deepened as she smiled. "Have I mentioned how much I like her?"

"Only about two hundred times," Suken said.

"Nice girl," Avara continued as if she hadn't heard. "Pretty, too. Got her head on straight." She pulled the cloth away and dunked it into the water bowl, wringing it out and pointedly not meeting his eyes.

"Avara," Suken said, his voice strained, "she's practically my *sister*. And in case you'd forgotten, I'm apparently dying of some kind of poison. Is this *really* the time?"

Avara's smile widened.

The door to the back hallway opened. Suken glanced up, glad

for the respite from this conversation. Greencloak soundlessly closed the door after himself, wearing an outfit about ten times too large for him. The thief eased himself down onto a stool near the door, concealed in the shadows. Avara met Suken's eyes, the smile fading. "What are you doing with him?"

"Helping him," Suken replied, glancing down at his shoulder and immediately looking away again, feeling sick.

"And doing a truly fantastic job of it so far," Greencloak called over. "What was the plan again? Use me as bait then circle around and take him out?" He snorted. "Worked like a charm."

Suken glared at him. "How was I supposed to know he'd come after me and not you?"

"'Following people's my job,'" Greencloak imitated Suken's earlier statement, his voice eerily similar to Suken's own. He fell back into his own voice and continued, "If you're half as bad at bounty hunting as you are at making plans to protect hunted criminals, it's no wonder your precious guild took your license."

"You," Avara said, raising her voice but not turning to look at Greencloak, "are in a mess of trouble, boy."

"Really?" Greencloak widened his eyes in mock surprise. "I hadn't noticed, what with all the hunters and guards and . . . oh, that's right. Assassins now, too, apparently."

"Don't give me that attitude," Avara said. "Especially not after what you did."

Suken winced again as Avara dabbed too hard with the cloth.

"Still looking for an apology?" Greencloak said, putting his feet up on the bench in front of him and crossing his ankles. His nonchalant motions were spoiled somewhat by a wince as he crossed his legs, but he recovered swiftly and leaned back against the wall, lacing his fingers behind his head. "Not gonna happen."

"You're lucky I didn't stab you as soon as you walked in the door," Avara snapped.

"Yeah," Suken put in. "It sure is a good thing she doesn't make a habit of injuring her patrons." He looked down pointedly at his shoulder.

"Don't you start," she said.

"You want me gone?" Fletch said. "Fine. I'm leaving. If the kitten's as good as he claims, he can find me after he gets his antidote." He slid off the stool and took a limping step towards the door.

Suken's heartrate picked up again, but before he could call out to Greencloak, Avara stood up.

"If you take one more step I'll have every damn hunter I know on your tail," she snapped.

The thief paused, hand on the door handle. "You wouldn't be the first to betray me," he said. "And I'm sure you won't be the last." He opened the door.

"Fletch," Avara said, her voice low and dangerous. "You. Owe. Me."

Greencloak didn't close the door. But he didn't step through it, either. "You sure you want to call that favor in?" he said quietly. "For *this?*"

Suken realized that his mouth was dry. It felt as if he hadn't had a sip of water in months. He licked his lips, and his tongue felt like sandpaper. "Hey," he said.

"Despite your penchant for melting months of hard work into useless balls of scrap metal, I don't want to see you hang," Avara said. "And if you're too gods-damned stubborn to admit that you need my help, then yes, I'll *force* you to admit it by calling in my favors." She tossed the blood-stained cloth into the bowl.

"Hey, um. My mouth is really, really dry all of a sudden," Suken said, starting to stand up. He made it halfway before he realized that his legs had about as much strength in them as cooked noodles and collapsed back to the bench. "Is . . . is that normal?"

"I'll get you some water once Jodrif gets here," Avara said, not breaking eye contact with Greencloak. "You'll be fine."

How comforting, Suken thought. He swayed slightly to one

side. Was there something wrong with the calibration of the city, or . . .

He swayed back the other way, his hands tightening on the wood of the bench he sat on. No. . . . Couldn't be the city, Avara and Greencloak were standing steady. He closed his eyes and took a deep breath, holding it for the count of ten, and when he opened them again the world had ceased swaying. Thank the Lady. He picked up the cloth and pressed it against his shoulder for a heartbeat before pulling it away. He glanced at the blood. Did it look darker than usual? No. . . . It was his imagination.

Wasn't it?

"You had a reason for coming here," Avara said to Greencloak. "Out with it."

Greencloak hesitated for another moment at the door, closed it, and turned to walk back over to her. He pulled Suken's drawing from his pocket and held it out.

"One of the people framing me had this," he said. "I need to know who made it."

She snatched it from him. "And your flavor-of-the-week couldn't tell you?"

Suken saw a brief pang of pain cross Greencloak's face.

"He's dead," the thief said. "We went to the Hollow Market to find out whose mark this was, and someone must have followed him back."

A brief expression of pity crossed her face, but Avara didn't say anything. Instead, she pulled her little spectacles down to rest on the bridge of her nose and turned her gaze to the drawing. Her eyes widened and she looked back up.

"This is mine," she said.

"What?" Suken and Fletch said at the same time.

"It's my mark," Avara continued, looking back down at the drawing. "Blue didn't tell you? He would have recognized it."

"No," Greencloak said slowly. "He didn't."

"This knife was in a batch I sold to . . ." she hesitated, brow furrowing. She shoved the paper back at Fletch and pushed past him, entering a long corridor filled with wooden boxes and vanishing around a corner, muttering the whole way.

Fletch folded the paper and tucked it back in his pocket, looking troubled. He glanced at Suken and raised an eyebrow. "Still bleeding?"

"Yeah," Suken said, pulling the cloth away and examining the fresh blood. "It'll stop soon enough." He shifted slightly. "How, um. How long until the poison . . . you know . . ."

"You've got at least another hour. Plenty of time for that lumbering ox to get back."

"And you're sure that this . . . this pav . . . pavala . . ."

"Pavendala root."

"Pavendala root will fix me?"

Greencloak limped over, settling down on Avara's abandoned stool and pulling the box full of medical supplies closer. "I know poisons," he said, rummaging through it for a moment. "Studied them, and their antidotes, for years. Pavendala root's what they call a panacea. The mages took over a hundred different herbs and plants, bound them together using whatever it is they do, and kept experimenting with different combinations until they found one that would cure most any poison. That's pavendala." He removed a curved needle and a length of catgut. "There are only a few poisons it can't cure, and those act so quickly that you'd be dead before you could get an antidote anyway."

"If it's so amazing, why have I never heard of it?" Suken eyed Greencloak as the thief threaded some of the catgut through the eye of the needle. "And what are you planning on doing with *that?*"

"It's expensive," Greencloak said, tying a knot in the end of the thread. "The mages keep it scarce so they can charge exorbitant amounts of money for it." He grinned at Suken. "Lucky you met me before you needed some."

"You never answered me about—"

"Shut up and lean forward," Greencloak said, picking up the needle. "It'll only take a couple of stitches."

Suken felt his blood run cold. He edged away from Greencloak and that wicked-looking needle. "Do you know how to—"

"Yes," Greencloak interrupted, shuffling his stool closer. "Come back here."

"It's fine," Suken said, leaning back. "I'll just—"

"You want to keep being able to use that arm?" Greencloak snapped.

"Yes. . . ."

"Then stop being a child and come *here*." He reached out and grabbed Suken's arm, pulling him closer. He jabbed the needle into the edge of the wound and Suken groaned, closing his eyes. "I'll have to tell all my criminal friends that if they want to scare you off their tails, all they have to do is bring along a needle or two," Greencloak said, pulling the catgut through the skin.

Suken swallowed as the needle jabbed him again, hot pain radiating out from the wound. "If you treat your criminal friends the way you've—ow!—been treating me, it's a wonder none of *them* have turned you in yet," he managed between clenched teeth.

"Oh, if I were treating you like I do them, you'd be moaning for a completely different reason, kitten."

Suken blinked once, surprised. Greencloak didn't meet his eyes, but Suken saw one corner of the thief's mouth twitch up into a grin.

So it's like that, huh? Suken thought. Fine. Two can play at that game.

"In frustration over your bad jokes?" He asked, putting a wry twist to the words. "Lady Chance, they're bad enough as it is."

The grin widened into a true smile for a fraction of a second before Greencloak's expression sobered again.

Score one for me, Suken thought, but any satisfaction was immediately erased by pain as Greencloak pulled the first stitch tight.

"What did you do to attract the attention of a sicario?"

Greencloak asked. "He followed you, not me. You must have done something to piss off someone rich." He tied the catgut off deftly and cut loose the excess with a knife he pulled from his belt. *He's done this before,* Suken thought, trying not to look at the raw bleeding edges of skin pulled together with small, neat stitches. *Did he teach himself to avoid having to go to a healer?*

"I don't know," he said as Fletch dabbed a bit of salve onto Suken's shoulder. It stung like caal-fire, but Suken managed to not wince.

"You don't have any enemies, then?" Fletch asked, pressing a wadded up piece of linen to the wound. "I find *that* hard to believe."

"I didn't say that," Suken said, running over the list of people who could possibly want him dead. It was relatively short. "But none of them are rich."

Fletch wound a roll of linen up over Suken's shoulder and around his chest a few times before tying it off. He was surprisingly gentle. *Probably only surprising in comparison to what I'm used to,* Suken thought, remembering with a wince the last time Terri had bound one of his injuries.

"Maybe they're trying to keep me from telling anyone else that you're innocent," Suken said.

"Maybe." Fletch's mouth twisted down in a frown. "That would explain Blue's death. If the sicario who attacked you is the same one who killed him, then it stands to reason that his orders are to keep anyone who knows the truth from talking."

The door to the lobby opened, and Jodrif ducked inside, holding a tiny glass bottle. His face was flushed and he was breathing heavily. "Powdered pavendala root," he said.

"I'll pay you for it later," Fletch said, holding out his hand. "With interest." Jodrif made his way over to hand him the bottle. Suken watched as the thief poured about half the bottle into a glass of water, swirling the dark powder around for a moment before handing it to Suken. "Drink all of it," he said. "And don't complain about the taste."

The powder was mostly dissolved, save for a brownish green layer of silt at the bottom of the glass. Suken tilted his head back, swallowing it all and shuddering at the bitterness on his tongue. As soon as he finished, he felt an immense wave of relief wash over him.

"I'll be fine now?" he asked, handing the empty glass back to Fletch.

"Probably," Fletch said. "Unless you're one of the five percent of people immune to the antidote."

"Five percent of . . ." All the blood drained from Suken's face. "Are you serious?"

Fletch smirked.

"You're a bastard, you know that?" Suken said flatly.

"Guilty as charged."

Suken took the little vial from him, tilting it to one side so the remaining powder shifted. "So does this have any—"

A triumphant cry from farther back in the workshop interrupted him. Suken looked up to see Avara duck under some sort of hanging contraption made of metal and wood, a ledger book in her right hand. "Found him," she said triumphantly, banging the book down on a table and flipping it open to a page about halfway through. Suken surreptitiously dropped the half-full vial into his case as she continued, "Lord Garron, of the High Mage's District."

Lord Garron. The man whose little girl had bled out in Suken's arms two nights ago.

Could it possibly be a coincidence?

"He's a merchant," Fletch said. "A particularly successful one. And adjunct faculty at the Academe, professor of economics."

Suken looked up slowly. "You're sure?" he asked Avara.

"Yes," she replied, adjusting her spectacles as she peered at the page. "Paid a sum of five hundred and thirty-three aerans, plus tax, for five custom-made metal-bound knives with dual caal and flauri-lei convergences, activated via touch-points on the top of the cross-guards." She closed the book, looking up.

"Know him?" Fletch asked.

"Yes," Suken said, feeling sick. "I was there when his daughter died."

"Have anything to do with her death?" Fletch asked, either not noticing or not caring about Suken's discomfort.

"No," Suken snapped, and looked away. "Well. . . . Yes. Sort of."

Fletch snorted. "None of your enemies are rich, huh?"

Suken ran a hand back through his hair, wincing as the movement pulled at the freshly-stitched wound in his shoulder. "If he knows about me, he's read the report, so he knows that I tried to save her," Suken said. "It might be nothing."

"I don't believe in coincidence," Fletch said.

Suken swayed, the world shifting from the gentle rocking he'd grown accustomed to for the last few minutes to a series of sudden lurches.

"We're going to need to stay here," Greencloak said as Suken lowered himself down onto the bench, feeling as if he hadn't slept in weeks. "Kitten's going to be out for a few hours, and I could use some rest too."

"Of course," Avara said in a brittle tone, her voice starting to fade in and out. "Please, use my shop as a bloody inn. It's not as if . . ." Her voice vanished into the blackness encroaching on Suken's consciousness, and he wondered blearily if Fletch might not have been lying about that five percent thing after all.

Chapter Sixteen

Fletch stood in darkness so complete that it made the deepest midnight of a starless night seem bright in comparison. He couldn't even see his fingers when he brought them up an inch in front of his face. He smelled nothing, heard nothing, tasted nothing on the air. The blackness around him seemed to have swallowed everything . . . light, sound, smell, taste, even temperature. He turned, feeling sluggish, as if he were submerged in water.

"Avara?" he called. His voice echoed back to him, but distorted, growing deeper and more distant with each repetition. By the time it faded completely, it was barely more than a low rumble, like thunder.

I'm dreaming, he thought. *This is too bloody strange to be anything* other *than a dream.*

"Hello, Fletch."

He whirled. Behind him, barely lit by some ethereal glow from within, stood Blue. He wore the same clothes he'd been wearing when he'd died, smudged with soot from the Hollow Market. And his face . . .

Gods below, his face. Fletch swallowed, hard. Those deep

gashes in his skin ran from forehead to neck. One blue eye gazed out at Fletch from the raw, bloody mess of flesh that had once been a face Fletch had kissed.

"Blue," Fletch said, feeling numb. The ring on his finger felt as if it were burning.

"It's your fault," Blue said, through lips split in three places by the gouges torn through his face. Blood dripped from the corner of his mouth, and what little remained of his skin had taken on the grayish pallor of death, a color that Fletch was unfortunately all too familiar with. *"Your fault."*

The guilt tried to take hold, but Fletch didn't let it. He lashed out instead, allowing the deeply buried embers of anger that continually warmed his soul to flare up. "I *warned* you," he said. "I said that—"

"You came to me for help," Blue said, stepping forward.

"You didn't have to give it," Fletch snapped back.

"Fletch."

Fletch whirled again, his heart in his throat. Now he found himself facing Vethin, wrapped in a white blood-stained sheet. The boy's throat had been slit from one side to the other.

"Turns out, this is how I die," Vethin croaked, his breath wheezing through the gash in his throat. A froth of pinkish-red bubbles leaked from the wound as he spoke. "Because I helped you. Trusted you."

"It's not my fault you let them catch you," Fletch said, taking a step back. "You can't blame *me* for *you* not being good enough." His voice caught on the last word, and he turned away so the apparition wouldn't see the tears in his eyes.

"You're right," a new voice said. Fletch didn't turn, not willing to see this boy's face, even in a dream. A face from his past, a face and voice he'd never forget. "We can't blame you for letting them catch us. But we *can* hold you accountable for your failures. We trusted you. . . . All of us. And you let us down."

Fletch started awake with a gasp, sitting up and banging his head against something hard. He cursed under his breath, reaching up to massage his head as he looked around, head tilted slightly to avoid whatever he'd hit.

He was in Jodrif's workshop, in the back of the shop. The big man sat a few feet to Fletch's left, behind a thick wooden table scarred with burns and gouges, fiddling with a tangled mess of wires. To Fletch's right, Anisaria sat with a battered sketchbook held open in one hand, his other holding a thin pen. He set the book down, looking at Fletch with one eyebrow raised.

"Dreaming?" he asked. He was pale, but otherwise looked fine.

"How long were we out?" Fletch muttered, leaning forward carefully to avoid hitting his head again on the cabinet above him. He vaguely remembered lying down on this bench before blacking out.

"A couple hours, according to Avara. I woke up a half an hour ago." He grimaced. "I feel like my head's been split open."

"Yes," Fletch said, squeezing his eyes shut. The image of Blue's ruined face faded slowly from his memory, like smoke dissipating in a strong wind. "Pavendala root will do that. You may notice a few other side-effects over the next few hours, depending on which poison that bloody bastard pricked you with."

"I'll live," Anisaria said, snapping his book closed. "Thanks to you."

The gratitude in the other man's voice was genuine. Any other time, Fletch would have taken advantage of that, but he simply couldn't muster the energy for banter right now. "Where's Avara?"

"She went home," Jodrif said from behind his bench. He looked up towards a sword dangling from the ceiling as if trying to recall something as he continued, "She told me to tell you that, 'if you get Suken killed, she'll find you and string your balls around your neck'."

That hit a little too close to the dream for comfort. Fletch bent over and hooked his boots with one finger, dragging them back towards him. "Where's the rest of the pavendala root?"

"I gave it back to you," Anisaria said, tucking his book into a case at his waist. "Don't you remember?"

Had he? Fletch patted his pockets, but found no little vial. He glanced at the cluttered room around him and sighed. Trying to find it in here would take hours. "Jodrif, when you find it, keep it safe for me. Shit's expensive."

Jodrif nodded once, not taking his attention from whatever it was he was working on.

"We need to get moving," Fletch said, pulling on his boots.

"To Lord Garron's manor?" Anisaria asked.

Fletch nodded.

"I assume you know a way there that doesn't involve being out in the open? That sicario never showed back up, but I don't trust that he's not out there somewhere, waiting."

"Avara's got an entrance into the undercity in a locked room in the back," Fletch said, finishing the last knot on his laces and taking a moment to massage his injured leg. "Did you pick up a weapon from her before she left?"

"Um . . ."

Fletch opened his eyes, looking at Anisaria. "What?"

"I don't have a license," the hunter said guiltily, not meeting Fletch's eyes. "It's illegal for me to carry any sort of weapon without one."

"Gods forbid you do something *illegal*," Fletch said rolling his eyes. "Like working with a known criminal, for instance."

"I'm not taking a weapon," Anisaria said. Fletch recognized that stubborn set to his features. He'd seen it in enough mirrors.

"Jodrif, talk some sense into him."

Jodrif grunted, his attention still fixated on his project.

"Fine," Fletch said, standing and wincing at the stab of pain in his leg. "You want to jump off the side of the city, it's none of my business. Let's get moving."

They entered the undercity through a small wooden trapdoor in the back room. For the first hour, Anisaria was blessedly silent. Fletch assumed that that had more to do with the headache throbbing in the kitten's temples than any sense of decent propriety. His mother had always said that pavendala root left you feeling as if you'd had your head cracked open on a blacksmith's anvil. Fletch himself had never had a chance to test that particular saying, nor did he want to.

"You're sure this is the way to Lord Garron's?" Anisaria asked, glancing at Fletch. He was sweating, and his pupils far too dilated. He held one of those stupid coins in his left hand, rubbing his thumb on it.

He's afraid of being down here, Fletch thought. *And trying— unsuccessfully—to hide it.* Fletch could have told him that being afraid of the undercity to some degree or another was smart, but doing so would probably open the door to five hundred and one questions about the criminal underworld.

"Yes," he replied. "I've been there before."

"You stole from him?" Anisaria didn't sound horrified, or even surprised. Just sort of defeated.

Fletch shrugged. Water dripped from the curved ceiling of the tunnel, the walls coated in the usual striations of moss and lichen.

Anisaria sighed. "So," he said. "How did you know Mage Bluvael?"

I knew the silence was too good to last. He never seems to shut up . . . unless he's unconscious.

"He and I did some business here and there," Fletch said

evenly, glancing up at a marking high on the wall to determine which branch to take at the next intersection of tunnels. "Over the table and under it, and occasionally under the sheets as well, if the mood was right."

Anisaria glanced at him, surprise flickering over his face for a moment before he visibly composed himself, turning to face forward. "I was under the impression that 'over the table' deals for your type were strictly limited to bribery and gambling," he said.

Not a bad rejoinder, Fletch thought with a hint of approval. *Quick recovery, and not going for the easy quip.*

"The broadsheets and the guards said that he was dealing in metal-bound weaponry in the Hollow Market," Anisaria continued when Fletch didn't reply. "Is that true?"

Gods, he was as transparent as a pane of glass. He was obviously trying to pump Fletch for all the information he could get, so he could try to catch him when this was all over.

"At the next intersection, we turn right," Fletch said.

"You haven't answered my question," Anisaria said, catching Fletch's eyes.

"Surprisingly perceptive of you, given your record tonight. Is one of the tests to get that vaunted license of yours on observational skills? If so, you must not have passed with high marks."

The bounty hunter raised one eyebrow. "Do all thieves take lessons in disambiguation and answering questions with questions, or are you unique?"

Fletch snorted. "We don't need lessons. All thieves are born with an innate skill in evasion. Some of us are just better than others."

Anisaria rolled his eyes. Fletch turned right and walked another fifteen feet before stopping at a rickety wooden ladder. He glanced at the marks carved into the stone, nodded, then started up, hopping in order to put as little weight on his injured leg as possible. He poked his head up into a cellar, rain water leaking from the narrow windows set in the stone near the ceiling. The rest of the cellar was filled with bags of sand and shelves lined with vials. Above him, he heard the movements of the student mages as they transformed the sand into glass. After they put it through whatever arcane process they used, it would be shipped all over the city for use as windows, awnings, decorations or jewelry. Fletch pulled himself up and walked over to the nearest window, easing it open as Anisaria climbed up out of the undercity behind him.

Fletch hauled himself onto the sill and squeezed through into an empty alley in the High Mage's District, near Craftsman's Square. The alley here was narrow but spotless, flowering bushes placed every ten feet or so. A cat yowled at Fletch, and he grimaced at it as Anisaria joined him. The hunter looked up at the sky and let out a sigh of relief.

As Fletch started climbing up a drainage pipe at the corner of one of the buildings, he decided to take pity on the kitten. Nothing about he and Blue's history would give Anisaria any hints about Fletch's life, or how to find him once all of this was over. He'd been true to his word so far, and Fletch hated feeling like he was in the other man's debt.

He turned when he reached the rooftop and offered the bounty hunter his hand, helping him up. "Blue and I went back a few years," he said, turning and leading the way towards a bakery near Lord Garron's estate. "He was a mage, but he wasn't like most of the others. On the surface, he sold metal-bound weapons. But he was also willing to give his wares away to people who really needed them, like Avara does." He paused. "Or like certain hunters who offer to hunt down rapists or lost kids for Valley dwellers for free."

Anisaria didn't look at him. The silence had the feeling of calculated ignorance. After a moment, the hunter cleared his throat and said, "There's a difference between what Avara does and selling weapons to the Hollow Market. She gives them away to people who need them for self-defense. Mage Bluvael, though . . . he was making convergence-loaded knives and bolts available to criminals. Criminals who undoubtedly went on to use them to murder or injure innocent citizens."

"That's one way to look at it," Fletch said evenly. "Another is that he was giving the poor a way to fight back against corrupt guards and mages. And hunters."

"He was making a profit off of the lives of others," Anisaria said. "He was no better than that sicario who came after us today."

Fletch stopped on the peak of a roof, turning to look at him, anger roiling beneath the surface of his thoughts like lightning beneath thunderclouds. "Say something like that about him again," he said coldly, "and you and I are through, hunter."

Anisaria winced and raised his hands palm outward in a defensive gesture. "I'm sorry. That was insensitive of me."

Fletch stared at him for another long moment, then nodded and continued, pausing to gauge the distance between one rooftop and the next. The roofs here in Craftsman's Square were closer together than anywhere else in the High Mage's District, but they weren't nearly as conveniently situated as those in the Valley. He stared at the roof, waiting for his anger to dim down to a manageable level.

"He must have meant a lot to you," Anisaria continued quietly. He put a hand on Fletch's shoulder. "If you need to talk about—"

"I don't need your sympathy, and neither does he," Fletch snapped, jerking out from under the hunter's hand. He took a deep breath, taking the anger and shoving it back. When he continued, it was in a calmer, more measured tone. "What he needs is vengeance."

Anisaria shot him a concerned look. "You can't kill the murderer when we find him. You know that, right?"

"Why not?"

"If you kill him, the guards will think you're guilty of *his* murder in addition to the ones already committed in your name.

When we find out what's going on, we have to bring in the man pretending to be you, so he can be questioned and proven guilty. If we don't, they'll keep hunting you. And when they catch you, they'll drag you to the Arrival Circle and . . ." he mimed hanging, complete with tilted head and gagging noises.

"Fair enough," Fletch said. "When we catch him, he's all yours. Happy?"

Anisaria smiled. "Usually."

You won't be when we find the bastard and I slit his throat after he tells us who else is in on this, Fletch thought, stopping and looking down on the bakery across the street. Justice was a luxury for the rich. Sooner or later, the kitten would wake up and realize that.

"For this next part," Fletch said, "you follow my lead. Do what I tell you, no questions. And play along."

"Right," Anisaria said, nodding. "What's the plan?"

"The plan is that you follow my lead, ask no questions, and play along."

Anisaria sighed. "You're never going to trust me, are you?"

Why would I? You're a bounty hunter. As soon as you clear my name and by association your own, you'll be using every scrap of information I give you to hunt me down.

That was what he told himself, anyway. Fletch realized that though he'd only known this man for a few hours, he wasn't entirely certain if that were true. Anisaria clearly had a deep respect for the law, and from what Fletch had seen, the man didn't seem to have much else going for him. No promise-bracelet, so he wasn't married. If he were anything like most of the hunters, he probably had few to no friends outside of the business. All he had was his job . . . and he'd put it on the line to help Fletch. If it was a ploy, it was very clever. And Fletch honestly didn't think Anisaria was a good enough liar to pull off a con of that caliber.

If his good-guy act with Fletch wasn't a ploy, then his charitable acts with the Valley residents probably weren't, either. He genuinely wanted to help them.

Clearly the kitten hadn't been a hunter long enough to get sucked into the politics and the corruption. He still thought he was doing the right thing. Hunting down evil criminals, bringing them to justice. He was an idealist.

Which presented Fletch with a rare opportunity. He could open this kitten's eyes to the way the world worked before the system had a chance to make him into one of the mages' lap dogs. Fletch found the idea strangely appealing.

He resolved to lay down a piece of bait or two over the course of this job to see what the kitten's reaction was.

Fletch pointed at the bakery. "They'll be closing in about ten minutes," he said. "We break in after they're closed and take some spare uniforms and use them to talk our way into Garron's estate."

"We're going to steal uniforms?" Anisaria said in a resigned tone.

"Yes," Fletch said. "I didn't complain about you using *your* skills for this job."

"*My* skills aren't illegal," Anisaria pointed out.

"They'll never notice they're gone," Fletch said, waving one hand. "Do you want to help with this, or don't you?"

The hunter sighed . . . but nodded.

Promising, Fletch thought. *Very promising.*

The smells of fruit pastries and sugars hung in the closed bakery down the street from the Lord's estate like a woman's perfume lingering in a room after she'd left. The sickly sweet stench made Suken's stomach roil, but he'd managed to keep from throwing up so far. He swallowed heavily for about the fiftieth time since they'd entered and looked down at himself, plucking dubiously at the front of the baggy white baker's uniform he wore. This was the only uniform that was big enough to fit him. . . . All the bakers at this particular bakery were much shorter than him. And apparently a lot wider around the middle.

"Isn't this going to make us conspicuous?" he asked. "I thought you thieves all wore black."

"Dark blue hides you better than black," Fletch said, running a hand back through his dark hair as he inspected his reflection in one of the bakery's windows. "But most of the time, the key to being unseen is looking like you belong. Someone in a mansion turns a corner and sees a guy skulking around dressed all in dark colors, what does he do?"

"Try to catch him?" Suken tried. "Raise an alarm?"

Fletch nodded. "But if he turns that corner and sees a lost delivery-man? He'll ask a few questions, sure. But he's not gonna jump to conclusions." He turned to give Suken a condescending look. "You want to catch a criminal, you'd better start learning to *think* like one, kitten."

Suken threw Fletch a dark look. He was getting tired of being called kitten. "I've caught—" he raised one hand to cover his mouth, closing his eyes as a particularly strong wave of nausea crashed over him. When it receded, he weakly continued, "plenty of criminals."

Fletch chuckled and bent to pick up a wooden box full of day-old pastries. They'd spent the last five minutes collecting them up from the shelves in the darkened bakery. Despite his flippant remarks about stealing while they'd been on the roof, Fletch had left a small pile of aerans on the counter, enough for the wares and the uniforms. Apparently he only stole from mages and nobles. That fit with what Suken had learned about him from the case-file. He was beginning to form a better picture of the man's personality than that which the guards wanted people to believe.

For starters, he was about five times as frustrating as Suken had expected. Sometimes Suken would feel as if there was someone loyal and human hiding behind that snide mask, like when Greencloak had told him about Blue, only to have the thief turn around and blithely imply that he'd have no problem killing someone. Suken bent and picked up his own box, full of sticky pastries with jellied-fruit centers and flaky crusts drizzled with sugar frosting. He pointedly looked away from the box as he shifted it slightly to put more of its weight on his right arm than his left. His shoulder still ached like caal-fire, in addition to the nausea and the headache still throbbing at his temples.

Getting poisoned, he thought, is most definitely now on my list of things to avoid, antidote or not. Right below working with known criminals.

"You," Fletch said, rummaging behind the counter, "have caught plenty of *mice*. Perfect prey for a kitten. If you want to be a *real* hunter, you're gonna have to learn to understand us."

Well, that was true enough. This . . . temporary alliance or whatever it was he had going with Greencloak offered him a valuable opportunity, but up until recently Fletch had been tight-lipped with details about his techniques. *Why the change?* Suken thought, eyeing the other man. *Ever since we left Avara's, he's been strangely forthcoming.*

It was almost as if he *wanted* Suken to get to know him. But that was ridiculous. Wasn't it? Was he deliberately feeding Suken false information? Or maybe all those comments about Suken's looks weren't as flippant as they seemed, and the thief was interested in him romantically.

Chance. The whole situation was making his head hurt worse than it did already.

"Why are you telling me this?" Suken said, following Fletch out the door, box under one arm. He threw a silent prayer of thanks to the Lady as they walked out of the reek of sugar and fruit and into the relatively clear, albeit humid air of the night street. "I wouldn't think that you'd *want* a capable hunter on your tail."

"Capable or not, you'll never catch me, Anisaria." He paused, the grin thrown back over his shoulder accompanied by a flippant tone. "Not unless I want you to."

Well, Suken thought with a sigh. *That certainly cleared things up.*

Either he wants to stab me in the back, or fuck me. Not that the thief wasn't attractive, in a sarcastic, mean-tempered kind of way. He was just . . . well, a *thief.*

Suken followed Fletch down the street towards the back of the mansion, the nausea abating more with each step. He still felt weak in the knees, and the damned headache didn't seem to be going away anytime soon, but at least he didn't feel as if he were about to lose whatever small amount he'd eaten in the last day. The moon hung fat and low above them, and the white uniforms they wore stood out like beacons, seeming almost to glow in the moonlight.

"I don't like this," Suken said, breaking the silence. He kept his voice low, in case anyone above had a window open. His heart started beating faster, and his palms grew clammy with sweat. Chance, he was about to break into someone's *home.* "What if they question us about more than our names and the pastries?" Suken was aware that his words were coming out quicker than usual, but he was unable to stop them from spilling out. "What if they ask about—"

"*When* they question us," Fletch interrupted, "you keep your mouth shut and let me do all the talking. Stand there and smile, give 'em something pretty to look at."

Don't let him get to you, Suken thought, taking a deep breath. *Learn as much as you can, while you can.* "Is this how you always do this?" The words came out stiff, but it was the best he could manage.

Fletch shrugged. "Most of the time. But I'm not gonna give all my secrets away to you just yet, kitten. You've gotta earn 'em."

The headache intensified. Suken reached up with his free hand to rub at his temple with two fingers. "I don't care about your secrets," he lied, hoping it wasn't too obvious. "I just want to catch this murderer and get my damn license back." *Then hunt down Shifter,* he thought, though he hadn't had time to find a single solid lead on the shifter yet.

"And the thought of grabbing me and bringing me in, innocence be damned, never crossed your mind? Be honest, kitten. You can't fool a thief; we build our lives on lies."

"You're innocent," Suken said. He paused, and continued dryly, "Well . . . of murder. If I turned you in, they'd hang you." They turned a final corner and found themselves facing a simple wooden door set into the stone wall around Garron's estate, a rope dangling beside it.

Fletch stopped and turned towards him, looking Suken up and down. "Here we go," he said softly. "What's my name?"

"Ollin," Suken replied, repeating what Fletch had told him while they'd been filling the boxes.

"And yours?"

"Sergin."

Fletch nodded once. "Good. Remember . . . let me do the talking." He turned and rested the box on his hip under one arm, reaching up to pull the rope. Suken heard a bell ringing somewhere far away, a door opening, and hurried footsteps. After a few moments, the wooden door creaked open, a young woman in servants' livery poking her head out to look at them. Her dark hair was bound up into a complicated-looking braid, and her eyes were red, as if she'd been crying recently. Her gaze flicked from Fletch to Suken and back again.

"Good even," Fletch said, dropping his voice down an octave and affecting the rolling accent of northern Majitan. "Cery, ain't it?"

"Yes," the young woman replied. "Ol . . . Ollin, wasn't it?"

"Ya remember me?" Fletch flashed her a smile far friendlier than his usual sarcastic grin. "Musta left an impression, aye?"

Suken eyed him. If he was trying to flirt, he was doing a spectacularly poor job of it.

"I suppose."

"Got some rolls n' pastries for ye master, from mine."

The young woman looked skeptically from Suken to Fletch. "We didn't order any," she said. "Master's not been in the mood for pastries. Not since . . ." She glanced back over her shoulder towards the house, but Suken caught a glimpse of the tears filling her eyes.

He felt a pang of grief. It had only been two days since Flower had died, though to him, it felt much longer. The girl must have been well-liked among the servants.

"Aye, the lil' lassie," Fletch said, nodding sadly. "Yerrio heard. That's why 'e sent us, y'ken?"

Her gaze shifted from Fletch to Suken again. She tried a small smile, though those tears still glinted in her eyes. He returned the smile, hoping that it might put her more at ease.

"I heard—" Suken began, but Fletch raised his voice and over-rode him.

"Call it an act o' charity, like. A little fine cane to bring some sweetness to the sorrow. Know it ain't gonna be much solace, but somethin's better'n nothin'. If your master ain't wantin' em, you and yer mates might, aye?"

"For free?" She looked at the boxes, twisting one of her apron ties around one finger. "Well . . . I suppose the lady might appreciate it. She ain't had much of an appetite." Her lower lip trembled, and she looked away again.

Suken stepped forward, ignoring Fletch's warning glance. He pulled a kerchief from his pocket and held it out to her. She took it wordlessly and dabbed at her eyes. "Thank you," she whispered, looking up and meeting his eyes. "It's been a hard week."

"I understand," Suken said softly. "I lost my parents when I was young. My little brother was devastated. I remember bringing him to the sweet-store a few days later. It was the only thing that seemed to cheer him up."

Cery nodded slowly. "I suppose it can't hurt to have them around the house." She dabbed at her eyes again and held the kerchief back out to Suken. He shook his head.

"Keep it."

She gave him a hint of a smile, hidden behind the tears. "This way," she said. "You can leave them with Cook."

As she turned her back to them, Fletch dropped a grudging nod to Suken.

"Would you like any more juice?" Cery asked. Suken gave her a tense smile.

"No, thank you."

She sat down opposite the table from him, resting her chin on the lattice of her fingers. The smells of roasting pork and spices surrounded them, coming from the half-open door to the kitchen to Suken's right. Huge copper pans hung from the beams in the ceiling, and the walls of the small room were covered with shelves holding everything from fine golden plates to ceramic mugs. Every so often a red-faced pudgy man with thinning hair poked his head into the room, scowling. The cook, unless Suken was way off his mark. Each time, he pulled back shaking his head. It was almost as if he expected Suken to be ravaging Cery, and was disappointed not to be able to use that wooden spoon he held to give him a sound beating. "How long have you been working for Master Yerrio?" Cery asked. "I remember Ollin making a delivery a few months back, but I haven't seen you around before."

"Um. A couple weeks?" he said, hoping that he wouldn't say anything blatantly wrong. "I . . . uh. Don't work many hours. Few here and there, to make ends meet. That sort of thing."

"Mm hmm." She tilted her head slightly to the side. "Do you live around here?"

Suken glanced desperately at the door Fletch had vanished behind. He'd excused himself almost immediately, asking to use the servants' privy. When Suken had risen, Fletch had waved his hand and insisted that he didn't need an escort. That had been fifteen minutes and two mugs of mango juice ago.

"Sort of," he replied, turning his gaze back to Cery. "Look . . . Ollin's been gone for an awfully long time. Maybe I should go check on him. He's been, um. Sick. Fainting fits."

Cery's face creased in concern. "Has he been to see an ardein?"

"Can't afford it, not on our wages," Suken said with a shrug. "The herbalists say that it's a passing thing. Should be fine in a few days. But I should check on him anyway."

"Of course." She stood. "I'll go with you."

The cook poked his head into the room again, his eyes narrowing. Cery ignored him.

"You don't have to," Suken said, getting to his feet. "I mean, I'm sure you have things to do, and . . ." he trailed off as she rounded the table and took his hand in both of hers.

"You won't know which way to go," she said with a bright smile plastered on over the ever-present tears. "It's no trouble, really."

He was going to kill Fletch for putting him in the position of having to lie to a grief-stricken, pretty young woman. Three hundred thousand aerans dead, wasn't it?

Suken sighed and nodded, letting her pull him through the door into a hallway. The cook watched them go, his expression full of seething disapproval. Luminaries set into metal brackets were spaced every few feet along the walls, the wooden floors giving off the soft sheen of years of careful polishing and buffing.

"Is Lord Garron here?" Suken asked as they walked.

Cery nodded. "Not for long, though. He's going to some sort of meeting tonight."

"At the Academe?" Suken said. "He's a professor, right?"

They turned a corner and started walking down a corridor narrower than the first. "I don't think so," Cery replied. "I think it has something to do with Lialla." At that, the tears rose in her eyes again and her hand tightened ever so slightly on his arm.

"I'm sorry," Suken said, his heart going out to her. "She was—" he caught himself and corrected, "She must have been a sweet girl."

Cery nodded. "She liked to cook with us," she said, grief causing her words to tremble. "She'd come down and ask us how to make things. Get more flour on herself than in the pans, usually, but it . . . it was sweet, you know?"

When I get my hands on Shifter, Suken thought, one hand clenching into a fist, *I'm going to make him regret ever thinking about taking that little girl.*

"Do you know why she was taken?" he asked as Cery stopped at a door. "Was it . . . ransom? Something like that?"

"That's what the guards said," Cery replied. She reached up and wiped at her eyes with Suken's kerchief, took a deep shuddering breath, and knocked on the door. "Ollin?" she called. "Are you all right?"

"Fine," came a voice behind them. Suken whirled, his heartbeat picking up to a race, to see Fletch standing behind him. Chance, he hadn't even heard the thief approaching.

Fletch was covered in dust and cobwebs, and had what looked like a bundle of fabric slung over his shoulder.

Cery's eyes widened. "What—"

Before she could finish, Fletch's hand darted out, jabbing her in the shoulder with something that briefly caught the light. She yelped in pain, one hand whipping up to clap against her shoulder. Her eyes rolled up in her head and her knees crumpled. Suken managed to catch her before her head hit the floor. He brought his fingers to the side of her neck, relieved to feel a heartbeat.

"What did you do to her?" he said, looking up.

"Relax," Fletch said. "Your little girlfriend will wake up in a few hours, right as rain." He held up the same type of narrow pin he'd used to demonstrate the sicario's poisoning technique, pinched between his index finger and thumb, the metal of the tip stained crimson.

Suken lay Cery down gently, then stood, narrowing his eyes. "You poisoned her?"

"Did I ruin a chance for a good lay? I'd say I was sorry, but we're on a bit of a tight schedule, kitten."

"You *poisoned* her?" Suken asked again, hearing the anger dancing on his words but unable to keep it at bay.

"It's only dreamshade," Fletch said, flicking the needle away. It embedded itself in the wood wall, quivering. "I've used it a hundred times. Get it straight from an herbalist I trust more than anyone else in this damned city. Never had a problem with it."

The anger faded, but only a little. He narrowed his eyes at Fletch. "You're *sure* it's safe?"

"Safe as a cup of tea."

Suken glanced down at Cery. She appeared to be sleeping soundly, her breath coming steady and even, her skintone normal. This wasn't the way he wanted to leave her, but how would they have explained the bag over Fletch's shoulder, and where he had been, otherwise?

And what *was* in that bag, anyway?

"If you're through playing the defensive suitor, we have business to take care of," Fletch said. "I overheard our good Lord Garron talking to his wife. He's getting ready to go to a meeting of the Coalition, along with a few trusted bodyguards."

"The Coalition? He's a member?" Suken was surprised by that. He'd thought that the Coalition was mostly comprised of the poor, and Lord Garron was one of the most powerful merchants in Adunare.

"Apparently." Fletch looked like a cat who'd discovered a bowl full of cream. "I'd say that there's a fair to decent chance that they're the ones who are behind all of this. Killing mage-born would certainly be in line with their agenda." Fletch patted the bag slung over his shoulder. "Picked us up a couple of disguises. I figure we can go in, listen in on some conversations, maybe find out which one of the bastards is masquerading as me. And if that doesn't pan out, we can get old high-and-mighty Garron alone after the meeting and question him more directly."

Suken didn't like the smile that accompanied that last. He closed his eyes, listing off the ten aspects of Lady Chance in order to calm himself down. By the time he'd finished, he didn't feel quite as much like reaching out and strangling Fletch. "So we just leave her here?" he said, his voice sounding brittle.

"Yes," Fletch said, his own tone growing serious, "Unless you plan on bringing her along."

Suken sighed. "Fine," he said. "But if there's going to be any questioning, I do it."

"Whatever you say, kitten." Fletch adjusted his grip on the bag and walked off down the hall, whistling an off-tune melody. Suken paused long enough to pluck the needle from the wall, putting it carefully in the case with his crossbow bolts and the half-full vial of pavendala root.

Chapter Seventeen

Suken looked through the iron gate of a rooftop garden towards the theater, peering through the haze of mist present even up here in the Mage's District after Descent. He'd never seen a show here, though he'd heard enough about them from Terri. She often stayed with her aunt for a night or two so the two of them could attend day-long performances put on by the troupes of actors, mages and musicians.

Water cascaded from the roof of the theater and poured down the carved columns supporting the glass arch over the main doorway. It wasn't raining—for once—so the owners of the theater must have installed some sort of system to make it always appear as if it were in the midst of a rainstorm, when you were inside. For the ambiance, he supposed. Wavery light spilled through water-coated windows to light the gilded statues standing in alcoves along the sides of the theater. Suken could barely make out chandeliers composed entirely of luminaries hanging inside.

Suken reached up and adjusted the tight collar of the stupid black tunic Fletch had stolen from Lord Garron's, pulling it away from his throat with two fingers. The embroidery on it itched, and the sleeve hems fell a couple inches too short for his arms. Fletch was still changing behind him. Suken had turned to give the man some privacy, though the thief hadn't afforded him the same courtesy. "This is a bad idea," Suken said over his shoulder, not turning. "We have no idea what sort of meeting this is. What if it's . . . I don't know. A . . . murderer's meeting, or something?"

A moment of silence behind him. Then, flatly: "A murderer's meeting?"

"What? It could be." Suken glanced back over his shoulder. Fletch was lacing up the front of his shirt, shaking his head.

"If you weren't so damn tall," Fletch said, "I'd say that you were no older than Tam."

"I'm twenty-two," Suken said.

"And I'm a High Mage."

"What is it with everyone questioning my age? I'm *pretty* sure I know how old I am."

Fletch snorted.

"If the Coalition is framing you," Suken said, "it stands to reason that the person who's been doing the killing is here. Or maybe it's more than one person, taking turns wearing your cloak."

"Gods forbid," Fletch muttered, easing his arm into the sleeve of a fancy brocaded jacket.

"So in that case it would be a meeting of murderers." Suken paused, then finished smugly, "A murderer's meeting."

Fletch stopped adjusting the front of the jacket and stared at Suken for a long moment, his expression unreadable.

"A conference of killers?" Suken tried, a smile flirting with the corners of his mouth despite the headache still lurking in his temples. "An assembly of assassins?"

Fletch shook his head and started doing up the buttons running up the front of the jacket. The outfit actually made him look dashing; like a prince in a fei tale.

"You'd better hurry up," Suken said, jerking a thumb back over his shoulder. "They could be starting any minute now."

"Old fat-and-mighty Lord Garron said the meeting would start at eleven."

"Bit late for a meeting on the up-and-up," Suken said. "That's another point in favor of it being a murderer's meeting."

"All the Coalition meetings start late," Fletch said, smoothing the front of the jacket. "Gods below, kitten, do you know *anything* about this city?"

"You mean aside from having memorized every layout map, law, and ordinance?"

"Congratulations, you're a walking textbook," Fletch said, reaching into the bag and pulling out two masks. "We'll have to wear these."

"Why?" Suken asked, catching the one Fletch tossed to him and turning it over in his hands. It looked like an Anchorage Day mask, simple and white, only covering the top half of his face, with little adornment save for a green feather arching over the right eye.

"What, none of your precious ordinances talked about this?"

Suken gave him a flat look.

"Coalition likes its anonymity," Fletch said. "Code-names, masks, the usual. Works out well for you and I."

Suken had never cared to do any research about the Coalition. From what little he'd heard, they were abiding by the law. Most of the members were Valley residents or poor merchants, but in order to rent the grandiose theater, they must have at least a few members who were High Merchants, like Garron. Maybe even some mages, though that seemed unlikely, seeing as how achieving their goal would put an entire branch of mage-craft out of business.

"I can understand why the Coalition would be interested in killing mage-born," Suken said, watching as a group of people walked through the doors, their laughter floating up to him. "I guess. But why frame you for it? If they're doing it, they'd want to take credit, wouldn't they?"

"That's what we're here to find out," Fletch said, pulling on his own mask, a dark blue one decorated with little swirls of gold embroidery. He turned to appraise Suken, looking him up and down. "I suppose it'll have to do," he said, reaching up to brush some dust from Suken's uninjured shoulder. "I doubt Garron's been able to fit into these for fifteen years, so he won't be likely to recognize them."

Suken looked over towards the theater again. A small group of people approached the open doors, nodding to the two men standing outside before walking in. All of the newcomers wore masks and somewhat nicer clothes than most you'd see in the streets, as if this were some sort of party. Two wore white sashes tied around their waists to offset the dull browns of their pants and buttoned vests, while another wore a tunic with tight-fitted sleeves. His black sash held the tunic closely fitted to his waist, where the fabric fell in four angled tails. It looked almost exactly like the one Suken was wearing, so at least he'd fit in.

Beneath the sleeveless tunic, Suken wore a collared white shirt with billowing sleeves tied at his wrists and a pair of black trousers. He tugged on the collar again, grimaced, and reached up and ran a hand back through his hair. It felt . . . odd not to be wearing a hat.

"Let's go," Fletch said. He wore a similar outfit to Suken's, with a brown tunic that fit his spare frame better than Suken's fit him. He made his way over to an ornamental iron ladder leading down from the roof, and Suken followed him down, wondering what anyone would think if they saw two well-dressed men in masks climbing down from a roof into an alley.

His shoulder flared in pain with each rung of the ladder, but he gritted his teeth and bore it until they reached the alley. Fletch adjusted his sleeves again and started walking towards the theater.

Suken glanced up at the garden where he'd tucked his normal clothes, sketchbook, and prayers, hoping they'd be safe.

Well, either they would be, or they wouldn't be. He'd have to hope that he and Fletch could learn what they needed and make it back out here to retrieve them before the owners of that garden went up and noticed a bundle of clothes that hadn't been there the day before.

Suken hurried his steps to catch up to Fletch. "I look like a bloody idiot," he whispered as they started crossing the street.

"No, you *act* like a bloody idiot. Half the time, anyway. You *look* like some high-and-mighty's son out for a romp with the commoners. Just act like everyone's a servant and you'll be fine."

The guards looked up as Suken and Fletch approached. Suken nodded to them, trying to look as if he knew exactly where he was going. *Act like everyone's a servant,* Fletch had said. Suken supposed it would have helped if he knew how servants were treated. Somehow he guessed that his and Terri's relationship wasn't exactly the norm. He straightened, squaring his shoulders and not glancing at the men as he passed them. It must have worked, because Suken and Fletch walked through the open door with no contest into an entryway filled with light and laughter.

His headache immediately intensified, but Suken squinted and clenched his teeth, doing his best to ignore it. He and Fletch pushed their way through groups of masked people holding glasses of wine and chatting with one another. Fletch slid around the groups gracefully, as if this were some sort of a dance and he'd been rehearsing it for years. Fragrant flowers were everywhere; adorning ladies' hair and the skirts of their dresses, pinned to the breasts of the mens' tunics or shirts, sprouting in riots of color from glass vases half as tall as Suken. The sheer number of blooms put the whorehouses of Orchid Street to shame, and their mingled perfumes made his stomach twist, a holdover from the nausea he'd suffered earlier.

As he made his way through the crowd, Suken caught snippets of conversations. Most seemed to be relatively innocuous; merchants talking about the current trends in grain import or poorer groups talking in hushed whispers about the movements of the various cartels in the Valley. They approached a group of finely dressed men and women standing around with glasses of wine in their hands, and Suken watched in horror as Fletch's hand darted into one of their pockets, coming out with something that sparkled in the light for a half a second before vanishing into the thief's own pocket.

The masks the Coalition members wore ranged from little more than strips of black fabric with holes for the eyes to one or two feathered, beaded contraptions which made their wearers look like gaudy birds of paradise. Several had been fashioned after flowers, spreading out from the wearer's noses in bright, stiff petals made of fabric. Suken felt as if he'd wandered into an Anchorage Day pageant, and wondered uneasily if the monsters in this particular pageant might not be real ones.

The chandelier he'd seen from outside cast bright white light over the gilded carvings running up the corners of the room and the paintings set cunningly into the walls between them. He and Fletch made their way up a set of tiers to a pair of large, intricately carved wooden doors. As they passed a cage constructed of thin glass and silver bars, the peacock inside let out a call that sounded unnervingly like a child screaming.

Now what? Suken thought, looking down into the room and feeling lost. He was used to the dark alleys, bars and warehouses of the Valley, or at best the well-maintained streets of the Mages' District. This was like walking into a story about Darashan, in the years before the mages were exiled to Majitan. Suken wished that he could rub his temple to relieve the headache, but the damned mask was in the way.

"Wine, sir?"

Suken started and looked to his left. A young man wearing servants' livery stood beside him, holding a large silver tray with several wine glasses on it.

Suken looked at the glass with a grimace, his stomach lurching.

"Thank you," Fletch said, picking up two of the glasses and dropping a pair of half-aerans on the tray. Probably ones he'd lifted from some of the Coalition members. The young man bowed, his left hand held behind his back, and wove his way back into the crowd.

"What?" Fletch said, catching Suken's dark look. "They'd be spending it here anyway. Not like it's ending up anywhere different."

Suken sighed and took the glass Fletch was holding out to him, though he had no intention of drinking it. He hated wine. Fletch turned and began heading towards a fountain flowing with molten glass, Suken following and wishing for a shot or two of gin to ease the aching in his head. Or at least to distract his attention from it. When they reached the fountain, they both turned their backs to it, looking out over the milling crowd.

"Is this headache ever going to go away?" Suken asked.

Fletch glanced up at the chandelier. "You'll be sensitive to light for a few days, probably. Best get used to it."

"Wonderful," Suken muttered.

"So," Fletch said, sipping his wine, "what now, oh great hunter?"

"You don't know?"

"I'd like to hear what your plan is. You're big on those, aren't you?"

For the first time, Suken realized that Fletch might be mining Suken for information on hunters just as Suken was doing to him for thieves. *So what if he is?* Suken thought. *Not like what we do is any big secret.* He looked towards the door where they'd entered.

"Garron ought to be here soon," Suken said. "Right?"

"Once he's done preening himself like one of these peacocks, yes." Fletch gave the bird in the cage beside him a disinterested look and took another sip of his wine.

"Once he arrives, we can eavesdrop on him, then follow him to wherever he goes after this. If the people framing you aren't here, Garron's bound to meet up with them eventually. In the meantime, we stay inconspicuous and try to learn as much as we can."

"Inconspicuous," Fletch said, giving Suken a speculative look over the rim of the glass. A grin pulled at the corner of his mouth.

Suken looked down at himself, annoyed. "I'm wearing what *you* told me to wear."

"It's not your clothes, kitten." He sipped his wine again, letting his gaze sweep out over the crowd.

"Then what is it?"

Fletch didn't answer. Suken shook his head and turned to look to his left and started. A painting took up the space between two fluted columns set into the wall. It was elegant work, a portrait of a historical member of the Sapphire School whose name Suken never could remember. The linework was smooth and fluid, the colors applied with a grace and fluidity Suken envied. He'd never been much good at painting.

"That's a late Fibonari," he said, surprised. "'Discovery of the Tribes.'"

Fletch turned and glanced at the painting. "And?"

"It's one of his most famous works," Suken said, staring up at it. "Why is it here, in a theater? I thought it would have been in the museum at Sciiren, or maybe the Academe."

A fat man standing in the group near them turned towards Suken, his ruddy cheeks nearly matching the red half-mask he wore. He looked a bit like an uakari, a type of monkey with a bright red face and bald head. He sported long, thinning grey hair ringing the bald section, held back in a tail. His chocolate-brown jacket appeared to be made of silk, with beads and bits of embroidery in stylized flower patterns looping over the shoulders.

"It was a gift," he said, stepping towards Suken. "From Mage Conlira some twenty years ago. She always did have an appreciation for the arts, whether they were on the stage or on the page." He chuckled at his own rhyme. "Art enthusiast, are you?"

"I've studied it a bit," Suken said, turning to give Uakari his full attention. "Don't have much time for it anymore, though."

Uakari laughed. "Who does? Well . . ." he paused, raising his wine glass to his lips, "I do, but I'm old." The eyes behind the mask sparkled with good humor. "Regardless, it's a pleasure to find someone else in this gaggle of uneducated louts who appreciates the intricacies of fine art."

Suken gave the man an exaggerated bow. "The pleasure's mine."

"Tell me," Uakari said, waddling up beside Suken and looking up at the painting, "What are your thoughts on the theory that Fibonari's use of red was a deliberate choice to highlight the undesirable?"

"Coincidence," Suken said. He glanced at Fletch, who was staring at him with one eyebrow raised. Suken pointed at the red light of the setting sun reflecting off the gates of E'dis City. "Here and in ten of Fibonari's other works," Suken said to Fletch, "red is used on objects that the artist would have found disagreeable. But in just as many, the red is simply that. . . . Red."

The rotund man chuckled. "I agree with you, m'boy. But the scholars must have their little theories, musn't they? Every shade and nuance a hidden meaning."

"Sounds about right," Suken said.

"And you, my friend?" Uakari said, raising his voice and looking at Fletch. "What is your opinion of this piece?"

"Depends," Fletch said, sipping his wine. "How much is it worth?"

Suken shot him a warning look.

"Hmm," Uakari rumbled. "The value of this piece is weighed in its history, young man. Some would say that it is priceless."

Fletch made a considering noise, his eyes scanning over the painting like a man looking a beautiful woman up and down.

"Will you excuse us for a moment?" Suken asked, forcing a smile.

Uakari rumbled an affirmative, nodding and stepping closer

to the Fibonari. Suken grabbed Fletch's arm with the hand not holding his wine glass and pulled him a few steps away, near enough to the glass fountain that the convergences whirring within it would mask their voices. "Don't even think about it," he whispered.

"Think about what?" Fletch finished his wine and tossed the glass into the fountain, where it promptly melted.

"We're in the middle of trying to find out who's framing you," Suken hissed. "I'm being hunted by a sicario for some reason, and you're being hunted by . . . well, everyone else. And you're thinking about stealing a *painting?*"

"Me?" Fletch reached over and deftly plucked Suken's glass from his hand, favoring him with a smile that looked entirely too innocent to be genuine. "I'm just admiring a priceless work of art. Like you and your high-and-mighty friend there."

"He's not my friend."

"Could have fooled me," Fletch said.

"I'm trying to get information. That's why we're here, isn't it?"

"I fail to see how information on shades of *paint* is bound to come in handy while hunting down the assholes who are framing me."

Suken reached up, realizing with his hand halfway to his head that he couldn't massage his temple due to the mask. He lowered it, settling for turning so the chandelier wasn't in his direct line of vision. "Do you know *anything* about how to deal with people?"

"Excuse me?"

Suken ran one hand back through his hair. "When you're trying to get information out of people," he said, "you can't come right out and ask. You have to work your way into their trust slowly." He hesitated and said, "Like . . . sneaking into a house you're planning to steal from. You wouldn't go running in the front door in broad daylight, right?"

Fletch snorted.

"What's your problem?" Suken asked, his annoyance rising.

"My problem?" Fletch said. "My *problem* is that these aren't pleasant people, kitten. I find it difficult to smile and play nice with them while they're plotting to kill the people I care about."

"You don't know for certain that anyone here is in on your frame-job except Garron," Suken replied. "Not yet. Why not give them the benefit of the doubt?"

Fletch leaned in close, lowering his voice. "Every man and woman is here for one purpose," he hissed. "Taking away the rights of every mage-born in this damned city, making them little better than animals. Whether or not they're in on the frame-job is neither here nor there. You want criminals, Anisaria? You want villains to arrest?" He waved one hand towards the crowd. "Have at them."

Any words Suken had been about to say dried up on his tongue. He turned away from Fletch to see Uakari eyeing them.

"Sorry," Suken said. "This is our first time here. He's a little nervous."

"Understandable," the man rumbled, folding his hands over the silver knob at the top of his black walking stick. "The masks do tend to be a tad unnerving, until you get used to them. Think of it as Anchorage Day, only for adults, eh?"

"And without the mazes," Suken said, but his mind lingered on Fletch's words. Suddenly, Uakari didn't look quite so much like a kindly old grandfather anymore. His words seemed condescending, his piggy eyes too considering. "So," Suken said, looking around and hoping his discomfort wasn't plain on his face, "what should we expect? Is this all there is, or . . . is there some sort of speech . . . ?"

"Oh, there'll be speeches," Uakari said. "They'll be calling us into the theater soon enough, I warrant." He glanced from side to side, leaned in closer, and said in a conspiratorial whisper, "One of the speeches tonight will be particularly special. You and your prickly friend chose a good night to join us. Though, I didn't tell you that." He smiled and laid one finger alongside his nose.

"Of course," Suken said. "Are there reserved seats? We weren't given any tickets or anything when we walked in."

"Oh, no no. Those of us involved with the inner workings have our own boxes, but everyone else finds their own seats down on the floor." Uakari paused, tilting his head to one side slightly. "My son and his wife couldn't attend tonight. Feeling under the weather, you know. They have their own box, beside mine. You look like a higher class of gentleman than most of this rabble. . . . If you like, you and your . . . *friend* could use it." Uakari glanced at Fletch, his gaze speculative.

"We're not . . ." Suken felt a flush rise to his cheeks and hoped that Fletch wasn't listening in to this particular part of the conversation. "It's not—"

"No judgments," Uakari said with a chuckle. "I'm Maji, boy, not some Darashanian prude."

"We're not a couple," Suken insisted. "Just friends. From . . . um. Work."

"My mistake," the man said smoothly. "Well, if you and your coworker would like to use the box, it's yours."

"Are you sure?" Suken said, his face still feeling uncomfortably warm. "We'd hate to impose. . . ."

"Otherwise it'll sit empty, and I'd rather leave a good impression on new members of the family than force you to sit down with the masses. Especially rich new members, eh?" He winked and jabbed Suken with his elbow. It felt something like getting buffeted by a leg of uncooked pork.

"That'd be great," Suken said. "Thanks."

"Not at all, not at all."

Fletch tapped Suken on the elbow. When Suken turned to him, Fletch raised an eyebrow. "Coworkers?" he said.

"Don't start," Suken muttered.

For a miracle, Fletch didn't push the matter. Instead, he nodded towards the doors to the street. A man walked in, wearing a black unornamented mask and a fine tunic and trousers, also of black. A woman wearing a thick veil that completely obscured her face hung on his arm. As soon as they walked in, people began whispering amongst themselves.

"Ah," Uakari said, sounding sad. "I didn't think he'd come, considering. . . ."

"Considering?" Suken asked.

The portly man shook his head. "The masks are to preserve our anonymity, but only for those new to the cause. Those of us who have been with the Coalition for years recognize each other. He," he looked towards the newcomer, "is a dear friend of mine. Lost his daughter two nights ago. Tragic accident."

Blue eyes. Blood. A small hand held in his, slowly turning cold.

Stop it, Suken told himself. *Garron has something to do with the people framing Fletch. Leave your guilt out in the rain and do your bloody job.*

"I see," Suken said, his tone more cold than he'd intended.

Uakari turned towards him. "I must go and offer my condolences. Tell the ushers to see you to box twenty-seven. Perhaps after the meeting you and your friend will meet with me? I'd be happy to answer any questions you might have about the cause."

"Sure," Suken said. "Sounds great."

Uakari bobbed his head and waddled off into the crowd towards Lord Garron and his grieving wife.

"Find out anything useful?" Fletch asked.

"Not really," Suken said. "But I did get us box seats."

"Lovely."

"Lords and ladies," a well-dressed man standing in front of the closed doors intoned. His voice carried over the din of conversation, which quieted slowly as people turned to face him. He was young, barely as old as Suken, and strikingly handsome. His brown hair was swept back from his bare face—he wore no mask. "The meeting is about to begin. If you please . . ." he stepped to one side, and the doors swung open behind him, revealing the velvet-shrouded dimness of the theater. The people pressed in around Suken and Fletch, talking quietly to one another, their voices tight with anticipation. They were swept along in a current of humanity towards the theater. Just inside the doors, a pair of staircases swept up to the right and left, circling towards the boxes. Suken stepped aside and told one of the ushers standing at the base of the steps the box number Uakari had given him. The man nodded, leading Suken and Fletch up the steps.

"Box twenty-seven, sirs," the usher said, stopping and gesturing to a curtain set into the wall. Suken thanked him, and he and Fletch stepped through into a small balcony barely larger than a wash closet, with four seats behind a waist-high wooden railing. It was blessedly darker in the theater than it had been in the entryway, and Suken felt the throbbing ache in his temples wane to the barest hint of annoyance. He stepped forward, leaning over the railing to look down into the theater.

Fifty rows of velvet-cushioned seats extended from the doors down to the stage, the walls covered with gilded carvings of flowers and vines. Luminaries rested in the hearts of those golden flowers, filling the theater with dim but warm radiance. Box seats like the one Suken and Fletch occupied lined the walls on either side of the floor, some filled by men and women in intricate clothes wearing equally intricate masks. Just as many stood empty. The stage spread out in two wide wings below, brightly lit by huge luminaries hanging from the wooden catwalks above it. The stage's floor was polished to a warm sheen, the musicians' and mages' boxes at the foot of the stage empty.

Fletch sat in one of the seats, looking around with a dissatisfied twist of his features.

"Do you see Garron?" Suken asked, watching the people as they entered below. Their chattering lapped like waves at the edge of their balcony.

"He's probably in one of these," Greencloak said, pulling a knife from somewhere and using it to clean under his nails.

"Once everything's underway I'll go and find him, if we haven't spotted him by then."

Suken sat down, feeling distinctly out of place. He almost wished that he could be sitting down in the floor seats, with everyone else. Those were the people he worked with day in and day out, the people he paid for leads, the people whose lost children he helped to find. They wore masks, but Suken could see beneath their poorly gilded exteriors. He saw the tattered hems of their skirts, the holes in the elbows of their sleeves, the soot from the incinerators beneath their fingernails. They all seemed so . . . normal, despite the masks.

And yet . . . they're here, Suken thought, staring down at them. *They're here, working together to try to remove the citizens' rights from others. Why? I'm certain they've worked with mage-born before, like I have. They have mage-born neighbors, or distant family members, or even just acquaintances.*

Everything he'd ever heard about the Coalition made him think that its goal was to make current mage-born little more than slaves and stop the mages from creating more of them. Suken supposed he could understand the latter. . . . The process by which normal people were made mage-born was dangerous. Only about half of those who undertook the process survived it. But why the former?

More importantly at the moment, what did they have to do with Fletch Greencloak and the people trying to frame him? All of the victims so far had been mage-born, which certainly implied a connection. Was the whole organization in on the plot? Suken didn't think so. The more people you involved in a plan, the more likely it was to fail. So maybe it was just a few like-minded individuals who had met at one of the meetings. But still, why frame Fletch? If they wanted to kill mage-born, why not just . . . do it?

Suken drummed his fingers on the arm of his chair. Then there was the sicario. The man had been after Suken, not Fletch, but—

"Careful, kitten," Fletch said dryly. "Think any harder and you're liable to break something in that pretty head of yours."

"I was trying to figure out why someone would be framing you," Suken said. Below, the lights dimmed and the hum of conversation around them began to fade.

"Obviously they're trying to use my reputation to their advantage," Fletch said, leaning his head back and closing his eyes. "Who better to frame for a series of murders if you want to keep doing them than someone who's uncatchable?"

"That doesn't make sense," Suken said, shaking his head. "You might be uncatchable—which is debatable, considering they caught you once already and I found you twice—but the real murderer probably isn't as good as you."

"Ah, but he hasn't been caught," Fletch said, gesturing with the knife. "Because everyone's bloody chasing *me*."

"But nobody knows who you really *are*," Suken insisted, leaning towards Fletch. "If the other hunters or the guards caught the killer while he was wearing your cloak, they'd assume he was you." He reached into his pocket and withdrew a prayer, flipping it over his fingers as he thought, turning to look towards the stage but not really seeing it. "And they kidnapped you. Why? If they wanted all of us chasing after you so they could kill mage-born with impunity, why hold you captive? Why ask you all those questions?"

"Maybe they're just trying to ruin my reputation before they kill me," Fletch said dryly. "I've pissed off a lot of people over the years. Maybe one of them finally had enough and wants to pull everything down around my ears, and make me watch."

"That still doesn't explain the interrogation. I—"

The well-dressed young man without the mask stepped onto the stage. Suken turned his attention forward. Beside him, Fletch rested his elbow on the arm of the seat and propped his chin on his fist. Suken would have to wait until the Coalition was done with whatever they were about to talk about before he continued his conversation with Fletch.

"Friends," the man on stage said, gesturing towards the seated people with one extended hand. His voice was deep and rich, and carried easily over the heads of those assembled. He wore a tightly cut vest of a rich purple so dark it was nearly black, the tiny glass beads sewn into the fabric catching the bright lights of the stage to glitter like miniature stars. His white shirt looked well-made, as did the trousers which belled out slightly above the tops of his knee-high boots. "We gather here today in joined purpose, united in a single desire. The desire for justice, for peace, for unity." A hushed murmur of assent rose from the crowd, people nodding their heads. "I see some new faces in the crowd to-day. Let's welcome them to our family, shall we?"

Suken glanced around, hoping he wasn't expected to stand up, or anything. But the only response to the man's words was a round of polite applause from the audience. When it faded away, the man bowed gracefully. "I am Teric," he said. "I lead these meetings, though not the Coalition as a whole. We govern ourselves through republican means, which are far better suited to government than those the high mages utilize. Those of you who are new to a meeting, know that you are welcome, and that your voice holds as much weight here as any other."

Fletch snorted. When Suken raised an eyebrow at him, Fletch whispered, "If they were a true republic, the high-and-mighties would be sitting down on the floor with the poor, instead of perched up here, looking down on them."

"As has been our tradition," Teric continued, "we'll open to-night's meeting with a testimonial. Lord Grey?" The man in the purple vest stepped aside, allowing a man in a dark grey tunic and unornamented full face mask to take the stage. The wide fabric ties of Grey's mask concealed his hair, falling from the knot at the back of his head halfway down his back. Lord Grey looked out over the crowd as he stepped forward.

He cleared his throat and began, his voice rough and husky. *Sounds rougher than should be normal,* Suken thought. *He's either sick, or trying to mask his voice. Maybe he's a famous actor, or singer, or orator.*

"Gathered Lords and Ladies," Grey said. "My story is . . . difficult to tell."

A moment of silence, in which he seemed to be gathering himself. "You're among family," a voice from the box beside Suken and Fletch rang out. Suken glanced in that direction, though there was a wall in his way. The speaker must be sitting with Uakari in the next box.

Fletch sat up. "That's our mark," he whispered.

"Garron?" Suken whispered back.

Fletch nodded.

"Speak, friend, and be at peace," Garron intoned.

Grey looked up in the direction of Garron's voice, the blank face of the mask hiding any expression he may have had. He took a deep breath, his shoulders rising and falling, and began. "Like many of you, my tale is one of tragedy," he said. His voice took on a biting, hard tone. "I was married twenty years ago. We had two little girls. They loved to sing." He coughed and looked down, and as he continued, his hand slowly curled into a fist at his side. "The creature attacked while I was at work. A shifter," he imbued the word with venom. "Mad, seeking money. It broke in, and finding my wife and children at home, it . . ." Lord Grey trailed off. Suken could see how violently the man was shaking from here. "I didn't recognize their bodies," he finally said, the trembling carrying through to his voice. It rose in anger, losing a little of the harsh masking quality. "It had taken a knife to them, while they were still alive. Carved out their eyes and their tongues. Chopped off their fingers. Scalped them. Raped them." A woman in the seats below let out a quiet sob, lifting one hand to her mouth.

"One of my daughters lived. She'll never be able to walk down a street without people staring and whispering behind their hands. She'll never bear children. She'll never hold my hand or sing. That . . . *creature* . . ." He clenched his jaw. The man who had begun the meeting put his hand on Grey's shoulder. After a moment, Grey looked up. "It gave her the same treatment as it did the others," he said harshly. "But she was strong. She held on, lying in her own blood beside the bodies of her mother and sister, until I arrived home to find them.

"I managed to get her to an ardein. By the grace of the Light, she was saved." He took a deep, shuddering breath. "Love?" he said, his voice now gentle and loving, but broken with grief. He held out one hand. Every head turned towards the curtains masking the side of the stage. Slowly, a girl in her early teens stepped out, her face covered by a white gauzy veil. Her dark hair hung in two thick braids, one over each shoulder. The dress she wore was made of simple grey silk, with long, wide sleeves falling down to conceal her hands and a high collar that hid everything from the edge of her jaw down. The man in the purple jacket, Teric, took her arm gently and led her to her father.

Lord Grey spoke to her quietly for a moment, and she nodded. Lord Grey raised one shaking hand to lift her veil. Suken swallowed and looked away. One of her eyes was little more than a dark hole carved into her head. Old scars crisscrossed her face in a web of pinkish, puckered skin. Her mouth was pulled up slightly on one side, revealing white teeth which seemed too perfect in such a ruined face. Suken heard several women and men in the audience let out shocked cries, and voices rose in angry murmurs.

Fletch let out another snort. Suken looked at him, aghast.

"Listen to 'em," Fletch said, his voice caustic but low enough not to carry. He lifted his voice into a falsetto. "'Oh, how horrid! Someone should save us from all those evil, evil mage-born.'" He shook his head, his mouth twisted into a dissatisfied frown. "As if so-called *normal* people haven't done worse." His eyes flicked to the box-seats opposite them briefly.

The murmur of angry voices below them dimmed back into silence. Suken turned his attention back to Teric, who was lowering his hands, having raised them to call for silence. Lord Grey lowered the veil lovingly over the ruin of his daughter's face. Before the veil fluttered into place, Suken thought he saw a single tear glistening beneath her good eye, and felt his heart wrench in sympathy.

"Thank you, Lord Grey," Teric called, his face drawn in anguish. "All of us will offer our prayers to the Light in the morning, for the peace of your wife and your daughters." The murmur of assent rose again. "We will be accepting donations in the entryway at the conclusion of tonight's meeting. Please remember that we are a community, a family drawn together by one unified desire. The pain of one is the pain of all." He waited a moment, watching as Lord Grey led his daughter off the stage, and turned back to the audience. "We have another in the audience tonight who needs our thoughts and our prayers. One who lost a child only two nights ago to a creature able to change its face, a creature more monster than man." He lowered his head, folding his hands. "We have all suffered loss in one way or another from the monsters roaming our streets, the monsters the mages have loosed upon us. One's suffering is not greater than any others, but the loss of a child is a grievous loss. Know that you are not alone, that we all share your pain, and that we are here to support you."

Quiet murmurs of assent. Suken glanced to his left, at the wall hiding Lord Garron. *How are you involved in this, Garron? Did the loss of your daughter drive you to . . .*

Suken's eyes narrowed. No. . . . That couldn't be right. Fletch had been kidnapped days before Garron's daughter had been taken. If Garron had been in on this, he'd been in on it from the start.

"And now," Teric continued below, breaking the solemn silence, "we move on to the night's main topic of discussion. We have an important matter to discuss, one which has the potential to affect us all."

The already hushed crowd grew even more attentive. Teric assumed a stiff posture. "I'm sure you've all heard the rumors of the thief known as Greencloak, and his current string of murders."

Suken glanced at Fletch. The thief sat with his chin propped on his fist, frowning.

"Earlier this week, we received a message from the man himself. I'd like to read it to you all here and now, as he asked that I do."

The reaction to this was almost as loud as when Lord Grey's daughter had removed her veil. Fletch's languid expression hardened. He leaned forward, his eyes fixed on the man on stage.

"Did you send them something?" Suken asked.

"No."

Teric cleared his throat and pulled a piece of parchment from his jacket. "Dearest members of the Coalition. I am Fletch Greencloak."

"They know your first name," Suken said.

"Yes, I'd gathered. Thank you."

"I thought you said you didn't give them any real answers."

"I didn't," Fletch replied, his expression darkening even further.

"You may have heard rumors of the murders I am accused of committing," Teric read. "They are true."

The hushed murmurs faded into dead silence. Teric continued, raising his voice. "But what the guards won't put on the warrants, what the broadsheets won't print, is my purpose for these murders. My motive. You see . . . my victims have only been mage-born.

"I have taken these steps only because all other measures have failed. I've watched you for years. The High Council refuses to listen to your pleas. Every day, more of your friends and family are lured into madness and corruption. They are forced to take steps no sane person should ever be forced to make . . . forced to become monsters who in turn prey upon you. That all ends now.

"Until today, I was one of you in purpose but not in name. I urge you to take up arms. Officially name me as one of you, and join me in cleansing our city of the darkness which has corrupted it for far too long. Join me . . . and help me to make the change which you've cried out for, cries which have until now fallen on deaf ears.

"Words have failed, so we are forced to take the only path remaining to us . . . that of action. We must create a movement the High Mages cannot ignore. We must raise not only our voices, but our *hands* in order to protect our streets, our children, our families. Join me . . . and we *will* succeed."

A moment of silence followed that. Suken felt a shiver run down his spine. Beside him, Fletch sat back in his seat, staring at the man on-stage. "They're trying to make me a fucking figurehead," Fletch said, sounding completely at sea. "Why in bloody glass and caal-fire are they trying to make *me* a figurehead?"

"Clearly, because they haven't met you," Suken said.

Fletch threw him a glare.

Suken looked down into the theater, where people were talking quietly to one another. The facts slowly came together in his mind, like pieces in a mosaic joining to form a picture. "Because the Valley District admires you," he said slowly. "There's a lot of anger at the mages down there. You steal from the people who oppress them, you flaunt that cloak of yours in the face of tradition. . . . You do what they all wish they could, and you get away with it." He looked at Fletch, seeing him in a new light. Seeing him the way the poor would. "No wonder none of them would talk when I went down there looking for information about you."

"That's because you're a cat," Fletch said dismissively.

"No," Suken said. "It's because they *love you,* Fletch. Or rather, they love Greencloak. Greencloak, the legendary thief. The man who doesn't adhere to the established rules, the man who shows the mages that they're not perfect, they're not infallible. You're a hero to them."

"A hero." Fletch snorted. "If they'd ever met me I'd disabuse them of that notion damn quick."

"Which is exactly why they captured you," Suken said, tapping his prayer on the arm of the chair. "To keep you from revealing yourself. If you suddenly showed up and refuted all their claims, think how stupid they'd look. They were asking you all those questions to learn about your personality, so the killer could pretend to be you believably to anyone who had actually talked to you, just in case."

"Once they knew enough about me, they were planning to kill me," Fletch said, picking up Suken's path of thought. "They were going to let that bastard who's wearing my cloak take my place, *become* me. Pick up the mantle of my reputation like he picked up my disguise, and become a leader for these deluded sons of bitches."

Below, Teric finally raised his hands for silence. "We have with us today several members of the city guard," the man announced. "Are this thief's claims true? Is he only killing mage-born?"

One man stood, turning to address the audience. "Yes," he called, his voice muffled by his mask. "It's true."

"Normally we wouldn't condone murder," Teric called, "but who can complain about one less mage-born thief or killer on the street? One less criminal to rape, or maim, or murder decent civilians like you, or I, or our children? Greencloak is right. The High Mages' Council refuses to listen to us. They ignore our pleas, turn deaf ears to the suffering of our children. The guards, even those sympathetic to our cause, can do nothing without the blessing of the Council. *We* are the ones who must stand aside and watch as the mage-born murder our children and rape our daughters and promised ones. *We* are the ones who must suffer.

Our hands are bound by the Council's greed and blind devotion to its own wicked creations.

"The question to be put before you tonight, brothers and sisters, is whether the actions of this thief should be condoned and embraced by the Coalition. Up until this point, we have kept our actions limited to matters of state. Greencloak's actions have the potential to fling the Coalition into the sight of every man, woman and child in the city . . . but will such attention help our cause, or hinder it? It is not a decision which should be rushed. Please take the next hour to discuss among yourselves which action we should take before we put the matter to a majority vote."

His voice faded to echoes, swallowed by the rising storm of voices from below.

Chapter Eighteen

Suken watched as the people below began getting to their feet, talking animatedly with one another, gesturing. The majority nodded slowly as they listened to their neighbors. Only a few stood with their arms crossed, deep in troubled thought. "They're going to vote in favor," he said, chilled.

Fletch muttered a curse under his breath and stood, staring down into the theater. "So I go down there," he said. "Right now. Do exactly what they hoped I wouldn't. Reveal myself, tell them who I am and that that bastard down there's full of shit."

"No," Suken said, shaking his head. "You don't have any way to prove that you're . . . well, you. And if you did that, anyone here who's in on the plan will know exactly where you are. As soon as you stepped off that stage, they'd kill you. The original plan is still the best. . . . We find the person they're setting up to be you. Grab him, bring him in to the guards. Once they get the truth out of him, they'll have to clear your name. Then we can begin dismantling the Coalition's claims, with the backing of the guards."

"And he's going to willingly tell them everything he knows?" Fletch said. "When he knows that he'd be facing the noose?"

"I can demand a Truthread," Suken said.

Fletch stared at him.

"What?" Suken asked, exasperated.

"You do know what'll happen to you if the person we haul in is innocent?"

Suken did. If he subjected an innocent to a Truthread and the insanity that inevitably followed, he'd be executed. Immediately.

"So we make sure he's guilty," he said. "Very sure."

Fletch snorted. "You want to risk your neck, fine by me. But we still need to find the bloody bastard."

"Lord Garron's in the next box," Suken said, jerking a thumb towards the wall. "He's the only one that we're certain is in on this."

"He's probably alone except for your fat friend," Fletch said, his fingers drifting to a small wooden case on his belt. "These boxes aren't big enough for all his guards. You and I can take him easily enough, make him talk."

"I'm willing to overlook a little thievery," Suken said, "but not torture."

"No? Even if it'll save your life, and mine?"

If I start down that road, Suken thought uneasily, *how far will it lead me?*

"No. No torture. But . . ." he sat back in the chair, considering. "Maybe I can convince him to let me in on the plan."

"How do you plan to do that?" Fletch asked. "Say, 'Excuse me, sir, you don't know me but I was responsible for the death of your daughter and I'd like in on your clandestine operation'?"

"Exactly," Suken said with a grin.

Fletch blinked. "That was sarcasm," he said. "In case you weren't aware."

"Trust me on this," Suken said, playing out the potential conversation in his head. "It'll work. I'll run into him on our way out and talk him into it."

"And what's my part in this little plan of yours?" Fletch said.

Suken drummed his fingers on the arm of the chair. "For the

actual conversation, you should probably hide," he said. "But you should follow us, in case I need help."

"I think you've let all that hero talk about me give you the wrong impression," Fletch said dryly. "I'm not one to go rushing in to save the damsel in distress. Especially not," he lifted his leg and propped it up on the railing, gesturing at the bandages wrapped around his lower leg, "like this."

"Didn't stop you from saving my life when that sicario came after me," Suken pointed out.

"Obviously you're a bad influence on me," he said sourly.

Suken looked down into the theater, thinking. Fletch was right. He was injured, and from what Suken had seen so far, not very good at hand-to-hand combat. Suken was on his own, then. Well, nothing new there.

"Fine," he said. "I'll do it alone. But stay nearby. I'll need to find you again once I find out who's framing you."

"So you use that ever-flapping mouth of yours to get him to open up, and I get to wait around with my feet up. You were right, kitten. You *are* useful. Or at least, your mouth is." He grinned.

Suken sighed, resolving to let that one lie.

"If you ever decide to start making an honest living," Fletch said, lacing his hands behind the back of his head, "Let me know. The world could use a few more thieves almost as talented as I am."

"If I *did* decide to be a thief," Suken said, "I'd be better than you."

Fletch laughed. It was a pure, genuine laugh, with none of the sarcasm or anger that Suken had grown so accustomed to hearing from Fletch. "Better than me? Keep dreaming, kitten."

"You know," Suken said, "I'm starting to think that you're not nearly as unpleasant as you seem to want people to think you are."

"You caught me on a bad week," Fletch said.

"So you're not usually this sarcastic and bitter?"

"No, I'm usually worse." He leaned back and propped his other foot on the railing, crossing one ankle over the other. "So, what do we do in the meantime?" He looked down into the theater where people still milled around, discussing the proposal. "We've got under an hour before they come to a decision down there." He eyed Suken. "I could think of a thing or two to keep us occupied. Provided you're quiet, that is."

"Not interested," Suken said, though some deep, dark part of him wondered if that were entirely true.

"Only because you haven't had me yet."

"Guess I'll never find out. What a shame. Don't suppose you have a set of cards on you?" Suken asked.

"Fresh out," Fletch replied evenly.

"Well, we could talk." He still hadn't managed to learn much about the thief.

"You? *Talk?*" Fletch affected a shocked expression.

"Very funny," Suken said dryly.

"I suppose it's better than sitting here in silence," Fletch said. "So. Why did you become a bounty hunter?"

"What?"

"You wanted to talk, kitten. I'm talking."

Suken looked away.

"Not exactly an easy job, bounty hunting," Fletch continued. "You bastards have almost as high of a mortality rate as thieves. So why? Why do it? I've always been curious, but I've never had the opportunity to ask one of you."

Suken didn't talk about his past to many people. Avara knew, obviously. And Terri knew most of it. But Suken didn't like saddling other people with his problems. Better to deal with them himself, and give everyone else a smile and a shoulder to cry on when they needed it. People had enough problems in their own lives without hearing about his, too.

"Why are you a thief?" he countered. "I imagine our answers would be pretty similar."

"I doubt it," Fletch said dryly. "You need motivation? Fine. You show me yours, I'll show you mine."

"You'll tell me why you became a thief?" Suken said, raising one eyebrow.

"Maybe. If your story's good enough."

The chance to learn Fletch Greencloak's history. Suken's interest immediately spiked. What *had* driven Fletch to become who he was? Where had he come from? Suken could learn it all. All he had to do was tell his own story. It was tempting. . . . Very tempting.

And there was something else, too. Something deeper than his curiosity. Of all the people he'd ever met in his life, Fletch might actually *understand* what had driven Suken to do what he'd done. He thought of the den, of the kids, of the way they looked up to Fletch. Thought of how Fletch was protecting them, just as Suken had when he'd refused to tell the guards about them. He closed his eyes for a moment. Could he open up, reveal his life to someone he'd only known for a day?

If he holds up his side of the bargain, he thought, it'll be worth it.

"It wasn't just one thing," he said, the words coming slowly despite the fact that he'd made his decision. "When I was young, my mother wanted me to be an artist, like her. And my father. . . ." It had been so long that he had trouble remembering their faces. But he remembered the rough calluses on his father's oil-stained hand as he'd ruffled Suken's hair, remembered sitting on his father's lap listening to stories as he drifted towards sleep. "He worked in the undercity. Structural engineer. I started school at ten, but when I was fourteen . . ." he paused, the words coming even more slowly, like syrup oozing out of a pitcher. "Both of my parents died. It was an accident. Just . . . a stupid accident. My mother had gone down to the undercity to bring my father some lunch. There was a cave-in."

"Afterward, my uncle took in my little brother and I." He lowered his voice, the memories flaring to life in intermittent bursts. "We both learned why my mother hadn't liked him. He was abusive. On top of that, he didn't know what to do with a couple of kids, and pulled me out of school to watch my brother. I spent all of my time trying to keep up with my classmates, burying myself in my studies. My friends brought me assignments and books and tried to help me, but I'd never been much of a scholar. My brother tried to talk to me, to spend time with me, and I . . . I resented him for it. For trying to take my attention and time away from where I wanted it to be." That hurt to admit. "There were good times between he and I after our parents died, but not many. So. . . . He ran away. Went to the Valley. Joined up with one of the street gangs, like yours. From what little I managed to find out, he ran with them for four years before . . ." the pain rose up, closing his throat and bringing tears to his eyes. He swore under his breath and looked away, hoping Fletch hadn't seen. Chance, it had been four *years* since he'd lost his brother. Was he ever going to get over it?

"Go on," Fletch said. "Your brother ran with the Valley kids for four years. That'd make you . . . eighteen. Then . . . ?"

"Then the warrants went up," Suken replied harshly. "For him and another of the kids. Supposedly they'd been involved in the death of a guard. I managed to track them down, with the help of one of my uncle's friends. It was my first warrant, really, though I was unlicensed at the time. I turned my brother and his friend over to the guards, intending to pay off their slave debts myself." He looked away. "But he and the other kid were brought before the High Council for some reason. It didn't make any sense. . . . They were only kids, barely ten years old. By the time I managed to get an audience with one of the High Mages, they were gone. Sold to the slave markets by some black market dealer working in the cells. And then they just . . . disappeared." Suken closed his eyes and ran a hand back through his hair. "My uncle's friend and I tracked them to the coast, but the trail vanished. There was no ship scheduled to arrive at that stretch of coast, and no one had seen one. It was like they turned into smoke and drifted away."

"So you became a bounty hunter in the hopes that you'd get good enough to be able to find him again?" Fletch asked.

"Sort of," Suken said quietly. "The mages know something. I know they do. There's a case-file about the event at the Guild, and I'm certain that if I could get my hands on it, I'd learn something. But it was marked as classified, first rank only."

"You hunters and your points," Fletch muttered, rolling his eyes. "Why don't you ask a first rank hunter to get it for you?"

Suken shook his head. "It doesn't work that way. If you don't have a warrant or some other connection to a case, you can't get access, and classified rank one files can't be brought outside of the record room. Once I'm first rank I can use a loophole in the Guild's bylaws to open it back up, because one of the marks was my brother. A direct relation. But no one else can. I'm the last person left alive in my family."

"Your uncle's gone?"

Suken nodded. "When we got back from the coast, we learned he'd been killed by one of the cartels. He waited too long to pay back his debts."

"Debts which were then passed to you, I assume."

"Yes." Suken shifted uncomfortably. "That's another reason I'm a hunter, paying off those debts. I didn't have time to finish my schooling, the cartel wouldn't give me that long."

"Anoltin?" Fletch asked, naming one of several active cartels in the city.

"O'Carfin," Suken replied, the name leaving a bitter taste in his mouth. "My uncle left me all his equipment, and I already had some contacts in the guild. So I signed up. And . . . along the way, I discovered I was good at hunting. Better than anything else I'd tried. That . . . felt good, you know?"

"Yes," Fletch replied quietly. "I know that feeling."

"I gave up on school and dedicated myself to hunting. I've been paying off my uncle's debts, but it's slow."

"So you do this because you're good at it and you make enough money to pay off the o'Carfins, but mostly because you want to work your way far enough up the ranks to get that file on your brother."

"Yes," Suken said. "I suppose that about sums it up."

Fletch stared down into theater, his face uncharacteristically solemn. "The most important thing I've learned about thieving," he said slowly, "is that there's *always* more than one way to get what you want." He looked at Suken. "Are you sure bounty hunting is the quickest path to getting what *you* want?"

Suken narrowed his eyes. "What do you mean by that?"

"I'm the son of a whore and a mage," Fletch said. "Bet you can imagine how much of my father I saw, growing up."

Suken felt as if his curiosity were pulling him in two directions. He desperately wanted to know what Fletch had meant with that question. . . . But now that the thief had changed the subject, Suken found himself just as curious about the thief's past.

"I went and found him once," Fletch continued. "Managed to convince my mother to describe him to me, hunted him down. Watched him at some ball one of his high-and-mighty friends held. Saw firsthand how affluent they are. How much money they waste on stupid things, like tapestries woven with silver thread, statues, jewelry. Things that serve no purpose except to make themselves seem more beautiful, or rich, or powerful. Or all three." His voice hardened. "He didn't give a damn about some tribal whore he'd once fucked, or her son. Even if he'd known I existed, he wouldn't have cared. He didn't care about anyone or anything outside of his own little circle of greed. If he and his high-and-mighty friends spent half as much money helping the poor as they did on their own trivial pursuits, the Valley District wouldn't exist. Not the way it does now, anyway." He leaned forward. "For years, that was what I thought. But as I got older, I started to realize the truth. The mages *do* think about the poor. They know damn well about the poverty and the disease and the starvation. They'd have to be blind not to. They walk past it every day, ignoring the beggars and the orphans holding out their hands and pleading for a dropped aeran or two. But they don't help. Do you know why?"

"I've never really put much thought into it."

"They want to keep the poor where they are," Fletch said, an edge of anger creeping into his voice. "They rely on poverty to gain new test subjects for their experiments and to line their own pockets, living in luxury. They force people into a life of crime, then sell them into slavery. This city," he emphasized the next words, "*is broken.*"

"What does that have to do with me and my brother's file?" Suken asked.

"What you said earlier was right," Fletch said, sitting back again, the rage fading from his face. "I steal from the mages and the merchants to show them that they're not infallible. They can be hurt. They can lose things too. They care so much about their bloody money and jewels and statues? Fine. I'll take them. Like they're taking the lives of the poor by not doing a damned thing to help them. And you," he met Suken's eyes, "lost something to them, too."

"The mages didn't kill my brother," Suken said. "It was a black market slaver who somehow got into the cells." He speared Fletch with a dark look. "A *criminal.*"

"So they didn't hand him over themselves," Fletch said. "They do allow the slave markets to exist, though. How noble, how compassionate, to turn a blind eye to people selling ten year olds to slave-masters."

Suken had harbored anger towards the slave market for years over what had happened, but he'd never extended that anger towards the system as a whole. Should he have? Was Fletch right?

It was a disturbing thought.

"Work with me, Anisaria," Fletch said softly, dropping his feet from the railing and leaning in towards him. "Turn this temporary alliance into a partnership. You're talented, and you've got a good head on your shoulders. But if you stay with the hunters, they'll turn you into one of *them.* They'll break that idealism of yours into fragments and turn it into something else. Something darker. Something dangerous. Give the Hunters' Guild a year and you'd have turned me in the moment you found me, innocence be damned."

No I wouldn't have, Suken thought, but a tiny portion of his mind whispered, *Are you sure? You were already planning on hunting him down as soon as this job was over.*

"Give *me* a year," Fletch said softly, "and I'll turn you into the best damn thief this city has ever seen, other than myself. Together, we could do anything. Steal anything. Show the high-and-mighties that they're not all-powerful." He leaned closer and lowered his voice. "I've got contacts, Anisaria. More than you can imagine. Once this business is all over, I could get those debts paid off in a day. I could even help you find your brother, if he's still alive. I know things about the undercity a cat like you will never learn, not if you asked a hundred sources. A thousand. Call it repayment for the help you've given me on this. All you need to do," Fletch's eyes seemed to pull Suken in closer, "is say yes."

Suken shook his head, his thoughts whirling. For the last five years, he'd worked tirelessly to become a bounty hunter. He'd practiced, and studied, and memorized, and passed the tests the guards and the guild insisted on for new hunters. He'd sacrificed money, time, friends, a normal social life. All so he could work his way up the ranks and get that classified file on his brother.

And now Fletch Greencloak offered him an alternative. Could Suken do that? Turn his back on everything he'd worked for, all the friends he'd made, everything he'd learned, and become a . . . a criminal? With Fletch's help, he could bypass years of effort. He was certain that together, even if Fletch's supposed contacts didn't work out, they could break into the guild and steal the file. Together, they might be able to find his little brother, if he was even still alive.

But by the time Suken found him, would Suken be the person he wanted to be? He'd always lived his life by a set of moral codes. He'd cut a few corners here and there, yes, but he'd never purposely done something illegal before tonight. Despite what Fletch said about the government, Suken truly believed that the law was just. Without it, the city would dissolve into chaos. Murderers like the one he and Fletch were hunting now would run free, people would take whatever they wanted. Then it wouldn't just be the poor who suffered. . . . It would be everyone. The merchants, the mages, the people going about their daily lives.

The system might be broken, but it was the only one they had, and without it, things would be even worse.

Below them, the man without the mask retook the stage. He lifted his arms, and the people in the theater began finding their seats.

"Can I think about it?" Suken asked slowly.

"Sure." Fletch sounded relieved, for some reason.

"All in favor," the man said solemnly, "of countenancing Greencloak's actions and inducting him officially into the Coalition?"

Almost every hand in the theater went up.

"Idiots," Fletch muttered.

"The motion passes," the man said with a broad smile. "The next meeting will be in two nights, when Greencloak himself will speak. Meeting adjourned." The people below stood again, chatting and smiling.

"The killer," Suken breathed. He looked at Fletch. "If Garron doesn't lead us to him, we know where he'll be, and when."

"I'd rather take him out before then," Fletch said darkly. "He knows about the kids, and there's more than one mage-born among them."

"I agree." Suken stood. "I need to catch Garron before he

leaves. Remember . . . follow me if you can, but be careful not to get spotted."

Fletch watched Anisaria step out of the box, staring at the curtain as it swished closed behind him. The kitten's story hadn't been what Fletch had expected. Money, fame, talent . . . all of these were understandable reasons for getting into the bounty hunting profession, and Fletch had expected at least one of them. But all that about his brother, and the case-file. . . . At first Fletch had bristled, thinking that the man was lying to him, coming up with a story that made him out to be some sort of hero. No one was so altruistic that they'd give up their entire lives in a misguided hunt for a lost family member. When you lost someone, you moved on. That was how it was.

But the longer Anisaria talked, the more Fletch had believed him. The kitten was a talented hunter, but a miserable failure of a liar. And there was something about the story, something that had struck true with a memory buried deep in Fletch's past. If one part of the story was true. . . .

So Fletch had made his offer. The words had left his lips with hardly any consideration, flying free like birds, as if they had minds of their own. And when he'd finished, he'd stopped, shocked at them. He'd expected and half hoped that Anisaria would turn him down outright. But at the same time, he'd found himself longing for the kitten to say yes.

I've never wanted a partner before, he thought. *What's so different about him? When did I start seriously considering this, and why?* He shook his head once, trying to clear the thoughts away. But one lingered like a scared child clinging to his parent's leg. *What has depending on someone else ever gotten me except betrayal, loss, and pain?*

Well, what was done was done. He couldn't retract the words, or the offer.

Nor do you want to, a part of him whispered.

If the kitten took him up on it, well . . . he'd have a partner. And the things he'd said back there hadn't been false. Things *would* be easier if he had someone else to work with. Someone to depend on, to trust. Someone to watch his back.

He'd thought that he'd had that once. He'd been wrong.

Fletch turned away from those memories and forced his mind back to the present. He opened the curtain a crack and peeked out into the hall.

"Excuse me, Lord Garron?" Anisaria called. The hunter stood a few steps down the hall, the receding backs of Garron, his guards, and the Fat Man just past him.

The man turned back, eyes narrowing behind his black mask. "Do I know you?"

"Newcomer," the Fat Man said. A thin film of derisive prevarication floated on top of the words like oil on water. Anisaria probably didn't notice the way the man humored him. Fat Man treated Anisaria like a base commoner, snide condescension lacing every word. It raised the hackles on the back of Fletch's neck. "I let him use my family's box."

"I'm sorry, but I have to admit that I lied about that," Anisaria said. Then, unbelievably, he said, "My name is Suken Anisaria. Lord Garron, I'm the bounty hunter who found your daughter."

Fletch resisted the urge to slap his forehead. He hadn't thought the kitten was *serious* about that.

Garron stiffened.

"I never got a chance to talk to you," Anisaria said.

"What makes you think I'd want to hear whatever it is you have to say?" Garron asked. His voice was cold. "You got my daughter killed."

"I can't imagine the pain you're going through," Anisaria said, "but your anger is misplaced. I tried to *help* your daughter. Tried to save her. To do so I had to let that fucking bastard run off. I might not want him taken down as badly as you do, but I don't ever want to see another little girl like yours die in my arms because of mage-born garbage like him. That's why I came here tonight. . . . Why I'm joining the Coalition."

Come on, Fletch thought. *There's no way he's going to buy—*

"You're serious about this?" Garron said.

You've got to be kidding me.

"Yes," Anisaria replied, taking a step closer to him. "I'm trying to find the bastard who did this to your daughter, sir. And . . . I wanted to ask, if I find him . . ." his voice roughened, and he clenched his fist at his side. "If I find him, would you prefer it if I brought him to you first?"

Garron didn't say anything.

"You might not want to see his face," Anisaria said. "I wouldn't blame you if that were the case. But if it were me . . ." he shrugged. "I thought I'd offer you the choice. A few minutes alone with the bastard who took your daughter." He lowered his voice. Fletch barely heard him as he continued, "Maybe more than a few minutes, if you take my meaning."

Garron didn't unlock his gaze from Anisaria's. The two men stared at one another for a long moment, the tension in the hallway as thick as the humidity outside. "Follow me," Garron said, his tone dark, "and we'll ascertain whether or not you and your talents will be an asset to this organization."

Chapter Nineteen

Fletch followed Anisaria as he and the others descended the stairs, joining the throng of people oozing towards the lobby. He stepped into the crowd and blended in with them, squeezing his way through until he was close enough to keep an eye on the group. Garron led Anisaria through the main doorway, turned right, and headed towards a door in the lobby. He said something softly to the Fat Man, who nodded and took up a post beside the door. The guards joined the crowd, heading for a table piled with food. The Fat Man made as if he were examining a vase standing on a marble plinth, but his true reason for being there was patently obvious to anyone with eyes.

Anisaria and Garron vanished inside, leaving the Fat Man to block Fletch's way.

Fletch growled a curse. There were other ways into the back corridors of the theater, but by the time he made it there, he'd have lost Anisaria's trail.

Gods below, I'm thinking like a bounty hunter. This kitten's definitely a bad influence on me.

He shook his head and reached into the case at his belt, palming one of his unpoisoned needles. Behind him, in clear view, hundreds of people milled about, chatting with one another. The guards were still back there, too, within shouting range.

Fletch walked up to the Fat Man and stabbed him in the shoulder with the needle.

The man spun towards him, raising his hand to his shoulder and letting out a squeak of surprise and pain. "What—"

"Quiet." Fletch lifted one hand so the man could see the needle glinting between his index and middle fingers. "I'd say you've got about ten minutes before you start feeling the effects of the poison I stabbed you with."

The Fat Man flushed a deep crimson. "Look here—"

"After that ten minutes," Fletch interrupted, "you'll have approximately three before you start bleeding from your eyes and nose and lose control of your motor skills. Another two of intense agony and you'll be dead."

The man's piggy little eyes widened.

"I have the antidote," Fletch said quietly. "And I might be inclined to give it to you, provided you cooperate."

"With what?" the Fat Man whispered.

"Your friend there went somewhere with my partner," he snapped. The next words died on his lips as he realized what he'd just said. *I'm already calling him my partner. Gods below.* He shook himself and continued, "You're going to bring me to them."

The Fat Man looked as if he were about to faint. "I . . . I don't . . ."

"Slow painful death, or antidote. Your choice."

The remaining color bled from his face, leaving it milky pale.

One of the guards sauntered over, a plate piled high with food balanced on one hand. "Everything all right?" he asked.

"Fine," the Fat Man said, his voice barely a squeak.

Fletch draped his arm over the Fat Man's shoulders, fighting back a grimace of distaste. "My friend here was about to bring me on a tour of the backstage area," he said, and dropped the guard a wink.

The guard raised one eyebrow.

"Yes," the Fat Man said. "Yes, that's, um. That's what . . . That's true."

"He's shy," Fletch said with as lecherous a grin as he could manage.

The guard rolled his eyes and turned away.

"Eight minutes," Fletch said, dropping the playful tone from his voice.

Fat Man gulped. "Follow me," he said.

He opened the door and led Fletch down a series of narrow, twisting hallways lined with curtains. Actors' changing rooms, no doubt. They passed a connecting hallway to their right through which Fletch glimpsed the lights of the stage through a complicated labyrinth of ropes, set pieces and curtains, and continued on down the hallway. The doors transitioned from curtains to solid wood, each labeled with a placard. There were two rooms for props, four for sets, one for lights and rigging, and, at the end of the hallway down the right arm of a t-intersection, one labeled simply "costumes."

Fletch waited as the big man pulled the door to the costume room open, reaching over to the wall to slide a small metal panel to one side. Luminaries hanging from the ceiling burst into light, illuminating a huge room lined with hundreds of metal racks on wheels. Costumes hung pressed so tightly against one another on each rack that some of the metal rods were beginning to sag downward from the sheer weight. The room smelled of dust and the herbs used to keep moths from eating fabric.

"They went down there," Fat Man said, waving one shaking hand toward a rack of clothes.

Fletch walked over to it and pushed the clothes aside to see a door set into the stone wall. He looked back over his shoulder. "Where does it lead?"

Fat Man wrung his hands. "A hallway," he whimpered, his voice reed-thin. "There are cells. We've been keeping the last victim there. Garron wanted him to suffer before we had him killed.

Based on what he said to your friend, I'd wager he's going to give him a shot at him, too."

"Last victim?" Fletch pressed. "What do you mean, last victim?"

The Fat Man started trembling. "Please, I've shown you where they went. The antidote?"

Fletch's voice hardened as he repeated his last question. "What do you mean, last victim?"

"I can pay you," Fat Man whispered. "As much as you want."

The idea of bleeding the Fat Man dry of both his riches and whatever information he possessed pricked Fletch's interest, but he discounted it. He didn't have time. And besides, if he wanted to transform Rich Fat Man into Poor Fat Man, he could do so any time he pleased. Later, when his reputation wasn't hanging in the balance.

"I don't want aerans," he said. "I want answers."

"Please, I—"

Fletch leaned in close. "It took us seven minutes to walk down here," he said, his voice flat and toneless. "You've got one more before it's too late. Talk. Don't, and I let you choke on your own vomit back here where no one will find you until you're good and ripe."

"Please," Fat Man whimpered, tears glimmering in his eyes. "If I tell you, and they find out, I'm a dead man."

"You're a dead man either way," Fletch snapped. "If you talk, you'll have a chance to make a run for it before they find you."

"He's the last one we're going to kill," Fat Man said, looking around as if he were worried that the other members of the Coalition were hiding around the room, watching him. "Then they're putting the next phase of the plan into motion."

"And that is?" Fletch said, his patience growing thin.

"At the meeting in two nights, the one who volunteered to do the killings will step forward and pretend to be . . . be . . ." Amazingly, his face paled even further. "Oh, Light. It's *you*. You're . . . *him,* aren't you?"

"Who's the killer?" Fletch snarled, stepping forward and reaching down to grab the man's half-mask. He ripped it off, revealing his face. "You've got thirty seconds left, and I haven't liked your answers so far."

"I don't know," Fat Man whimpered, shriveling back away from Fletch. "Only the Hooded Lady knows his name!"

"Is it Garron?" Fletch asked, stepping even closer.

"I told you, I don't know! Please!" His chin wobbled, and tears leaked free of his eyes. "Please, the antidote? I . . . I don't want to die."

Fletch let out his breath in an annoyed exhalation, breath hissing between his teeth. He glanced aside at one of the racks and started. "Is that my cloak?" he asked.

The question had been rhetorical—Fletch knew his cloak when he saw it. But Fat Man glanced over, sweat beading on his forehead and running down his face. "Yes," he said. "Who would think to look for it here?"

Fletch walked over and disbelievingly ran his fingers over the thick green fabric, from the hunter green of the shoulders down to the pale leaf-green at the hem.

He pulled the cloak from the hook and swirled it around to settle on his shoulders. As soon as it touched him, he felt a great weight seem to lift from his mind.

This was who he was. Greencloak, notorious thief, master criminal. A man who took what he wanted, when he wanted. A man whom nothing could stop, not locked doors or walls or steel vaults. He wasn't a wounded man, hunted, scared, running for his life from the cats and the pearls. He was a *legend*, gods damn it.

He let out a slow sigh of relief and felt his mind clear. This cloak was his identity. He'd never let anyone take that away from him again. And those who had this time?

He'd make them pay.

He turned back to Fat Man, who looked as if he were about to faint. "Last question," he said, stalking forward. "And I better like the answer to this one, because your time's almost out."

Fat Man whimpered.

"Ralor Bluvael," Fletch said, his voice barely louder than a breath. He reached down and touched the ring on his finger, remembering the face of the man who had given it to him. "Did this killer of yours murder him, too? Or was it someone else in your organization?"

"Who?" Fat Man whispered. But knowledge lurked in those watery eyes of his. Knowledge, and fear.

Fletch grabbed him by the front of his tunic and pulled him close. "Ralor," he said through gritted teeth, "Bluvael. Also known as Blue. Did you bastards kill him?"

"I d-don't know who th-that is," Fat Man said, voice shaking. "Please . . . the antidote. . . ."

Fletch shoved the man away. "I didn't poison you, you fat fuck," he said as the man staggered back to collapse on his prodigious ass. "Yet."

He flung a needle—poisoned this time—with a lazy flick of his fingers. It flew through the air, straight and true, and stabbed through the Fat Man's tunic, piercing him in the shoulder. "When you wake up," Fletch said, watching as the man fell to his knees, his eyes already drifting closed, "tell your colleagues that I'm coming for them. All of them. And Fletch Greencloak always gets what he wants."

A few minutes after the Fat Man succumbed to sleep (a sleep filled with nightmares of thieves hunting him through the city, Fletch vehemently hoped), Fletch crept down the tunnel into the undercity, his cloak a comforting weight draped over his shoulders. The stone walls here had been covered with wood paneling, making this section of the warren of caves and tunnels beneath the city seem like an extension of the theater above.

He set his teeth, recognizing the hallway. *This is where they kept Vethin and I.* Anger, dark and violent, boiled in his chest. He forced it down.

No time for that. Not now.

He passed several wooden doors, pausing at each and listening for a moment before moving on. On the third try, he heard muffled voices. They weren't raised in anger, but there was a tense timbre to Anisaria's voice, though Fletch couldn't make out any words.

He glanced around. The hallway was lit only by a few dim luminaries. But it was straight as an arrow and offered no hiding places whatsoever if someone were to come and check up on Garron and Anisaria, and whatever it was they were doing in there. Fletch didn't like that.

The room Garron and Anisaria were in had been Vethin's room, once. And that meant . . .

He opened the door beside it. The storeroom, where they'd kept his things. He eased the door shut behind him, throwing the room into blackness. Blackness . . . except for a ray of light shooting out from a crack in the wall between the two rooms. Vethin's blood, barely visible in the dim light, stained the edges of the wood.

Fletch knelt beside it, peering through the crack between the boards.

"—you find him?" Anisaria said. He stood facing the wall behind which Fletch hid, his eyes fixed on Garron. Between them, a man sat tied to a chair, his chin resting on his chest, his long dark hair falling forward to shield his face. The simple shirt he wore was soaked with blood, most of it dried to a deep rust-red.

"It was only a matter of time. We have hundreds of contacts in the Valley," Garron said, circling the seated man like a vulture. He rested one hand on the prisoner's shoulder. "Don't we, Berron?"

The prisoner groaned.

Garron looked up at Suken, his gaze predatory and sharp. "They're filthy," he said, rage trembling beneath the words. "When the mages change them, they break their minds. They're not human, not any longer. What he did to my daughter proves that. You were there. You saw it." He grabbed the man's hair and yanked his head back, revealing a face so covered in bruises that Fletch couldn't make out any features save his obviously broken nose. Both of his eyes were swollen nearly shut, and blood dripped from lacerations along his cheek.

"Barely better than an animal," Anisaria agreed, his voice hard. His face was drawn, his eyes fixed on the prisoner. "And like any rabid animal, he deserves to be put down."

Garron stepped back and folded his arms. "You said you wanted a chance at him," he said. "Well. Here's your chance."

He won't— Fletch thought, but Anisaria drew his fist back and punched the bound shifter in the face.

Fletch blinked, taken aback. Nothing he'd seen of the man up until now had prepared Fletch for that. He'd thought Anisaria was too noble, too honorable, to . . .

The thought trailed off as a realization struck him. *He watched this man kill a little girl. The kitten's letting his anger blind him to what he should be doing . . . getting answers.*

Or . . . was he?

Fletch narrowed his eyes as Anisaria drew back his fist and punched the man again. He clearly wasn't holding back. The shifter rocked in his seat with the blow, blood spattering the wall beside him.

What if I misjudged him all this time? What if he's been playing me, working with the Coallition this whole time, waiting to get me back into one of these cells? He saw it all playing out in his head. Anisaria would feign making a mistake, and Fletch would rush in to help him. Then the jaws of the trap would close around Fletch, and this time there was no Vethin to save him.

The notion was ridiculous. Anisaria had had plenty of chances to betray him before now. But the part of him that was always looking for the next betrayal screamed that he should run, *now*, before it was too late.

"That's enough," Garron said, and Anisaria stopped, blood-stained fist raised, his face dark with anger.

"What are we waiting for? Why not kill him now?"

Garron's smile was familiar. Fletch knew that if he had had a mirror, he'd have seen the same smile on his own face whenever he thought about killing Blue's murderer, and Vethin's.

"He's going to be the last victim," Garron said. The prisoner's head lolled forward, as if he hadn't the strength to hold it upright. Blood trickled from his mouth to drip on his leg. "We need Greencloak to kill one more mage-born. Who better than the shifter who murdered a little girl three nights ago?"

We, Fletch's mind whispered. *He said we.*

"Fuck you," the prisoner whispered.

Garron shot him a venomous look. "You killed my daughter, you fucking bastard. You've bled for that, and now you'll die for it." He looked up at Anisaria. "The Ruddy Amapola," Garron said. "You know the place?"

"Yes."

"Bring him there and leave him gagged and tied in one of the rooms. Wait outside, watching to make certain he doesn't escape. Our man will arrive at half past midnight. He'll ensure that he's seen by a witness or two. After that, make your way back to my manor.

"As for your license," Garron continued, "We'll ensure that your status within the guild is fully reinstated, providing you live up to your end of the bargain regarding the real Greencloak."

"I've already worked my way into the bastard's trust," Anisaria said, still in that cool tone. "He should be showing himself any time now."

"And as soon as he does, your license will be returned to you," Garron said. His tone hardened as he continued, "but not a moment before."

Fletch's blood ran cold. . . . Then hot. The anger surged to the surface like water boiling over, making his heart beat faster and his hands begin to tremble. The thoughts came quickly, bubbling to the surface, his anger building.

He should have known. Given the chance to reinstate his precious license, Anisaria had turned on Fletch. Just like everyone else.

Fletch longed to shove the board aside and rush in, to bury his knife in Anisaria's chest. But cold hard reason steadied him. *He's a better fighter than you. You're injured. And he's got Garron there with him.*

"And if he doesn't show himself?" Anisaria asked. "Does our bargain stand if that sicario you sent to the orphans gets to him before me?"

Fletch started, the blood heated in anger cooling now in sudden horror.

Garron waved one hand dismissively. "Yes, yes. It would be no fault of yours if a plan already set into motion came to fruition."

"Well then," Anisaria said, a smile spreading across his face as he held his hand out to Garron. "Nice working with you, Lord Garron."

You fucking bastard. . . .

Fletch turned and crept out of the store-room, hurrying down the hallway towards the hidden door leading back up into the theater. The pathways would be faster than trying to limp his way through the undercity. Fletch's hand tightened into a fist. He'd warn the kids, get them out of the den and into the safe-houses they had prepared for such an eventuality.

Then he'd make his way to the Ruddy Amapola and pay Anisaria and the bastard who was impersonating him a visit they wouldn't soon forget.

Chapter Twenty

As soon as the door closed after Lord Garron, Suken heaved a sigh of relief, leaning against the wall and closing his eyes, his hands trembling.

Chance. He'd been so certain that Garron would see through him. But he hadn't. Hitting the shifter had taken every ounce of acting ability he'd been able to muster. Suken pushed away from the wall and bent to examine the wall where he'd seen movement earlier. The crack between the boards was empty now.

"Fletch?" he whispered.

Silence. Suken stood, unsurprised. As soon as he'd realized Fletch was there, he'd tried to steer the conversation back to where it had begun, making certain that Fletch heard that the den was in danger. He must have left to go warn them.

Good. In the meantime, Suken would bring Shifter to the precinct for safe-keeping, and head to the Ruddy Amapola. Hopefully Fletch had heard that part of the conversation too, but even if he hadn't, Suken was relatively certain that he could bring in the murderer on his own. Then this whole bloody mess would be over with.

He crossed to the chair where Shifter was tied and looked down at the man. "Well," he said. "Fancy seeing you again."

"Fuck you," the man muttered.

"You know," Suken said, crossing behind the man and kneeling to pull a knife from his boot, "that's an exceptionally stupid way to talk to the person who's saving your life, especially considering how our last meeting ended." He slit the ropes binding the man's hands, noting that the skin around the rope was red and inflamed.

Shifter raised his head and turned it slowly, watching Suken as he rounded the other side of the chair to saw through the thicker ropes around the man's ankles. "You're . . . not bringing me to the whorehouse?"

"No," Suken said, the ropes parting in a cluster of frayed ends. He tucked the knife back into his boot and stood, his voice hardening as he said, "But don't think that the guards will go much easier on you. That girl was ten years old."

Shifter massaged his wrists. "Didn't have a choice."

Suken stepped forward, fists clenched. "Of course you had a choice," he said. "You could have chosen to put the knife away and come with me willingly. If you had, you'd have been in a nice warm cell eating gruel right now, instead of being tortured by the father of the girl you killed."

Shifter barked a laugh. "You fucking idiot," he said, squinting up through bloodied, swollen eyes. "You ruined everything. If *you'd* just turned and walked away, six people would still be alive today, and thousands more wouldn't be in danger."

"Don't try to turn this around on me," Suken warned. "There's no excuse for—"

"I didn't kidnap her for money, you deluded sap," Shifter snarled. "I found out what the Coalition was planning a month ago and kidnapped the girl to try to blackmail her father into turning himself over, along with the rest of these murdering sons of bitches." He stood, swaying before finding his balance. "I was *trying,*" he continued harshly, "to save the lives of every fucking mage-born in this gods damned city. Men, women, children. And that's just the start. I had to put one little girl's life in danger to save *thousands*. Would you have chosen any differently?"

Suken stared at him, at a loss for words. He sat down on the edge of the thin bed, his legs seeming to have stopped working. "How did you find out?" he asked shakily.

"I heard rumors," Shifter said. "Lots of people in the Valley talking about the Coalition lately. So I decided to infiltrate one of their meetings, find out what they were really up to." His face shifted, the bruises remaining but the nose straightening, the eyebrows growing bushier, his hair lightening to grey. As quickly as it happened, Shifter changed his face back with a low groan of pain. "They talked about how they were going to make Greencloak into a martyr," he said, sinking down into the chair again, obviously too weak to stand. "They said they'd contacted him, but he'd turned them down. So they were going to capture him, find out everything they needed to know. They already had a plant, someone close to him, someone who knew him well enough to be able to find him."

"Who?" Suken asked, a chill running down his spine.

"I don't know. They never mentioned any names. After they'd killed him, they were planning on setting up a new Greencloak in his place. Once they'd firmly established him as a hero of the Coalition, they'd let the guards hang him and use the people's outrage over his death to further their own cause."

"The extermination of the mage-born," Suken whispered.

"No," Shifter snapped, looking up. "That's only the first half. The Coalition plans to use the government's execution of Greencloak as a springboard to set into motion a revolution against the mages. They're planning a full-on *coup*, hunter. They're using the blood of the mage-born to grease the gears of war."

Suken stared at him in shock. He remembered his discussion

with Marxen in the Lady's Face days ago. *"I made a mistake. I expected a criminal to do the right thing,"* he'd said.

Chance. Shifter *had* been trying to do the right thing. "Their plan couldn't really work," Suken said shakily. *Could it?*

"The poor are looking for a reason to rise up," Shifter said. "And can you blame them? If the Coalition bastards weren't planning on using the lives of me and my friends to begin this, I'd be marching into battle with them."

Lady's breath. He's right. Suken thought of the people he knew in the Valley, about how dissatisfied they were with the current state of the country. Born Talented was born lucky, as the saying went. And if you weren't Talented, well . . .

Suken stood. "Get up," he said. "I'm taking you to the guards."

"Thought you said you were *saving* my life," Shifter said harshly. "Bloody guards will hang me for killing that little girl."

"No," Suken said, "they won't. With no evidence or witnesses or a full written confession, they'd have to pardon you."

"They have a witness," Shifter said slowly. "You."

"Only if I testify."

Shifter stared at him in obvious disbelief.

Suken grabbed the man's arm and hauled him to his feet. "After I leave you with them, I'm going to get the bastard who's been doing all the killing, and I'm going to haul him straight to the High Council chambers and demand a Truthread. Once they pull the truth from inside his bloody head, along with the names of all the other members of the Coalition, the lot of them will be arrested for treason. Then, during your trial, I'll testify in your defense. Tell the judge how you tried to stop it all." He pulled the man closer. "You'll still have to answer for that little girl's death," he said his voice harsher than he'd intended. He forced himself to soften his tone as he continued, "But I'll tell them why you did it. You'll get off with a steep fine, probably a slave sentence. But it's better than the gallows."

Shifter stared at him.

"What?" Suken snapped.

"You'd do that," Shifter said slowly, "for a mage-born murderer?"

"I wouldn't do it for someone who murdered out of greed, or spite, or anger," Suken replied. "But for someone who made a bad choice in order to try to save hundreds of lives? Yes. I'll testify in your defense. Provided," he raised one finger, "that you, in turn, tell them everything you told me. Especially the part about Greencloak being framed."

"He your friend, or something?"

"Or something," Suken agreed, sending a silent prayer to the Lady for Fletch's safety.

Chapter Twenty-One

Fletch ran through the undercity, his limp growing more pronounced as the pain in his injured leg steadily grew worse. He panted for breath, hoping that he wasn't too late.

Another three turnings, he thought, passing the Red Lady and slowing to turn into a tunnel so narrow his shoulders brushed the moss-covered walls.

Now two.

If he hadn't gotten here ahead of the sicario . . . well, he'd deal with that possibility if and when it presented itself. For now, he concentrated on running, on putting one foot ahead of the other, on ignoring the pain that shot down his leg with each step. As he passed one section of wall, he ripped a piece of his shirt sleeve free, wrapping it around his hand to snatch some bloodmoss. He folded the fabric around the moss and held it in his left hand.

Better to be prepared than not.

He made another turn, his steps slowing as he crossed the narrow stone bridge over the rushing water in the cavern. Water often condensed on the bridge, making the footing precarious. He only slipped once while crossing. The act of catching his balance wrenched his wounded leg even further. He gritted his teeth and continued on towards the wooden barricade.

As it came into view, Fletch slowed to a stop, his sides burning and his leg aching so badly that it might as well have been on fire. He gasped for breath, leaning his shoulder against the wall, and examined the barricade.

No one called out for him to identify himself.

He felt a chill run down his spine, but pushed himself away from the wall and began limping towards the barricade none-theless. There were other entrances, more hidden ones, but get-ting to them would take time, and several required some rather strenuous climbing. The idea of more running through the tun-nels followed by hauling himself up slippery stone outcroppings was frankly unthinkable.

He'd have to make do. He gripped the moss he'd grabbed more tightly and reached out with his other hand to shove aside one section of the barricade, bending double and limping through. The next two barricades were empty as well.

Fletch pushed his way through the last one and crawled into a far too silent cavern. Kids sat in large groups of ten or more, turning to look at him when he walked in, their eyes huge and terrified. Other than their heads, they didn't move, their bod-ies tense, stiff. Fletch hesitated in the entryway, every instinct in his body screaming at him to flee.

He couldn't. He couldn't leave them here, in danger because of him.

"All right," he said, raising his voice. It echoed from the arched stone roof of the cavern. "I'm here. Come on out, you bloody-handed bastard."

A man stepped from behind one of the hanging tapestries, a man wearing a hooded cloak and holding Tam by the hair. The little girl cried in quiet, hitching sobs, blood trailing from the corner of her mouth to stain her dirty over-sized tunic. The si-cario held a metal disc in his other hand, extended outwards so it was clearly visible. Fletch's eyes darted over the room, taking in unfamiliar glints of metal. Silver spikes, driven into the walls.

No wonder the kids were so quiet. Those spikes were undoubtedly metal-bound. The sicario could bring this whole cavern down around their ears with a single twitch of his fingers.

How in the gods names did he find out where the den was in the first place? Fletch wondered, but the thought was followed immediately by the most natural answer.

Anisaria. His face drew down into a scowl, anger licking at his mind like the flames of a fire. *He knew about the den, knew where to find it.*

The sicario tossed Tam forward between them, the girl crying out in pain as she landed, hands splayed out in front of her.

"Bind the thief's hands," the man said to her. "Then divest him of whatever weapons he might be carrying. If you tie him less than securely, or conveniently forget a weapon, I'll know." He raised the metal disc. A warning.

Tam scrabbled to her feet, but Fletch held up a hand towards her, palm out, to forestall her. "You blow this cavern, you kill us all," he said, his eyes fixed on the sicario. "Yourself included."

The man didn't reply. Tam stood between them, glancing back over her shoulder at the assassin.

"We both know this is a bluff," Fletch said, struggling to keep his voice calm. "You're not going to risk killing yourself to get me."

"If I fail in my mission, my own guild will see to it that I am eliminated. We have certain standards to uphold." His voice held a hint of a Tyrodamian accent.

"They're *children*," Fletch said.

The hood turned slightly, taking in the children huddled around him. "I have killed children before." His voice was flat, toneless.

Fletch looked at Tam. "Do what he says."

"No," she whispered, shaking her head, her eyes huge. "Fletch . . ."

"Do what he says," Fletch repeated sternly.

"They'll kill you," she said, her voice barely more than a breath.

"Tam," a voice said from one of the groups of kids. Fletch glanced over to see Rossin, sitting cross-legged with the smallest kids in the den huddled behind him. His voice was harsh. "He'll be fine. Take care of the *family*, remember?"

"He's family too," she said softly.

"No," Rossin replied, throwing a hard look at Fletch. "He's not. Family doesn't put one another at risk. Family doesn't run off and leave with no explanation. He," his eyes narrowed, "isn't family. He doesn't care. Not about you, or me, or any of us. We're just something to entertain him, like a puppet show."

Tam looked back and forth between them. Fletch kept his face carefully blank. Those words hurt far more than he'd expected, but he couldn't let Tam know that. She was emotional, scared . . . and she'd always been one of the more naïve kids in the den. He briefly imagined the possible conversation between them. Him telling her he'd be fine, her rejecting it as she had earlier, because she cared about him. She'd refuse to do as the sicario ordered, and if she did, the other kids would band together with her, as they usually did. Rossin would try to stop it, but one man couldn't stop a pathway car. They'd stand together, like a family. . . . And they'd die that way as the sicario activated those convergences and killed them all.

He only had one choice. One shot at saving them.

And that was to break a ten-year-old girl's heart. If she survived this, she'd hate him.

But she and all the rest would be *alive* to hate him, and that was all that mattered.

"You found us," she said, looking at Fletch with desperate hope in her eyes. "You found us, and—"

"Oh, for all the gods' sakes," Fletch said, rolling his eyes. "I *found* you the way a dog finds fleas. I'd lose you all in a heartbeat if I could figure out how without bleeding myself dry." His heart wrenched as the hope in her eyes faded.

"Fletch," she whispered.

"'Fletch,'" he repeated mockingly. "'Show us how to pick pockets, Fletch. Play games with us, Fletch.' On second thought," he said to the sicario, "I'll come willingly. If your masters kill me, I won't have to listen to their bleating anymore."

He could *see* the moment her heart broke, the tears gathering in the corners of her eyes, her lower lip trembling. Rossin, sitting off to one side, gave Fletch a small nod, his eyes still hard.

"Tie him," the sicario said to Tam. "Now."

Fletch held his fists out in front of him, wrists together, the fabric-enshrouded clump of moss still hidden in his left hand. "Go on," he said to Tam. "Do it, so I can get out of here."

Tam stepped forward, eyes downcast, and began wrapping the rope around his wrists. She did a good job, tying them securely and tighter than was strictly necessary. Fletch flinched as she pulled them tight. Tam brought the trailing end of the rope to the sicario, holding it out to him. He took it in the hand not holding the metal disc.

The man didn't say anything, didn't move. Tam returned to Fletch, pointedly not looking at him as she began stripping him of his weapons. She pulled the last hidden knife from Fletch's boot, tossed it aside, and stepped away.

She hadn't touched the wooden box at his belt.

She knew what was in it, of course. She'd seen him use the needles before, had even used one herself once. But she'd left it there, despite the fact that he'd hurt her deeply.

"That's everything?" the sicario asked.

"Yes," Tam whispered, looking down.

The sicario's hood turned back towards Fletch. "Open your hands."

Fletch coughed. As he did so, he flicked the packet of moss up his sleeve, just as he would hide a lockpick or a stolen purse. He opened both of his hands palm out to the sicario, who nodded and tugged on the rope. Fletch walked over to him slowly. The sicario backed up towards the barricade, and Fletch followed.

The kids watched solemnly, all except Tam. She sat down on one of the bundles of tattered blankets, crying into her crossed arms.

They reached the barricade, and the sicario met Fletch's eyes. "You and your hunter friend shouldn't have fought back in the weapon shop," he said. "Our reputations are far more fragile than those of thieves."

"Fuck your reputation," Fletch snarled.

The sicario smiled. He shifted his thumb over the silver inset into the metal disc.

Fletch felt horror slide over his mind like a cold veil. "I came willingly," he said.

The sicario's thumb hovered over the silver, and Fletch's gaze darted out to scan over the frightened faces staring at them.

Witnesses, he thought, the veil descending fully. *He can't leave any witnesses.*

He lunged at the sicario, flinging the bound packet of moss at the man's face.

He was too late.

The assassin's thumb pressed on the silver as the moss puffed out of the fabric to whirl around his face in a cloud of swirling motes. He screamed as the moss began eating at his skin, lurching back against the barricade and dropping the rope. Behind Fletch, the cavern exploded into a chaos of fire, screams and falling rock.

Chapter Twenty-Two

Suken sat beside Shifter in the guard's station, waiting for Corporal Niden. He was beginning to grow impatient. They'd been sitting here for nearly an hour, and midnight wasn't far off.

He didn't want to risk leaving Shifter here with anyone but Corporal Niden, or maybe Captain Weyav. Suken couldn't be sure if any of the other guards here were Coalition members. So he waited, flipping a prayer back and forth between his hands and growing more and more worried about Fletch.

Had he managed to get to the den quickly enough to warn them? Suken hadn't heard anything, but he hadn't really expected to. If the Coalition had caught Fletch, they'd have killed him and dumped the body. He flipped the prayer again, catching it and glancing at the symbol.

The Noose, which meant danger, or that your plan was ill-advised.

Thanks, Lady, Suken thought, rolling his eyes and flipping the coin again. *You've sure been good at telling me what I already know this week.* He caught it and looked down. The Noose again. He flipped the prayer around, looking at the other side.

Both sides were inscribed with the Noose. Suken felt a shiver run down his spine. The placement of the symbols was completely random, meaning that the same pair of symbols didn't always necessarily correspond on a prayer. One might have the Star and the Lady's Face, while the next could be the Star and the Cloud. A prayer bearing the same symbol on both sides was exceedingly rare; an incontrovertible omen.

He glanced at Shifter. The man sat beside him in nervous silence, still rubbing absently at the chafed skin on his wrists. His face was a mass of purplish-red bruises and scabbed-over cuts, his hair greasy and hanging around his face.

A few people sat in the station, keeping their distance from Suken and Shifter. That one in the corner, though . . . the one with the serape tattered at the hem and the hair pulled back into a tail. Had he been staring at them more than he should? Suken watched him out of the corner of his eye, but the man yawned, tilted his head back against the wall and closed his eyes.

We're in the guard's precinct, Suken told himself firmly. *Not even the Coalition would dare attack us here. If any of the guards are working with them, they could make Shifter disappear quietly. But they're not going to attack us in the lobby. It's just that prayer, making me jumpy.*

Kora sat at the main desk, her head bent, scribbling on a piece of paper behind the raised counter. She'd snapped at Suken to go and have a seat when they'd first arrived, insisting that Niden was due to come check in.

Come on, Suken thought, looking out the nearest window at the moon, wreathed in clouds. *It's got to be almost midnight by now.*

The front door banged open, a group of bedraggled guards led by Niden entering. All of them wore their cloaks and sideswords. "Jotor," Niden said, not slowing as he strode across the room towards the door leading to the offices and cells, his eyes scanning over the room in a cursory fashion, "have that report filled out and on my desk in ten minutes. Heshin, go and collect the ardein's testimony and—" he cut off as his gaze passed over Suken and Shifter. His eyes widened, flitting from Shifter to Suken and back again, and his expression darkened. "Anisaria," he said. "This had better not be what—"

"I haven't been carrying a weapon," Suken said, standing. "Or doing anything I shouldn't have without a license." *Except for breaking and entering, impersonation, a little property damage and some petty theft.*

The fact that he could justify all of those things, Suken thought with a wince, probably meant that Fletch Greencloak was a terrible influence on him.

"I found the man responsible for killing Lord Garron's daughter," Suken hurried on. "I think you'll want to hear what he has to say, sir."

Niden waved one hand dismissively. "Fill out the report and I'll see to it tomorrow."

"Sir," Suken said, stepping forward. "I *really* think you'll want to talk to him now."

He held the Corporal's gaze for a moment. The older man sighed and turned toward his officers. "Go on," he snapped. "You don't need me to tell you your jobs, I hope. Get to them."

The officers scattered and Niden turned back to Suken and Shifter, beckoning. Suken helped Shifter to his feet and led him after Niden down the hall towards an empty cell. Niden pulled a ring of keys from his belt and unlocked the cell with a clank of metal on metal, swung the door open, and gestured for Suken and Shifter to enter.

Suken had never been present for an interrogation before. He supposed that it made more sense to hold one in a cell than in an office, but it still made him feel nervous as Niden pulled the door closed behind them with a clang.

"Talk," he said, leaning against the door and crossing his arms.

Suken took a deep breath, then began telling the story he'd concocted during his wait in the lobby. "After I left here without my license," he said, "I decided to look for the man involved in that botched case."

"The shifter," Niden supplied, voice flat.

"Right. I figured that everyone else would be too busy chasing after Greencloak, and he might slip through the cracks."

"Despite my expressly ordering you not to."

Suken swallowed. "Yes, sir."

Impossibly, Niden's expression darkened. "Go on."

"I thought that maybe if the kidnapper had tried to ransom Lord Garron, they'd try again, so I followed Garron, and tonight he went to a meeting at the theater, and after I followed him in, I found out that he was keeping this man," he gestured to Shifter, "down in the tunnels under the theater and that he'd been torturing him."

"So I see."

Suken forced himself to take a deep breath and continue in a more measured tone. "Garron was torturing him in retribution for killing his daughter," he said. "I waited for Garron to leave, then went in, intending to bring this man right to you. I think you're going to want to hear what he has to say."

Shifter, true to his word, told Niden everything he'd told Suken, staring at the floor the whole time. Niden listened, leaning against the door with his arms crossed. Suken glanced out the small window in the cell as Shifter finished telling how Lord Garron had personally hired a group of ten bounty hunters to track him down and bring him in alive.

Half an hour until midnight, Suken thought, sweat breaking out on his forehead. *I can still make it to Orchid Street in time, but I'm going to be cutting it close. Very close.*

Silence fell in the jail cell, Niden staring at them flatly. No surprise, or confusion, or disbelief. Just . . . nothing.

"Let me see if I've got this straight," the corporal finally said. "Greencloak *wasn't* responsible for killing three men, an orphaned haunt child, and destroying a valuable shadow-sprite.

He's being framed," he glanced at Suken, "by a political organization planning to make him a martyr to inspire the poor to revolt against the mages."

Something about that tickled the back of Suken's mind, but he couldn't quite place it. "I know it sounds crazy," he said. "But I know where the real killer will be in under an hour. If you help me to catch him, we'll be heroes."

"Heroes," Niden said, emotion finally creeping into his voice. It wasn't consideration, or confusion, or anything else Suken had expected. It was bitterness and disgust.

A horrible suspicion bloomed in Suken's mind, but before he could say or do anything, Niden pushed away from the door towards Shifter, his right hand dropping to draw his sword. It flashed from its scabbard as quickly as a hummingbird darting from flower to flower.

Suken leapt to try to put himself between Niden and Shifter, but he wasn't quick enough. The blade cut a shallow slice along the side of Suken's ribs, but the point buried itself in Shifter's upper chest, sinking deeper as Niden shouldered Suken roughly aside and shoved the blade forward, one palm flat against the pommel.

Suken regained his balance and turned. Shifter stood very still, the tip of Niden's bloodstained sword poking out the back of his shirt. The man looked down; silent, disbelieving.

No, Suken thought, frozen in place.

Niden pulled his sword free and Shifter fell to his knees. The battered man looked up at Suken, his swollen eyes questioning.

Suken read something else in that look before the man's face softened like melted wax and his eyes took on the glaze of death. Accusation.

I brought him here, thinking that the guards would keep him safe. My plan, my choice. My misplaced trust. A shiver ran down his spine. *I assumed that Niden would be untouchable. Principled.*

A memory surfaced, that of a drawing Suken had seen in

Niden's office. A family portrait, of Niden and a wife and two little girls, and two remembrance blooms peeking out from under the hem of Niden's sleeve, one on each wrist.

"I was married twenty years ago. We had two little girls." Suken closed his eyes, the words floating across his memory, along with an image of the man speaking them. A man dressed all in grey, a man with the same height and build as the one standing in front of Suken now. A man who had been masking his voice, because he hadn't been certain who in the audience might have heard him speak.

"It's a shame," Niden said casually, flicking his sword to one side to leave an arc of blood spattered on the wall, "that a young man with such a promising career ahead of him would throw his life away so easily."

Suken stared at him, his hands clenching into fists.

"How much did Greencloak pay you to try to assassinate me?" Niden continued, turning hard grey eyes on Suken. "He must have hundreds of thousands of aerans put away. How much of that did it take to buy your loyalty? Enough to pay off those debts to the cartels that your uncle left you?"

"You know damn well that Greencloak didn't hire me," Suken said, his voice, low, dangerous. "He's innocent. You bastards are framing him."

"We were closing in on him," Niden continued evenly. "So he hired you, a bounty hunter with enough debt on his shoulders to buy half the city. When you couldn't convince us of his innocence, you decided to take a different approach. You captured the man responsible for poor Lord Garron's daughter's death and beat him within an inch of his life before bringing him in. Everyone out in the lobby will testify to the fact that the man was battered. You used him to get a private audience with me, then attempted to kill me. Thankfully," he said with a humorless smile, "I'm an accomplished swordsman. When you realized that I wouldn't be an easy mark, you pushed him," Niden glanced at the body hemorrhaging blood onto the floor, "towards me, in an attempt to buy yourself some time to escape. I struck him. A terrible accident on my part, but I'm certain no one will care about the death of the killer of a child."

A child. The killer of a child. That tickling in the back of his mind, almost forgotten under a wave of anger, abruptly unfurled petals of icy realization.

Earlier, Niden had listed Greencloak's victims. *An orphaned haunt child,* he'd said. But the kids in the den had taken Vethin's body. The guards only found a puddle of blood on the ground and the ever-present word written in blood on the wall. The only people who could have known that one of the victims was a haunt child were the orphans, Suken, Fletch . . .

And the murderer.

Suken darted towards the cell door. He nearly made it, his hand closing around one of the bars, but Niden was too quick. He grabbed Suken's tunic, spinning him around and catching Suken under the jaw with a savage uppercut. Suken tried to lash out in retaliation, but his head was swimming and the floor kept seeming to try to pull itself out from under him. He felt a blow slam into his side, then another, and another. He fell, crying out.

Niden grabbed the front of his shirt, hauling him upwards. "Tell me where the thief is and I might be persuaded to tell a different story, when the others arrive," he whispered.

"Fuck . . . you," Suken said through a mouthful of blood.

"Where . . ." Niden drew his fist back and buried it in Suken's gut, "*is* he?"

Suken coughed and fought for breath, spraying blood all over Niden's face. He managed a grin, hoping it looked ghastly. "Even . . . if I knew . . . I wouldn't tell you."

Niden released him, letting Suken drop back to the cold floor. He pulled a kerchief from his pocket and carefully wiped the blood from his face.

"You'll . . . never find him," Suken said, trying to push himself up. He collapsed back down to the stone floor with a groan, and looked up through a haze of pain.

Niden knelt and leaned down, tilting his head to look at Suken. "I think," he said softly, "that I know *exactly* where he'll be. I think you told him where the murderer would be tonight, and that he's supposed to meet you there, as backup."

Suken's blood ran as cold as ice.

Niden's smile widened. "Ah," he said. "You *did* tell him."

"I didn't," Suken said desperately as Niden stood up. "I—"

Niden's boot lashing out towards his face was the last thing Suken saw before darkness and pain claimed him.

Chapter Twenty-Three

Fletch rolled to one side, a chunk of rock bigger than his body crashing to the floor where he'd been. He staggered to his feet, hands still tied, amid roiling smoke and rock dust and the panicked screams of children.

He looked to his right in time to see the sicario vanish into the barricade. Fletch spared a moment to savagely hope that the man didn't make it to the surface in time to find an antidote for the bloodmoss. The thought of following the man briefly crossed his mind, but he couldn't leave the kids to fight for their lives alone.

Gods *damn* it. He stood in the mouth of the tunnel between the barricade and the den, as blind and helpless as a newborn kitten, while the children he'd saved screamed.

He growled deep in his throat and ran the ten feet to the barricade, grabbing a jagged piece of wood and sawing his wrists back and forth across its edge, listening as the thuds and crashes of falling rocks slowly tapered off, replaced by cries for help and pained screams.

The last piece of rope parted and Fletch whirled, his cloak flapping behind him as he ducked into the smoke and rock-dust. Calls for help echoed in the cavern, mingling with crying and the voices of others trying to help or calm the injured. The worst of the destruction was nearest the cave's mouth. At the back of the cavern, the massive edifice the kids used to practice jumping and climbing had provided some shelter from the falling stones.

Fletch didn't speak. He worked at a feverish pace, digging his fingers into piles of rubble and hauling them aside as older children pulled the trapped ones free. Later, he remembered only vague impressions of blood, and pain, and pangs of deep sorrow mixed with a black anger so deep and violent that he trembled with it as he pulled rocks aside only to find still, silent bodies.

He didn't know how long he worked. He only knew that he continued well past the limits of endurance, until a hand grabbed his arm and pulled him away from the still corpse he was trying to unearth.

He growled and whipped his head around to see who had stopped him, and found himself looking into the dust-coated face of Rossin.

"Enough," the young man said, his voice brittle. "He's gone."

The boy Fletch had been working to free lay half under a rock as large as a carriage, his entire left side from his shoulder to his hip buried beneath it. Bits of his ribs poked up from the mess that had been his chest, and frothy blood dribbled from the corner of his half-open mouth. His eyes stared up sightlessly at the ceiling.

I found him on a street corner two years ago, Fletch thought, numb. *Planning to pick a guard's pocket.*

He stood slowly, exhaustion sweeping over him as he looked around, the haze that had been blinding him fading into cold hard clarity. The children had been busy as he'd worked, carrying the injured over towards the rear of the cavern and dragging the bodies to another, covering their still forms with ragged, dust-coated blankets.

Fletch staggered over to the line, lifting each blanket in turn to examine a still, ashen face. There were ten. He knew all their names, remembered each and every one of them. He hadn't brought them all here himself. But he had *known* them all, spoken to them, watched in amusement as they learned or played or practiced. He looked away, one hand clenching into a fist at his side, pain lancing up his arm.

When I find you and your friends, he thought viciously towards the sicario, *you're going to have plenty of time to regret each and every life you've taken, directly or otherwise. And that goes double for you, Anisaria, you two-timing bastard.*

Coughing and weak sobs rose from the injured group. Fletch walked over to them, looking over the line. Nine children, sitting or lying on their backs. Bloodied. Covered in dust. Shaking or crying or staring at the ruins of their home. The uninjured ones weren't much better. Rossin knelt beside one of the smallest, holding a dirty, blood-soaked rag against the boy's head. Fletch walked over to the older boy, looking down at him. "Bring them to Temiran Street," he said, his voice raspy from smoke, inhaled dust, and unspent rage and sorrow. "There's a clinic there. Tell them I sent you." Rossin glanced up at him, his gaze shifting briefly down to Fletch's hands. Fletch looked down to see that he'd torn the skin from most of his fingers, leaving them raw and bloody.

"So you're just going to leave them?" Rossin asked, his voice low. "We could use your help to get them all there, you know."

"Thought I wasn't family," Fletch snapped.

"If you leave," Rossin said, his face dark, "you won't be. Never again."

Fletch looked over the injured group again. He saw Tam sitting there, blood running down her face from a gash in her forehead, looking dazed.

The longer he stayed, the worse it would get for them. Tonight proved that. He needed to cut his ties, once and for all. "You'll be better off without me," he said.

With that, he turned his back on the lot of them and walked away.

It was the single hardest thing he'd ever done in his life. But it was necessary. He focused his thoughts on where he needed to go, what needed to be done next.

The killer would be arriving at that whorehouse on Orchid Street sometime soon, to meet with the traitor Anisaria and that poor bastard who was doomed to die. Fletch narrowed his concentration down to a pinpoint of cool, calm clarity.

They wanted Greencloak? Fine. They'd get him. He'd be there waiting, and then the bastards would pay. All of them.

Especially Anisaria.

Chapter Twenty-Four

Suken?" The voice was small, barely more than a whisper. Suken had been lying on his back, staring at the ceiling, but he looked over towards the doorway at that tiny, familiar voice.

"It's past midnight," Suken said. "You should be sleeping."

"So should you." The figure standing in the doorway was little more than a shadow. Suken sighed and shifted over in his bed, making room for his brother to join him. The boy padded into the room, clambered onto the bed, and snuggled in close against Suken's side.

"He hates us," Jandin whispered. "I wanna go home."

Suken knew how he felt, but wishes weren't going to change their situation. They wouldn't make Uncle Lorrin care about them, they wouldn't stop him coming home reeking of gin to either flat-out disregard them or yell at them, and they certainly wouldn't change the fact that Suken couldn't keep up with his studies now that he'd been pulled from school to care for his little brother.

"This is home now," Suken replied, though he took care to keep his voice soothing. He had no desire to yell at his brother, especially not after the harsh words their uncle had thrown at them over the table tonight. "We've got to make the best of it, Din."

The boy buried his face against Suken's shoulder. Suken felt the warmth of his brother's tears soaking into his shirt. His brother annoyed *him more often than not these days, but at this moment he felt a surge of protectiveness and love so strong that it nearly took his breath away. Jandin was needy, but he was the only family Suken had left. He tightened his arm around his brother's shoulders.*

"Hey," Suken said. "Want me to tell you a story?"

"You're no good at it," Jandin replied, his voice muffled. "Not like mom was."

"Better than nothing, right?"

The boy sniffled. Suken stared up at the dark ceiling, feeling his brother's tears wet against his shoulder, and began.

"In the Valley," Suken started, "there's a bounty hunter."

"I don't want to hear about hunters," Jandin whispered.

"This one's not like Lorrin," Suken said. "He helps people."

"What kind of people?"

"All kinds of people. Anyone who needs help."

Jandin fell quiet, so Suken continued, vividly imagining it as he spun his tale. The hunter he made up was the polar opposite of their uncle. A good man, honest and kind and compassionate. A hero. A man who did the right thing, who helped the helpless, who refused to let the violence corrupt him. Somehow, it made their own situation seem less dark, less hopeless, to think there might actually be someone out there like that. Someone who helped others for no reason other than that it was right.

When he finished the story, which had been about a warrant Suken's fictional hunter took to find a man's missing kid, Jandin remained quiet for a long time. Suken thought that maybe he'd fallen asleep. Then his hand tightened around Suken's upper arm. Jandin pressed his face tighter against Suken's shoulder.

"That was a good story," he whispered. "Mom would have liked it."

Suken swallowed hard, remembering her. Her face was becoming harder and harder to imagine, but he could still clearly remember her voice, the way she'd stroked his hair as she told him and Jandin stories after dark.

How long before those faded from his memory as well?

He wasn't a good enough artist to capture her likeness, as she could have done. Maybe if he practiced enough...

He turned on his side and wrapped both arms around his little brother, holding him close.

Suken blinked back tears, pulling himself from the bittersweet memory. He sat on the thin mattress in his cell, his elbows on his knees and his face in his hands. The moon had dropped behind the line of rooftops across the street hours ago, leaving only the single dull luminary set into the stone of the ceiling to illuminate Suken's last hours.

He'd been an idiot. Chance, how could he have been so stupid?

He'd told himself for years that he was going to be the best bounty hunter this damn city had ever seen. He'd help the less fortunate, save lives, and build a name that would cross continents, bridge seas. And maybe, if the case-file didn't help him track down his little brother . . . just maybe . . . if Jandin were still alive out there somewhere, he'd hear about Suken, and how much he'd changed. And come back.

But none of that would happen. Because in less than four hours, he'd be dead.

He pushed his hands up into his hair, his eyes closed.

The hour after he'd woken from Niden's beating had been hectic. He'd only been out for a few seconds, apparently, as he'd awoken to guards swarming over him, binding his hands, dragging him by the arms into a room where a sleepy-eyed judge had listened to Niden's report (given by one of his subordinates). The judge had cleared his throat, reading off a list of charges.

Assault against an officer. Attempted murder. Accomplice to the notorious Greencloak in a further five murders.

Suken had tried to tell them the truth. The judge had asked if he had any proof to back up these 'ludicrous claims.' Suken had demanded a Truthread. But the judge had rolled his eyes and declined his request. Then he'd declared Suken's sentence.

Death. By hanging. At dawn.

They didn't want to give Greencloak an opportunity to 'steal' him, apparently.

Suken glanced out the window. It was well past midnight now, maybe closer to two or three. If Greencloak *had* gone to the whorehouse to try to catch Niden, he'd either have had to fight his way free, or he was dead. Suken fervently hoped for the first option, but he knew better than to expect a reprieve from his current situation. Even if Fletch had managed to capture Niden somehow, without Suken he had no way to safely turn him in. He had no one he could trust, no one to help him. . . . And who would trust the word of Fletch Greencloak over that of the esteemed Corporal Niden? Once he realized that, Fletch would probably wind up killing him in revenge for Vethin and that mage lover of his. Suken would hang with the rising sun, and Fletch surely wouldn't be far behind him. He couldn't run forever.

Suken closed his eyes again, memories drifting across his mind like clouds. His mother's smile as she'd taught him how to hold a pencil, and her delighted laughter at the first drawing he'd given her. His father's dirt-stained hands, huge and strong, and how Suken's mother had scolded him whenever he'd tousled Suken's hair, leaving it coated in dust. His brother, giving him a gap-toothed grin.

Those memories faded into others. His brother's bruised and tear-streaked face as Suken snapped at him to leave him alone, he was studying. The day when he'd vanished, and how panicked Suken had been, how guilty. If only he'd spent more time with him . . . listened to him instead of dismissing him. The months he'd spent prowling the Valley District in between his combat lessons and target practice sessions with Avara, looking for a lead after his brother had vanished into thin air. Then the heart-rending despair of finding him only to lose him to the slave markets.

He thought of the friends he'd made, of Terri, Avara, Marxen, and a half-hundred others. He thought of hunters, and whores, and orphans, and thieves. He thought of Fletch Greencloak and his ever-present grin.

Who would remember him, after he was gone? How many would weep for him?

Terri would. Of that he was sure. And Avara. Marxen would likely hold a day of remembrance for him at the Lady's Face, as he did for all fallen hunters.

Or would he? Suken grimaced. They were saying that he'd been working with a murderer, that he'd tried to assassinate a decorated officer of the City Guard. Would the hunters believe that? Would they curse his name, mock him? Mutter into their drinks that he'd always thought he was better than everyone else, that he deserved what he'd gotten?

If they did, they'd be right. He *hadn't* been as good as he'd thought he was. He hadn't been able to protect Greencloak. He hadn't been able to save Shifter. He couldn't even save himself.

Suken stood and limped across the cell towards the hallway, wrapping his hands around the cold steel bars and pressing his face between them as far as he could to peer down the hall. Two guards sat at a table at the end of the hall of cells, bent over a game of towers. One of them was Captain Weyav. Unlike the other guards, who had stared at Suken with outright disdain and anger during the short hearing, Weyav had regarded him with sadness and a hint of betrayal.

"Kel," Suken called. "Can I talk to you for a minute?"

One of the criminals in the opposite cell growled and curled into a ball on his cot, pulling a pillow over his head. Suken ignored him. Weyav looked down the hall towards Suken and stood, placing his hands at the small of his back and arching it before turning to walk down towards Suken's cell. As he approached, his eyes lost his usual good-natured humor and turned wary. He stopped out of arm's reach and regarded Suken.

"What do you want?"

"Kel," Suken said softly. "You know me. I'm no murderer. I can't even stand to watch Chance kill the damned lizards she catches."

"Ain't you kept us awake enough tonight?" the prisoner snarled, turning to spear them with a hard-eyed look.

Weyav crossed his arms, ignoring the other prisoner. "You've been sentenced," he said harshly. "It isn't my place to question it."

Suken sighed. "All right. Look, could you just . . . answer a few questions for me? Call it a parting gift for a dead man."

Weyav didn't say no.

"Corporal Niden," Suken said. "He's got a wife and two kids, right?"

The kidnapper threw his pillow at the bars. It hit with a solid *thwack* and fell to the ground.

"He did," Weyav said. "Five years ago, a man broke into his house while he was working. Raped and murdered his wife. Killed one of his little girls, and left the other one wishing she was dead." He shook his head. "It was a terrible night."

Well, that verified that. Niden was Lord Grey.

"He was mage-born," Suken said. "The killer."

Weyav nodded. "Haunt. Someone saw him fleeing the scene, though we never caught him." His eyes narrowed again. "How'd you know?"

Suken closed his eyes and pressed his forehead against a bar. "Lucky guess."

The man in the next cell let out a frustrated exhalation and turned away from both of them, muttering curses under his breath.

"Suken?" Weyav stepped closer, lowering his voice. "Did Greencloak have something on you? Threaten Terri, or some other type of blackmail? If so, you can trust me. I could call for a leave of execution."

"No," Suken replied, eyes still closed. "It's exactly like I said in the hearing, Kel. Greencloak's not a murderer. And neither am I."

Weyav turned and walked away. Suken listened to his boots tapping on the stone until the guard reached the end of the hallway and resumed his game, then he turned and walked back over to his cot, sitting down.

Three hours.

He put his head in his hands and descended into his past.

Some time later, he heard voices down the hallway. The man across the hall groaned and pulled his pillow over his head. Suken looked up as footsteps echoed down the hall. Weyav and Terri stopped outside his cell.

Suken squeezed his eyes shut, looking away. He'd hoped that she wouldn't have heard, wouldn't have come. He didn't want to have to say goodbye, not to anyone, but least of all to her.

"You've got a visitor," Weyav said. He turned towards Terri. "Ten minutes," he said. He started to walk by her, but hesitated briefly to lay a hand on her shoulder before walking away.

"Suken," Terri said, her eyes brimming with tears. "What did you *do?*"

"I failed," he replied, not standing. He looked down at his hands. "Guess I'm not as good as I thought I was."

"Stop that," she snapped, stepping up to grab a bar in each hand. "You stop that *right now.* There's got to be a way out of this."

Suken shook his head. "I tried to convince them. Told them everything, the whole story. They didn't believe me."

"Tell me what you told them," she said, her voice fierce. "If I know what's going on, I might be able to help. I can—"

"Terri," he said, looking up at her and feeling tears stinging the corners of his own eyes. "It doesn't matter. I'm sentenced, and nothing's going to change that."

"This is because of Greencloak, isn't it?"

"Just go," he said. "Get out of here."

"No," she snapped. "Tell me what happened or I swear by all the gods, Suken Anisaria, I'll find a way to break these bars and beat you senseless with them."

That pulled a reluctant smile from him. He knew that she wasn't going to leave him alone until he talked to her, so he recounted the events of the last few days as quickly as he could, and for once she listened without a word. When he finished, he spread his hands to the sides. "There's no way I'm going to be acquitted in the next three hours, and Fletch is undoubtedly too busy saving his own life and the orphans to help me. It's over, Terri. I'm sorry." He met her eyes and tried a smile. "You were a great housekeeper, and a better friend. You should know that—"

"Don't you dare," she snapped, her expression dark. "Don't you *dare* say goodbye."

"If that's what you want. But . . . you've been practically a sister to me, and—"

She turned on her heel and stalked away down the hall. Suken sighed, the rest of the words dying unspoken on his lips. *And I'm glad you came. Wherever it is I'm going, I'll miss you.*

He lay back on his cot, staring at the ceiling and waiting for the dawn.

Chapter Twenty-Five

An hour after leaving the den, Fletch nodded to the bouncer, Jor, and pushed aside the cloth curtain shrouding the doorway to the Ruddy Amapola. He stepped into a warm, cozy entry-way littered with plush cushions, flowers, and half-naked women. One courtesan wearing an outfit composed entirely of orchids fed grapes to a slim young woman wearing the tunic of a mage of the Sapphire School.

The unoccupied courtesans looked up when he walked in, leveling seductive smiles at him. As he walked into the faint light and they recognized him, the smiles changed from alluring to genuine warmth.

One woman rose fluidly from her cushion to approach him, and rested her hand on his elbow. Ayal-ia wore a loose light gown which fell from her shoulders to plunge almost to her waist at the front, revealing more skin than it concealed. The strings of seed-beads in her hair clicked as she tilted her head to examine his face.

"Little Finch," she said warmly, her dark eyes glittering beneath lids painted with blue and gold. Her Tyrodamian accent was still strong, despite years spent living here in Adunare. "It is pleasant to be seeing you, though I am afraid that our offerings tonight are . . ." she paused and looked around at the women, a smile playing across lips painted as dark as midnight. "Not to your liking."

The women here had taken to calling him Finch years ago, after the small birds whose penchant was stealing small bright trinkets for their nests. He'd spent most of his childhood on Orchid Street, following his mother from one brothel to another. The women had doted on him, and he suspected that many still saw him as the wiry five-year old they'd showered with praise and flowers.

Fletch wasn't in the mood for playful banter tonight. "We need to talk," he said, keeping his voice low. "Alone."

Ayal-ia's expression sobered, and she nodded. She led him toward the stairs leading up to the rooms on the second floor. Several of the unoccupied women sent taunting little whistles after him, imitating bird-calls. He ignored them, following Ayal-ia in silence, walking past the faint sounds of pleasure coming from curtained doorways. Eventually she came to an empty one, and pushed aside the thick brocaded curtain to let him in ahead of her.

The small room smelled of scented candles, sweat, and the unmistakable scent of spent seed. Dark gauzy curtains encircled the wide cushion which served as a bed, and the window at the far end of the room was concealed by a pair of wooden screens inset with faint luminaries. The impression it gave was one of closeness, warmth . . . intimacy. Which was, of course, the point.

As soon as the curtain swished closed behind Ayal-ia, Fletch turned to her. "Someone would have made an appointment for one of your women tonight," he said. "He might be here already. I don't know who made the appointment, but the client would be beaten to shit, and maybe in the company of a bounty hunter." That last came out harsh. "Hunter'd have hazel eyes, short brownish blond hair. About a head taller than me. Clean-shaven. Goes by the name Anisaria."

Ayal-ia's brows shot up nearly to her hairline. "Suken?"

Somehow, Fletch wasn't surprised that the whores of Orchid Street were on a first-name basis with Anisaria. He suppressed a trembling chord of anger at the thought of the bastard and pushed on. "Have you seen him yet tonight?"

"No," Ayal-ia said slowly, her dark eyes measuring. "Fletch, are you being all right? You are smelling of smoke, and blood."

Fletch walked over to the window, pushing the curtain aside to look at the street. He scanned the people walking arm in arm or staggering along drunk, whores leaning from windows tossing flower petals down on their heads invitingly. No sign of Anisaria or his charge out there yet, either.

Ayal-ia let out a gasp. Fletch whirled, his heartbeat picking up, but the woman only strode forward, grabbing his hand. He'd bound his fingers with strips of linen as he'd made his way here, and they were soaked through with blood. "What is this?" she asked, looking up and meeting his eyes.

"Blood," he snapped. "Being a woman, I'm sure you've seen plenty of it." He snatched his hand away. "I'm going to rent a room for the night. When the two I mentioned arrive, bring them to me."

Ayal-ia narrowed her eyes. "And what is it you will be doing?"

Fletch considered her. The brothels were known as places of safety, even among the criminal underworld. If a murder or a theft happened under one's roof, the brothel in question often didn't last long.

"You've heard what they're saying I am?" he said.

"Yes," Ayal-ia said carefully. "But we are knowing better than to believe it."

"Anisaria's working with the people who are framing me."

Ayal-ia arched one slim eyebrow. Fletch ignored her expression of disbelief.

"The real killer will be arriving here soon," he said, glancing out the window again. Still no sign. "He's going to kill Anisaria's prisoner under your roof, unless I stop him. I'll draw them away, into a position where I can turn the tables on them."

She regarded him, raising one hand to touch her mouth and cupping her elbow in her other hand.

"You have my word," he said. "No bloodshed here, if I can help it."

"Fletch," she said slowly, as if she were talking to a small child. "Are you being *certain* that Suken is—"

"Yes," Fletch snapped. "I'm certain. The fucking cat stabbed me in the back, Ayal-ia. You should know better than to trust one of them."

Like I should have.

One corner of her mouth twisted down into a dissatisfied frown, but otherwise she seemed to accept his word. "You are injured," she continued. "Have you been to see—"

"I don't have time," Fletch interrupted. "They'll be here soon. If you don't want 'Greencloak' killing another mage-born in one of your rooms, you'll help me."

She considered him for a long moment, sighed, and nodded. "We will be seeing that they come to this room," she said. The mother-of-pearl bangles on her wrist clicked against one another as she gestured towards the screens hiding the windows. "You may be waiting there. I am knowing that you are never seen unless you are wishing to be. But remember, if you are breaking your word, we will be finding you."

Once, Fletch had seen a specimen of one of the giant fish that swam in the waters east of Majitan in the market. He remembered staring at those rows of sharp white teeth with his mouth hanging open. Ayal-ia's smile now was like that . . . predatory and bearing more than a hint of the icy darkness of deep waters.

"And if that is happening," she continued, her voice barely audible, "you will be wishing that you had never sung your songs here, Little Finch, no matter who your mother is being."

Fletch nodded. She started to turn, but he called out, "Ayal-ia, one other thing. If the hunter comes in with him, distract him."

As much as Fletch wanted to slit Anisaria's throat, he knew that he was at the limit of his endurance. He was relatively certain that he could get the drop on the killer and dispose of him quickly and easily, but the bounty hunter was another matter. Fletch would have to deal with him later.

"This may not be so easy," Ayal-ia said with a shake of her head. "I am doubting that he will be partaking of our offers if he is to be working. He is a diligent one."

"Get him to drink some dream-sap or something, I don't care. Here . . ." he pulled out his box of needles and handed one to her, careful not to jab her with the point. "Use this if you have to. Just keep him out of here."

"I am not liking to be pulled into the middle of these games," she said, pinching the needle between her fingers and giving it a distasteful look. "It is being dangerous for my girls, and for our clients."

"If this bastard has his way, he'll murder a man under your roof," Fletch snapped. "You'd lose every client you ever had in under a week, and your girls will wind up selling themselves in the Hollow Market."

She regarded him for another long moment, nodded, and left, closing the door behind her.

Fletch waited by the window as the moon sank behind the clouds. Midnight came and went, and with every passing minute he grew more uneasy.

Anisaria and his mage-born prisoner were late.

Something was wrong. They'd been tipped off, somehow. Maybe Anisaria had realized that Fletch had been listening.

The man impersonating me will be at their damned meeting tomorrow night, Fletch thought, gently drumming his injured fingers on the windowsill. *Going up before the Coalition. I'll have to try to get to him there. It'll be more difficult, but better than waiting around here to meet whatever Anisaria sends my way.*

A courtesan leaned out a window across the street, tossing

flower petals down onto the heads of passerby. A street orphan made his or her way along the street with one hand outstretched, begging for half-aerans. Dozens of men and women strode down the street in groups or alone, heading for the pleasures that the brothels would give. Fletch hopped up onto the windowsill, preparing to make his escape. Then he saw the shadow on the rooftop across the street.

It detached itself from the night to shift to a new position. Moonlight gleamed for a brief moment on something metal.

Anisaria?

The figure moved enough for Fletch to make out that he was wearing a hat. The foreboding strengthened into downright surety. *Go,* his mind screamed at him. *Get out now!*

Fletch was many things, but stupid wasn't one of them. When his instincts were this clear, he always listened to them. He readied himself to jump, hoping to all the gods old and new that the convergences stored in the ring that Blue had given him hadn't been drained of energy in the days since he'd gotten it.

"Greencloak!" The voice came from behind him, in the hallway outside the cloth hanging that served as the room's door. It was deep and rough and full of authority. "We know you're in there!"

Fletch snarled. Anisaria had sent the bloody *pearls* after him. A crossbow bolt slammed into the wood beside his right hand, throwing up splinters. One jabbed painfully into the web between Fletch's thumb and index finger. He drew his hand back with an intake of pained breath.

The hunter knelt on the roof, moonlight glinting on the tip of another bolt aimed at Fletch. On the street below, guards in iridescent armor melted out of the crowd to look up at his window with expectant expressions and raised crossbows of their own. He heard the clanking of armor and the thuds of heavy boots entering the room behind him.

Fletch did what he always did when his plans crashed down around his ears. He stopped planning and *reacted*.

He dropped back into the room and stepped to one side to avoid any further bolts from the hunter on the roof and pulled his needle-box from his pocket, grabbing two of the thin slivers of metal. His fingers were numb from the salve he'd slathered over the torn skin, but he managed to get a good grip on the needles.

He took a deep breath and kicked down the wooden screen, dropping into a crouch. Six guards stood in the room already, resplendent in their opalescent armor. More clustered in the hall behind them. Thankfully, none of them wore helms. Another bolt hissed into the room from behind him, and Fletch felt his belt jerk as if it had been hit, but the lack of pain meant that that was a secondary concern. Fletch flung his arm at the guards, sending one needle to bury itself in the lead guard's neck. The man let out a startled shriek and raised his hand to his throat even as his eyes began to roll back in his head. Fletch's hand darted out again, and the second needle vanished into a guard's red beard. The man gagged, dropping the metal-bound club he'd carried to scrabble at his throat.

Fletch drew a pair of small throwing knives he'd lifted from someone on the street and held them as he'd been taught so many years ago, thin blades pinched between thumb and fore-finger. He tapped the disks of silver set into each to activate the metal-bound convergences within them, crossed his arms over his opposite shoulders, and flung the knives to *thunk* into the wooden floor in front of the guards.

Caal-fire burst from them in a deafening explosion, bursting the glass spheres on the pommels of the weapons. The guards threw their hands up to protect their faces and took several steps back towards the hallway. The wave of heat hit Fletch like a physical blow, tightening the skin on his face and hands. Smoke began to fill the room as the liquid contained in the glass spheres interacted with the heat. He whirled back towards the window.

Cries from below and behind. The shadow on the roof rising to stand. But now the smoke was beginning to pour around Fletch towards the window, obscuring the archer's sight. Fletch pulled his cloak up to cover his nose and mouth, giving the smoke another few seconds to reach the window. His eyes stung and watered, but he blinked to dispel the tears and leapt onto the windowsill as dark smoke began to billow out of it, balancing himself with the hand he wasn't using to hold his cloak over his face.

Thirty feet to the ground. Five to the rope running between this building and the next, strands of flowers hanging from it to brush against the heads and shoulders of the people below. Fletch reached down and tapped the ring that Blue had given him five times, activating the convergence.

The smoke ceased to pour around him, slowing instead to a sluggish crawl. Voices raised in panic became low-pitched drones, like the wings of giant bees. He gathered himself and leapt.

He flew five feet through the still air before catching the rope, the rest of his body jerking to a sudden halt and the flowers swinging wildly on either side of him. He winced as the muscles in his shoulders strained with the weight and his hands burst into bright flares of pain, but forced himself to ignore it. He pulled himself hand by hand along the rope towards the next building, his boots dangling twenty-five feet over the crowded street below.

Tidi-lei slowed the flow of time itself in a small radius from the object containing it, allowing the bearer to appear to move with supernatural quickness to those outside of its influence. It was also the least conductive of the types of energy, fading more quickly than its two counterparts. Even the largest iron metal-bound objects could hold at most a few minutes' worth of time.

Fletch's ring could hold about a minute, when fully charged. It should be enough time for him to get himself out of situations like this, if he used it wisely.

His fingers caught the eave of the next building as the convergence's stored power ran out. The voices below took on the normal shrill cadence of people panicked by fire. He pulled himself up to the roof and found himself face-to-face with a hunter.

It wasn't Anisaria. This man was older than most of the cats, his hair beginning to go grey at the temples, fine wrinkles branching out from his eyes and the corners of his mouth.

A crossbow string twanged, and Fletch felt a bright bloom of pain in his left shoulder. He winced, raising a hand to clap against the bolt sticking out of his skin, as the hunter's hard eyes narrowed. He dropped one hand to hang the bow from a hook at his belt, the other lifting a stout club.

Fletch spun, throwing himself into a run along the rooftops away from the hunter. Pain vanished. The limp vanished. Everything faded into an eerie clarity fueled by the knowledge that if he didn't outrun this man, his life would be over. He knew every steeple, every window, every entry into the undercity and all the paths through them. He wouldn't be caught. He *couldn't.*

He heard the hunter's heavy footsteps behind him, falling slowly behind as Fletch leapt from roof to roof. He ducked around chimneys, ran along metal rails ringing roof-top gardens, and wove his way through a small forest of steeples on the roof of a Temple, his boots tapping on the glass roof of the worship hall. He caught a glimpse of shocked faces looking up at him from below through the glass, bathed in candlelight. And all the while the footsteps behind him faded.

He was certain that he was in the clear . . . until another hunter stepped out in front of him, crossbow leveled directly at his heart. This man was younger than the first, his long dark hair hanging in a braid over his left shoulder. Fletch snarled a curse and dodged to one side, but he wasn't quick enough to avoid the bolt entirely. It slammed into the same arm the older hunter had hit, above the elbow this time. Fletch cried out and dropped into a roll, coming up in a crouch to find himself facing a third hunter. This one was a woman. She knelt four feet in front of him and wore all black. Her eyes were as dark as her long hair, and she held a pair of wicked-looking blades which curved around the outsides of her hands.

Fletch had seen hunters work together before. But never in more than a pair. The price on his head must have been incentive enough for them to put aside their greed for a change.

Lovely.

He reached down for his case of needles, only to find it shattered, a crossbow bolt embedded in the leather of his belt. He dimly remembered feeling something hit him in the whorehouse, and growled a curse under his breath. His needles were undoubtedly scattered all over the floor back there, and he had no reserves.

"Greencloak." A smile spread over the female hunter's face. It was predatory and dangerous, even more so than Ayal-ia's had been. "We've been looking for you."

"Come tomorrow, you still will be," Fletch snapped. He pushed off to his right, only to come to a skidding stop as a *fourth* hunter stepped out from behind a chimney. This one was Eldressi. His skin was the color of burnt molasses, his metallic gold hair bound in hundreds of tiny braids.

Fletch stood and turned in a slow circle, his body tense.

The first man, the eldest one, had finally caught up with the others. They stood around Fletch, four points of a square, the woman rising to her feet with languid grace.

Used my last convergence, he thought, turning to try to keep them all in sight. *No needles, no knives. They're not leaving any gaps between them, and I can't tell if any are weaker than the others.* And, to add insult to injury, the adrenaline was beginning to wear off. His leg ached. His hands burned. The arm that had been shot was worse than both of those combined. He glanced down, clenching his teeth. He stood on the ridge of the roof. The older man and the Eldressi stood in front and behind him, respectively, straddling the ridge. The other two stood on the downward slanted tiles to Fletch's right and left. All of the tiles appeared to be firmly affixed, for once. Of course.

"Looks like a half-dead rat," the woman said, a sneer twisting her face into a grotesque mask. "Chance. No challenge in taking him like *this*."

"Then why not . . . come over here and . . . try to take me," Fletch said between pants for breath. "Even half-dead rats can . . . bite."

"Shoot him, Eril," the woman said, never taking her dark eyes from Fletch. "Bounty's near as good dead as alive, and he'll be less trouble as a corpse. He's halfway there already anyway."

The man with the graying hair gave her a sharp look. "No, Ria."

"She's right," the man with the crossbow and the braid said harshly. A scar marred his face from his temple diagonally across to his opposite jaw. "Greencloak ain't no normal mark, Ezin, even injured. We oughtta do him. Safer that way."

Ezin, Fletch thought with a sinking feeling. *Gods below. Of all the bloody—*

"I said no," Ezin said, interrupting Fletch's thoughts. "When you chose to work with me, you swore to abide by my rules. Well, this is one of 'em. I've never brought in a mark dead, and I'm never going to."

Fletch turned to look at the older man, trying to ignore the throbbing waves of pain radiating up from his arm and the burning in his lungs in order to exude confidence. "Ezin o'Fairis," he said, looking the man up and down. "I thought you'd be taller."

Ezin grunted, but his eyes narrowed ever so slightly.

Fletch straightened, his breath finally beginning to come more naturally. "Word is that . . . you're the best hunter in Adunare," he said. "Too good for amateurs like this." He gave the man with the crossbow a withering glance before turning back to Ezin. "How about you and I settle this like the men we are? You and me. No kittens, no weapons."

"Do you take me for a fool, Greencloak?" Ezin asked, his expression darkening.

"I take you for a man of honor and integrity." *Which is the same thing, really, but I doubt you'd see it that way.* He nodded towards the woman with the knives. "I take *them* for fools."

He heard a low growl to his left. Good. He shifted his weight, preparing himself.

"You've obviously been in this business long enough to know that you can't depend on unreliable shit-for-brains hunters like them," Fletch continued. "I bet they shoot at anything that moves." Ezin's eyes darted to Fletch's left.

"Erillis," he said sternly. "Stand down."

The man with the crossbow growled again deep in his throat, taking a step towards Fletch. "Y'ain't my father," he said, his eyes fixed on Fletch but his words directed to Ezin. "And y'ain't my boss, neither. We found 'im, and we ain't gonna lose him now 'cause of your stupid—"

Fletch shifted his weight and made a half-lunge towards the man, as if he were about to dash at him. The hunter flinched, and the finger he'd curled around the trigger of his crossbow reflexively jerked. Fletch had already dropped to his knees, expecting this reaction, and the bolt screamed by over his head. He felt the wind of its passing kiss his forehead. A single heartbeat later, the woman with the blades let out a harsh cry of pain. Fletch didn't turn to see if she fell. He lunged to the side to grab Erillis's ankle, yanking it out from under him. The man toppled over backwards with a thud and began sliding, his hands desperately scrabbling for purchase but only breaking bits of tile that clattered and slid around him as he continued on his slide towards the street.

The Eldressi man cursed and ran at Fletch from behind. Fletch turned, taking in the pair of short swords the man carried. Each was barely as long as his forearm. Fletch reached up with his uninjured arm in the seconds he had before the man reached him, unclasped his cloak, ducked, and flung the thick fabric upwards into the Eldressi's face as the man lunged at him, blade extended. The steel slid across Fletch's cheek instead of burying itself in his chest, leaving a line of searing pain in its wake. Fletch grabbed the Eldressi's shoulder and fell back, rolling and planting his foot in the man's stomach as he went.

The hunter was heavy, but his momentum carried him over Fletch's head easily. He landed on his head with a sickening crunch and slid bonelessly down the roof after the man with the crossbow. Fletch reached out and snatched his cloak from the man's tangled limbs before the Eldressi vanished over the edge of the eave with a shriek. The woman was nowhere to be seen.

That left Fletch alone with Ezin. Fletch stood slowly, whirling his cloak back around his shoulders and clasping it with bloody fingers as he stared at the hunter. The man had his crossbow aimed at Fletch's leg. "I don't want to shoot you, son," he said, his expression dark.

"I must be more charming than usual tonight," Fletch replied, feeling a bit more sure of himself now that it was only him and Ezin. "Usually I don't hear that until at least the fourth date. If you like, we can skip straight to the sixth. By then they all want to shoot me again."

"You've murdered five people," Ezin said dangerously, and glanced at the eave over which his kittens had tumbled like cards. "Maybe more. And you've gotten a friend of mine shut away in jail, facing the noose in the morning. And you expect me to laugh at your *jokes*?"

"Do you think I'd be funnier if I killed more often? Because I suppose I could arrange that." His bloodied fingers darted into his pocket, fumbling at the thing he found there. One of Anisaria's prayers, symbols scratched into its flat surfaces. A smile twitched at the corner of his mouth at the irony.

"Hey hunter," he called. "Catch."

He flipped Anisaria's prayer directly at Ezin's face. The hunter's eyes widened and his left hand reflexively shot up to swat at the projectile. Fletch took the momentary distraction to turn and dash five steps to the edge of the roof. He didn't stop to think. He jumped.

It was a good twenty feet down to the street. He landed hard and rolled to break as much of the fall as he could, but his injured leg buckled under him when he tried to stand and another wave of blinding pain shot up his arm. He forced himself up, sparing a glance at the female hunter lying on the street, moaning and holding one hand over the crossbow bolt jutting from her shoulder. Her face changed with each panting breath, as if it were melted wax. Fletch aimed a half-hearted kick at her side before limping for the entrance to the undercity which he knew lay around the corner.

People on the street gave him surprised looks as he pushed past them. Warm blood coated his cheek, running down his neck. Apparently that cut hadn't been as shallow as he'd thought. He winced with every step, but managed to make it to the alley without hearing any sounds of pursuit behind him. He ducked in and made his way to the metal gate at the back, shoving it open on squeaky hinges and stepping into the darkness. He paused long enough to look back through the bars into the alley.

It was empty. Ezin hadn't followed. *Probably picking up his kittens,* Fletch thought as he turned and began limping into the darkness, counting his steps and running his right hand along the wall beside him. He had no light. Thankfully, he didn't need it. Four intersections and five hundred thirty-two steps later, he figured he was far enough to be safe. He stopped and sagged against the wall, sliding down it to sit on the cold stone floor in the pitch blackness of the tunnel. The stone thrummed slightly beneath his hands.

His arm throbbed, and his leg burned. His hands joined their voices to the chorus of pain as the last dredges of adrenaline wore off. Fletch leaned his head back against the wall, squeezing his eyes shut against tears.

He was tired. Tired, and well past the limits of his endurance. But he had one more shot, just one, to catch the murdering bastard who had done all of this to him. The bastard who had killed Vethin, and been responsible for those ten still bodies in the den . . . and for Blue's death, he had no doubt.

The meeting. Fletch opened his eyes in the darkness, looking up towards the unseen roof of the tunnel.

He had to make it to that meeting. It was his last chance, the only place and time where he knew for certain the murderer would be.

He no longer had Anisaria, and the hunter's assurances that turning the killer over would clear Fletch's name.

Killing the bastard would have to do. It would be his vengeance against the whole sorry lot of them. He'd ruin their plans, even if he had to give his own damned life to do it.

But to do that, he'd need weapons.

He used the wall to get to his feet, resting his weight against it until the pain faded and the dizziness passed. Then he limped into the darkness, his jaw clenched.

Chapter Twenty-Six

Fletch stood in the shadows across the street from the Paress's weapon shop, his arm in a sling and several tinctures and poultices numbing his pain. He'd made one brief stop along the way to procure the necessary medical supplies and bind his wounds, then spent an hour making his way through the undercity step by painful step, but he'd finally arrived.

Fletch gritted his teeth, staring at the shop. A year ago, he'd stolen a batch of prototype metal-bound weapons being sent to one of the High Council members. Every five years, the mage in question held a competition for the weapon-smiths of the city. The one with the most innovative new weapon would be eligible for a year's worth of financing towards the creation of new weapons, a veritable fortune. It was only after Fletch had taken the lot to Blue to be destroyed that he'd learned that one of the items, a glass globe covered with a complicated web of thin silver wires, had been the work of Jodrif.

Such globes were fairly commonplace, but the gas inside was something truly special. Blue had exclaimed over it before reluctantly destroying it, telling Fletch that, when heated by the wires, the gas would render anyone breathing it unconscious for up to an hour, maybe more, with no lasting effects. It was extremely volatile, extremely potent, and extremely expensive. There was enough gas to fill a large room.

Or a theater.

Fletch remembered seeing Jodrif standing in the doorway with an exact replica of that globe the day the sicario had attacked Anisaria. Apparently he'd spent the last few years re-creating his work. Avara would likely have Fletch's head on a plate if she knew that he was planning on stealing it. Again. But this time he wouldn't be destroying it to make a point to the mages.

Dim light shone through the windows at the front of the shop. Someone was there, though Fletch couldn't imagine why. Dawn was two hours away, and he knew that Avara didn't usually arrive until an hour after sunup.

Oh well. Even injured and exhausted, he could sneak in and steal the weapon without Avara being the wiser.

He made his way carefully around to the back door, kneeling in front of the lock and drawing in a sharp breath at a jab of pain from his leg. He pulled one of his lockpicks from his belt and paused.

He reached up with his good hand, gently turning the handle.

The door opened. Fletch hesitated, the door open only a crack. He heard voices inside, Avara's and Jodrif's and someone else's, though he couldn't make out what they were talking about.

Fletch had been in the back of Avara's shop often enough to know that a hallway stretched from the back door, lined with doors leading to various store-rooms, a forge, and a small room with a cot for when Avara worked too late at night to want to head home. The last door on the left led to the workshop where Jodrif worked. Judging by how faint the voices were, Fletch guessed that that was where they were.

He pushed the door the rest of the way open and limped silently into the hallway. The globe would be in one of these store-rooms, unless he was completely off his mark. He opened the door, watching the end of the hallway out of the corner of his eye in case Avara, Jodrif or their mystery guest finished their conversation and headed back here. He stepped into a room lined with racks of half-finished weapons and shelves stacked with metal wires, wood, bone, and steel ingots. He scanned the shelves, searching for the globe.

He found it on the third set of shelves beside the door, inside of a wooden box carved with delicate traceries of flowers. Two other small globes rested beside it, barely the size of luminaries. Jodrif had been experimenting with making smaller, more portable versions, apparently.

Fletch picked the two small globes up, carefully tucking them into a pouch at his belt. They might come in handy. Then he reached into the box with both hands, his fingers brushing the cool glass.

As he began lifting it out, he heard something behind him. A slight footfall, perhaps. He started to turn . . . and with another blinding wave of pain, the world went black.

Unconsciousness gave way to pain. Fletch groaned, not opening his eyes. Maybe if he kept his eyes closed, he could sink back into blissful sleep and leave all this pain floating on the surface of his mind, like a skim of soap on water. He could sink back down into the dark depths and let them claim him for a time, then—

Something cracked against his face, launching him up from the depths to burst into the bright light of pain. He forced his eyes open, squinting. Someone stood over him. They were fuzzy, blurry, barely a silhouette against the light.

"Avara?" he asked, blinking rapidly. The word felt thick and cumbersome, as if his tongue were swollen.

"No," a feminine voice snapped. He flinched at its loudness. An unfamiliar face came into focus, the face of a woman bending down to look Fletch in the eyes. Her own were dark and full of anger, her long brown hair falling forward to screen the sides of her face. He tried to lift his hand to push her away, but found that he couldn't move either of his hands. He groaned again, twisting his wrists against the ropes binding them.

Bloody glass and caal-fire.

"Looks like you've had a rough couple of days, boy." *That* was Avara. Fletch looked away from the unfamiliar woman to see the weapon-smith standing beside Jodrif. The rest of the room slowly came into focus, resolving itself into Jodrif's workroom. "Care to explain why you were trying to steal from me?" Her eyebrows drew down into a scowl. "*Again?*"

"I don't care why he was stealing from you," the unfamiliar woman snapped. "Knock him back out and leave him here until we get back, then you can question him until the city falls, for all I care."

"Not a good idea," Jodrif rumbled. "We leave him here alone, he'll have those ropes undone in ten minutes flat."

"Ten?" Fletch said, though his mouth felt as if it had been stuffed full of cotton and his tongue felt twice its normal size. He didn't know whether he was more insulted by the man's under-estimation of his abilities or the fact that they'd tied him in this chair.

"So what?" the woman rounded on Jodrif. "We don't have *time* for this! Suken's going to be executed in an *hour!*"

Executed? A glimmer of dark satisfaction flitted across Fletch's mind. *Good. Serves him right.*

But something wasn't quite right about that, and deep down, he knew it. If Anisaria was going to be executed, it meant that he'd been caught by the guards. Doing what? Bringing the mage-born to the Ruddy Amapola, maybe? No. . . . That didn't make sense.

It doesn't matter why the traitor's going to get his neck stretched, Fletch thought to himself viciously. *He'll be dead. That's enough for me.*

Avara walked over to look down at Fletch. "Do you have any idea what's happening?" she asked coldly.

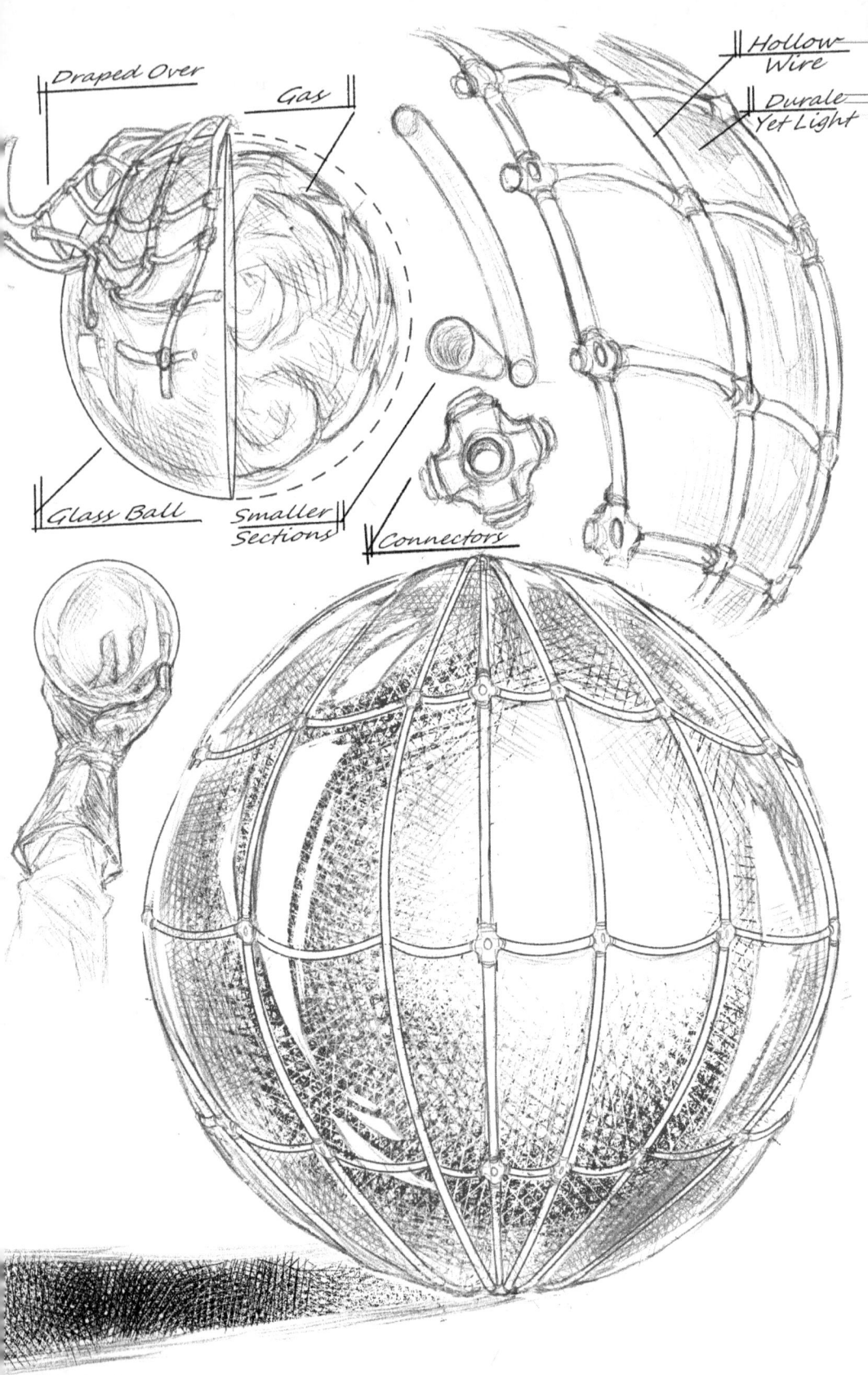

Draped Over

Gas

Hollow
Wire

Durale
Yet Light

Glass Ball

Smaller
Sections

Connectors

"I'm being framed by the Coalition," he said. "Everyone and their mother's hunting me, and if I don't make it to their bloody meeting tonight to kill the man impersonating me before he gets up on that stage, they'll turn the name Greencloak into a banner behind which the poor will march, killing every last gods-be-damned mage-born in the city."

Avara stared at him.

"Didn't know that, did you?" he said. "Guess the great Avara Paress, mistress of whispers and rumors, isn't—"

Her hand flew out to crack him upside the face. The world swam for a moment before settling back into sharp, throbbing pain.

"Ow," he said flatly.

She leaned forward, her nose nearly touching his. "You've got it mostly right," she said. "Only the Coalition's not going to stop with killing the mage-born. They're planning on turning this into a full-blown bloody revolution against the mages."

"About time somebody did that," Fletch said, almost on reflex. But the words rang hollow. As much as he'd love to see the mages go down in a hail of their own caal-fire, that line of still bodies in the rock-strewn cavern reminded him that he hated the Coalition far, far more than he'd ever hated the mages.

"More importantly," Avara continued as if she hadn't heard him, "Suken's going to be executed at dawn for aiding and abetting you."

"Aiding?" Fletch barked a laugh. "The bastard stabbed me in the back. He—"

"He knew you were listening," the strange woman cut him off. "In that room underneath the theater. He lied to them to get into their confidence, then brought that poor man to the guards to testify, to clear *your* bloody name."

Fletch looked up at her. "Who *are* you, anyway?"

"The woman who's about to give you another smack in the head with this," she picked up a half-carved club from the workbench beside her, "if you don't *shut up and listen.*" Anger flashed in her eyes, anger every bit as strong as Fletch's own. He had no doubts that she was serious.

"Fletch," Avara said, and there was something different in her voice this time. She almost sounded as if she were *pleading.* "He was trying to help you. And they're going to hang him for it."

"He knew what he was getting into," Fletch said, but as the words left his lips he felt a chill run down his spine.

"I warned you," he'd told Blue in his nightmare.

If Avara and the woman were right, and Anisaria hadn't betrayed him . . . If he'd known that Fletch was listening in, and thought that Fletch would trust him enough to know he was bluffing . . .

He thought back to earlier tonight, watching the conversation as it played out in that room. *He deliberately turned the conversation to the Coalition's plan for the den,* he realized. *Gods, he was warning me. Trying to give me the jump on them, so I could get there before them.*

A wave of guilt washed over him. Could Fletch turn his back on Anisaria, let him die for trying to help him? Like Blue had? Could he let this end the same way, when this time he had a chance to stop it?

Gods below. This was why he preferred to work alone.

Avara shook her head and turned to the other woman. "He's not going to help us. Go ahead and knock him out. We'll have to hope that he's still here by the time we get back."

"Hold on a second," Fletch said, looking back and forth between the women. "Are you planning on trying to *break him out? Of a guard's precinct?*"

"What do you care?" Avara snapped. "You're just as willing to let your friends die as you are to steal from them, apparently."

I never said he was a friend. Fletch couldn't quite bring himself to say the words aloud. They weren't true, and he knew it. He'd offered Anisaria the chance to work with him because he'd seen something in the hunter, something that he admired, something that drew him. Potential. And not only the potential for a business partner, either. Potential for friendship. Real, true friendship.

Or maybe more.

He pulled away from that thought like a child snatching his fingers back from touching something hot.

Friendship. A partner. Trust. Things Fletch hadn't had in . . . gods below. So long that he could barely remember what they were like.

"Which precinct is he in?" Fletch said, hopping the chair an inch to the side away from the madwoman with the club. "Fifteenth?"

"Yes," Avara said. "Why?"

"If you're going to try to break him out, you need me," Fletch said, his mind already whirling with half-formed plans he'd laid years ago. "It's practically theft, isn't it? Stealing him out from under their noses. You know I'm the best, Avara."

Avara held up one hand, forestalling the club-wielding lunatic. "Now you change your mind? Why?"

"It's a challenge," Fletch said, forcing a flippant tone. "I love a challenge. Especially if it involves stealing from the high-and-mighties. Or, in this case, their lapdogs. I've already put some thought into this, in case I ever needed to—"

"That's a load of shit," Avara snapped. "The truth, Fletch. I want to hear you say it."

"We don't have time for this," the woman said, looking at the small window set high in the wall.

"She's right," Fletch said. "If we want to do this we—"

"There *is* no we," Avara said, leaning forward, "until you tell me why you changed your mind. Otherwise I won't be able to trust you not to vanish as soon as we untie those ropes." Her eyes narrowed. "The truth, Fletch Greencloak. I know it's like trying to squeeze water from a bloody rock to pry the truth from those lips, but unless you do, we're doing this without you."

Fletch stared at her, gritting his teeth.

Forty-five minutes 'til dawn, give or take. This is going to be close enough as it is.

"The handsome bastard tried to save my life," he muttered, looking away and feeling like a chastised five-year-old boy. "With practically nothing to gain, and everything to lose. I owe it to him to return the favor."

Avara leaned back, obviously pleased as a cat with a bowl full of cream.

"And gods know that if I let you do this alone, you'll botch the job and wind up hanging next to him," Fletch snapped. "Bloody amateurs, the lot of you. Now untie me." Avara pulled a knife from her belt and knelt beside his chair. "And Avara?" Fletch said as the ropes parted. He began massaging his left wrist. "We're going to need a portable metal-bound furnace-stone."

Avara cocked an eyebrow. "Why?"

"You'll see."

Chapter Twenty-Seven

The floor of the cell began vibrating, rousing Suken from a sleep plagued with nightmares. He sat up, glancing out the window as the clouds rolled back across the city to reveal light slowly bleeding into the sky.

This is it, he thought. *Any minute now they'll be coming down that corridor. Then a brief ride on the pathway to the Arrival Circle, and then.... After hours of thinking about his past and the future he'd never see, he felt strangely ... at peace.*

He'd never find his brother, if Din was even still alive. But he'd done the best he could, and he'd helped a lot of people along the way. He supposed that he'd have to be content with that.

Something flashed in the morning light as it passed between the bars of the window, turning end over end. It bounced to the floor beside him. Suken stood, looking down at a prayer. It lay on the stone in the middle of the cell, glinting in the early morning light beaming in through the window. He bent with a wince and looked at it more closely.

The symbol carved into the prayer was the Mountain. Suken picked it up and flipped it over. Someone had folded a piece of paper into a tiny square and stuck it to this side. Suken unfolded it, keeping his back to the bars of his cell. *Stay near the window,* the note said in cramped text. He walked over to the window and raised himself on his toes to look out.

The street was empty. Suken looked back down at the prayer, hope kindling in his heart. He brought it his lips and looked up at the sky.

"Thank you," he whispered.

Before the words even finished leaving his lips, the air shook with a concussive blast somewhere nearby, the floor beneath his feet shuddering, dust trickling from the stones of the ceiling. He heard cries of alarm outside in the street and within the station.

Stay near the window.

Suken did, turning to see Weyav darting down the hallway, glancing from side to side as he went.

"Kel," Suken called. "What's—"

But the guard was already gone. Suken grabbed the bars of the window and pulled himself up to look out.

A harsh red flickering light underlit a bank of smoke rising into the sky from what must have been a burning building a block away. People began flowing out of nearby buildings, most half-dressed, clustering in packs. He heard the sound of boots thunking on cobblestones, and soon a full regiment of guards raced towards the fire, Weyav among them. One of them shouted for someone to connect the flame-hose to the pump which pulled water up from the undercity aqueducts.

Fletch, Suken thought, a grin crossing his face. *Who else could it be?* He wasn't sure which he was more relieved by: the fact that the thief must have gotten away from Niden and his men, or that Suken's own impending death now looked like less of a certainty. *I knew he wouldn't leave me to die,* he thought.

Well . . . earlier in the night he hadn't been so certain. But those doubts had apparently been baseless.

What was Fletch's plan? The fire was a distraction, obviously. But Fletch was a thief, not a fighter. There was no way he'd be able to take out whatever token force the guards had left at the station. The prayer told Suken to stay near the window, so Fletch wasn't planning on destroying the wall. So how . . .

The floor beneath his feet was hot. Suken looked down, only now noticing that he could feel the heat even through the soles of his boots.

What the . . .

He grabbed the bars of the window, pulling his feet up off the floor, the bruises on his ribs aching with the exertion. Within a matter of seconds, the stone in the center of the room began to glow red, then it . . . *melted.*

Suken watched in horrified fascination as an uneven circle about three feet wide began to liquefy like hot candle wax, sagging downwards. Another moment and it dropped into darkness, a hiss and cloud of billowing steam rising up through the hole after it.

"Hurry the fuck up," a voice called from the steam-enshrouded darkness. "And don't touch the edges."

Suken dropped down from the window, glancing at the prisoner across the hall. He stared at Suken with his mouth hanging open.

"See you," Suken said, touching his fingers to his temple in a salute, feeling almost giddy with relief. He took a deep breath and jumped into the hole.

He landed in ankle-deep scalding water, hot steam pressing against him on all sides, sweat immediately breaking out on his face. Someone grabbed his arm and pulled him a few feet to one side, the water growing cooler with each step. Finally, they exited the steam and Suken looked up to see Fletch bathed in the light of a luminary hanging around his neck, sporting a deep slice across his cheek, his left arm hanging in a sling. He was coated in soot and his fingers were bandaged. He must have found his cloak somewhere, because he wore it now, hood down, the hem being pulled in the current of the water running around his ankles.

Ten minutes ago he'd been certain that he was about to die. And now . . .

Now he had a second chance.

"Took you long enough," Suken said, a stupid grin spreading across his face. He couldn't help it.

"Typical," Fletch said. He sounded exhausted. "Save a hunter's life, and get paid in insults."

Suken laughed. "Would you rather I kissed you?"

"Yes," Fletch said, as if it were obvious.

I might take you up on that later, Suken thought.

"But we'll have to save that for a time when we're not in danger of drowning," Fletch continued. "Come on."

"Drowning?"

Fletch started jogging, his limp heavier than it had been the last time Suken had seen him. "Fighting that fire is going to draw all of the water out of this aqueduct for the next few minutes," Fletch said, his voice echoing in the damp tunnel. "But as soon as it's out, this place is going to start filling back up."

"You set the fire?" Suken asked, splashing after him.

"Avara," Fletch said.

Suken's grin spread wider. He'd have to do something special for her when this was all over. Bring her and Jodrif out for a nice dinner. Or maybe a few drinks.

"Well," Fletch called back over his shoulder a moment later, "Hate to say I told you so, but . . ." he paused. "No, actually, I don't. I told you so. This is what you get for trusting pearls."

"Very funny," Suken said, rolling his eyes. "Did you get to the kids in time?"

Fletch was uncharacteristically quiet for a moment, splashing along the tunnel ahead of Suken. Then, "No."

Oh, Chance.

Suken hurried his steps until he was jogging alongside Fletch in the narrow tunnel. "Are they all right?"

"Most of them are," Fletch replied. "The ones who aren't, died quickly."

"Tam?" He could barely get the name past the lump in his throat.

"She's all right."

A flash of relief, but anger burned it away at the thought of the kids who hadn't made it. "Bastards," he hissed.

"Yes. It was that sicario. The one who attacked you at Avara's."

"We'll get him, too," Suken assured him.

"If the bloodmoss didn't do him in already," Fletch replied darkly. "What I can't figure out is how they found the den to begin with." He rounded a corner. Suken had no trouble keeping up with him. As he jogged, he noticed that Fletch had been right. The water was swiftly rising. When he'd landed down here, it had been up to his ankles. Now it was nearly to his knees.

"Did you catch Niden?" Suken said.

"Who?"

Fletch's luminary illuminated a metal gate blocking the tunnel ahead of them. They pushed their way towards it, the water's current helping to push them along. It lapped against the backs of Suken's knees now, and every so often he saw things float by his legs, bobbing in the water. Judging by the smell, they certainly weren't fresh fruits.

"Corporal Niden," Suken said as they reached the gate and sloshed to a stop. Fletch dug into a case at his belt and pulled out a lockpick. "He's the murderer. The one who's impersonating you."

"Why am I not surprised that it would be a pearl," Fletch muttered, and continued, raising his voice to be heard over the rushing water. "He never showed up at the whorehouse. But about fifteen of his friends and four of yours did." He plunged his hand under the water. "I might have left them a bit worse for the wear." His expression took on an air of concentration, his eyes staring sightlessly at the metal gate as he worked beneath the surface of the water.

Suken looked back over his shoulder. He thought he heard shouts echoing down the aqueduct, but he couldn't be certain over the rushing of the water. "You can open this, right?" he asked.

"Yes."

"Are you sure? Because—"

"I would probably have it open by now if *someone* didn't keep breaking my concentration," Fletch snapped.

Suken swallowed his next question, remaining quiet as the water steadily rose to his chest, swirling around him in dark, stinking eddies. A thin layer of yellowish foam floated on top. He watched Fletch, standing with his shoulder pressed against the gate, his right arm submerged. The water lapped at the shorter man's chin. The luminary around his neck had been submerged, masking its light and making it look like a wavering glowing ball beneath the surface. Suken grabbed the cord, snapping it to hold the luminary over the surface, where it would actually do them some good. Fletch didn't take any notice.

If Fletch didn't open the gate soon, they'd certainly drown down here. The current was far too strong to swim back, even if they could have made it that far by the time the water rose high enough to submerge them.

"Look, I hate to bother you," Suken said as Fletch tilted his head back to avoid the water rising above his mouth, "but—"

"Bloody lock's half rusted over," Fletch muttered to himself. He looked up at Suken. "Come over here and hold out your hand." Suken stepped closer to him and did so. Fletch raised one dripping hand out of the water and pressed a tool into Suken's palm.

"I don't know how to—"

"I know that," Fletch snapped. "Just hold it where I put it." He took a deep breath and ducked under the water. Suken felt the thief take his hand, guiding it towards the gate. He felt Fletch's hand around his put tension against the metal tool, and adjust the position of Suken's hand slightly before letting go. Suken froze, holding the pick exactly where Fletch had placed it as the water rose to his neck. He felt the other man doing something, his hand grazing Suken's knuckles in a series of quick movements. As the water rose above Suken's mouth, the pick in his hand jerked violently and the gate swung open.

Fletch surfaced, his expression grim, clinging to one of the bars of the gate. He spat some water to the side and nodded forward. "Go," he said.

Suken pushed his way past the gate, Fletch following him.

Exit, he thought, eyes sweeping over the tunnel walls desperately, *exit, we need an exit. . . .*

"Fifty feet," Fletch said, sounding out of breath. He was having to hop now to keep his head above water, bobbing like a cork, his uninjured arm stroking the water to his right. "There'll be a—"

His voice cut off in a strangled gurgle. Suken glanced back over his shoulder. Fletch was gone.

Suken swore and took a deep breath, ducking his head under the water, keeping the luminary with him. He opened his eyes in a murky land of swirling, distorted images and tried not to think about what was in the water currently touching his eyes. He felt around until his questing hands found Fletch. Suken could barely make him out, but he saw enough to realize that the thief was struggling with something around his neck.

His cloak, Suken realized. *It's caught on something.*

He forced his way further down under the water, grabbing Fletch's belt to keep from being swept away with the current, and held the luminary closer. Part of the fabric had snagged on a broken piece of the metal gate protruding from the floor of the tunnel. Suken put the luminary's cord between his teeth and grabbed the cloak with both hands, pulling.

Nothing happened. Suken gritted his teeth over the cord and

pulled himself down hand over hand along the cloak to where it was caught, his fingers seeking out a way to free it. His lungs started to burn. He longed to take a deep breath, but he knew that to do so would be suicide.

Not to mention disgusting.

Finally, after what seemed like hours, he managed to tear the fabric free. The current began pulling them down the tunnel. Suken grabbed Fletch, wrapping an arm around his chest, and planted his feet on the floor, pushing himself towards the surface.

His head hit the roof of the tunnel without breaking the water.

He blinked back a few bright little flashes of pain, and the luminary fell from between his teeth as he exhaled an involuntary gasp of pain, bubbles escaping to brush against his nose and forehead.

Fifty feet, he thought desperately, running his free hand along the rocky ceiling as the current carried him along. His lungs felt as if they were on fire.

It can't be much farther. I need to find—

His fingers lost contact with the stone. Suken punched his hand upwards, grabbing onto the edge of a vertical hole in the ceiling before they were swept past it. He pulled, injuries screaming in protest, Fletch a dead weight under his arm, hauling them inch by inch closer. He managed to get his elbow up, and his fingers blissfully closed around the rung of a metal ladder. Just as he thought he couldn't possibly hold his breath any longer, his head broke the surface of the water.

Suken gasped in a lungful of sweet air, stars dancing in front of his eyes, but he didn't have time to revel in it. Fletch's head was still under water, and he'd been under longer than Suken had. He managed to get his shoulder pressed against the inner edge of the hole, letting go of the rung briefly to snatch at the one above it.

The next rung was easier, as less of the water was pressing

against his lower half. Fletch's head broke the water. Suken looked up. Three more rungs led to a metal grating, through which morning light filled the bore.

"Fletch?" he asked, adjusting his grip around the thief's chest.

The thief didn't reply. His eyes were closed, and his skin looked entirely too pale.

Suken felt his heart pounding like a drum. He had to get Fletch out of here and onto a flat surface. He somehow managed to reposition Fletch so the thief was slung over Suken's shoulder, and pulled them up the last three rungs. He gritted his teeth against the horrid aching pain in his injured shoulder, now bearing the full weight of an unconscious thief. He looped his arm through one of the rungs and shoved at the metal grate with his other hand.

It creaked upwards, thank the Lady, falling back to the street with a clang. Suken pulled himself up another rung and flopped Fletch's body to the street, pulling himself the rest of the way out of the hole after him. Dirty water cascaded from him to pool around Fletch's still body as Suken turned the other man onto his back.

He bent over the thief, pressing his head to Fletch's chest. He wasn't breathing.

"No," Suken whispered. He made a fist and slammed it against the other man's chest. He'd seen someone do something like this once for a child who had fallen into one of the fountains. "Come on," he said through gritted teeth, slamming his fist down again and hoping to every god he knew of that he was doing it right. "Come *on*, damn you, breathe!"

Nothing.

Suken let out a frustrated sob as he brought his fist down again. "*Breathe,* you fucking bastard, breathe! I know you're too stubborn to die, so come on!"

Fletch spasmed and coughed, water spewing up from his mouth, and began choking on it. Suken hurriedly turned the man onto his side as Fletch alternately coughed and retched water onto the street. It was only then that he looked up to see where they were.

People stood in a loose circle around them, staring with wide eyes. They were on the edge of the Valley District, and the people were all poor, wearing moth-eaten ripped serapes or soot-stained workers' uniforms.

Suken glanced down at Fletch, who was still hacking and coughing. And wearing his unique, namesake cloak. He looked back up.

The name passed amongst the crowd like a gentle breeze, whispered by one person after another. *Greencloak.*

"Get out of the way," a familiar voice said somewhere nearby. Suken turned in time to see Terri shoving her way through the crowd, muttering under her breath. Her clothes were stained with ash, and a long smudge of soot marked her forehead like a brand. When she pushed past the last person and saw Suken, a flash of relief passed over her face. She hurried forward and knelt beside him, reaching out to steady Fletch's shoulders as the thief continued to retch into the street.

Suken stood slowly, looking at each face in turn. Men. Women. A few children. All poor. The last time most of them had seen a bath-house was obviously weeks, even months past. They wore clothes little better than rags and expressions ranging from curiosity to greedy consideration to outright awe.

He remembered walking through the streets days ago, asking after Greencloak. Remembered the stories the people had told, the way they'd protected him. Remembered how quickly the poor members of the Coalition had rallied behind the *idea* of him, the legend of Greencloak, the man who flipped the wealthy a rude gesture as he fleeced them blind.

"You know who this is," he said simply, meeting each member of the crowd's eyes in turn. "He needs help."

"Is that *really* him?" a woman carrying a basket of moldy bread asked, her eyes fixed on Fletch.

"Thought he'd be taller," a man said, crossing his arms.

"And better lookin'," another man replied skeptically.

Murmurs swept the crowd, people leaning close to one another.

A whore pushed her way between an incinerator worker in a soot-smudged uniform and the woman with the moldy bread. She wore an open-fronted serape over filmy trousers and a shirt that barely concealed her unmentionables, her red hair bedraggled and her makeup smudged. She bent, tilting her head to peer at Fletch's face. Then she nodded and straightened. "That's him," she said, her voice steady. The murmurs quieted.

The whore narrowed her eyes and looked Suken up and down. "What you doin' with Greencloak, cat?"

The energy in the street shifted from curiosity to tense menace with that one word. All eyes turned to Suken. He saw several hands drop to what were undoubtedly the hilts of illegal, concealed weapons.

"I'm helping him," he said, keeping his hands in plain sight and taking care to make no moves which could possibly be construed as dangerous. "We need a place to stay for a few hours until he gets back on his feet, somewhere where the other cats and the pearls won't be able to find him. Food, water. Maybe some medicine and fresh bandages." Fletch had finally stopped retching, but he seemed to have fallen unconscious. Terri was now sitting on the street with her legs crossed, Fletch's head in her lap. Suken looked at the whore. "Please," he said, lowering his voice and taking a careful step towards her. "Just a few hours. You can even tie me up until he wakes up, if you want to be sure that I'm not up to something."

Silence, save for the pattering of rain on the street and the ever-present hum of humanity nearby. The whore nodded once.

She turned to the crowd. "Any of you bloody bastards get it into yer heads to turn 'im in for the bounty yerselves," she said, turning slowly to look at them, "I'll find ya, and I'll set the fuckin' cartels on yer hides so quick ya won't know what hit ya."

Dropped gazes, shuffling feet. The whore turned back to Suken. "Pick 'im up," she said, "and follow me."

Chapter Twenty-Eight

Fletch awoke in a dimly-lit room, the smell of soot heavy on the air. He sat up, his head pounding, and looked around. The room was tiny, barely larger than a closet. The bed he lay on—if it could be called a bed—was stiff and hard, and a dirty blanket had been draped over him.

He raised one hand to rub his temple. Where was he? The last thing he remembered was the aqueduct under the station . . . his cloak getting caught, the water filling his lungs, the panic as he realized that he was about to die.

"You probably shouldn't be moving," a familiar voice said. Fletch looked towards it and barely made out Anisaria sitting in the shadows on a rickety chair, a dark blanket draped over his shoulders. He yawned, raising one hand to cover his mouth, and stretched. Before he could stretch his left arm to the fullest, he winced and drew it back.

"Where are we?" Fletch asked.

"The Valley," Anisaria said, glancing at the ragged curtain hanging in the doorway. Dark circles stood out under his eyes, and a shadow of stubble marked his jawline. "After I hauled you up out of the aqueducts, someone was kind enough to take us in." A sour look crossed his face. "Apparently she's a Coalition member."

"*What?*"

"Calm down," Anisaria said. "Most of them think you're a hero, remember? It's only the leaders we have to worry about." His expression darkened. "And Corporal Niden."

"How did we get out of the aqueduct?" He could probably guess, but he needed to know for sure.

"After I got your cloak untangled, I found the exit and dragged you up after me."

He says it as if it were simple, Fletch thought, staring at Anisaria. *But that can't have been easy, with me unconscious. He saved my life.*

And less than twelve hours ago, Fletch had been plotting his death. He realized that he was ashamed of that, of not trusting the hunter, of jumping to the wrong conclusion without giving him the benefit of the doubt.

As soon as he'd realized that the hunter hadn't betrayed him, all those rejected plans of getting the man to turn to a life of crime as Fletch's partner had come surging back, but did he really deserve as good a partner as Anisaria had proven himself to be?

Fletch was unnerved to realize that he wasn't sure.

He leaned back against the wall, closing his eyes and forcing all that shame and doubt to the back of his mind. "What time is it?"

"Late afternoon. You were out for a while. Figured it would be better to let you get some rest."

Late afternoon. They still had plenty of time to come up with a plan on how to wreck the Coalition's little party.

Well, maybe not *plenty* of time. But enough. Especially now that he knew who the killer was. Even if the man managed to get away from the meeting, Fletch would be able to track him down easily enough.

Anisaria shifted, not looking at Fletch. "I haven't thanked you yet," he said.

"For what?"

"Saving my life." His voice was solemn.

"Well, we don't have much time, but I suppose we can make do." He gave the kitten his most lecherous grin.

Anisaria gave him a smile. "Maybe later."

Fletch raised an eyebrow, but Anisaria continued as if he hadn't said anything unusual. "Look, I . . . Thank you. Really. I . . ." he rubbed his arm, looking at the window, his expression haunted. "If it weren't for you, I'd be dead right now."

Fletch shrugged. "Least I could do, for a partner." His tone was flippant, but he watched Anisaria carefully, to see what his reaction to that would be.

The man looked troubled. "I'm still considering your offer," he said softly.

Fletch let the subject lie, knowing better than to push, and reached to his waist for his belt. His bandaged fingers encountered only thin fabric, and he started, looking down. Under the dirty blanket, he wore only a stained linen shirt about six sizes too large for him and a pair of trousers that would probably fall off of him if he stood up. Both were darned and patched, and so thin in a few areas that the fabric was practically sheer.

Anisaria stood, holding the blanket around his shoulders closed in the front. "Your things are next to the bed," he said. "Including your cloak. Our host was gracious enough to lend us some of her brother's clothes while ours dried out."

"You stripped me while I was unconscious?" Fletch said. "There's hope for you yet, kitten."

Anisaria actually blushed. "Both of us are tired and injured," Anisaria said. "I figured that catching a cold was the last thing we needed."

"Admit it," Fletch said, leaning forward. "You just wanted to see me naked."

Anisaria cleared his throat and walked over to the window, pushing aside the dark curtain shrouding it. Through the thin oiled paper which served as a substitute for glass, Fletch made out the dull light of late afternoon. "At least one good thing came out of this," Anisaria said. "We know who the killer is, and we know where he'll be tonight."

Fletch sobered at that. "What did he do when you showed up with that shifter?" he asked.

"He killed him," Anisaria said flatly. Fletch knew the kitten well enough by now to hear the anger buried beneath the words, but he moved on with hardly a pause. "If I can get Niden to the High Council, I can request a Truthread directly, but getting to the bastard's going to be tough." He let the curtain fall closed. "He knows we're out here, and that we know about him. He's not going anywhere alone from now until the Coalition makes him their martyr."

"Martyr?"

"They're going to let the guards execute him," Anisaria said. "Use his death to incite the people to rise up against the government."

Fletch blinked slowly. "They actually think that will work?"

Anisaria shrugged. "Historically, it's viable. When people feel oppressed, it doesn't take much to push them over the edge."

"I find it hard to believe that he's willing to let himself be killed. Why not hire a shifter, like your dead friend? Why not threaten someone else into it?"

"You're underestimating the power of a unifying cause," Anisaria said, shaking his head and sitting down. "Niden's wife and daughter were killed by a mage-born, his other daughter crippled. He *truly believes* in what he's doing. Anyone they hired or threatened could turn on them at an inopportune moment, tell the guards or the Council the truth. That's why they couldn't have turned you, the *real* Greencloak, over to the guards. But Niden?" Anisaria leaned forward, resting his elbows on his knees. "Niden *believes*. I bet he thinks that he's giving his life to stop anyone else from suffering the same pain he did."

"That's khanna-shit," Fletch said. "Mage-born are no more or less likely to be killers than anyone else."

"You and I know that. But Niden . . . he's obviously lost sight of reality, Fletch. He might not even care about the Coalition's greater plan, so long as he accomplishes his goal of eliminating the mage-born. He'll become Greencloak and willingly walk up to that noose, knowing in his heart that he gave his life for the greater good."

"What an idiot," Fletch muttered.

"There's nothing you'd risk your life to save?" Anisaria asked, staring at Fletch. "No one you would die to protect?"

"You can't protect anything after you're dead."

"Strange," Anisaria said, leaning back and eyeing him. "I seem to remember you putting your life at risk earlier today to save those kids."

"So Niden's going to give his life for the greater good, blah blah blah, et cetera," Fletch said, hoping to steer this conversation back to more productive territory. "Why not kill the bastard ourselves? I know about a few poisons that would—"

"No," Anisaria snapped.

"He's a *murderer*," Fletch said. "You said it yourself. . . . The guards will execute him anyway, so why not make it easier? Why not do it for them? Just you and me. Make him pay for what he did to Vethin, and all those other mage-born."

"You're talking about murder," Anisaria said flatly.

"I'm talking about *justice*."

"I said *no*," Anisaria said, turning his head to give Fletch a dark look. "We need to take him to be Truthread in order to clear your name and convince the High Mages of what the Coalition is planning. After they read him and get the names of all the people he's working with, they'll try him for his crimes and execute him. Justice is found through due process, not at the end of a knife in a dark alley."

"Need I remind you what *due process* got you yesterday?" Fletch said. "Here's a hint. It involved a rope around your neck and a big man in a black hood."

"This is different," Anisaria said. Gods below, he was stubborn. "Niden was a Coalition member. Chances are pretty damn high that a High Council member won't be, since the Coalition is working to bring them down."

The man's naivety was truly amazing. "Let me give you a life lesson, kitten," Fletch said. "If the High Council gets their hands on Niden, they're not going to allow a Truthread. You know why?" He leaned forward. "Because they're going to wonder, 'what if Niden only knew false names? What if he's in the dark about who the leaders are?' That's certainly how I would have done it, if I were in charge of this little party they're running. Code-names. Masks. No one knows anyone else's names, so no one can sell out the others. But," he raised one bandaged finger, "if they have Niden alive and sane, they can cut him a deal. His life, in exchange for leading a group of Mazarine Guards to a meeting of the Coalition leaders. They'll make him a double agent, a spy, in return for his sorry hide." He leaned back, watching the kitten's expression. So far, he hadn't turned to look at Fletch. That could either mean that Fletch was getting through Anisaria's thick head, or that he was stewing in stubborn silence. Fletch pressed on, hoping for the former.

"The Council doesn't give a damn about justice for a bunch of poverty-stricken dead mage-born," he said. "They can always make more of those. But finding the leaders of a treasonous re-bellion?" He clenched his fist, barely noticing the pain as his torn and bruised fingers tightened. "You better believe they'll care about *that*. They'll cut him his deal, and Vethin and the others will never get justice. The Council will catch the leaders in their little snare, and either pay them off or hire sicarios to dispose of them quietly if they can't be bribed. They won't make any sort of a public announcement . . . wouldn't want to give the rest of the people in the city any *ideas*. And they'll still need someone to pin Niden's murders on, since they promised him his life. I've already been framed like a bloody painting, so they'll let the guards execute me when I eventually get caught. Why not? I'm just a thief." His mouth twisted into a dark parody of a smile. "I'll die, Niden will live in captivity or exile, and the Council will get everything they want. Like they always do. *That's* what will happen if you go running off to the Council. But we have another option."

He paused, trying to read the other man's expression. Anisaria stared out the window, his expression carefully blank. "You were right about one thing," Fletch said. "The other leaders of the Coalition deserve to be brought down, too. This wasn't only Niden. So here's what we do." He reached down, picking up his cloak and running his fingers along the fabric. "First we kill Niden," he said, "and whoever's guarding him. Put my cloak on him, and let some Valley residents find him and start planting rumors that the *Coalition* killed him. Everyone except for the Coalition's leaders will think I'm dead, so the warrants will go down. They might hire some sicarios to come after me, but I'm sure that together, you and I can take care of them. Over the next few weeks or months, however long it takes, we hunt down the rest of the leaders, one by one. If you're so concerned about justice, we can do it by framing them, making certain that the guards raid their homes and find information which leads them to the truth. Then, once we're certain that all of the leaders are dead or behind bars, I go and commission a new cloak." He lifted one corner of it with a smile. "Greencloak returns from the dead, and everything goes back to the way it was. I get vengeance, you get the other leaders prosecuted or whatever it is you want, and then you and I start looking for that brother of yours." He paused, and continued carefully, "If that's what you want."

"What you want," Anisaria said, finally turning, "is vengeance. Not justice."

Fletch didn't answer.

Anisaria's expression turned cold. "This isn't a debate," he said. "We find a way to get Niden alone or almost alone, capture him alive, and I bring him to the Council. That's how this is going to work. Understand?"

And if I said no? Fletch thought. *What would you do?*

Probably knock him out and leave him tied up somewhere safe until this was all over. Fletch finally realized with a dull pang of remorse that no matter what he said or did, Anisaria would never come around to his side. He was too stubborn, too set in his ways, and above all too . . . well, too *good.* But those ethics of his, those morals, were part of what made the kitten so damn interesting. Fletch was surprised to realize that if the kitten *had* taken him up on his offer, he wouldn't have been nearly as interested in him.

As fascinating as all of that was, though, it wouldn't help Vethin. It wouldn't fill the deep need in Fletch's heart to see Niden and all of the rest of the leaders of the Coalition suffer for what they'd done; not only to the mage-born victims, but to Fletch himself. They'd ruined Fletch's life, killed Fletch's lover, and forced Fletch to drive the orphans away. And Fletch wouldn't, *couldn't,* take the chance that Anisaria's little plan would backfire on him. However, he couldn't do this alone, either. He knew that now. He needed Anisaria, needed his help, needed his trust.

So he'd do what he did best, though not without a bit of regret for what could have been. He shrugged and let out a sigh, feigning acquiescence. "Not leaving me much of a choice, are you?"

"No."

"Then fine. Whatever you say, as long as you promise me that he winds up dead."

Anisaria leaned down, putting one hand on the bed and looking Fletch in the eyes. "I have your word that you won't try to kill him?"

"You have my word that I won't try to kill him." *Because I'm not going to try. I'm going to* succeed.

Anisaria stared at Fletch for a long moment, nodded, and straightened. "We need to find a way to get him alone."

"The only place we know for certain he'll be is masquerading as me on that bloody stage tonight," Fletch said.

"In front of two hundred people," Anisaria replied dryly. "That's not exactly *alone.*"

Fletch swung his legs over the side of the bed, wincing and glancing at his left arm. The bandages wrapped around his fingers and arm were clean, new. Anisaria must have replaced them while he was changing Fletch's clothes. "He's got to be alone sometime," Fletch said. "When he uses the privy, for instance. I doubt he's going to want guards watching him while he shits."

"True, but they'd be waiting right outside, and most privies don't have a back exit," Anisaria said, starting to pace. The room was only wide enough for him to take three steps before turning and retracing them. "The Coalition's going to have every guard and street tough they can hire on him tonight. But . . ." he stopped. "What if we could draw those guards away from him? Not all of them, of course, but most of them?"

"How?" Fletch asked. "If I had access to my money I could hire a veritable army of thugs, but I can't risk trying to get at any of it. I'm relatively certain that you're broke, and as pretty as your smile is, I doubt it's going to get us the kind of help we need."

"We don't need to hire an army," Anisaria said, a smile spreading across his face. "We already have one."

Fletch blinked. "We do?"

"Greencloak is supposed to be giving a speech tonight, right? Well . . ." He looked at Fletch. "What if he does?"

"It sounds," Fletch said slowly, "like you're suggesting that I go up on that stage myself. But that can't possibly be what you're suggesting, because it's bloody stupid."

"Hear me out," Anisaria said, starting to pace again. "If you got up on that stage before Niden and told the people the *truth.* . . . Chance, if you worded it right, they'd be outraged. Someone trying to frame and kill their beloved Greencloak? You could incite them into a riot. They'd want the leaders of the Coalition's heads on bloody plates. Any guards they put on Niden would have to split up, help the other leaders to get out with their heads still attached to their shoulders." He quickened his steps and started talking faster, the words almost spilling out of him. "I'd be backstage, watching. I'd follow at a distance, wait until Niden got far enough away, then take out however many guards he had left and capture him."

"And if he's got more than one or two?" Fletch asked. "What then?"

"I'll figure something out. I always do."

Very reassuring, Fletch thought. "And while you're playing with Niden and his unknown number of guards," he said, "I'm supposed to do what, exactly?"

"After the chaos breaks out, you could sneak backstage and catch up with me. Help me take him down."

Fletch started drumming his fingers on the edge of the bed, but stopped with a wince as the pain reminded him that his fingers were still torn to shit.

It wasn't the *worst* plan he'd ever heard, but there were still a lot of things that could go wrong. But then, what plan didn't have potential to go astray? And he had to admit that the thought of turning all the Coalition's little lapdogs against them had a certain . . . vicious appeal.

After he and Anisaria got Niden alone, he could knock Anisaria out and kill Niden, put his cloak on the corpse, and all of the Coalition members would believe that their leaders had killed him in the aftermath of his revelation.

Gods below, he might not even have to hunt down the Coalition's leaders. Their own members would do it for him.

All he'd lose was Anisaria's trust.

That made him hesitate. First the orphans, now Anisaria.

Sacrifices need to be made, he told himself, though that buried shame writhed below the surface of his mind. *If I have to destroy every friendship I have to get vengeance for Vethin and Blue . . . so be it.*

He stood, wavering for a moment before he caught his balance and holding up the waist of the pants so they didn't fall. "If we're going to do this," he said, "I'm going to need better clothes than what I was wearing when I broke you out. Or these." He looked down at what he was currently wearing. "And you're going to need a weapon. Probably more than one. And don't tell me you're still insisting on not using one because you don't have your bloody license."

"I think the High Council and the Guild will understand that these are extenuating circumstances," Anisaria said solemnly. "That's why an hour ago I sent Terri to go out and get everything we'd need." He grimaced. "Apparently she'll be using the last of my money to do it, but at least the weapons will be free. She seemed certain that Avara would lend them to us."

"Terri?"

"My housekeeper," Anisaria said. "She said that you two met earlier. Something about a club?"

"She's your *housekeeper*?" Fletch shook his head. "You're either very brave or very stupid to keep that rabid excuse for a woman under your roof."

"A little of both, I guess."

Fletch bent and picked up his cloak, folded neatly on top of the pile of his other clothes. "This had better work, kitten."

"It will," Anisaria said. He pulled a prayer from his pocket and held it up to the dim light. It was the one that Fletch had written the message on and thrown in his cell window. "We've got the Lady on our side."

"Lovely," Fletch said. He picked up his belt, and the case attached to it, flipping it open and glancing inside.

The two small spheres from Avara's were still there. He nodded and closed it again.

If Anisaria's plan didn't work, Fletch at least had a backup, a way to get himself out of that theater in one piece. And if the plan *did* work . . .

He had a way to knock Anisaria out and finish the job himself. He grinned and lay back down on the bed, intending to rest until the kitten's psychotic housekeeper showed up.

Chapter Twenty-Nine

Suken crouched beside Fletch on the familiar rooftop overlooking the theater an hour past Descent, his abused shoulder aching less now that he'd taken numbroot to dull the pain. Vines coated the railing with thick leaves and the scent of orchids was strong in the twilight air. Thirty feet below, two guards stood outside of the theater, but otherwise the street was empty save for mist. The meeting was probably about to begin inside, and most of the law-abiding middle-class citizens in this district were safe in their homes behind locked doors, unaware of what was being planned in their midst.

Suken leaned to one side, trying to see what was happening through the wide, high windows of the lobby. "They're still in there," he said, watching as the people clustered into groups, some breaking off to join others or to pair off like partners in some incredibly intricate dance. "But it won't be much longer now."

"Good." Fletch crouched beside him, idly playing with one of Suken's prayers. Suken wasn't certain where he'd gotten it—the thief had probably picked his pocket at some point. Fletch wore a midnight blue tunic cut in the mage's style, cinched tight to his waist with a forest green sash. His cloak was turned right-side out to display the green, the hood up to shroud his face in shadows. Even under the bright lights of the stage, no one would be able to see much of his face. In the dim light of twilight, he seemed less like the man Suken had gotten to know for the last few days and more like the infamous Greencloak.

That's who he's always been, Suken reminded himself. But he couldn't make himself think of Fletch as another heartless criminal anymore. He knew him now. Knew what drove him. Understood his passions, his loyalty, his talent. He was a criminal, yes, but he wasn't *only* a criminal. His life was every bit as complicated and complex as Suken's own.

Suken turned his thoughts back to what they were about to do. Fletch had taken more numbroot than Suken had, but then, he was more badly injured. Suken was honestly surprised that the thief was still able to walk, let alone do what he had to tonight. He'd removed all of the bandages from his fingers. In their place, he wore black gloves.

"Once they're all inside, we move," Suken said. "I'll stay with you, pretending to be hired muscle, until we reach the stairs up to the boxes."

"At which point you break off and head backstage and I go and make my grand entrance," Fletch said. "We've been over this, kitten. Nervous?"

"Yes," Suken said, wiping his sweaty palms against his pants for the tenth time. "Aren't you?"

"Why would I be? I'm stealing the loyalty of the people, then throwing it back in the faces of those smug bastards running the show." Suken could barely see the thief's grin in the shadows of his hood. "Sounds like just another night's work to me."

Suken thought he heard the lie behind those words, but he couldn't tell if Fletch was nervous about the speech, or about whatever it was he was obviously planning to do to Suken.

He'd agreed to Suken's plan far too easily back in the whore's bedroom, especially after all that time trying to convince Suken to kill Niden. He was going to backstab Suken somehow, use him to further his own plan. Whatever Fletch was planning probably wouldn't leave Suken dead, not after Fletch had risked his life to save him from the executioner's noose, but it certainly wasn't going to help Suken get Niden to the Council, either. So Suken had resolved to keep a close eye on him, as much as he could, anyway.

Through the huge windows, Suken saw the mask-less man from the previous meeting step onto the dais before the doors to the theater. Everyone in the room turned towards him.

"They're moving," he said. He turned to look at Fletch, his fingers creeping down to brush against the familiar weight of the crossbow strapped to his leg. He felt much more at ease now that he had the weapon, despite the fact that it was illegal for him to be carrying it. *I suppose that makes me a criminal now, too,* he thought uneasily. He turned towards Fletch. "Ready to make your first public appearance, Greencloak?"

Fletch rolled his eyes, turned, and made his way through the rooftop garden to the ladder hanging down into the alley. Suken followed him down, his boots making dull clangs against the metal as he descended, and joined Fletch in standing in the alley across from the theater. Mist beaded on Fletch's cloak and on Suken's serape.

"This is it," Suken said, glancing askance at the other man. "Once we walk out of here, no turning back." He paused, and continued quietly, "Are you sure this is what you want to do?"

He wasn't talking about the plan, of course. He was giving Fletch one last chance, hoping that the thief would confess to whatever he was planning . . . or maybe decide not to do it at all. *He saved my life,* Suken thought, trying to peer into the shadows of that hood. *Do I feel that I owe him for that, or . . . is there something else going on here?*

"It's either this, or being hunted by cats and pearls until I'm too wounded and tired to keep running," Fletch said. He glanced down at his hand, flexing the fingers and wincing. "Which wouldn't be too far off." The hood turned towards Suken, inky blackness beneath the hood impenetrable. "You looking to back out, kitten?"

"No," Suken said. "I'm in." *But don't think for a moment that I'm going to sit back and let you do . . . whatever it is you're planning to try.*

"Good. Let's go," Fletch said, and stepped into the street.

The men at the front door stared at Fletch as he approached, their eyes wide. He stopped at the top of the steps, staring at them.

"Um. . . . Meeting's already begun," one of the men said.

"You a bloody idiot?" Anisaria said, gesturing at Fletch and doing his best to imitate a Valley accent. He did a passable job. "This is fuckin' *Greencloak*. Ain't your superiors told you he's speakin' tonight?"

The men stepped back as one, their eyes growing wider.

"I'm s-sorry, sir," one of them said. "We, uh, we thought you were already here, in the back."

Thanks for the information, idiots. Fletch swept by him without a word, cloak flapping. One of the doormen called after him, but Fletch ignored him, pushing open one of the doors and stepping into the nearly-deserted lobby. Servants in black flitted about, picking up empty wine glasses left on tables.

One looked up. The wine glass he'd been holding dropped from his fingers to shatter on the marble floor. Fletch continued toward the closed doors to the theater, walking slowly to hide his limp, though the wound sent little jolts of pain up his leg with each step. His arm burned too, but the numbroot was keeping the worst of the pain closed off behind a wall of fog. Anisaria followed in his wake.

He reached the double doors leading into the theater, pushing one open to reveal the dimly lit entryway, stairs sweeping up from the right and left towards the boxes, the aisle between the floor seats stretching down towards the bright stage below. The room smelled of dusty velvet and sweat. Someone on the stage was speaking, his voice barely more than a low monotone up here.

"Remember," Fletch whispered over his shoulder. "Try to get Niden to the costume room, if you can." *That's where the entrance into the undercity is. Easiest way for me to make a getaway after I slit the bastard's throat.*

Anisaria didn't move. He stared at Fletch, his gaze searching the shadows of the hood. Fletch felt a brief pang of worry, looking at those narrowed hazel eyes.

Does he suspect? he thought. If he does, this is all going to get a whole lot harder.

Anisaria shook his head, as if shaking free a thought that was bothering him, and that damned handsome smile flitted across his face. "Good luck," he said. He held Fletch's gaze for another moment, and Fletch wondered if the kitten was going to kiss him for luck. But Anisaria didn't. He turned and started up one of the stairways towards the boxes.

Fletch looked down at the stage, taking a deep breath and putting thoughts of troublesome bounty hunters with handsome smiles behind him. This was a performance, like any personality he assumed while casing a potential target or fencing some stolen goods. The difference was, this time the mask was himself. This legend he'd unwittingly built around himself, that of Greencloak. . . . Tonight he decided exactly who that man was. Self-serving thief? Hero? Murderer bent on vengeance? Should it be Fletch himself? Or should it be someone else entirely, someone the people could rise up behind, someone they could admire?

Fletch wasn't stupid, or blind. He knew that he wasn't a likable person. He was sarcastic, and self-contained, and didn't really enjoy being around other people very much. He repelled people more often than he attracted them, though there were a few who were stubborn enough to stick around long enough to see through the snide veneer.

And most of those I've either gotten killed or driven away, he thought, thinking of Tam, of Blue, of Avara.

Greencloak couldn't be Fletch, that was for certain. He needed to be someone else, at least for tonight. So who?

He'd once heard that Greencloak had once stolen a woman's undergarments while she was wearing them without her noticing. He wasn't certain why he'd ever have wanted to do so, but he supposed he might have been capable of it, in the right circumstances. He'd heard the one about the statue in the Academe (it was mostly true), and dressing the mages in the incinerator workers' uniforms (not true, but he'd seriously considered doing it after he'd heard it).

The people also apparently thought that he was giving his stolen money to the poor, albeit discretely. That last was most certainly *not* true, but if perpetuating the myth would help him to turn the people against the Coalition, that's who he'd have to be. Who he would *become,* for as long as he was on that stage, anyway.

Cocky, daring. A flair for the dramatic. All of those things would come easily to him. Coming across as charitable would be harder, but wasn't impossible. Personable, trustworthy . . . those would be the hardest to convey. He thought of how easily Anisaria had struck up a conversation with that fat mage in the entryway last night, how he'd even managed to breach the high walls around Fletch himself and get him to trust him enough to offer him a partnership.

With a start, Fletch realized that he'd need to become a mix of his own personality and Anisaria's. Fletch's bravado and wit, with Anisaria's easy smile and ability to gain people's trust.

If it works for the alias, it works, he thought. He straightened his back, let his new-found personality drape over him like its namesake cloak, and strode down the aisle.

Suken stepped into the empty hallway at the top of the stairs, his boots sinking into the thick blood-red carpet. The hall swept ahead of him in velvet-swathed, dimly lit opulence. It was eerily silent, save for the echoes of voices rising up from the theater behind the curtains lining the left-hand wall.

He knelt outside one of the curtains, pushing it aside to peek into the box. He saw the heads of two people above the backs of the seats, and let the curtain fall back into place. He moved on to the next one, knowing that he should be making his way backstage, but unable to move on without knowing that the first part of their plan was going well.

He opened the next curtain a couple of inches, enough to see that this box was empty. Suken made his way to the balcony overlooking the theater just in time to see Fletch striding down the darkened aisle, his cloak billowing behind him as he walked. At first, no one noticed. The hundreds of faces angled up to stare at the man on the stage were intent. But as Fletch made his way closer to the stage, people began to glance at him and nudge their neighbors. A hum of curious voices rose, interrupting the man onstage, whose speech trailed off as he lifted one hand to shade his eyes from the bright lights.

Fletch reached the base of the stage, vaulting over the waist-high wall separating the seats from the mage's effect box, and pulled himself up onto the stage itself. Suken winced, knowing how much that had to hurt. But the other man didn't let on.

"Actually," Fletch said, his voice echoing through the quieting theater as the voices of those in the seats trailed off into silence, "I'll be speaking now."

No one shouted, or leveled crossbows at him, or cried for the guards. Suken scanned the faces in the boxes opposite him, but all of them were wearing masks. He couldn't tell if they thought that Fletch was Niden, or if they were displeased. None of them were moving, though, so that was a good sign.

Good enough for Suken. He pulled a prayer from his pocket, kissed it and laid it on the balcony railing. *Keep an eye on him for me, Lady,* he thought, and ducked out of the box.

Suken turned left into the section of hallway which led towards the stage, glancing back over his shoulder every few seconds. Once he got backstage, he was certain that he'd begin running into guards. But it was entirely possible that one or two had been stationed up here, too. The Coalition wouldn't have wanted to take any chances with Niden's safety, not with what was at stake for them.

He made it to a simple wooden door at the end of the hall without encountering anyone. He took a deep breath, steadying himself, and reached down to turn the handle. It wasn't locked. The door swung inwards on well-oiled hinges to reveal inky blackness. . . .

And the sicario who had attacked him in Avara's shop, the one Suken had named Hawk.

The sicario seemed to have been having as rough a couple of days as Suken and Fletch. His face was puffy and red, covered in weeping sores and scratches. But whatever had happened to him clearly hadn't affected his reflexes or his speed.

His fist flashed out, and Suken barely managed to dodge to his right, tripping and falling on his side. Bruises flared into bright flowers of pain as he rolled and came up to his feet, unhooking the crossbow from his belt before he was finished coming to his feet. His other hand dropped to work the lever to load the weapon, his eyes fixed on the assassin straightening in front of him. The man stood a few paces away, a small throwing knife held in one hand, the other up in a guard position near his throat.

Hawk had sliced the skin below each eye, probably to let out some of the blood so he could see, but the cuts looked inflamed.

"Didn't your mother teach you to stay away from bloodmoss?"

Suken's next words were harsher, tainted by the memory of Fletch telling him that this man was responsible for ten still, small bodies in the undercity. "Maybe you should have eaten it and saved us all some trouble."

The assassin's eyes narrowed. "Where's the thief?"

"Behind you," Suken said, stepping to one side, crossbow trained on the other man's heart.

The man didn't turn.

Oh well. It was worth a shot.

"You must be the worst sicario in the history of Majitan," Suken said, taking another small step to the side. He slowly, carefully reached into the case hanging from his belt, his fingers seeking out the tiny needle he'd put there for safekeeping yesterday night, the one Fletch had used on the young woman in Lord Garron's manor. "I thought you people were supposed to be *dangerous.* You couldn't even manage to kill an injured thief and a hunter without a weapon."

"A situation I will now be remedying," the man replied between bleeding lips.

"Given your record so far?" Suken snorted. "Might as well surrender and save me some time."

Hawk's fingers tightened on the knife he held.

"Can't say I didn't give you a chance." Suken whipped his hand out, throwing the needle in his hand directly at the assassin's face.

The man cursed and slapped it out of the air, but by the time he returned his attention to where it should have been, Suken had stepped into the shadows of the doorway leading to the backstage area of the theater.

The Coalition's spokesman's voice echoed around Fletch as he walked down the wide central aisle.

"—so glad to announce that our testimonial speaker tonight

will be none other than Greencloak," he said. A round of polite applause followed his words. "He'll be speaking later, after we've discussed some other matters. Now, I . . ."

People in the audience had begun murmuring to one another as Fletch passed them, and now the man onstage finally seemed to notice. He paused, one hand shading his eyes. Fletch reached the edge of the stage and pulled himself up, only somewhat hampered by his injured leg and arm. The man—Teric, Fletch remembered—stared at him with a dumbfounded expression as Fletch clapped a hand to his shoulder in a friendly fashion, turning towards the people.

"Actually," Fletch called, "I'll be speaking now. But thank you for the kind introduction nonetheless."

"My friend," Teric said under his breath through a wide smile, "this isn't what we discussed. I . . ."

"Shut it," Fletch whispered, dropping his hand from the man's shoulder. "You want Greencloak to speak? Well, he's speaking. Try to stop me and watch how well it goes over with them." He nodded towards the whispering people in the seats.

All of the color drained from Teric's face.

Sit back and watch, asshole, while I single-handedly ruin everything you've tried to build. Just like you did to me.

Fletch turned to the assembled Coalition members. "Lords and Ladies of the Coalition," he called. "I am Greencloak."

The reaction was immediate and deafening. Half of the people in the room surged to their feet, clapping and cheering. Fletch turned his head towards Teric, tilting his head back enough for the lights of the stage to illuminate his slow smile.

Teric, predictably, stepped forward. "And how do we know that you are who you say you are?" he yelled over the applause, an edge of desperation to his voice.

"You invited me here," Fletch said, pitching his own voice up to be heard by the whole theater.

"Many people knew that you were to speak tonight," Teric said, giving Fletch a vicious sidelong glance. "You could be anyone."

"What would convince you?" Fletch asked. "A display of my skills, perhaps?" He raised his hands towards the audience. Cheers sprinkled with some good-natured cat-calls rose around him.

"I . . . that's not . . ."

While Teric was stumbling over his tongue, Fletch called, "Where's your pin?"

"You . . ." the man blinked. "What?"

"Your pin," Fletch repeated. "The one you had on your lapel when I came up here with you."

Teric's hand went up to his empty lapel. Fletch raised his left hand, the stage-lights glinting on the pin in his hand.

"Oh," Fletch said, the smile playing across his lips again. "Here it is."

Scattered laughter from the audience.

A brief flash of fury crossed Teric's face, almost immediately replaced by a calm mask. "So you stole my pin," he said, raising his voice to be heard over the laughter. "Any second-rate pick-pocket could have done that!"

Fletch carefully affixed the pin to his cloak. "Unseen, on-stage in front of hundreds of people?" He sighed theatrically and shrugged. "I suppose you're right. Any pick-pocket could have done that. But could any pick-pocket have taken these?" He reached back into his cloak and withdrew six masks, each taken from one of the people seated along the aisle as he'd walked by them.

This time the audience reaction was a moment of stunned silence, then surprised shrieks or exclamations as six people's hands flew to their bare faces. Teric stared at him, his hands balling into fists at his sides. Fletch tossed the masks to the stage as a renewed wave of laughter rose from the audience, louder this time, and accompanied by thunderous applause.

Fletch spread his hands towards the audience. "Are you convinced?"

The floor vibrated with the strength of their cheers.

Fletch looked out over the sea of faces, suddenly at a loss for words. He'd never intended to be seen as a hero. When he had begun thieving, he had done so for the sheer vicious joy of taking what the high-and-mighties loved best. . . . Their money, their possessions, their precious reputations. He'd heard the rumors about himself when they began, of course, but he hadn't much cared about them. Let people say what they would. . . . It didn't affect him, or his job. But slowly he'd come to realize that that wasn't true. More and more often as time passed, he'd discovered that his marks had heard of him, knew the legend of the infamous Greencloak. They took extra precautions with the safekeeping of their goods, making his job more difficult. . . . But that made it all the better when he circumvented those precautions and shoved their failures in their faces, time and time again.

And with each successful theft, his legend grew. His marks took increasingly extravagant preventative measures against him, and as he circumvented them, the rumors and stories grew wings and flew from mouth to mouth until the entire city was aflutter with his name.

It had been unexpected, but not wholly unwelcome. And now . . . now, he looked out over the faces of hundreds of people who admired him, looked up to him, relished in his successes almost as much as he did.

And he discovered that he liked it.

These people, the ones in the floor seats below him with tattered skirts and coal-smudged faces behind their masks, weren't like the orphans. They weren't depending on Fletch, didn't see him as family. They simply watched, silently cheering him on for doing what they couldn't.

Kindred spirits, one and all. Kindred spirits who had been misled and manipulated by those in the box seats above them.

"Now that my identity is proven," Fletch said, "I'd like to tell you why I'm standing before you tonight." The cacophony slowly faded into echoes. "For years I've worked from the shadows. I live among you in the Valley, and I've seen the things which the Coalition stands against."

Teric, who had been sidling off towards the wing of the stage, stopped, staring at Fletch.

I have to try to draw this out, Fletch thought. *Give Anisaria enough time to find Niden before I loose the dogs on their masters.* He'd seen enough plays to know that the best way to do that was with pretty words.

"Since the exile three hundred years ago, the mages have fed us a story. A floating city where magic is made available for all. Equality for Talented and untalented, for followers of any religion, any nationality, any romantic proclivities. Freedom." He paced to one corner of the stage, sweeping his gaze over the rapt crowd staring up at him. "Lies. Pleasant lies, yes, but a corpse in a ballgown is still a corpse."

Approving mutters in the crowd to that.

"Most of you were drawn to this theater by promises of a better city, a better future," Fletch continued. "The Coalition gave you a unified purpose, a place full of others who understood your pain, the pain of loved ones taken too soon." Solemn faces in the crowd nodded.

"You thought that you found family," Fletch said, warming to the subject. "And who can blame you for that? You wanted to believe that you'd found a purpose, something to work for. The mages turned a deaf ear to your pleas for aid, so you resolved to stand up and fight for the future you wished to create.

"I applaud you for that. But I'm afraid that in your eagerness to find family, to find freedom and vengeance and justice, you have been misled by the very people you trusted to help you. And *that* is why I am here tonight. To shed light on the depth of the deception that *they,*" he glared at Teric, "have led you to believe."

The silence following those words was so thick, Fletch thought he could have drowned in it. But it was shattered by a single small voice from the rear of the audience.

"Liar!"

A figure leapt up onto the seat of her chair, pulling the mask from her face, meeting Fletch's eyes defiantly. A blood-stained bandage encircled her head like a crown.

Tam, he thought, his heart sinking.

Chapter Thirty

Suken ducked behind a suspended piece of scenery on the platform inside the doorway, taking in his surroundings as his eyes adjusted to the darkness. To his left, he could make out the lights of the stage far beneath a complicated mass of wooden catwalks, curtains, dangling pieces of scenery and ropes. To his right the platform he stood on continued for another ten feet before ending abruptly at the outer wall of the theater. A set of wooden stairs stretched down into the darkness of the backstage area directly opposite the open door.

The assassin stepped through, looking warily to his left and right but not catching sight of Suken. He reached back and pulled the door to the hallway shut, plunging the platform into darkness lit only by the lights from the stage below and to his left. Suken heard the echoes of someone talking from the theater below. Fletch. Well, at least he'd managed to keep their attention so far. Suken hoped he'd be able to continue to do so for a while, because it didn't look like Suken was going to be able to find Niden anytime soon.

Hawk walked carefully along the platform, darting quick glances behind scenery pieces and curtains.

Suken reached down, his eyes trained on the sicario, pulling a metal-bound bolt from his case and setting it gently into the channel of his crossbow. He gritted his teeth as he slowly pulled the lever back, praying that it would be quiet enough.

As the lever reached the extent of the string's pull, the bolt fell into place with a dull thud. The assassin whirled towards him as Suken raised the bow, his finger squeezing the trigger. As the string twanged and the bolt loosed, Hawk's fingers twitched in the air, then he was . . . gone.

"Damn," Suken whispered, his eyes sweeping the dark platform. Tidi-lei convergences were notoriously difficult to metal-bind, but this sicario didn't need to rely on binding. He was apparently a mage in his own right. He must have sketched out the convergence before he'd even stepped out into the hallway. That meant that he had anywhere between one and twenty seconds of heightened speed until the energy ran out.

Well, Suken had time to think, *at least he can only use it once.*

He heard a sudden rushing of wind, and jerked his head to one side in time to dodge Hawk's knife. Instead of cutting his throat, the hilt of the knife caught Suken square on the chin, the blade grazing Suken's collarbone. The blow caught him off his guard despite the fact that he'd been expecting it, and he stumbled back a step, dropping his crossbow. Hawk stepped into Suken's guard with a grin, obviously thinking that he'd gained himself a moment, but Suken had been hit harder than that a hundred times in practice. As the sicario swung his knife in a back-handed slice, Suken snatched the man's wrist and hooked his right foot around the other man's ankle, lunging to the side to knock the assassin hard in the chest with his shoulder.

The resulting pain was worth it. Hawk staggered two steps towards the wall, thrown off-balance. Suken whirled, yanking a knife from his belt as he did, and flung it at the sicario, staying in a crouch. Hawk dodged, Suken's knife slamming into a piece of wood painted to look like a tree a mere fingers-breadth from Hawk's arm. Suken snatched his crossbow from the floor and pulled the lever back with his right hand as he stood, dropping a mundane bolt into a firing chamber. Hawk took a careful step to his right, keeping five feet of space between them.

"We really going to have this dance again?" Suken said. "I seem to remember leading the last time."

"You're a dead man," Hawk said coolly. "You just don't know it yet."

Suken resisted the urge to reach up and touch the shallow cut on his collarbone. *Poisoned again. Great.*

"I don't know," Suken said. "I feel pretty lively. Lively enough to take you down for the second time this week, anyway." He still had the rest of the powdered pavandala root in his case. He couldn't take it now—he remembered all too well how it had knocked him out last time. So he had an hour to find and capture Niden—then he could take the antidote.

As if things weren't hard enough, he thought with a grimace. *Now I have a deadline.*

Hawk took another step towards the stage, nearly reaching the edge of the catwalk branching out from the platform on which they stood.

"As much as I'd love to continue dancing with you," Suken said, mirroring him again, "I've got places to—"

Hawk stepped smoothly behind the giant wooden tree, and suddenly it was careening at Suken in a flurry of trailing ropes and screeching metal wheels somewhere above. He dropped to the floor, barely avoiding getting clipped on the top of the head by the base of the thing, and when he stood back up, Hawk was gone.

Fletch stared at the small figure standing on the chair, the momentum he'd been building collapsing like a house of cards in a strong wind.

"Don't listen to him," Tam cried, pointing. "He's a liar! A murderer and a liar!"

Bloody glass and caal-fire, Fletch thought. *This is the absolute worst time for you to be confronting me about this, Tam.*

Murmurs rose from the crowd. Those sitting around Tam gave her angry glances. Fletch supposed that he should have been thankful that they were siding with him and not with her, but he didn't want to see some ardent Greencloak supporter haul Tam away and beat her for daring to speak ill of him, either.

He glanced to his right, and started.

A man stood in the shadows of the wing behind the curtain, out of sight of the audience. He was wearing a cloak identical to Fletch's, and surrounded by armed guards.

Niden.

Anger swept over Fletch like a storm, dark clouds of rage with flashes of murderous intent striking and demolishing the rational parts of his mind like lightning. He took two steps towards the man before he realized what he was doing and stopped, both hands clenched into trembling fists at his sides.

Vethin. Blue. Ten still bodies enshrouded in dust and blood-stained sheets.

No, he thought. *Not now. Killing him isn't good enough. I need to make certain that the Coalition's control over these people is smashed beyond repair. Then I make him pay for what he's done. But only then.*

Besides, he'd never get past the guards flanking the man. Fletch forced himself to look away. He had to deal with Tam, and quickly, before he lost control of the crowd.

"Why don't you join me up here, little lady?" he called. "It'll be easier for you to—"

"Shut up!" Tam cried, her hands balled into shaking fists at her sides. "Shutupshutupshut UP!"

Dead silence from the crowd. Every eye was fixed on either the child or on Fletch. Out of the corner of his eye, he saw Niden push back the hood of the cloak which was a twin to Fletch's own. The bastard's eyes were steel, his gaze iron. He leaned to his right to whisper something to the guard standing beside him.

"Come up here," Fletch called to Tam, putting every ounce of authority he could muster into his voice. "If you have a grievance with me, we can discuss it like—"

"No! You're trying to fool them, like y'did us! Well, I won't let you!"

"Shut up, kid," a man in the audience shouted. "Let him bloody talk!"

Tam whirled towards the voice. "He made us think he cared about us! But then he led people to us, and they hurt us, and he didn't care! He *left us!* He doesn't care about NOBODY! He makes you think he does, but he doesn't, not really!"

Two of the guards standing with Niden stepped out from behind the curtain and began descending the steps towards the seats. The murderer gave Fletch a slow, cold smile.

"This isn't the time for a game of *Two by Hand*," Fletch said, emphasizing the phrase.

Get out, Tam. Get out now!

She didn't see the approaching men. She was too busy addressing the crowd. "Whatever he's going to tell you is a fuckin' lie! Don't believe him! He ain't never given us nothing, not money or—" one of the men grabbed her upper arm, and Tam cut off with a squeal of surprise.

There was some polite applause as Tam struggled against the man, and a few calls of approval.

"Don't hurt her!" Fletch shouted, taking a step towards the edge of the stage. The people in the front seats looked at him warily, and he took a deep breath. His next words were in a far calmer, albeit forced, tone. "Bring her here, if you please."

The guard hesitated while Tam spat insults at him and tried to pry his hand open.

"Bring her," Teric said, his voice brittle.

The man hauled Tam, twisting and clawing like a bedraggled alley-cat, up onto the stage. She hung from the guard's hand, glaring at Fletch with a gaze that looked capable of melting steel.

"Let go of her," Teric said, stepping up to Tam. When the guard did, Tam pulled away from them, rubbing her arm but continuing to glare at Fletch. "You claim that this man is not who he says he is?" Teric asked in a voice intended to carry to the entire theater.

"He's Greencloak," Tam said reluctantly, then shouted, "But he's lyin' about everythin' else!"

With a start, Fletch realized that he could use this to his advantage. He turned back to the audience and looked at the box seats. "Bribing children? You'd sink so low, to discredit me?" He shook his head. "I suppose I shouldn't be surprised, considering everything else you've done."

The people in the audience leaned to the sides, whispering with their neighbors, looking from Tam to Fletch to the box seats.

Time to stop playing coy, Fletch thought. *Let's see how you like this, you bastards.*

"You've all followed the Coalition thus far without knowing who led you, save this one," he said, gesturing to Teric. "But why would they need anonymity from you, their faithful followers? Their family?" He looked up at the boxes and raised his voice. "I challenge the leaders of this movement to stand, now, and remove their masks. Reveal yourselves, so the people can see exactly who leads them."

How loyal would your followers be if they realized you're all high-and-mighties?

Tense whispers in the audience as almost every head turned to look up at the people in the boxes. The leaders shifted uncomfortably, but none stood. Fletch grinned. No matter what the high-and-mighties did now, they'd lose the crowd. If they demasked, they'd be revealed as those the poor so despised. If they didn't, the poor would cease to trust them.

Niden stepped onto the stage, having discarded the copy of Fletch's cloak. Fletch glanced over at him.

Go ahead, he thought. *Do it.*

Niden reached up and pulled the grey mask from his face. "My name is Kefris Niden, Corporal of the fifteenth precinct of the Adunare City Guard," he said. "You know me as Lord Grey."

A hush fell over the crowd, and Fletch had to bit his tongue to keep from laughing out loud. *Oh, you've done it now.*

"I am one of the founding members of the Coalition," Niden continued, and turned his head to spear Fletch with a black look. "Our trust in Greencloak may have been . . . misplaced." He gestured to the guards, who started advancing on Fletch.

Immediately, the people rose from their seats, shouting. The guards halted, weapons undrawn.

"Don't you touch him!"

"Greencloak's a bloody hero and—"

"—ain't got no right—"

Fletch gave Niden a slow smile.

A man in the audience wearing a simple black leather mask leapt onto his seat, raising his voice over the cacophony. "You pearls ain't much better'n the mages! I came to you when my son was taken and you told me you couldn't do nothin'!"

"You work for *them!*" a woman cried. "Don't you pretend like you give a diseased shit about us!"

"Get off the bloody stage!"

Scattered shouts of agreement. Niden growled a curse under his breath. While the audience made its disapproval known, Fletch stepped towards Tam, never taking his eyes from the bastard who had murdered Vethin.

"Tam," he said barely loud enough for her to hear him, "get back to the others."

"No," Tam shot back at him, her shoulders square and her brows drawn down. "You're just tryin' to—"

"I'm trying to save your fucking life," he hissed. "*He* killed Vethin, Tam. He sent the man who attacked the den. Trust me. I'm trying to help you."

She glanced at Niden and transferred her gaze back to Fletch, her eyes narrowing. She didn't move.

He turned his attention back to the audience but kept himself between Niden and the girl, raising his hands for silence. Slowly, the people quieted, seating themselves.

"He's trying to stop me from telling you the truth," Fletch said. He took a single step towards the edge of the stage, subtly inching his hand towards the case at his belt where he'd put Jodrif's globes. "But I won't be intimidated, not by the mages in their fancy Council Chambers, and not by the rich bastards who run the Coalition. I was approached three weeks ago and asked to take part in this endeavor, and I *refused*. The leaders of this group captured me. They beat me and tortured me, they stole my cloak and my identity and *this* man," he pointed at Niden, "began killing mage-born in my name. When I escaped, they tried to kill me, and they *did* kill ten of the orphaned children I protect in order to try to draw me out!"

He swept his eyes over the crowd. "Why do all of this? Why frame me, make you believe that I was a killer?" He glared at Niden. "They knew that you looked up to me, so they coldly used that to gain your trust. Your support. They wanted you to love Greencloak, so that when they turned the man impersonating me over to the pearls to be executed, you would rise up in righteous anger and follow them to whatever end they wished." He stopped, giving them a moment to process that. Then he said slowly, "You have all been played for fools."

People in the audience began whispering to one another, but Niden's voice bellowed out over it, blanketing their doubts in anger.

"You're going to listen to this *thief*? A man who makes his living lying and stealing? I've spent my *life* protecting you!" He turned to Fletch, his face frozen in a rictus of rage. "You talk about truth, and masks, but *I'm* the one who's standing here unmasked! I've shown them who I am! Have you? No! Your claims sound little better than the stories in the bloody broadsheet serials!"

Silence fell over the theater again, and all eyes went to Fletch.

Showing the people his face would disprove Niden's point, yes. But it would also make Fletch's future far, far more difficult, and Niden damn well knew it. Fletch would never be able to show his real face in public again. He'd be forced to don a disguise every time he left the privacy of his own home, except when he was thieving.

But showing his face was the last card to play in a hand which would completely topple the trust the people had in the Coalition.

It would ruin everything Niden had worked for.

He let out a slow breath and pulled his hood back, removed the mask from his face, and blinked in the sudden bright light of the stage. "I," he said, his voice carrying over the uplifted faces of the people, "am Fletch Greencloak. And I am *not* lying." He dropped the mask and heard a quiet gasp from his left, where Tam stood.

Faces in the crowd looked back and forth between them. Fletch turned his head to look at Niden, and found the other man glaring at him. "Didn't expect that, did you, asshole?" Fletch said quietly.

"I'll see you rot in the pits for this," Niden hissed.

Fletch took a deep breath, intending to land the final blow and order the people to take down the leaders. But before a word left his lips, a scream rang out from above. He and Niden both looked up, and Fletch's mouth dropped open.

Suken searched the darkness of the platform, turning slowly. Hawk was here somewhere, waiting. Probably sketching convergences, too, the bastard. *Assassins,* he thought sourly, looking up. *I am really, really starting to hate assassins.*

He had to start looking for Niden. His time was running out, and he knew it. But he couldn't turn his back on Hawk. That was a sure way to get a knife between the shoulder blades. He'd have to incapacitate the sicario before he moved on. . . . But first, he had to find him.

More scaffolds and catwalks hung above him, vanishing up into the inky darkness. A single ladder leading up to them stood beside the closed door. The man probably hadn't gone towards the stage—too much light that way, Suken would have seen him. And in order to get to the steps, he'd have had to go around Suken. Unlikely.

That left up. Suken eyed the rickety ladder. *No*, he thought. *No way in Lady Chance's ten brothels am I going up that way.* It was exactly what the man would expect . . . and what he'd have planned for. But those ropes to the right of the ladder . . . those looked promising. Suken went to them, glancing down but keeping his crossbow pointed up towards the catwalks. Huge sandbags hung from the ends of the ropes, some touching the floor of the stage, others nearer the ceiling. *Yes. Perfect.*

He reached down and pulled a metal-bound bolt from the case at his belt, concealing it in his left hand and being careful not to touch the silver nub that would activate the convergence. He strapped his crossbow to his leg, pulled out a second small knife, and grabbed the rope. He wound it once around his wrist, gripping it in the same hand that held the metal-bound bolt, and heard a whispered curse from above.

Before Hawk had a chance to stop him, Suken sawed the knife through the rope below his hand in one clean stroke, sending a silent thank you to Avara for the sharpness of her blades. He was yanked upward as one of the sandbags plummeted towards the stage, the rope tightening around his wrist and his already injured shoulder protesting the additional strain. The upper level of catwalks rushed towards him. As he shot by them towards the shadowed ceiling, he released the rope to drop ten feet to the shaky wooden structure, reaching out with one hand to grab the railing before he could fall.

A sudden sharp pain flared between his shoulder blade and neck. Suken hissed and shuddered once convulsively. He spun, the catwalk rocking violently as he shifted his weight. Hawk darted back away from him, a small throwing knife clutched in his hand. *Another one of those is probably what's sticking out of my back right now. Great.* Well, at least it hadn't been metal-bound.

The other man leapt from one catwalk to an adjacent one, the wooden planks creaking and swaying. He darted away from Suken, running bent at the waist out over the catwalks hanging over the stage.

Suken followed him, ducking under taut ropes and leaping over hanging pieces of sets, the catwalks rocking treacherously under him.

Hawk stopped abruptly at the far end of a section of catwalk and turned. Suken warily came to a halt at the near end of the same section of catwalk, ten feet of wooden plank hanging from ropes separating them. He saw no good reason for the man to have stopped. A knife glinted in the assassin's hand, but that was hardly a surprise at this point. Then Suken happened to glance down. Fletch stood on the stage fifty feet below them, gesturing widely as he addressed the audience. And . . .

Suken blinked.

Was that *Tam* standing beside him?

"Ah," Hawk said. "There he is."

"Well done," Suken replied, looking back up. "You found a man standing in the middle of a well-lit stage."

"Throw your weapons backstage," Hawk said coldly. He lifted his own knife, holding it between his index finger and thumb. "Or your friend down there dies."

"Oh, nice try," Suken said, taking a step closer. "Very nice. But you're bluffing."

"Am I?" Hawk said.

"Your bosses need Greencloak to be their martyr," Suken pointed out. "You *were* hired by the Coalition, right? Gonna be hard to convince those people that the government killed Greencloak with an assassin's knife in his back."

"Unless I tell them that the High Council hired me." He lifted the knife ever so slightly, the threat in his eyes clear.

Point, Hawk, Suken thought wryly. He lifted his hand to show the knife to the sicario, keeping the metal-bound bolt concealed in his other palm. He curled one finger inwards to tap the silver nub and clenched his fist around it, trying not to wince as the building heat began burning the palm of his hand. "All right," he said. "All right, fine." He flung the knife into the darkness backstage. "You win." He reached down and flipped open the strap holding his crossbow to his leg next. The weapon plummeted towards the stage, and Suken winced at the thought of what Avara was going to do to him when she learned he'd wrecked *this* one, too.

He didn't have long to think about that, though. Hawk's hand whipped out towards Suken, sending the knife towards him with a whistle.

For a half a second Suken waited, his eyes following the steel hurtling towards him. Then his empty hand snapped out and snatched the knife from the air by the hilt. *Thanks, Avara,* he thought, and whirled to slice one of the two ropes supporting his side of the catwalk.

The wooden planks shifted as one corner of the catwalk abruptly dropped. Suken staggered as the whole thing shifted to the right, but he'd been ready. He grabbed the intact rope with one hand and flung the activated bolt at Hawk with his other as the assassin swayed, struggling to keep his balance.

It hit him in the leg with a loud crack of discharging force, bright purplish-white arcs of energy streaking over his black clothes and sparking off of his teeth as he opened his mouth to scream. If the bolt had hit him in the chest, the man would likely have dropped dead instantly. As it was, he'd recover from the shock in a matter of moments.

Suken started towards the sicario, meaning to knock him unconscious while he was stunned. But the man's head snapped up, and he lunged blindly across the wooden planks to catch Suken in a bear-hug. His momentum took them both off the edge, hurtling them towards the stage fifty feet below.

Anisaria managed to twist in mid-air, putting the body of the sicario between himself and the floor. They landed on the stage with a crash and a sickening thump imbued with the cracking of bones. Fletch winced, but he didn't have time to worry about the kitten now. He flung the globe in his hand into the orchestra box at the base of the stage. It shattered, unleashing a cloud of bluish smoke which hung between the crowd and the stage. That done, he lashed out with a kick that caught Niden above the ankle as people in the audience began shouting, getting to their feet. Niden snarled and threw himself at Fletch, slamming his shoulder into Fletch's chest. Fletch stumbled back, looking up in time to see Niden grab Tam by the wrist. He hauled her back with him to rejoin his group of guards.

"Half of you go to the boxes," he shouted. "The other half, with me."

"Tam!" Fletch shouted, and the girl screamed something unintelligible in reply.

Half the twenty men obediently split off, running towards a flight of steps backstage as the people in the theater milled about in general chaos. The other half of the guards surrounded Niden and Tam as the killer dashed backstage.

Fletch took one step in the direction Niden had gone, and stopped.

He wasn't going to be able to take on all those men alone. He turned and hurried to Anisaria's side instead.

The bounty hunter lay on top of the sicario, one hand pressed to his side, his face pale. A small knife jutted from his back near the shoulder, and a bruise was beginning to darken his jaw.

"I thought cats were supposed to land on their feet," Fletch said, having to raise his voice to be heard over all the shouting.

Anisaria's eyes fluttered open. He looked up at Fletch with an expression of frustrated disgust overlaid by flickers of pain and groaned. Fletch glanced back over his shoulder. Behind a screen of blue smoke, he could see that the audience was roiling towards the doors, the box seats conspicuously empty. Anisaria pushed himself to his hands and knees with a sharp intake of breath and sat back on his heels, his breath coming in quick, jagged pants. He reached up to touch his chest and winced. The assassin lay still and unmoving on the stage, one of his arms bent at an extreme angle and his eyes staring sightlessly at the ceiling. When Anisaria looked up, his hazel eyes were clouded in pain. "Was . . . was that Niden?" he asked.

"Yes," Fletch said, standing and looking towards the shadows of the backstage wing. "He took Tam." Niden was too smart to risk using any of the rear exits from the theater, not with the possibility of a lynch mob waiting out there for him. That left the entrance to the undercity concealed in the costume room.

Anisaria stood, swaying visibly before gaining his balance and pressing his hand against his side. "Think . . . think I've got . . . a broken rib. . . ."

"You'll live." Fletch started towards the darkness behind the curtains. He nearly tripped over a sandbag, then stopped, raising an eyebrow.

"This your crossbow?"

Anisaria nodded, apparently in too much pain to speak. Fletch grabbed the weapon and tossed it to the hunter, who managed to catch it.

"Hurry up, kitten." He ducked behind the curtain into dust-cloaked stillness, and a club swung by a huge, brawny arm whistled toward his head. Fletch jerked to one side and reflexively raised his injured arm to block the blow. A flare of white-hot pain blinded him for a moment and he staggered back three steps, tripping over the sandbag and sprawling to the floor. He heard a cry of shocked pain, and shook his head, looking up.

Anisaria stood over Fletch, crossbow held in one outstretched hand. Five feet in front of him, a man in dark clothes and a mask was looking down in almost comical surprise at the crossbow bolt sunk to the fletching in his shoulder. The man looked up at Anisaria and dropped to his knees. Anisaria looked down at Fletch.

"You all right?" he asked.

Fletch winced and sat up. Pain flared in his shoulder with every breath. Anisaria offered him his hand, helping to pull Fletch to his feet with a wince of his own.

"Arm's not working," Fletch muttered, gritting his teeth, trying to move it. It stubbornly refused to comply.

"You'll live," Anisaria said. He looked as if he were about to be sick. "And you're *not* going . . ." he shuddered and winced again, pressing a hand to his side, but continued, "anywhere without me."

"Better keep up, then," Fletch snapped, limping backstage.

They made their way as quickly as they could through the warren of ropes, set pieces and piles of costumes backstage until they reached the hallway leading deeper into the theater. No guards or assassins attacked them, and as they continued Suken struggled to get a handle on the pain stabbing him in the chest with every step. The blade buried in his shoulder was little more than a dull ache in comparison, though he could feel a trickle of blood making its way down his back, sticking his shirt to his skin. The injury he'd sustained from the fall was much, much worse. Each breath sent stabs of pain through him, stealing his breath and making his vision blur. He didn't try to ignore the pain—doing so would be impossible. Instead he focused on putting one foot in front of the other, on the shallow breaths he was forced to take, on the crossbow in his hand that had miraculously escaped the fall unharmed.

The only good thing about the pain was that it kept him from thinking too hard about the man he'd killed.

Fletch limped beside him, his own breath coming in sharp gasps. He must be in almost as much pain as Suken was. He'd managed to pull his limp arm over to tuck it into the front of the tunic he wore, but his face was pale and drawn. And determined.

No matter what happens, Suken thought, gritting his teeth as the pain intensified, *I can't let him get Niden alone.*

The doors on either side of the hallway stood closed, signs on them indicating that they were actors' and actresses' private dressing rooms. The hallway ended ahead at a T-intersection. Suken heard voices, but he couldn't determine which branch of the hall they were coming from. He and Fletch staggered to a stop before the intersection. Fletch pressed himself against the right wall and ducked his head around the corner.

Suken panted for breath, trying to do so as quietly as possible, and listened. One of the voices, muffled by the door, was obviously Niden, though Suken couldn't tell what he was saying.

Fletch held up two fingers, then mimed holding a crossbow and pulling the trigger twice. Suken lifted his crossbow and raised his eyebrows. Fletch nodded, pointed to himself, and made a circling gesture.

What in the Lady's name does that mean?

Suken blinked and shook his head. Fletch rolled his eyes and beckoned him closer. Suken leaned in, and Fletch breathed in his ear, "There's a doorway in that room," he nodded towards the door at the head of the intersection directly opposite them, "that leads into the costume room, I saw it the last time I was here.

You go around front and take out the two guarding the door, I'll circle through and cut them off."

"No," Suken whispered back. "We stick together."

Fletch leveled a flat look at him.

Suken returned it. "I'm fast," he said, "but not . . . fast enough to take them both down before they can raise some sort of alarm. Especially not . . . injured like I am. We're not going to be able to sneak up on Niden and his . . ." he winced, shuddering as another wave of pain swept over him, "his men, so we might as well stay together."

"Don't be dense," Fletch hissed. "You distract them, I take them from behind. It's the best plan, and you know it. Especially since he has Tam. He'll use her as a hostage, unless I can sneak behind him."

Suken glared at him. "Don't try to make this about her. While I'm dealing with the guards, you're going to try to get him alone, to kill him. Don't deny it."

"Fine," Fletch said, expression darkening. "I won't."

He grabbed Suken's shoulder and shoved him into the hallway.

Chapter Thirty-One

Suken stumbled into the hallway, Fletch barely more than a green blur darting into the door beside him. He cursed as he regained his balance and turned to see two guards standing in front of the closed door snapping loaded crossbows towards him.

Suken hesitated for the amount of time it took for his mind to remind him that these men had families. Friends. Lovers. They'd chosen to work for the Coalition, but they were still men. He couldn't kill them. But he had to get into that room, he had to do it before Fletch had a chance to do whatever it was he was planning to do, and he had to do it as quickly as possible. His finger squeezed the trigger, his other hand flying up to draw back the lever. The crossbow was reset before the first bolt found its target, and Suken swiveled slightly on the balls of his feet to let a second bolt loose. For one brief moment, the pain was nothing but an echo on the horizon of his mind, dampened by concentration.

The bolts found their homes in the guards' knees, one swiftly followed by the other. Both of them squeezed their own triggers. One bolt whistled past Suken's ear close enough for him to feel the wind of its passing. The other buried itself in his thigh.

Suken gritted his teeth against the pain and lurched forward. One of the guards was struggling to reload his bow, the other had fallen to one knee, blood-stained hands clenched around the bolt protruding from his knee. Suken reached the kneeling man first and brought the haft of his crossbow around in a wide circle, slamming it against the guard's temple. The guard fell to the floor as the second finally got his crossbow reloaded, bringing it up to point at Suken. Suken ducked under the raised crossbow and came up with a savage uppercut to the man's chin. The impact caused a flash of pain in his knuckles, but compared to his rib and leg, the pain was infinitesimal. The second guard collapsed beside the first, and Suken straightened, panting in pain and exertion.

Suken took a deep breath and reloaded his crossbow before he reached out to open the door.

Racks of costumes stood in tight rows, filling the huge room with everything from gaudy feather-covered gowns to simple garb like you'd see in the Valley. Rows of shelves lined the walls, filled with masks and realistic-looking weapons and huge fake stones and leather-bound books. Three men stood in the central aisle, whatever conversation they'd been having obviously interrupted by Suken's arrival. They all turned to face him with grim expressions. Niden stood with one hand gripping Tam's shoulder.

The girl let out a choked gasp, taking a single step towards Suken. But Niden pulled her back, pressing a knife to her throat.

Suken stopped dead in the doorway, feeling as if he'd been punched in the gut. In his mind's eye, he saw Flower, standing in a smoke-filled factory, Shifter's knife to her throat.

This won't end the same way, Suken told himself. *I won't let it.*

He stepped into the room, his crossbow aimed at Niden's heart. "Hey Tam," he said. "Sorry I'm late."

Tam tried to jerk her shoulder out of Niden's grasp, but the corporal tightened his grip. "You're a hard man to kill," Niden said flatly.

"What can I say? I like breathing." Suken's gaze swept over the room, but he didn't see Fletch anywhere. "As fun as this little chase has been, it's over now. Let the girl go and I'll put in a good word for you when I haul you in to the High Council."

"You and I both know that they're going to execute me for treason no matter what you tell them."

"True," Suken said. "But I might be able to convince them to give you a nice quick beheading instead of a hanging." *Which would be better than you deserve, you bastard.*

"Given my options, I'd prefer to kill you now," Niden said.

"You're an asshole, you know that?" Suken said.

"That depends on your perspective." Niden looked at the men flanking him, and swept his gaze around the room. "You're outnumbered, and you're injured. Even if that green-cloaked bastard is hiding in here somewhere, you'll never take me." His eyes narrowed. "I'm willing to offer you a deal. Walk away. Forget everything you saw here and buy yourself passage to Darashan, or maybe Tyrodames."

"You know, that's a nice offer," Suken said, mock-thoughtfully. "But . . . I think I'd rather put a couple bolts in your friends' kneecaps, then drag you to the Council."

Tam let out a bark of laughter, but Niden's expression only darkened.

"Let the girl go," Suken said. "She doesn't have anything to do with this."

Niden didn't move.

"If you kill her," Suken said, his voice growing dark, "you're no better than the man who killed your own family."

"That wasn't a man. It was a monster," Niden said in a level tone. "An abomination."

"Which is exactly what you're on the verge of becoming," Suken snapped. "You've already killed so many. Are you really willing to add the murder of an innocent girl to your sins? Look at her. She can't be much older than your little girl was."

Niden hesitated, looking down at Tam.

Come on, Suken thought, his grip on his crossbow damp with sweat. *Make the right choice, Niden.*

Another man stepped out of a costume rack beside Niden, and the corporal seemed to shake himself out of his thoughts. He tossed Tam towards him. The girl stumbled, but the new man grabbed her arm and pulled her in front of him. "Take her to safety," Niden said.

Suken started to smile, but the expression froze on his face at Niden's next words.

"Kill him," he said.

One of the two men took a step forward, the tip of his sword rising a half an inch. Suken's hand guided his crossbow to point at the man, his eyes ever leaving Niden's. "I wouldn't take another step, if I were you."

The man stopped. Suken pointed the crossbow back at Niden. "Your men are smart enough to realize that close-range weapons are no match for a good crossbow."

"Or maybe," one of the men said with a smirk, "we're distractin' you 'til our friends get in place behind you."

Oh. Well, that would make sense. Suken itched to turn and look behind him, but he managed—somehow—to restrain the urge. "You're bluffing," he said.

"You sure about that?" A voice said from behind him.

Shit.

"You're outnumbered," Niden said again. "And surrounded. Last chance, hunter."

"Go fuck yourself," Suken said.

Niden stepped back, the man holding Tam keeping pace with him, and the two men flanking them stepped together to close the gap.

"Hey," Suken called to Niden as the two men took another step towards him. "You just going to run and let your men fight for you, you bloody coward?"

Niden didn't answer. He simply walked away. Tam hissed like an enraged cat and lashed out at the new man with her fists, but he ignored her blows, dragging her after him.

Suken looked back over his shoulder. Three more men were behind him, two with crossbows, one with a wicked-looking sword. "You guys willing to die for him?" he said, training the crossbow on each of them in turn as they advanced. "A man who's killed children?"

The two men with the crossbows stopped. Suken watched out of the corner of his eye as one's finger tightened on the trigger. *You first, then,* he thought. *Lady . . . hope you're with me now, because I'm gonna need you.*

He took a deep breath, every injured muscle in his body crying out as he tensed.

And Fletch Greencloak stepped out of a costume rack.

Suken turned towards him with the beginning of a smile, then he noticed the small glass globe in Fletch's hand. Suken recognized it immediately as a miniature version of whatever Jodrif had been about to use in Avara's shop the day the assassin had first attacked him.

The smile faded.

If Fletch threw that now, it would knock out all the guards in the room. It would also knock out Suken, which would leave Fletch free to murder Niden.

Fletch, no. . . .

Fletch grinned, his eyes meeting Suken's. "See you around, kitten."

He hurled the glass globe at the floor.

Suken dropped his crossbow, reaching down to pull his shirt up over his mouth and nose as bluish-grey smoke billowed up from where the globe had hit. It expanded far more quickly than Suken could have imagined was possible, washing over Suken after only a single heartbeat.

His eyes began to sting and his throat to itch. Something

metallic and harsh coated his tongue and throat, and he began to cough, each cough sending a fresh wave of devastating pain through his injured side. He sank to his knees, desperately pressing his shirt over his mouth and nose.

He saw a flash of green through the smoke, heading in the same direction Niden, Tam, and the last guard had gone.

Then . . . nothing.

The smoke enveloped him, masking the world in grey, and he felt everything begin to fade.

The poison, he realized numbly as he collapsed slowly to one side, as if he were trapped in a tidi-lei convergence. When he hit the floor, he barely felt it. *I haven't taken the antidote yet. If this knocks me out longer than a half an hour . . . I'm dead.* His hand went to his bolt-case slowly, as if he were trapped in molasses. His fingers touched bolt . . . bolt . . . a cork. He grabbed the vial, only fumbling with it for a moment before getting a grip on it, and slowly . . . so slowly . . . brought it up towards his face.

The world faded to a mere pinprick of smokey light as he grasped the cork between his teeth, pulling it free.

I will not *die this way,* he thought, spitting the cork aside. *I . . . I won't . . .*

I can't.

He tilted the vial back, swallowing the contents, and his hand dropped to the floor beside him with a dull thunk. He stared at the empty vial clutched in his fingers as the darkness enfolded him in soft, painless sleep.

Chapter Thirty-Two

Fletch felt a brief stab of guilt as he watched Anisaria crumple to the floor. But Niden was running for the door to the undercity, and regret vanished under a wave of steely determination. Fletch darted forward, slamming into Niden's guard with one shoulder and wincing at the pain in his arm. The man cried out in surprise and lost his grip on Tam, who immediately dashed deeper into the room, out of the smoke. Niden shoved aside an armful of costumes with a screech of hangers against metal rod to reveal the small, simple wooden door Fletch remembered from the last time he'd been here, hanging ajar. He ducked into it as the smoke began filling the room.

The guard lashed out with a fist, dealing Fletch a glancing blow on the jaw. Fletch managed to hook his foot around the man's ankle and pulled his leg out from under him, then dealt him a savage kick to the face that probably broke the man's nose. Fletch held his breath to avoid inhaling any of the smoke from Jodrif's sphere and stepped through the doorway after Niden into the hallway where he'd been held captive. Gods below, it felt like years ago. Had it only been a week? He closed the door behind him and took a deep breath of damp, untainted air as he glanced from side to side. To his left, he caught a glimpse of

Niden before he turned a corner. He was going in the opposite direction Fletch had taken the last two times he'd been here.

If Niden thought that he'd lose any pursuit in the undercity, he was sorely mistaken.

Now we end this, Fletch thought, limping after the murderer. *Now you pay.*

"Suken."

Suken groaned, the voice pulling him from a dream in which he'd been reunited with his brother. A hand shook his shoulder, pulling him the rest of the way into the waking world . . . and into pain.

"Go 'way, Terri," he muttered, and tried to turn over. Pain crashed over him, lancing up from his ribs and stealing his breath. He shuddered convulsively, his eyes flying open.

He wasn't home. Where was he?

He looked to his right to see a young face staring down at him. For a heartbeat, he thought it was Flower, in her torn white dress. But then the girl's face resolved into Tam, her eyes full of concern.

"You're hurt bad," she said, sounding as if she were on the verge of tears. "Should . . . should I go an' get an ardein, or—"

"No," Suken said, rolling to his uninjured side and forcing himself to his feet, wincing. "No time. Have . . . have to stop Fletch." How long had he been out? He looked around. All five of the men lay unconscious around him, their hands tied with various bits of costume. The smoke seemed to have dissipated.

"Forget him," Tam said viciously. "He's a jerk. And a liar."

"Yeah," Suken said. "But if he does what . . . what I think he's going to do, he's . . . going to be caught and . . ." Chance, could he finish a single sentence without the pain sending shuddering convulsions through him? ". . . and executed."

"Good," Tam spat. "Serves 'im right."

Suken shook his head, forcing himself to his feet. The clothes on one of the racks had been shoved aside, revealing a small wooden door. He started towards it, but Tam grabbed his hand, holding him back.

"No," she said. "He ain't worth it. He don't care about us, he said so. And he don't care about you neither!"

"He lied," Suken said simply. He pulled his hand free from Tam's grasp. "He does care about you, Tam. All of you. That's why he's doing all this." She didn't look convinced. Suken didn't have time for this, but he couldn't leave her here, thinking the worst of Fletch. Especially if things went badly. "He knew that assassin was heading for the den," Suken said softly. "He went back to save you. He *lied* to save you."

Her eyes filled with tears, her lower lip trembling.

"Keep an eye on them for me," Suken said, nodding towards the unconscious men. "If you . . ." he winced, pressing a hand to his ribs, "if you hear anyone coming, hide until you're sure they're friendly."

Suken made his way over to the door as quickly as he could, opening it and stepping into the wood-paneled tunnel.

"Suken," Tam called. Suken looked back over his shoulder at her. She stood alone in the middle of the ring of unconscious men, dirty and bedraggled and tiny. "Help him," she whispered. Suken gave her a strained smile, then turned and started down the tunnel.

Fletch ran through the undercity, his right hand trailing along the wall. They'd left the wood-paneled section of tunnel about ten minutes ago and entered the damp, unlit tunnels Fletch was so familiar with, and he'd been pleasantly surprised to realize that he knew this section of the undercity well. The tiny luminary around his neck cast enough pale light to dimly illuminate a two-foot sphere around him. That was all he needed. His eyes darted from the ground, where the moss had been scuffed by hurried footsteps, to the barely visible symbols carved high into the walls of the tunnel.

These particular marks told Fletch that Niden was heading for Lord Garron's estate, near the edge of the city. *Running back to your financier?* he thought. *All the aerans in Adunare won't get you out of what you have coming, you bastard.*

Niden apparently knew the way well, as the pair of footsteps scuffing the moss showed no signs of hesitation. But Fletch was willing to bet he didn't know about the side-passage that ran parallel to this one, cutting across it several hundred feet farther down.

When he reached the branching of the tunnels, Fletch turned down the new path, quickening his steps to a dead run. His left arm and leg sent shocks of pain through him with every jarring step, but he gritted his teeth and bore it.

Vethin, he thought. He remembered the night when they'd first met, the boy lying in a dingy alley half lit by moonlight. Remembered how bloated and swollen Vethin's stomach had been, how he'd sluggishly tried to blend into the shadows. The shifting grey and black patterns on his skin had reacted slowly, the boy's face screwing up in pain as he'd desperately tried to hide himself, tears tracking down his cheeks. Fletch remembered bending to pick the boy up, how light he'd been as Fletch had carried him to the nearest ardein. He remembered the months after, in which the child had slowly regained his strength. How he'd always been ready with a smile or a joke, like a boy Fletch had known in his own childhood. He remembered Vethin saving Fletch's life that night they'd escaped from the Coalition, how he'd never given up, dragging Fletch along the tunnels with him despite Fletch's many muttered insistences that he leave him.

The other ten children hadn't died by Niden's hand, but they might as well have. Memories of them flitted through his mind, boys and girls ragged and starving and bleeding on the streets, their exhausted gratitude as he'd taken them in, their wonder when they'd seen the den for the first time.

And Blue. Ah, gods. Blue. He remembered nights of pleasure, the calluses on the mage's hands, how quick with a laugh or an off-color joke he'd been. How he'd blushed the first time Fletch had seen him naked, how he'd loved to run his hands through Fletch's hair when the sex was over. Fletch hadn't loved him—he didn't love anyone, love was a commodity he couldn't and didn't want to afford—but he'd enjoyed Blue's company, and he'd trusted him.

The Coalition had killed them all. Fletch felt a growl building deep in his throat. The anger built in him as he ran, like the strengthening wind preceding a storm. Snatches of memories flashed in his mind, borne on the wind of anger like whirling leaves. Blue trying to explain to him how metal-bound convergences worked. Vethin learning how to pickpocket, Fletch rebuking him when the boy was too obvious. A masquerade ball Blue had brought Fletch to, and how mortified he had looked when Fletch revealed the hundreds of articles of jewelry he'd lifted during the course of it. Then his laughter, starting as a chuckle and evolving into a deep, full laugh that had ended in more pleasant activities.

The tunnel around him began to grow brighter, the gentle curve of the wall hiding the source of the light. He took five more limping steps before bursting out onto a wide ledge on the outer edge of Adunare. He stopped, wind buffeting his hair and snapping his cloak behind him. The cold wetness of the clouds enshrouding the city dampened his skin and stole his breath as he stood there gasping, his heart thundering and his shoulder aching as if it had been set afire.

He looked down, then up. The bottom of the city looked something like a mountain turned upside down, the grey rock patched in many places with sections of glittering or rusted metal. Far below, he could barely make out glimpses of green through the mist and clouds. The ledge Fletch stood on was a hundred feet below the flat top on which the city had been built, and was dotted with entrances into tunnels, some small, some as large as small buildings. Dirty water poured from one of the larger openings to fall in a curtain through the mist towards the ground somewhere below. Fletch glanced at the glyphs carved over the entrance he'd come out of, then looked right, and left.

Yes. . . . Niden should be exiting that tunnel entrance to his left . . . and running past him along the ledge to re-enter the undercity through the tunnel to Fletch's right.

Fletch melted back into the shadows and mist of the tunnel, pulling the luminary from his neck and stuffing it into a pocket.

The engines thrummed somewhere far, far away, sending gentle vibrations through the stone to quiver against the soles of Suken's boots as he limped down the tunnel. His breath came in labored gasps, the pain in his side, shoulder, and leg making his head swim and his steps falter. He kept his eyes fixed on the moss lining the floor of the tunnel. It was thicker here than in any part of the undercity he'd been in before, for which he was thankful. He could clearly see two sets of boot-marks, one of which was obviously left by a heavier man, and places where someone had occasionally brushed their hand or shoulder against the wall. He followed them, trying to ignore how close the walls of the tunnel seemed to be.

Then the boot-marks split. Suken came to a halt, his lungs burning. The smaller person had turned from the main tunnel into a narrower, branching one.

Suken looked down the tunnel. Fletch had stopped following Niden. Why? Why take a different path, unless . . .

Unless he knew this was a shortcut, and is planning to cut Niden off farther along.

The roof of this new tunnel was considerably lower than the

main one. Fletch had likely been able to run along it just fine, but it looked like its ceiling was low enough to force Suken to duck slightly, or else risk banging his head against the stone with each step. His stomach clenched, and he glanced back towards the main tunnel. If he were right, and he knew that he was, both Niden and Fletch would wind up in the same place eventually. But Fletch's way would be quicker. If he followed Fletch, he'd stand a better chance of catching up quickly enough to have time to talk Fletch out of doing something he'd come to regret.

But . . . oh, Chance. He looked down that tunnel, realizing that the walls were close enough to brush against his arms. And if it grew narrower, or if the ceiling dropped further . . .

Suken reached into his pocket and drew out a prayer, his last save for the one that Fletch had attached his message to. He raised it to his lips, kissing the metal as he stared into that rock-lined darkness. *Little Lady,* he thought, *I know you can't do much for me down here . . . but luck above, watch out for me if you can.* He clenched his fist around the prayer tightly enough for the metal to dig painfully into his palm. The pain was nothing compared to the pain in his side, but its presence was a comfort to him, strangely.

He had the blessing of the Lady of the Winds. He wouldn't die in a hole in the ground. She wouldn't let him.

Suken took a deep breath and ducked his head, running into the smaller tunnel after Fletch.

Niden exited the tunnel. The murderer stopped for a moment, looking out into the clouds. The wind whipped his graying hair around his face as Fletch watched from around the corner, pressed tight against the wall of the tunnel, a rock clenched in his left hand. After a moment Niden shook his head, then began jogging along the ledge. He picked his steps carefully along the damp rock. Fletch waited, the anger smoldering in his chest like a bank of red-hot coals. Niden passed Fletch's tunnel, continuing on towards the one leading to Lord Garron's estate. Fletch waited another breath, then stepped out.

Niden whirled, but Fletch was ready for him. He lashed out with a savage kick, catching Niden between the legs.

The murderer cried out, one hand going to his groin and the other to the hilt of the sword he wore belted to his waist. Fletch followed the kick with a swift uppercut, rock still clenched in his hand. It caught the bigger man under the jaw, and Niden staggered back against the wall, his eyes glazed over in pain.

Fletch didn't give him time to collect himself. He slammed his fist into the man's stomach, gaining a harsh grunt of pain. His next strike connected with Niden's head again. One of the sharp edges of the stone in his hand broke the skin on Niden's temple, sending a trail of blood trickling down his face.

The corporal fell to his knees, reeling. Fletch dropped the stone and reached down to grab the hilt of the man's rapier, drawing it. Niden tried to make a grab for it, but in his pain he was too slow, and grabbed the blade instead of the hilt. Fletch drew the blade back, slicing Niden's hand, bright blood welling from between the murderer's fingers.

Vethin's blood had once stained this man's hands. That thought caused the embers of hatred, guilt, pain and grief to burst into the full-fledged fire of rage.

Fletch whipped the blade to one side, droplets of blood whisking from the thin steel to be caught by the wind and carried out into the mist. He drew back and carefully placed the tip of the blade against Niden's shoulder, relishing the pain in the bastard's eyes as he slowly began to push the blade forward. The rapier's tip broke the skin, then vanished inch by slow, painful inch, working its way toward the nest of bones and tendons in Niden's shoulder.

The murderer screamed, reaching up to try to grab the blade

of the rapier, to halt its slow, inexorable progress. For the second time, blood welled from between his fingers. Finally the blood-stained point emerged from Niden's back, poking through the fabric of his grey uniform. The sound of his screams reverberated against Fletch's rage. It brought no closure, no joy. It only pulled Fletch deeper into the depths of molten hate, and made him lust for more. He left the sword embedded in the man's shoulder and reached down to grab Niden's hair, pulling him forward and leaning down until their faces were inches apart.

"Is this how your victims sounded while you spilled their guts from their stomachs?" he snarled, shaking Niden once savagely by the hair. "Did Vethin scream when you gutted him, you fucking bastard?" He leaned in closer, his voice growing harsher. "Did you enjoy it? You must have, because only a fucking lunatic would do the kinds of things you did to them." He grinned, his hand clenched into a trembling fist in Niden's hair. "Well, I guess I must be a lunatic too, because I'm damn well going to enjoy this."

He brought his knee up to connect with the bottom of the man's chin, hearing the satisfying click of his teeth snapping together. Fletch hoped his tongue had been between them.

He let go of Niden's hair. The man swayed on his knees, looking up with eyes dulled by pain, blood running in a thin trail from the corner of his mouth to merge with the blood from his temple. "You better not even think about passing out," Fletch said. "Because we're just getting started."

The tunnel around Suken began to brighten slightly. At first he thought it was his imagination. . . . Wishful thinking, after ten minutes of running with his head bent to one side and his heart hammering in his chest. But then he began to hear the distant roar of wind, and he quickened his steps.

Thank you, he thought, directing the prayer upwards.

He rounded the final bit of curve and nearly ran into a wall of mist. He staggered to a stop and stepped forward more slowly onto a narrow ledge. Fresh pain throbbed between his temples, probably due to the pavendala root, but Suken ignored it.

Ten feet to his right, Fletch stood, Niden kneeling before him with his back to the expanse of mist, the toes of his boots hanging over the lip of the ledge. He swayed slightly, both of his eyes swollen shut. His lips were puffed and bloodied, and Fletch had carved a long, deep cut along his jaw which wept blood down his neck. One of the corporal's arms hung limply at his side, a patch of his tunic dark with blood below his left shoulder. A bloodstained sword lay on the stone behind Fletch, and Fletch's hand was curled around the collar of Niden's shirt, holding him upright. He was saying something, but Suken couldn't hear the words over the wind.

Suken took a deep breath, ignored the drop to his left, and started towards them. "Fletch," he called.

Fletch turned his head slowly. Suken didn't like what he saw in the man's eyes. He'd seen it before, in the eyes of Shifter that night in the dye factory. Desperation. Anger. No. . . . Anger was too light of a term. *Rage.* Suken let his gaze drop briefly to Niden, and inexplicably felt pity stir in his heart.

"That's enough," Suken said, close enough now to not have to yell to be heard over the wind. "You've—"

"Stop." Fletch's voice was hard. Suken halted, a different kind of fear than that he'd felt in the tunnel touching his heart with cold, icy fingers. Blood caked the knuckles of the glove Fletch was using to clutch Niden's shirt. "Stay right where you are."

"Fletch," Suken said, not moving. "That's enough. Look at him."

"It's *not* enough," Fletch snarled. "Not until he's dead." He turned his gaze back to Niden. "I needed him to feel what Blue and Vethin felt. What the rest of the kids felt as his damned assassin buried them in rock and rubble. He's paid for their blood with his own, and now he'll pay for their deaths with his life. It *still* won't be enough. . . . But it'll be a damn good start." A mad grin played across his face. "He'll have a long time to regret what he's done before he hits the ground."

Lady preserve me, Suken thought, chilled. *He's let the anger drive him mad.* He drew a deep breath, then said, "No."

Fletch whipped his head to the side to turn that fevered glare on him. "No? *No?* You want me to let him *live?* You know what he did. He *deserves* to die. And I deserve to kill him."

I know you, Suken thought, meeting Fletch's eyes. *You're better than this.*

Is he? Another part of his mind asked. *You thought Shifter was better, too. Not to mention Niden. And look where both of those got you. One with a little girl dying in your arms, the other with an execution sentence.*

This is different. He's different.

Suken realized that sometime over the last week, he'd stopped viewing the world as black and white, right and wrong. Things had taken on shades of grey, variances he'd never considered before. Guards could be corrupt, and thieves could be honorable.

"Yes," Suken said, squinting against the wind. "He does deserve to die. But not at your hands, Fletch. Look at yourself. Look what it's made of you." He dared to take one small step forward, holding Fletch's gaze. "You've become like him."

"No," Fletch snapped. "I haven't. I'm killing to prevent him from doing to anyone else what he did to Vethin, and all those other poor bastards he and his Coalition slaughtered."

"Funny," Suken said, his voice far harsher than he'd intended. "That's exactly what he said."

For the first time since he'd stepped out onto the ledge, Suken saw a flicker of uncertainty in Fletch's eyes.

"He," Suken went on, gesturing at the broken man Fletch was keeping from toppling over the ledge, "says that he was only killing mage-born to keep them from killing anyone else."

"It's different," Fletch said, but some of the rage had faded from his voice. "He killed innocent people!"

"And he'll pay for that," Suken said. "I give you my word, Fletch. I'll see that he pays. But not by your hand."

Fletch set his jaw. "Why *shouldn't* I do it? The outcome is the same."

"No. It's not. He'll be dead. But what will it do to you?"

Fletch snorted. "I'm not *you.* I'll sleep better tonight than I have since this whole thing started." His lip lifted in a snarl. "You think that if we play nice with the Council and hand this bastard over, they'll clap their hands and exclaim over what a good boy you are, and waive my charges?" Fletch pushed Niden slightly. The corporal sat back on his heels, leaning precariously back over the edge. He didn't seem to realize what was happening. He hung from Fletch's grip like a broken doll, little bubbles of blood at the corners of his mouth, his eyes glassy with pain. "They don't give a shit about the people of this city, Anisaria, and they don't give a shit about you. You're fooling yourself if you think they'll listen to morality over money. They'll betray you. Like *this one* did."

"You want to talk about betrayal?" Suken snapped. "You were planning on backstabbing me the whole time, using me to get what you wanted. How are you any better than them?"

Fletch stared at him, his eyes widening.

"You have a family to get back to," Suken said. "People who depend on you."

"What do you know about family?"

"I know that the only family member I had left, I drove away because I was too damn self-absorbed to see his pain. I don't want to see you make the same mistake. Those kids love you. They need you."

Fletch turned back to look at Niden, his lip lifting in a snarl.

"I understand," Suken continued more quietly. "It's hard to trust, after you've been hurt. Hard to believe that someone else cares enough to not let you down. I might not be willing to become a thief, but . . . You and I, we're not so different, Fletch. I can help you. I *want* to help you." He paused, the wind buffeting him. "Do you trust me? If you do, then you know that I'll fight to ensure that he faces justice. Fight until my last breath, if I have to."

Fletch stared at him, his expression unreadable.

Suken took another small step. "Do you *trust* me, Fletch?"

"It's not you I'm worried about," Fletch said, turning his gaze back to Niden. "It's *them*."

"I know what I'm doing," Suken said. "I can clear your name. I can get justice for the dead. I can bring the Coalition down, but only if you'll trust me with his life, right here, right now. I promise you that the victims' families will find peace." He paused, and when he continued it was so quietly he wasn't certain if Fletch would be able to hear him. "*All* of the victims' families. Including you."

He took one more step forward, within touching distance. Fletch's cloak snapped around his legs, and his dark hair whipped around his face. "Vengeance won't bring you peace, Fletch," Suken said quietly. "It'll just bring you more pain."

Fletch stood there for another long moment, his head lowered, his eyes dark as they stared at Niden's face. Then he sighed and pulled Niden forward enough so the man was no longer leaning back over the edge, and let go of his shirt.

A wave of relief swept over Suken. *It's over,* he thought, meeting Fletch's eyes. *It's over.* He smiled. Somewhere behind him, he heard the distant rumble as the engines of the city kicked in, beginning Ascent. "Thank you," he said. "I'll prove that—"

Before he could finish, the city lurched into Ascent and Niden's hand shot up and grabbed Fletch's wrist, the bloody fingers gripping so tightly that Suken heard the bones grind together. "If I die," Niden hissed, blood dripping from his lips, "you're coming with me."

He threw himself back over the edge, pulling Fletch with him. Suken cried out, his hand instinctually jabbing forward into the air after them. His fingers wrapped around fabric, and he was yanked forward and down, the weight pulling him flat on his stomach against the damp stone of the ledge.

Pain lanced through his chest like a bolt of fire. He panted, unable even to scream, but kept his fingers locked tight on whatever he'd grabbed, hoping that it was Fletch and not Niden. He felt himself slowly sliding along the ledge, the weight pulling him towards a drop of Lady knew how many thousands of feet, and he scrabbled with his other hand on the stone ledge.

His hand found purchase on a small outcropping of rock as he slid far enough to be able to see over the edge. Three feet below him, Fletch hung from his cloak, grasping it in both hands. He was staring up at Suken in stark fear and desperation. Niden was nowhere to be seen.

"I've got you," Suken said through gritted teeth. "Climb!"

Fletch swallowed, then began pulling himself up his cloak hand by hand, his legs swinging in the mist below. Suken closed his eyes and concentrated on holding on, doing his best to ignore the pain that seemed to be assaulting him on all sides. He focused everything on his hands, on holding the cloak and the rock, on keeping his friend from dying.

I won't fail again, he thought, remembering Flower. Remembering his brother. *I won't.*

He felt a hand grasp his wrist, and opened his eyes to see Fletch gritting his teeth a foot below, bringing his other arm up to grab Suken's forearm. The thief looked as if he were in as much pain as Suken was, but he took one labored breath and swung his arm up again, grabbing the ledge. Suken felt the pressure on his arm blessedly lessen as Fletch put his weight on the stone. He let go of the cloak, his fingers trembling, and grabbed Fletch's arm, helping him to pull himself up onto the ledge.

Suken pulled himself forward enough to look over the edge, but there was no sign of Niden. He reached one trembling hand into the pouch at his belt and pulled out his last prayer.

He rolled over onto his back, hearing Fletch still panting for breath beside him, and looked at the sky. "Thank you," he whispered, and tossed the prayer over the edge.

Suken closed his eyes and imagined it falling, the wind playing with it, whirling it back and forth and flipping it end over end before it vanished into the clouds.

Chapter Thirty-Three

A few hours after Niden's death, a crowd gathered along the sides of Alwin Avenue, pointing and whispering as Suken and Tam led their captives up the street toward the Council Chambers. The wide stone avenue was lined with trees, sprouting up from well-tended patches of grass to spread their fronds over the street and the small wooden carts some food vendors had set up. Some of the people stopping to watch were mages, obviously on their way to the Academe adjacent to the Council. One or two had shadow-sprites trailing after them like pets, carrying armloads of books, boxes full of plants, or bags of sand to be melted into glass. Most of the spectators were students, dressed in simple white tunics belted at their waists with their major and minor fields of study embroidered on the breasts in colorful threads. They watched the strange procession with wide eyes and many a whispered conversation behind raised hands.

A week ago, Suken would have relished the attention. He probably would have waved to them with broad smiles. But now he found it difficult to care. He was in too much pain, too tired.

Tam marched at the head of her bedraggled chain of captives with a wide grin, occasionally turning to bark at them to hurry up. Suken had allowed her to lead them only because they were all still woozy from whatever smoke had been in those glass globes. He sent up a silent prayer to the Lady for the fact that the antidote had apparently worked as well on the smoke as on the poison the assassin had used on him, though the headache currently splitting his skull made it difficult to be *too* grateful. Beside him, a man in a black hooded cloak walked, face hidden and silent as the grave.

Convincing Fletch to come had been easier than Suken had expected, probably because the thief was mentally and physically exhausted. He'd insisted on keeping his face hidden, but other than that he'd come along without much of a fight. Any other time, Suken would have been concerned, but for now he counted the Lady's blessings that Fletch wasn't making this harder than it had to be.

The pain in his side had dulled to a throbbing ache, but Suken suspected that after this was all over, he'd probably be bed-ridden for a month, maybe more.

The Council and the Academe rose up before them, twisting white and gold spires and domes catching the early morning sunlight. More trees and flowering bushes lined the streets leading off from the main avenue, and each immaculate building boasted an expanse of green grass and beds of flowering plants. The smells of roasted pork, grass, molten glass, and thousands of perfumed mages and nobles pressed in around Suken, Tam, and their charges. News of their coming must have spread, because the crowd was larger here. Hundreds of mages, students, merchants and nobility packed the Academe Green, staring. Suken winced and rubbed at his temple. The noise and smells certainly weren't helping the headache. He tried to ignore the crowd's shouted questions, keeping his gaze fixed on the glass blocks that made up the street in front of his feet.

When they reached the bottom of the steps to the Council

Chambers, Fletch stopped. Suken stepped closer to him, trying to pierce the darkness of that hood.

"You all right?" he asked.

"No," Fletch replied, his voice thick with exhaustion. "I'm about to get sentenced to a life chained up in the pits." He took a step away, as if to turn and flee.

"Fletch," Suken said, gently putting his hand on the other man's shoulder to stop him. It didn't take much force. "I'll make sure you walk out of here a free man. Trust me."

The hood turned towards him, and Suken caught a glimpse of Fletch's face in the shadows. "I trust *you*," he said. "But you're putting your own trust in the wrong people, Suken. That's how you're going to die."

"Guess it's a good thing I'll have you watching my back, then," Suken said with a ghost of a smile.

Fletch looked at him, his expression unreadable. Then he shook his head and let Suken help him up the steps.

Ten long, painful minutes later, they reached the closed gates of the Council Chambers.

"All right," Tam said, turning towards her charges and putting her hands on her hips. The five men looked sluggishly up at her, squinting. "Sit yer asses down, and don't even think about tryin' anything." Suken helped Fletch to sit on the steps and approached the silver and steel gates leading to the Council Chambers, where five members of the Mazarine Guard stood. The sunlight made their armor and helms shift from white, to blue, to pink, and the azure capes clasped to their breastplates at the shoulders draped down behind them to brush against the marble. They eyed the group warily, their swords sheathed but their hands gripping the hilts.

Suken looked the one in the middle in the eye. "Send for High Mage Hanran," he said, unable to keep the weariness out of his voice. The guard reached up and pulled the ornate helm from her head, tucking it under one arm to reveal a young woman with long curly brown hair. She gave Suken a skeptical look which swept behind him to take in the entire rag-tag bunch of prisoners.

"Do you have an appointment?" she asked.

"No," Suken snapped. He could still hear the hum of curious voices behind him from the Green. "Tell Hanran that Suken bloody Anisaria's here to see him, and that I've got five traitors to the state in custody, with information about hundreds more. Whatever he's doing can wait."

The guard's eyes widened as if something he'd said surprised her, which was probably true. It wasn't every day that someone demanded a personal appointment with one of the High Mages. But she turned to one of the other guards and made a curt gesture. The man snapped a bow, then vanished through a small door set into the gate. The lead guard turned back to Suken. "It may take some time," she said. "The Council is in session this morning." Suken turned away, making his way back down the steps. He glanced at Fletch to make certain he was still there, then sat down carefully beside Tam, wincing.

She sat with her knees pulled up to her chest, ropes clutched in one hand, staring at the Academe.

"Never thought I'd be so close," she said. "Big, ain't it?"

"Yes," Suken said, following her gaze. "It is."

"Heard all the floors have rugs," she said. "But that's rubbish, ain't it? Who'd clean 'em all?"

"There are servants," Suken said, shifting his shoulders. Something felt . . . wrong. He reached back over his left shoulder and winced. That damned knife was still sticking out of his shoulder. No wonder all those people had been staring at him.

Well, it had already been there for over an hour. What would another hour hurt?

He sighed.

"Wish I coulda been born Talented," Tam said.

"It's not as great as you'd think," Suken said, trying to find a comfortable way to sit that didn't result in sharp jabs of pain lancing up from his ribs. "People telling you what to wear, and eat, and drink. Having to study all day, nose buried in a book instead of outside in the sun."

"Yeah," Tam breathed wistfully.

Suken glanced at her. "Tam," he said softly. "Whatever he said to you . . . it was to keep you safe. He wouldn't have done all this if he didn't care about you. All of you."

She sniffed and rubbed at her nose with the hem of one sleeve. "Tam?"

"Heard you," she said, still staring at the Academe.

All right, then. Suken looked out over the Green, where teachers were making their way through the crowd, sending students off towards their classes with sharp rebukes and gestures. The merchants and nobles began to make their way back to wherever they'd been heading as well. Suken saw a heavy-set man with curly red hair and a broadsheet band pinned to his sleeve break from the crowd and mount the steps.

"Excuse me," he said, eyes darting from Suken to Tam. "My name's Curtwell, from the LeiLine. I, um. Was wondering if—"

"Not now," Suken said. The last thing he needed was a half a hundred questions.

"But—"

"I said not now," Suken repeated, his tone harsher than he'd intended. The broadsheet reporter paled, fumbling his notepad and nearly dropping it. He stuttered over an apology, and when Suken didn't reply, turned away. Suken watched him as he scurried away, then noticed a short woman pushing her way through a crowd of students, all of which looked shocked at the epithets falling from her lips.

She carried a battered hat in one hand and a folded serape in the other.

Suken smiled as Avara approached the steps, steel-grey hair

pulled back into a practical bun as always, and surveyed the line of prisoners.

"Productive night?"

"Guess you could say that," Suken said.

"Fletch?"

Suken nodded towards the cloaked figure fifteen feet away.

Avara raised one eyebrow. "How'd you manage to get him here?"

"Saved his life," Suken said.

"Again?"

Suken smiled as Avara sat down beside him, settling her brown skirts around herself and handing him his hat. He pulled it on, the brim blessedly blocking the damned sun and bringing some relief to his aching head.

"Rest of the Coalition's in shambles," she said, her voice barely louder than a whisper. "I think most of the Valleys are sidin' with Fletch, and the leaders are scatterin' to the—"

She cut off, her eyes widening. "Is that a *knife* in your back?"

"Yeah," Suken replied, glancing back at it. "Little harder to catch 'em when you don't see 'em coming."

"Do you want me to . . ." she trailed off, nodding at the knife.

"Do you have any bandages?"

Avara shook her head.

"Then it's probably best to leave it where it is."

"You're turning into a bloody pincushion, boy," she said.

Suken smiled again, unable to help it.

"Talked to your guildmaster," Avara said. "Wasn't happy to hear that he'd been fooled by Niden. Seems he's grateful to you for taking him down. I have it on good authority that your license has been reinstated, providing you keep quiet about the fact that Ulric got played like a newborn kitten."

Suken leveled a dubious look at her. "I find it hard to believe that—"

"Ain't you learned yet not to question it when a prayer lands in your bloody lap? Shut up and be grateful."

Suken sighed, but accepted it. Whatever she'd done, she'd done because she cared about him, and he had to admit that he was relieved. Having his license back was one weight off his mind, at least.

"Speaking of Fletch," Avara said, eyeing him. "We need to have a chat about you lying to me and tailing me in order to find him in the first place."

"Later," Suken agreed, unable to keep the exhaustion from his voice.

She seemed to realize that he was too tired for playful ribbing. "I'm grateful to you," Avara said after a moment, uncharacteristically quiet. "I know what you risked, helping him. Are you two . . ." she trailed off, searching his face.

"I don't know," Suken replied, uncomfortable. He glanced over at Fletch again, but the thief hadn't moved. "We're . . . friends, I suppose."

"I see," Avara said slowly. "Be careful. If word should get around . . ."

"I know," Suken replied. "The other hunters would use me to get to him. But I'm not certain that he'll want anything to do with me after this, depending on how it goes." He was surprised at how badly that thought hurt. He wanted . . .

Chance, what *did* he want? He was too damn tired to figure it out.

"What are you planning to do in there?" Avara asked.

"Something stupid," Suken replied, meeting her eyes. "What else?"

She snorted.

"Suken," Tam called.

Suken turned to see one of the gates behind him swinging open. The guard nodded to him. "The Council will see you now," she said.

Suken's footsteps echoed as he walked down a set of marble stairs into a recessed section of floor, above which loomed a half-circle dais. Six people were seated at a long table on the dais, backlit by luminaries. Fletch stood beside him, still enshrouded in his black cloak. Behind him marched the five captured men, ten members of the Mazarine Guard, and Tam.

Suken swallowed. He'd spoken to one of the High Mages before, but that had been in the man's personal study, not the Council Chambers. This was where matters of state were decided. Where people brought grievances too important for the individual precincts and judges to determine.

Where people were sentenced to execution.

He and Fletch stepped forward, the others remaining near the doors.

"Boy," High Mage Hanran of the Amber School said solemnly, his aged voice breaking the silence. "You look like you got into a fight with a jaguar. And lost." He wore a crimson tunic with thick bars of black and gold embroidery on the hems of the sleeves, his white hair short and his clean-shaven face lined with a hundred wrinkles, most around the corners of his eyes. There were considerably more wrinkles than the last time Suken had seen him.

"It's been a long week," Suken said.

"Suken Anisaria," one of Mazarines said, sounding annoyed that her announcement duty had been interrupted. "Bounty hunter, fifth rank. With him are five men in custody, an orphaned girl from the Valley, and . . ." She hesitated. Suken hadn't told her who was in the cloak.

"Fletch Greencloak," he supplied. "Here of his own free will to testify to his innocence." Out of the corner of his eye, he saw Fletch glance at him. All of the High Mages shared looks, some curious, some clearly surprised.

"You claim to have knowledge of high treason?" one of the High Mages, a balding man in an emerald tunic, intoned.

"I do," Suken said. He took a deep breath, then relayed most of the events of the last few days. When he reached the part about Lord Garron's estate, High Mage Hanran interrupted him.

"You broke into a Lord's estate?"

"Technically, they let us in," Fletch muttered under his breath. Suken pressed his lips together to suppress the laugh that tried to escape.

"We were invited in as guests," Suken finally managed. "Which doesn't fall into the realm of trespassing. Under Article twenty-seven, subsection G, anything we may have seen in plain sight is admissible."

The High Mages looked down at he and Fletch imperiously. When none of them disputed that, Suken continued. As he reached the end of his story, one of the High Mages leaned back in her chair and folded her hands in front of her.

"You make claims which cast a decorated member of the guard as a killer with no evidence," she said in a musical voice. "Do you have witnesses to back your claim, Anisaria?"

Suken glanced at Fletch. Fletch looked back at him, and Suken saw enough of his face to see that his jaw was clenched. Suken took a deep breath. He'd have to play this carefully. "I do," he said. "Fletch Greencloak can corroborate all my claims."

Silence met his words as every eye in the room turned to Fletch.

"Bastard killed twelve of my friends and tried to frame me," Fletch said venomously. "I hope he rots in the Dark."

The High Council continued staring at Fletch.

"I tried to bring him in alive," Suken continued. "But when he realized that I had him cornered, he killed himself, and tried to take Greencloak down with him."

"So what you're telling us is that you have no evidence, and the only witness is the criminal accused of the crime?" The Sapphire School High Mage shook his head. Suken felt his heart sink. He'd hoped that it wouldn't come to this. "Bring in the TruthSeer," the High Mage continued. "He'll get to the bottom of this."

Beside him, Suken saw Fletch stiffen. He knew exactly what would happen to him if he was Truthread—insanity.

"You can't Truthread him," Suken said.

"Oh?" The Diamond High Mage leaned forward, lacing her fingers together. "Why not?"

"If you do, that means that you're accusing him," Suken said. "Are you willing to suffer the consequences if he's innocent?"

Those consequences being, of course, execution.

Silence from the mages. For one fleeting, horrible moment, Suken wondered if he might have taken this too far.

"We are above the law," the Emerald High Mage intoned. "It is our right to demand a Truthread without punishment in order to ascertain guilt or innocence in matters of treason."

Was that right? Suken tried to remember, but he'd only skimmed over the sections of the Articles dealing with treason. He'd never expected to need them.

Well. That was a bloody mistake.

If they Truthread Fletch, he'd be driven insane. Suken's stomach twisted at the thought of it. He couldn't see a way out of this, unless . . .

Unless he believed that the leaders he'd placed so much faith in were truly just. Unless he placed his trust in them, as he'd begged for Fletch to trust him. He took a deep breath and stepped forward, between the mages and Fletch. "Truthread *me*," Suken said.

Once again, silence fell in the Council Chamber. Suken felt every beat of his heart pounding against his chest, and his palms were slick with sweat. Fletch grabbed his arm.

"What are you *doing?*" he hissed.

"Clearing your name," Suken replied, not bothering to lower his voice or tear his gaze from the mages. "Because I know you're innocent, and I'm willing to put my own sanity on the line to prove it." He shook Fletch's hand from his arm and stepped forward, looking up at the Council. "I believe in due process," he said, meeting each of their eyes in turn. "I believe in the law, and I believe that you're doing what you think is best for this city. I *know* this man is innocent, but I understand that you can't take my word for it. That's fine; the law's the law. But I won't stand aside and watch you subject an innocent man to insanity, same as I wouldn't stand aside and let him hang, even when my guild tried to revoke my license for helping him. I'd rather give up my own sanity than see that happen. So if you really believe that I'm lying, that this man is guilty of murder . . ." Suken took one more step forward, looking up at the shocked faces above him, "Then do it. Call the TruthSeer. I'm ready."

He stared up at the shocked faces above him for a full minute before Hanran turned to the man next to him and whispered something.

"Please excuse us for a moment as we discuss this," the Sapphire Mage said. All five of the High Mages clustered together and began speaking in hushed tones.

"Suken," Fletch said, stepping forward and grabbing Suken's arm to turn him towards him. "Stop it. It's not worth this."

This time, Suken lowered his voice. "They're not going to go through with it. You'll see."

"And if they do?"

Suken shrugged. "Your name will be cleared of murder."

Fletch stared at him for a long moment.

"What?" Suken asked, irritated.

"You're unbelievable."

"I keep telling everyone that, but—"

"Shut up," Fletch said. "I don't want to be in your debt any more than I am already. I don't want your sanity or the lack thereof on my gods damned conscience, Anisaria."

"It won't be," Suken said levelly. "Because no matter what happens next, this is *my* choice."

"Whether or not it's your choice, I'll know that—"

"Anisaria."

Suken turned back towards the High Mages. Despite his

flippant words to Fletch, his heart was racing. *Please,* he thought, *be the people I know you are. . . .*

High Mage Hanran stood. "Due to your years of service and your frankly unbelievable willingness to put your life on the line to prove a point, the Council has decided to accept your version."

Suken let out a shaky breath in relief.

"But," Hanran continued, raising one finger, "we are currently sending members of the guard to apprehend Lord Garron. We *will* be putting him to a Truthread due to your accusations, and if he is not guilty of all you claim, you *will* be executed. Is this understood and accepted?"

"Yes, sir," Suken said.

"And as for Greencloak . . ." Hanran snapped his fingers, and five members of the Mazarine Guard melted out of the shadows to surround Fletch. "He is cleared of the murder charges, but will stand trial for his other crimes."

Fletch threw Suken a black look as the guards snapped a pair of manacles around his wrists. "Hope you're happy," he said, but the menace was sapped by his obvious exhaustion.

Suken watched as the guards led Fletch away. He looked back up at Hanran. "So," he said. "Let's talk about my compensation, shall we?"

Suken sat in High Mage Hanran's study, rubbing the bridge of his nose between his thumb and index finger. His hat lay on the desk on top of a clutter of papers and books laid open to pages covered in maps and complicated diagrams. Light fell from the windows behind the desk to illuminate dancing motes of dust and shelves stacked high with books, scrolls and reams of paper.

The room brought back bad memories. Memories of pacing here as a younger man, twisting his serape between his hands, waiting to hear what was going to be done with his brother.

The door opened behind him, and Suken turned to see High

Mage Hanran enter, a single member of the Mazarine Guard behind him. Hanran paused long enough to gesture for the guard to remain outside, then closed the door and rounded his desk, his walking stick thumping heavily with each step. He didn't sit. . . . He simply stood there staring at Suken, his hands resting on the head of his cane. He looked tired. Worn.

"That was an incredibly brave thing you did in there," he said.

"It was worth it."

Hanran gave him a skeptical look, but didn't refute it.

"Did you find Lord Garron?" Suken asked.

"Yes." Hanran sat down heavily. "Light, boy. I shudder to think of what would have happened if you hadn't uncovered this."

"Did you find out the names of any of the other leaders?"

Hanran shook his head. "They're operating under code names. As soon as you and I are done, I'm calling an emergency session of the Council. I'm going to move to enact a decree stating that all members of the Coalition are wanted for treason. Anyone attending a meeting or found to be working with them from this day forward will be subject to immediate execution." He tried a smile. "I expect it will make a great deal of business for you and your friends."

Suken shrugged.

"The Council owes you a debt of gratitude," Hanran went on.

"Gratitude won't pay my taxes," Suken said. "Or my uncle's cartel debts." He reached over to the desk to grab his hat, placing it back on his head. "I expect to be well compensated, old man."

Hanran looked up at him for a long moment, then sighed, raising one shaking hand to his head. "How many times must I apologize before you forgive me for what happened with your brother?"

Suken clenched his fist, biting back the response which leapt to his lips. He took a deep breath, then tersely said, "How much will you be paying me?"

"Enough to keep you living in luxury for the rest of your life," Hanran said, though his face was pale. "If that's what you want."

Suken turned and left High Mage Hanran sitting in his study.

Chapter Thirty-Four

Fletch sat in a jail cell, staring at the bars and trying to decide which method of murder he'd most like to use on Anisaria. Strangling him with his own crossbow string was tempting, but so was making him choke on that stupid hat he always wore.

Footsteps approached. Fletch looked up to see a guard with a huge ring of keys standing outside the bars.

"Fuck you," Fletch snapped.

The guard raised his eyebrows. "What did I do to deserve that?"

"You exist."

The guard turned to someone down the hall Fletch couldn't see. "Maybe I should leave him in here for a while longer. Teach him some respect."

"I wouldn't be opposed," a female voice said dryly.

Fletch stood and tried to peer through the bars, but they'd chained him to the wall in addition to locking him in. He couldn't get close enough to the bars to see around the corner.

"Avara?" he called.

She stepped into sight. She had his cloak and a set of clothes draped over one arm.

Fletch narrowed his eyes. "What's going on?"

"You're being released," the guard said, unlocking the cell door.

Fletch blinked. "Why?"

"Someone paid your slave-debt," the guard said, walking into the cell and gesturing for Fletch to turn around.

Someone . . . who could possibly have . . .

Fletch looked at Avara as the man began unlocking the manacles around his wrists.

"Don't look at me, boy," she said. "I don't have that kind of money."

Then who . . .

The thought trailed off as realization slowly dawned on him.

How much did Anisaria get paid for bringing him in? Surely not enough to pay off Fletch's entire slave-debt.

But he didn't just get paid for bringing me in. They would have paid him for uncovering the Coalition, for taking care of Niden, for the five Coalition members he brought in with him that day . . .

The manacles snapped open and Fletch rubbed his wrists, a sinking feeling settling into his stomach.

Avara tossed him his cloak, and Fletch caught it clumsily. "Welcome back to the world of the free," she said.

Gods below, I hate being in someone's debt.

Five days later, Fletch sat on a rooftop overlooking the Arrival Circle, his hood pulled up to hide his face and his cloak turned inside out to hide the green. The ten great Gates lay around the outside of the cobblestoned circle, looking like nothing more than spilled puddles of molten silver ten paces across. Carts piled high with food and wood trundled their way up out of the Gates, as if they were rolling up out of puddles of water.

He sighed and pulled an envelope from the pocket inside his cloak. The drizzling rain had stopped, leaving the roof lit by grey light from the overcast sky above. He opened the envelope and pulled out the single sheet of paper inside it.

Jandin Anisaria. Birthdate: 1299. Known living relations: Suken Anisaria, Lorrin Anisaria. Rank: one. Last known sighting in the year 1307. Wanted for conspiracy to commit murder. All further details classified as per High Mage Hanran's orders. If found, detain and contact the High Council immediately.

Scrawled on the bottom in cramped script was one last line.

Associated case: Wellspring Subject. Highly classified.

Fletch stared at the paper for a long moment, then slipped it back into the envelope.

Jandin, he thought. *Similar. Too similar to be a coincidence. The name he gave us must have been a pseudonym.* He couldn't remember much of the boy's physical appearance save that he'd had darker hair than Suken's, and a somewhat thick build. As Suken had told him about his past that night in the theater, Fletch had wondered if the boy who had spent so much of his time with Fletch's old partner might have been Anisaria's lost brother. The stories were remarkably similar. But he hadn't been certain. Now he looked down at the envelope and the file he'd stolen from the Hunter's Guild, drumming his fingers on the roof.

This Wellspring Subject was clearly a secret the High Mages didn't want to reveal.

Which meant that he might be able to use it against them.

That was good. Fletch never regretted finding information that might prove useful down the line. But it didn't answer the question of what he should do with the case-file. He'd stolen it with the intent of giving it to Anisaria to repay him for everything he'd done for him. But now . . .

Anisaria obviously thought that the file would give him some sort of clue to work from. But there was nothing here. Nothing save that cryptic code phrase, and Fletch doubted that old high-and-mighty Hanran was going to cough up the meaning behind that to a bounty hunter, no matter how high a rank Anisaria got. If he'd wanted Anisaria to know, he would have told him already.

The hunter was working his way up the ranks to get a useless piece of paper.

Fletch reached up and rubbed at his forehead, closing his eyes. Suken was well on his way to becoming a renowned hunter, one with a conscience and a genuine desire to help the downtrodden. Over the last few days, Fletch had spent a good deal of time thinking about it, and had come to the realization that he *wanted* to see Anisaria succeed. He wanted to see Suken become the person he had the potential to be, someone the common people could look up to, someone who had the drive and the talent to save hundreds of lives. But if Anisaria found out how little there was in this file, he might very well give up. He might join with Fletch, become a thief, work with him, if only to potentially find out what this Wellspring Subject was. But Fletch didn't want that anymore.

Or did he?

Gods, he didn't know *what* he wanted, and Fletch Greencloak *always* knew what he wanted.

"I'm a bloody idiot," he muttered to himself, tucking the file back into the pocket in his cloak. He'd return it to the Guild tonight, and find some other way to repay Anisaria for his gods-be-damned generosity.

Someone crept up onto the roof behind him, little footsteps padding across the tiles. The kid settled down beside him, and they sat in silence together for a full minute before she spoke.

"Took awhile to find you," she said. Fletch turned to look at Tam. She pointedly didn't meet his gaze, watching as the carts full of food wound their way towards the Market District. "We found a new den," Tam said. "Bigger. Had to kick another gang out, but Rossin says they won't be back."

Fletch didn't answer. He didn't know what to say.

"It'll be better than the other one," Tam went on. "More exits, and a bigger Bruiser." She glanced at him. "You could come see."

He wanted to. But he couldn't. He knew that now.

"No," he said.

Tam screwed up her forehead in obvious thought for a moment, then the creases vanished. She pulled her knees up to her chest and wrapped her arms around them. "I talked to Dusty, you know. After the theater."

"Dusty?"

"Suken. Dusty's a better name for a cat. Anyway, he said you lied. He said you did it to keep us safe. That you really do care about us."

Gods below, Anisaria. You and your ever-flapping mouth.

"Listening to cats, now?" Fletch said. "You know better than that."

"So what you said was true, then?" She hesitated, and when she continued, her voice trembled. "We're like fleas? You wanted to get rid of us?"

He sighed, unable to break her heart a second time. "No."

She nodded, all the tension bleeding from her expression to be replaced with an easy smile. "All you have to do is say sorry, then," she said. "And then everything will go back to how it was."

"No," Fletch said, standing. "It won't."

"Why?" she looked up at him.

"Because I got eleven of you killed."

"That wasn't your fault. It's cuz all those people were chasing you."

"The entire city will know my face soon," he said. He hadn't done anything to get any new warrants yet, but he had plans for a few heists that would begin to repair the sizable dent in his fortune he was about to make. "And I never found out who led that sicario to you." That still bothered him, but every possibility he'd hunted down had led him to a dead end. "It's not safe to be around me."

She chewed the inside of her lip. "So visit less often," she finally said. "Wear masks."

"No. You have each other, and Rossin. You don't need me. You never did." He turned.

"You're family," she whispered. "We'll always need you, Fletch."

Family. He'd never wanted it, or expected to miss it so much once he'd lost it. But he did. He sighed and turned back. "Once a month," he said, raising one finger. "And only through the most secret entrance you have. Never on the same day. And if I so much as hear one of you calling me boss, I'm gone."

She grinned. He rolled his eyes and turned again, but stopped as she called his name.

He paused, not looking back. The rain started again, pattering against his cloak and leaving clean spots in the soot staining the tiles of the roof.

"How do you die?" Tam asked.

He stood there for a long moment, thinking, twisting the ring on his middle finger.

"Trust," he finally said. "That's how I'm going to die. Trusting people I shouldn't."

He pulled his hood up to hide his face and walked into the rain.

A week after Niden's death, Suken walked into the Lady's Face Tavern to be greeted with a round of cheers and raised drinks. He smiled and carefully raised his hand to tip the brim of his hat, then made his way to the bar, the other hunters clapping him on the back as he walked past them. Every so often one landed on the stab wound below his shoulder or jarred his bound ribs, but Suken smiled to hide his winces, nodding as he pushed his way through the crowd. Finally, he made his way to the back and sat on one of the unoccupied stools, pulling his hat off and placing it in front of him. Marxen walked over and eyed him from behind the bar.

"Rank?" he asked. He was obviously trying to hide the smile hiding behind his gruff exterior, and failing at it.

"Really, Marxen?"

"Rules are rules, boy."

Suken smiled. "Third," he said, pulling his license from his pocket and holding it up so Marxen could see.

Marxen's own smile broke free, and he chuckled as he placed a glass in front of Suken, turning to take a bottle of gin from the shelf behind the bar. "Feelin' better?"

"No. But I was hoping a few drinks would help with that." He'd spent almost the entire week in bed, Terri alternating between doting over and chiding him for his carelessness. His ribs still ached, and he had to change the dressing on the stab wound on his shoulder once a day, but he no longer felt as if he'd been run over by a rail-car.

He pulled a heavy leather pouch from his belt and placed it on the bar next to the glass as Marxen finished filling it. Marxen glanced at it and raised one eyebrow. "I'll be in here a lot for the next month," Suken said. "Figured I might as well start a tab." Marxen nodded and took the pouch, not bothering to open it. He tucked it away behind the counter somewhere.

"So it's true? The Council paid you the entire Greencloak bounty?"

Suken nodded again, picking up the glass and bringing it to his lips. "And then some. Apparently uncovering a city-wide treasonous rebellion is as good as finding a vein of silver ore." He tilted his head back, the gin burning all the way down. Chance, but that was good. He let out a long breath in satisfaction, his eyes closed.

"Fair number of warrants went out for members of that Coalition," Marxen said. "Guess the boys you brought in decided it'd be in their best interests to talk to the Mazarines, get lower sentences. Everyone's been busy this past week." A burst of laughter rose from somewhere behind Suken as some hunter made a joke at the expense of one of the others. "When do you think you'll be back to work?"

"It'll be at least another month," Suken replied, tapping his index finger on the bar once. "Still not up to running. Or much of anything else, for that matter. It's bloody boring."

Marxen refilled his glass. "Terri know you're here?"

Suken snorted. "Chance, no. She thinks I'm buying more dressings for my wound. She cleared out all the gin in the house, too."

Marxen shook his head, smiling. The door opened behind them, some of the other hunters calling out greetings to whoever had entered.

Marxen set the bottle on the bar. "Don't go drinkin' it all," he warned. "If Hop has to carry you home, Terri'll have both our hides."

Suken grinned and waved the man away. Marxen bobbed his head once and hurried off to deal with another customer. Suken picked up the glass, staring into the gin for a moment before taking a mouthful.

Someone took the stool to his right. "So," a voice said. "Rank three."

Suken turned to look at Ezin. The older man was staring at the bottles lining the shelves behind the bar. "Yeah," Suken said, finishing his drink and shuddering as the liquor slid down his throat. "Sorry."

"For what?"

"Rendering the Greencloak murder warrant null and void. I know you were after him."

Ezin chuckled. "Part of the business. And besides, word is that someone paid his slave-debt, so he's back on the streets."

Suken pointedly avoided looking at the other hunter, examining his glass.

"Only a matter of time before he starts stealin' again," Ezin continued, "so I'm sure I'll get another shot at him." The older hunter finally looked at Suken. His eyes were a bright, ice blue. And quite obviously brimming with pride. "Wish your uncle coulda seen this. Would have knocked that stupid, conceited grin right off his face."

Suken blinked. "I'm sorry," he said slowly. "What?"

Ezin lifted his hand, signaling to Marxen. "Why do you think

I hung around with that abusive bastard as much as I did?" he said. "Before he adopted you, I wanted nothing to do with him. I got close to him to keep an eye on you, and your brother." He shook his head. "Wish I could have stopped your fool brother from running for it, or found him myself. When you found him, I knew you were something special. Well, now you've proven it, despite what your old fool of an uncle always said about you. And you're going to keep proving it."

Marxen filled a tall glass half full of rum and some sort of sugar-water, then slid it down the bar to Ezin, who grabbed it. He turned a grin to Suken.

"Keep up the good work," he said, lifting his glass in a salute. He slid off the stool and joined some older hunters at another table. They shuffled their chairs aside to make space for him as he seated himself with them.

Huh, Suken thought, bringing the glass to his lips again. *I wonder if—*

"He seems tolerable," a familiar voice said. "For an old tom-cat, that is."

Suken choked on the liquor, nearly spitting it across the bar.

It can't be, he thought, turning his head slowly to look to his left. But sure enough, Fletch had taken the stool beside him. He wore an outfit similar to Suken's; dark brown pants, knee-high boots, a simple white shirt covered by a serape. His dark hair was pulled back into a tail at the base of his neck. The cut across his cheek had been neatly stitched, and his beard was trimmed. He rested his elbows on the bar and leaned forward over them, turning his gaze from the bottles lining the shelves to the one in Suken's hand.

"Least you could be drinking something decent." He nodded to the bottle. "That Darashanian stuff could probably eat a hole through steel."

Suken managed to swallow the gin and glanced back over his shoulder before meeting Fletch's eyes, leaning in closer to him. "Are you insane?" he hissed. "This is a bar for *bounty hunters.*"

"Is it?" Fletch raised one eyebrow. "What are *you* doing here, then?"

Suken gave him a withering look. "Half of these people would kill for the chance to bring you in," he said. "And the rest would maim for it."

"Bring me in for what? I've got no warrants on my head at the moment." Fletch gave Suken an artfully innocent look. "Don't suppose *you'd* know who paid off all my slave-debts?"

Suken threw the innocent look back at him. "Someone paid off your slave debts?"

"Cute." Fletch reached over and took the bottle of gin, looking at it skeptically. He shrugged and poured himself half a glass full. "You pay off those cartels before you decided to get all altruistic?"

Suken looked away. He'd had barely enough to cover the slave debts, but he didn't want Fletch to know that. The way he figured it, now that he was a higher rank he'd be making a lot more aerans, more than enough to work off his uncle's debts.

"Didn't think so. Well, don't worry about it. I took care of them."

Suken felt as if he'd swallowed a lead weight. "Took care of them, like . . ."

Fletch rolled his eyes. "I *paid them off*, you idiot. I'm not fool enough to take on the cartels. The way I see it, that makes us even."

I suppose it does. Suken felt disappointed in that. He'd rather enjoyed having the higher moral ground, though the realization that he was finally free from the cartels was . . . well, it was frankly unbelievable. He'd expected to be paying that debt for most of his life.

"Why are you here?" Suken asked, trying to change the subject.

Greencloak tossed the drink back and shuddered. "Awful. Like drinking a bunch of ground up leaves mixed with piss." He set the glass down and met Suken's eyes. "Had to wait for you to leave home. I'm not going anywhere near that snarling house-hound you keep, but I had something for you."

He pulled a leather pouch similar to the one Suken had given to Marxen from his belt and set it on the bar. Suken edged away from it. "Is that stolen?" he asked.

The look Fletch gave him could have withered leaves on the vine. "What do you think?"

Suken pushed the bag back towards Fletch. "I don't want your stolen aerans."

"Never said it was from me," Fletch replied, pushing it back towards Suken again. "It's from Tam. She said something about having hired you to clear my name. Tried to talk her out of it, but the little fucker's as stubborn as . . . well. You."

Suken shook his head. "I can't take it. They've got it hard enough as it is." He slid the pouch across the bar for the third time. "Tell them I took it, but use it to buy them food, or something. And tell them thanks."

Fletch gave him an appraising look, shook his head and took the pouch back. Suken reached for his glass and found it missing. He paused for a moment, rolled his eyes, and pulled his glass back from in front of Fletch, pouring himself another drink. They sat in silence for a few minutes, passing the gin back and forth, before Suken cleared his throat and said, "Don't know if you heard, but they executed Lord Garron."

Fletch's expression darkened as he stared into the glass. "I know." He tossed the gin back and passed the empty glass to Suken. "Wish they'd drawn and quartered him. Or that thing with the live rats. Hanging was too quick and clean."

"Regardless, he's dead. Along with another four leaders of the Coalition they've managed to find." Suken paused, then said, "I told you they'd do the right thing."

Fletch rolled his eyes. "'I told you so'? Isn't that a little juvenile?"

"You said it to me when you broke me out of prison."

"Did I? Well, it must have been warranted, then." He snatched the glass back and refilled it. "We still need to talk about your little Truthread stunt."

Suken set his jaw. "I'm not going to apologize for that."

"Your high-and-mighty mage friends might have made the right decision that time," Fletch continued, "but only because it was in their best interests. Don't trust them, kitten. It'll get you killed." He swirled the gin in the glass, glaring at it.

Suken wasn't sure how to respond to that in a way that wouldn't start an argument, so instead he said, "The people know that the Coalition was framing you, and the Council publicly declared that working with them is punishable by death. That's bound to dissuade all but the most serious of them."

"Great," Fletch replied caustically. "So they're turning a group of activists into an underground resistance. I'm sure that'll turn out splendidly for them."

"Some of us have been given permits specifically for Coalition members," Suken said, pulling his from his bolt-case and setting it on the table. Fletch glanced at it. "If we find a meeting in progress, we're legally permitted to bring in as many of them as we can catch."

"Good for you," Fletch said. "Have fun with that."

Suken grinned. "I plan to," he said, and paused. "Well. As soon as Terri lets me get back to work, that is."

Marxen returned from the other side of the bar, giving Fletch a skeptical look. He turned to Suken and raised one eyebrow. "He's with me," Suken said, though his heart fluttered against his ribs as he said it. Fletch's description was beginning to spread amongst the people, but Suken had yet to see any drawings with his face on them. Chances were good that Marxen had no idea who was sitting at his bar.

It was still nerve-wracking, though.

"You want your own glass, son?"

"No," Fletch replied. "I won't be here long."

Marxen gave Suken a knowing wink that Suken couldn't begin to decipher and took the half-empty bottle. As soon as he was out of ear-shot, Fletch turned back to Suken.

"Listen to me, Suken," he said. His brown eyes were dark and serious. "What I said before still stands. . . . As long as you're working for the High Mages, you're working for a broken system. How many other murderers are out there on the streets right now, walking free, because they've got the money to buy off the guards and the judges?"

"And you think overthrowing the Council would fix that?" Suken said. He shook his head. "It wouldn't, and you know it. People are greedy, Fletch. There'll always be someone willing to look the other way for a handful of aerans. I'm doing the best I can, and I'm going to keep doing it my way. On the right side of the law."

Fletch shrugged. "Can't blame a man for trying. If you insist on walking into caal-fire, so be it." He slid off the stool to stand beside Suken. "You're not bad, you know. For a hunter. You ever change your mind and decide to make an honest living as a thief, you let me know."

Suken snorted. "The guild's recognized me as a third rank hunter now, you know. Won't be long before I'm highly ranked enough to take *your* warrants, when they start going back up."

"And if you ever get half as good as that housekeeper of yours, you might even stand a chance of catching me." He paused, reached over, and took the glass, still half-full of gin. He downed the liquor in a single swallow, shuddered, and replaced the glass on the bar. Then he turned back to Suken and leaned forward, planting a quick kiss on Suken's lips. Suken drew back, startled.

"I look forward to the day you catch me," Fletch said, grinning. "'Til then . . ." he flipped a prayer to Suken. Suken caught it instinctively. "Good luck. You'll need it."

He turned and made his way towards the door. Suken turned and watched in horrified amusement as Fletch picked the pocket of every hunter he passed before exiting.

"Friend of yours?" Marxen asked with a smirk.

"Yeah," Suken replied, turning back towards the bar. "Something like that." He flipped the prayer into the air, caught it, and looked down at it with a smile.

Suken and Fletch will return in
Book Two:
Crimson Intent

Acknowledgments

A great many people helped with the writing of this novel, so many that over the years and multiple revisions I am certain that I will have forgotten a few. If I have, let me know and I'll add you into the acknowledgments of Book Two (yes, there will be a book two!)

First and foremost, I'd like to thank Salvatore Virgilio, without whom this book certainly would not exist. He played the Fletch to my Suken in the D&D campaign which inspired this whole world, and to this day some of the best Fletch lines in the book are from his amazingly talented mind. He helped brainstorm scenes, write lines, and critiqued my worldbuilding on several early drafts of this novel and I will never be able to thank him enough.

Also high on the list is Kylah ("Terri") Coffey, who has been a stalwart friend and fan through thick and thin and has always encouraged me to continue writing (often times with threats to my well-being, as only the best friends are wont to do).

Some professionals looked at this novel and offered invaluable critiques, but by far the best was Hannah Bowman. She read the entire second draft and without her insightful criticism, this book would not be nearly as good as it is today. I want to thank her immensely not only for her advice, but also for the boost of self-confidence that her offer to read the novel gave me at a time when I really needed it.

Other people who have given me guidance, criticism, and bolstered my self-esteem include my wonderful husband Joe Zusi, who has had to put up with way more rants and monologues about my novels than anyone should and did all of the digital formatting for the book; Peter Ahlstrom, who continued to tell me that this book was good on the many occasions I doubted it and offered some great editorial insight on the ending and on the physical design; Nathan Spence, Frongi, Megan F. and Jess Jespersen for being the best damned writing group in existence; my partner Andrew Prete for his frequent commiserations on the difficulty of being a working artist; and Nikki Ramsay, Gary Singer, and Christine F. for being the most enthusiastic beta readers I've ever had. I'd also like to thank David Burke, Karen Zusi, Kevin Berstene, Nightwing White-head, Jedidiah W. Thompson, Eliza Lewis, Ravi Persaud, Mark "Marxen" Lindberg, A. Forbes, Kyle Gorman, and everyone else who's read the novel either for fun or with the intent to critique over the last four years.

Many many thanks go to Mario Bueno for agreeing to do the audiobook narration on this novel, and to Sean Sorensen and Linnea Lindstrom for helping with some of the audio proofing. Linnea has also earned the title of "Empress of Ellipses" alongside her cohort Robert "King of Rivers and Stacks" West for their hard work on the formatting of the print copy.

Huge thank you to Trenten Rose and Ben McSweeney for the interior art. J. Caleb Design did this amazing cover art way back after I'd finished the first draft, and it's still fantastic.

I'd also like to thank Patrick Loveland and Georgia Dunn for inspiring me to begin writing fantasy back in grade school. Without our study hall creations and hours-long phone calls, this adventure would not exist.

Early kickstarter backers for the audiobook version and interior art of this novel are as follows: Jory "Jor" Phillips, Ross "Rossin" Newberry, Joe "Jodrin" Deardeuff, Becca Reppert, Darci Cole, Paige Vest, Jacen Rukh Ulfric, Veronica Bailey, Deana Whitney, Kalyani Poluri, Danielle DeCesaro-Virgilio, Ted Herman, Shannon Halpin, Brian and Sarah Magnant, Kara and Isaac Stewart, Scott Williams, Jennifer L. Pierce, Ted Herman, Ben and Becca Reppert, Susan J. Voss, LantisEscudo, Rebecca Ramsey, Drew Brisco, Jenijellybean, Alison Bird, Ryan "Lyndsey's sometimes husband" Pagella, Lahman Marcel, Marija and Justin Corriveau, Ashley Shaffer, Matt "Papa Dragon" Neyssen, Julie Anderson, Beck "rawr" Hubschwerlin, Adam Ferraro, Cori Leyden-Sussler, Patt "Your Majesty" Miller, Sean Sorensen, Stephanie Meier, Mathias Rotestam, Rebecca Lovett, Simon and Christine Strauss, Katrina and Jack Doucette, Rosemary Williams, Tom Fulgione, Alice Arneson, Qudsi, Jackson Kane, Arianna Kosoff, Tanya A, Camille, Taylor Simpson, Author Michael J. Sullivan, Nathan Strom, Pamela "Izumi" Larsen, Marcel de Jong, Andrew Waskiewicz. Pat S., Darci and Brandon Cole, John H. Bookwalter Jr., JKK, Alberto, Lisa Sussenberger, Aaron Falis, Jacqueline Collins, Kevin Kastelic, Nichole Pelletier, X, Caleb Duvall, Dan Orlowitz and Sarah Gabriel, Erin Woodard, Camie, Alissa "Honk" Murray, Tony, Chris and Dyann Zusi, Bao and Aubree Pham, Ketki V., Rachel J, and BJ Clinton.

I wouldn't have been able to create this story, or any of the ones to come, without all of your support. Thank you.

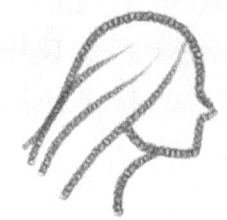

LADY'S FACE

TREE

MOUNTAIN

CROWN

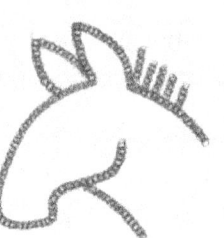

FOOL

JEWEL

NOOSE

CLOUD

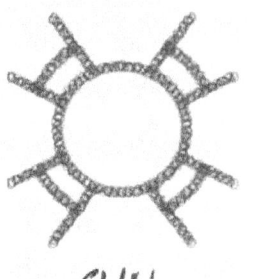

SUN

STAR

Lyndsey Luther *lives in Connecticut with her husband, son, and two rescue dogs. She has been writing since her teens and is a frequent contributor to TOR.com. She is a professional actress and stage combatant, proud rennie, fire-dancer, cosplayer, and unabashed geek. Greencloak is her debut novel.*

YOU CAN FIND HER ONLINE AT THE FOLLOWING PLACES:

www.lyndseyluther.com

Facebook: Lyndsey Luther – Author/Cosplayer

Instagram: kiarrens